Alexander K. McClure

Three Thousand Miles Through the Rocky Mountains

Alexander K. McClure

Three Thousand Miles Through the Rocky Mountains

ISBN/EAN: 9783337286842

Printed in Europe, USA, Canada, Australia, Japan

Cover: Foto ©Andreas Hilbeck / pixelio.de

More available books at **www.hansebooks.com**

THREE THOUSAND MILES

THROUGH THE

ROCKY MOUNTAINS.

BY

A. K. McCLURE.

PHILADELPHIA:

J. B. LIPPINCOTT & CO.

1869.

PREFACE.

In presenting these letters to the public in book form, I do not claim for them any measure of literary merit. They were written hastily, during a journey of three thousand miles through the Rocky Mountains, and often in the midst of annoyances not favorable to epistolary perfection. The letters embrace two distinct series: one published in the New York "Tribune," and the other published in the "Franklin Repository," which will account for the treatment of the same topics in different letters, although always substantially varied. I need hardly say that they were not written with the design to collect them in book form; and now, when the wide-spread interest felt in the rapidly-growing Great West seems to demand reliable information of the people, resources, progress, and destiny of the Rocky Mountain Territories, I find it impossible to revise the letters so as to conform them to the exactions of the critical without depriving them of much of their freshness, and, probably, some of their usefulness. Fully conscious of their many imperfections, I have consented to their publication only because I hope thereby to afford, in some humble degree, the long-delayed justice to the pioneers of the West, and, at the same time, give some little additional strength to the growing disposition to make the boundless mineral and agricultural wealth of the Territories available to benefit our common country. He who aids, in any measure, in advan-

(3)

eing our people and our government to a just appreciation of the limitless riches which the Great West has so long offered to the nation, will not have lived without benefit to his people; and it is to contribute my mite to that great end that these pages are presented to the public. I am fully sensible that, in another decade, scores of new records of the West will be written by abler pens than mine; and each new advocate will have brighter fields to explore and more dazzling pictures to present, as the nation is made to grasp its matchless prize of wealth toward the setting sun. Before that brief time shall elapse, these crude pages will be forgotten,—unless by the few who preserve the erratic foot-prints of Western progress. Three through-lines of railroad will span the continent from the Atlantic to the Pacific, dotting their lines with new cities, new settlements, new churches, new schools, new communities, and new and mighty States; and the freshly-inspired commerce of the ancient empire will be turned from its westward course toward the Great Republic in the East, and mingle with the newly-created millions of products of our new-born Commonwealths, as united they sweep across our continent to our commercial centres, and thence to the Old World. To hasten the events that will cause these letters to be forgotten, is now their mission; and their faults may be freely condemned, if they shall render the humblest aid to enlarge the stature of our Western empire.

A. K. M.

PHILADELPHIA, April, 1869.

CONTENTS.

(5)

THREE THOUSAND MILES

THROUGH THE

ROCKY MOUNTAINS.

LETTER I.

From Chambersburg to Pittsburg.—Parting with Old Friends.—
The Juniata Valley.—Crossing the Alleghanies.—The Progress
of a Quarter of a Century.—A Day in Pittsburg.

PITTSBURG, May 1, 1867.

A TRUCE with politics and law for a season. I have
long wished to see the Great West, to gaze upon its virgin
beauties, learn its gigantic progress, and mingle with the
sturdy pioneers who are laying the foundations for future
empires. All intelligent people have read of them, and
read of them more now than ever before; but to see them
as they are, to mess with them, shelter with them, travel
with them, and share their life as it really is, has long
been a strong desire with me; and, if blessed with health
and safety in travel, I shall devote the summer to the study
of this great lesson with nature and nature's first help-
mates themselves.

I need not say that I turned regretfully from the beautiful Valley of the Cumberland, with its heartsome homes,
its fields green with the promise of future plenty, and its
people congenial and kind. Many parted with me with
emotions I shall not soon forget, and the sadness of ex

3   (17)

changing the comforts of home and the blessings of friends
for a long and perilous journey was brightened by the
many earnest aspirations given for a pleasant trip and a
safe return. Many greatly magnified the dangers of the
tour, and seemed painfully impressed that it was but an
invitation to danger or death; but, while no such journey
can be free from peril, we have the promise of peace on
the Plains this season, especially on the great overland
route. Still, it is exposed to perils not known in the
boundaries of civilization, and they are, therefore, ever
present in the recollections of friends, and give rise to fears
for the safety of friends who thus journey. Let us all be
mindful that "there is a Divinity that shapes our ends,
rough-hew them as we will," and that even the perils of
the wilderness and of the deep are controlled by Him who
numbers the very hairs of our heads. I fondly hope to
return again renewed in vigor myself, and with renewed
health for those I most love; but, if it cannot thus be, I
trust that there will be a few, at least, who will not leave
me unlamented, and who will feel that I have not lived
entirely in vain. If I shall merit such a tribute from the
lowly and the children of sorrow, some measure of my aim
in life will have been fulfilled.

But enough of sad forebodings. They belong not to the
hopeful, the earnest, the useful. They will in a time, brief
enough at best, present their reality, as all in turn accept
the inevitable doom; but till then life has its duties, its
sufferings, its pleasures, and each should be welcomed or
borne with the fortitude of manhood.

I never saw the Cumberland Valley more beautiful
than when I passed through it on Monday last. It seems
the home of contentment, of plenty, and of all that should
make man better from year to year. And after we turned
our way toward the setting sun from Harrisburg, winding

along the beautiful Juniata, there were on every hand the
same evidences of thrift, of order, and of happiness. Now
and then we would find our wild mountains towering
over us; but soon again the beautiful fields and the blossoms of spring would break upon the view. Thus following the sinuosities of the river, still growing smaller and
smaller as we approach its source in the Alleghanies, we
had alternate wilds and blooming fields until we landed at
the very foot of the mountain at Altoona. Wishing to become used to our journey by degrees, we stopped for the
night, and took the morning for crossing the famed Alleghanies. Less than a quarter of a century ago it was deemed
impossible to cross these great barriers to trade, except
by inclined planes, at great cost and peril. Slowly the
weary passenger would be dragged from level to level by
stationary engines and powerful wire ropes, and hundreds
of lives have been lost in passing them. Now the iron
horse may be heard ploughing through the gorges and
climbing these steep declivities, from the far North down
to Tennessee. On the North the Philadelphia and Erie
winds through the great wilderness of our State, bringing
its vast wealth to the lap of commerce. Here the sound
of the locomotive is ever heard, bringing its untold measure of trade and travel to and from the coast. In Virginia the Baltimore and Ohio spans the mountains again;
and still farther South the Virginia Central (I believe it
is) finds its way through and over them to Knoxville, and
thence to the Gulf. Thus in the matchless progress of a
quarter of a century have the great mountains of the East
been leveled, as it were, by the handiwork of man, and
have ceased to retard the whirl of commerce or the stream
of travel as we swarm westward to fix new stars of the
galaxy of the States of the Republic.

It is worth a week of delay for any tourist to cross the

Alleghanies by daylight. I have passed them often, but each time I gaze on their bewildering beauties more intently than before. A span of iron horses stood hitched to our train, as the crowd filed out from breakfast to nestle down comfortably again in the seats. They stood there, quietly humming their voluntary, as if to denote that all was in readiness. At the signal from the conductor, they belch forth their black column of smoke, hiss off their steam, and, after a short, shrill, double scream, move off with their immense load with a majesty that is sublime. Slowly, but steadily, they climb the steep grade, wind around the famous horseshoe, pass on up the mountainside so high that the dwellings below are scarcely perceptible, and finally plunge into the bowels of the earth, nearly three hundred feet from the surface, and for seven-eighths of a mile there is total darkness, save as an occasional column of smoke brings with it a shadow of dull light to break the gloom about you. Soon again the train emerges on the western side, and the great Alleghanies have been ascended so gradually and so quickly that those who had not been attracted by the scenery would be ignorant of the exploit. Thence the descent is made at a high rate of speed, following the windings of the Conemaugh, which starts in a little spring on the mountain-top, and courses its way to the Gulf. From the mountains to Pittsburg there is everything to remind the Pennsylvanian that he is still in Pennsylvania. The same thrifty agriculture and slow but steady progress are observable everywhere, until the dark cloud of smoke that begins to search its way into the cars reminds us that we are about to enter Pittsburg.

I have spent a day here most pleasantly, devoting my spare time mainly to friendly chats with the editorial brethren. I found Brigham, of the "Commercial," full of energy, and hopeful of everything — of politics, of the country, and of the "Commercial." I was pained to find Foster, of the "Dispatch," an invalid. He is about to start for France and the Holy Land, with the hope of saving for a time the only lung he has left. May he have many years yet in store for him! Caldwell, of the "Commercial," long the Washington correspondent of the "REPOSITORY," I fear has cut his local reports short for to-morrow by his kind attentions to me, and as I write at one of the "Commercial" editorial desks, Brigham emerges now and then from his pile of exchanges in the adjoining sanctum, to talk a little more of politics. At two I leave for Chicago, and, as the clock points to one, I must send this just as it is, without even attempting to read it, much less correct it.

3*

LETTER II.

CHICAGO, May 3, 1867.

WE left Pittsburg by the Fort Wayne and Chicago Road
at three P.M. yesterday, and arrived at this place at eleven
this morning. It is a pleasant journey. The cars are
elegant, the road mostly straight and in good order, and
the sleeping-cars are called "palace cars" with some warrant for the high-sounding title. I took a farewell of our
noble Pennsylvania mountains as we were whirled into
the Buckeye State. They have no fellows east of the
Mississippi, and as we passed westward the level plains
became painfully monotonous. In Pennsylvania and Eastern Ohio vegetation was pretty well advanced; the
cherries, peaches, and pears were in blossom, and the
apple was thrusting out its leaves, soon to be followed by
the beautiful harbinger of its valued fruit; but as we approached Indiana the country seemed to be frost-bound,
and the farther we got west the more dreary and winter-
like the fields and vegetation looked. Ohio looks cosy,
despite its want of mighty mountains. It has majestic
forests—too much so, often, for the comfort of the husbandman—and her fields have an old-fashioned Pennsylvania
look that makes me feel quite at home among them. But,
as we shorten the distance between us and the Missis-

(22)

sippi, the fields and houses become more and more strange, until the steady old-time ways of the East are entirely lost sight of. They do nothing in the way of progress out here just as we do it East. They are restless, impatient, and original. If they need a house, they build it at once; put up a place to cook, eat, and sleep in first, and finish it off afterward. A Pennsylvanian must plan and think; then he must prepare; then he must dig, and lay the foundation; then he erects the walls, the roofs, and finally finishes it for a residence. While he is thinking and planning, the Buckeye or the Hoosier or the Sucker will move into his new house. True, it will have no cellar, no foundation but four blocks, perhaps but partly weatherboarded, but he has a house, and he finishes it when and how it suits him; so with his fences, his out-buildings, his everything. Even the children out this way look older for their ages than do ours, and would seem to be born much after the general Western style of go-ahead-ativeness. They seem to be born frequently in most families, and I should judge, from their independence of manner, that they don't consume any great quantity of Winslow's Soothing Syrup, and that they don't average above one occasional nurse to a household. They climb up the bumpers of the cars, crawl under the locomotive at the stations, look in at the doors, and frequently strut through the cars as if they owned the train and were prepared to make a respectable bid for the passengers. A man needs to pass through the West but once to understand that those who talk about a hundred millions of population in this country in less than half a century, are not very wild arithmeticians after all.

We had a delightful sleeping-car, as I have stated, and I passed the night in comparative comfort. I never could get a good refreshing sleep in a car, and never hope to do so. But, whether sleep can be wooed successfully or not in them, they are a great institution, and a luxury to the traveler. A sleeping-car always makes a jolly, family-like company, and there is nothing that destroys the conventionalities of society so speedily and so thoroughly, in the matter of getting acquainted, as "turning in" on board of one of these wandering lodging-houses. When we start out, all or most of the company strangers to each other, all, of course, observe due dignity, and allow acquaintance to win its way by gradual approaches. Now and then a rollicking baby will force a smile from some sympathetic mother distant from her loved ones, and the mothers at once become friends, relate their travels, discuss their homes, husbands, babies, houses, pullets, and poodles, and share their lunch-baskets. A wayward boy, or a lovely girl with sunbeams dancing on her face as if playing upon a rippling stream, will insensibly break the reticence of the bachelor, gather the spare candies, nuts, and cakes from the pockets of the fathers, and end the campaign by a friendly chat between the old folks. One little, blue-eyed, taffy-curled girl emptied my pockets of the debris of my last campaign among the children of Alleghany, and made me a willing purchaser of all the jim-cracks the train vender had to tickle the fancy or palate of these miniature editions of ourselves. Of course the mother was appreciative, and a pleasant acquisition was added to our party, to last till we reached the Plains. Thus do the genial and the obdurate alike surrender to railroad acquaintances in a sleeping-car, and, when night comes, we all seem much as one family, mutually sympathetic and generous. A woman may even crimp her hair before the bachelor without provoking a surly remark, and prodigious waterfalls, and hoops, and ribbons, and the thousand other things which pertain to female adornment may be scattered in wild profusion around the car, swinging from hooks, and impeding locomotion by side blockades; but all is taken in good part, and there is peace and good will in the great family thus im-

provised upon a few hours' acquaintance. Occasionally a
coy damsel or a veteran spinster seems to rebel against the
free-and-easy manners of the sleeping-car; but they merely
make themselves uncomfortable, and are sure to provoke
just that notice and comment they least want. I pity a
fastidious old maid in a sleeping-car. She always keeps
watching everybody else with such palpable suspicion that
she compels everybody else to watch her, and her most
studied efforts to protect herself from profane eyes and
speech make a score of eyes peer in upon her from behind
curtains and by side glances, while the lady who accepts
the situation goes free. If a mishap falls to the lot of any
in a sleeping-car, it invariably falls to the one who tries
most spasmodically to avert it, and there are few who do
not enjoy it when the moment of confusion comes. When
people do their best, they cannot secure the privacy that
most persons would prefer; but when all agree to do the
best they can, the great mantle of charity hides what the
more tangible fabrics fail to protect from the gaze of the
curious or rude. We were waked at half-past four, with
notice that we must be ready for breakfast at five precisely;
and I need not say that at that unromantic hour the Greek
Slave might have been personated in any of the berths
without arresting the heavy yawns which mingled with
the hurried preparations for breakfast.

When within about twenty miles of Chicago, the monotony of the low, marshy, ill-improved prairie of this
section was broken by a regular locomotive race. The
Pittsburg, Fort Wayne and Chicago, and the Michigan
Southern, come together on the same time, and for twelve
miles the two roads are rarely over one hundred feet apart.
The country is perfectly level, the roads straight, and there
is every incentive to a trial of speed. It seems that they
have a daily race, and it is neck and neck between them.
Whichever train happens to have the best locomotive or

the lightest train, usually wins. We had ten cars and the Michigan Southern but seven, so the odds were against us; but our engineer, brakesmen, firemen, porters, newsvenders, baggage-masters, conductors, all entered into the spirit of the race with boundless enthusiasm, and I need not say that most of the passengers watched with intense interest the issue of the struggle. The baggage-master of the Michigan Southern was first seen standing on the lowest step of his car, with a roll of bank-notes in his hand, trying to make himself understood by pantomime, in the midst of the thunder of two large trains flying at their utmost speed, that he would bet either his cash or drinks on his train. I could not see whether his banter was accepted or not, but, if it was, he must have been winner, for we were distanced the length of our train in the race. Both trains stopped at several stations during the run, but both always stopped at the same place, and it was ludicrous to see how old women, and their bundles and baskets, were hustled in and out of both trains to prevent unnecessary delay. One old man on our train wanted to get off, but he had one question too many to ask the conductor, and he was sent whirling along to the next station, in spite of his violent gesticulations. At last the iron horses divided in their course as they entered Chicago, and both seemed to forget the friendly strife, as their shrill song told us that our journey was ended.

I would like to write about Chicago, but I cannot. It seems to be a second New York. Although it has but two hundred and fifty thousand population, its main streets rival Broadway in magnificence and life, while its beautiful Wabash and Michigan Avenues tell the story of its wealth in social life. The train leaves at 8.15 this morning for Omaha, and I must hasten away. I hope to be there by Saturday noon, as the road, recently torn up by the floods, is again in running order.

LETTER III.

OMAHA, May 6, 1867.

I HAD a pretty fair inside view of Chicago. I got there in the midst of the great riot on Thursday last, and left it the next morning in the midst of a grand fire. It is a fast place—fast in a fight, fast in a fire, fast in business, and fast generally. They do up a riot in the most improved style, and can make more noise at a fire twice over than Philadelphia. The laboring-men got up a flurry over the inauguration of the eight-hour law on the 1st instant, and had, as was appropriate and commendable, speeches from politicians and dignitaries, and processions with banners, etc. But they committed the fatal error of supposing that, because no man could compel them to work more than eight hours per day, they could compel every fellow-laborer to work just that number and no more. It was on this difference that they threw Chicago into disorder and did themselves the dishonor of attempting anarchy.

As I left Chicago, I left all news behind. By making

(27)

several efforts along the railroad at the telegraph-stations, I managed to learn the result of the fire that was raging when I took the train; but as for keeping posted in the events of the day, beyond this single fact, I might as well have been in China ever since. As yet there are no papers here later than New York of the 29th ultimo, and Chicago of the 1st. There are daily papers published in most of the Western towns of any size; but they afford but a meagre outline of the events of the world which we are used to enjoy so fully in the East with our breakfast or tea. I judge that as I go westward I shall learn to dispense pretty much with general news; but the force of habit will make me break in upon far-western rules on this point as often as a newspaper or a telegraphic operator can be captured.

We had rather a variable time from Chicago to this place, and, upon the whole, quite a jolly trip. As variations are the spice of travel, I do not regret that we took the widest latitude in reaching and crossing the Missouri. At Chicago we were assured that the train would go through on time to the Missouri; but, if the princes of old, against whom the world was cautioned, were less to be trusted than railroad managers out West, those who had to deal with the princes should not have needed the Divine injunction. From Chicago to this point it is four hundred and ninety-four miles by rail, and the line runs almost directly west, thus bringing trade and travel to the plains by the shortest route. Until last winter, the emigrant and sojourner for the mountains reached the Missouri at some point below this, and generally left Omaha out of their programme; but the construction of the Union Pacific Railroad for two hundred and ninety miles west of this place, last fall, necessitated the hasty construction of the connecting link between this and the Mississippi at Fulton, so as to open an unbroken and direct railroad line from the Atlantic to Platte City, the point to which the Pacific Railroad is now run. The result was that the Chicago and Northwestern road was forced through last fall in the most imperfect manner. It was flung down on the prairie at the rate of two miles per day, and, while the bed remained frozen, it did tolerably well; but, when the thaw and spring floods came, it imitated the Dutchman's milk in lying around loose generally. The flood of the Missouri this spring was more extensive than usual, requiring, it is said, the oldest inhabitant to remember its counterpart. It put a score or more miles of the Chicago and Northwestern road completely under water, and floated it about, with its occasional rude embankments and improvised culverts, as if it was but a plaything for the Western elements. As the tide of spring travel had set in for the plains—ten times greater than ever before—the management could not afford to wait to repair the road and have trade seek a southern line to St. Joseph or St. Louis. Accordingly, it was announced officially, a week ago, that the road was repaired, while miles of the track were still frolicking with the frogs and other occupants of the ponds and lakes of the prairies.

Although still doubting, I ventured to try the road on Friday, just four days after it was pronounced to be thoroughly repaired, hoping that we might do rather better over it than to strike St. Joseph and have to stem the boisterous tide of the Missouri to this point. It is well that I had some doubts,—sufficient at least to distrust the regular railroad eating-stations to satisfy the demands of hunger. I had a bountiful lunch put up in Chicago, to guard against accidents in the way of "square meals;" and but for that precaution we must have had a protracted fast. All went well until we got to Dennison on Saturday morning, where we had our last regular meal

4

during the journey, leaving us a period of thirty-six hours
without any food but what we had with us and what we
foraged from the scant larders of the pioneers. Be it remembered that Western Iowa—at least along the line of
the railroad—has scores of miles at times without the sign
of an inhabitant. Often during the tedious journey over
the monotonous prairies, broken occasionally only by bleak
sandhills, I looked in vain in every direction for a house
or a field. It has no timber, is but poorly watered, and
until now has presented no inducement to the husbandman to break up its fertile soil. The transition from the
luxurious tables of the East to the "square meals" of the
West is, fortunately, gradual, and by the time the traveler
reaches Omaha he is prepared for "hog and hominy," or
whatever may be presented. The last cooking I found fit
for a table was in Chicago. As we got out into Iowa,
the Western style grew more and more original, until a
break in the road brought us right into genuine pioneer
living. Our last meal was at Dennison, Iowa, where we
had the inevitable bacon and eggs, with hot, heavy, greasy
biscuits, made apparently with flour, corn-meal, hog's fat,
saleratus and water, and served up smoking hot. This is
the favorite bread of the Far West. They usually have it
at every meal—always hot, and their children begin on it
before they have teeth to masticate it. But it seems that
travelers in the West, however fastidious about their diet
at home, are able to accommodate themselves to a diet
here that would require the force of medical attendants to
be doubled if used in the East. The active life, pure air,
and the magic effect of change of scenery, habits, exercise,
association, etc. fit most persons for living in Western style
with comparative comfort.

When within fifty miles of Council Bluffs, we were
stopped by the wreck of a mixed burden and passenger

train, that was piled up on and all about the track. But two miserable shanties were in sight in a circle of twenty miles, and scarcely a shrub was visible. It was eight miles to the nearest station, and fifty miles to the nearest point from which the necessary machinery could be had to clear the wreck. It was about ten o'clock in the morning, and the cold, sharp wind was sweeping a hurricane over the prairie. The passengers got out, and, in spite of the repeated assurances of the conductor that we should "get right along shortly," it was clear to all that we were in for the most of the day. I walked along the track for half a mile, to take a look at a Western railroad, and I think it well that my inspection of the road did not occur until I was over most of it. I think I would have walked in preference to spending two nights on such a road. The bed was made by throwing up an embankment some three or six feet above the level of the prairie, of the soft loam dug up alongside of the track. Light, indifferent ties were then thrown upon it, the rails spiked down, and the space between the ties was not even filled up with dirt. The hard freeze of the winter kept the road in fair order until recently; but now the track seems as if laid on a bed of hard dough. In walking over it the ties would sink down in the earth from my weight, and a glance along the rails showed that it had settled irregularly, crooked, and disjointed, and in places seemed to have slid bodily to one side or the other. There was no help, however, then but to go over it, and as it was just as bad to go back as to go forward, and the shortest part of the road was ahead, I had no choice but to wait patiently and philosophically for the end of the journey.

In the mean time, the question of provisions became a serious one. Our party had a clever-sized lunch-basket filled; but there were thirty others in the car, some of them women and children, who had no supplies. Misfortune soon breaks down all reserve, and the provisions on hand were divided around as if we were all of one family. How quickly a lunch-basket in a hungry crowd makes everybody sociable! First, all the children of the car will gather around it, in spite of the threats and frowns of tender mammas, and through them the way is easy to an intimate acquaintance with all. But our supplies were insufficent for the party, and we improvised a foraging corps. There were but two shanties within sight, and they were most unpromising for a successful foray in the provision line; but they were the only possible points of attack, and we charged on them. One of them was entirely out. They had no eggs, no meat, no bread, no milk, no butter—in fact, nothing. The other had a few hard fat biscuits and some cold bacon, which were purchased at a price that would have made the Continental cashier blush. It was but little we got, but that little was somewhat like the widow's cruse—it went a great way and lasted well. I made a satisfactory dinner on half a biscuit and a small cut of bacon. After nearly ten hours' delay, the welcome sound of the locomotive whistle was heard, and "all right" was called by the conductor. As most of the road had been submerged between that point and the river, and part of it swept away and but temporarily repaired, I felt but little confidence that we could get through that night,—if we could get the train through at all. I amused myself, as we passed along, watching the soft sides of the road and calculating the probable loss of life and limbs that would follow a run-off. Our conductor and engineer seemed, however, to value their own lives, and the train proceeded with great caution—at no time running at the rate of over ten miles per hour, and generally not exceeding six. We were not interrupted in our course for some thirty miles,

when at the village of Honeybrook we came upon another
wreck, and had to stop for repairs. It was now getting
dark, and, as we had dined very sparingly, and had no
prospect whatever of supper, I renewed my foraging efforts.
There were half a dozen shanties scattered about the place,
including an Irish railroad boarding shanty, so I hoped to
be able to gather some eggs and potatoes—the only things
they could cook without rendering them unfit to eat by
dirt and grease. An ex-member of Congress went with
me, while the others divided off in squads to raid upon
the different houses. The Congressman had a child in his
party, and milk was requisite to its comfort, and we drove
the cows with us up to the door of the house we assailed.
We went in to negotiate, and found the lady of the house,
with a blooming daughter just doing up her hair in the
last weekly paper, preparatory to frizzing it for Sunday.
We asked in turn for eggs, meat, potatoes, bread, and milk,
but they had none of most of the articles, and none to
spare of any of them. "But my child must have milk,"
said the grave national legislator. "So must my calves,"
said the Western matron, with a dignity and independence
that showed her to be master of the situation and determined to keep it. The Congressman became patronizing, and proposed that he would milk the cow, and that
I would nurse her baby, if she would consent to sell enough
to give the young Congressman his supper. Finally the
lady came in; but she would not trust either of us with
the cows, and she milked a quart, which she gave for half
a dollar. While the milking was going on, I negotiated
with the daughter for a loaf of bread by a tempting offer;
and was glad to get it, notwithstanding the untidiness of
the bakery, and the general air of filth about them. We
next got two dozen of eggs, boiled by a man who had a
sort of a boarding-car to feed the hands making repairs, at

4*

the modest price of one dollar and a half; and the same generous gentleman made us a gallon of what he called tea, for another half a dollar. We called it tea, because he said it was tea, and we could not prove the contrary. We then tried the Irish Biddy of the shanty to get some potatoes roasted, and finally got her to agree to roast us two dozen for half a dollar, in advance. She put them in the stove—so much I saw of the potatoes; but I do not know that they ever came out. There were cakes—the inevitable fat biscuit—in the oven, the fire was bad, the cook was mad, and I saw that if there was any chance for the train to get off within an hour or two, the potatoes would not be done until just after the train started. An hour afterward, the whistle sounded, and we left the potatoes and the half-dollar with Biddy. She had a supper to her liking, if we did go hungry for want of them.

From the romantic village of Honeybrook, we got along slowly but safely to the river. We arrived within a mile of Council Bluffs a little before ten o'clock at night, and there our conductor, engineer, and everybody but the car-boy left us to take care of ourselves. We were ticketed to Omaha, on the western side of the river; but the only answer we could get from any one was that we had better stay where we were, as we could not get rooms in Council Bluffs, and would not cross the river before the next morning. We had all become patient by this time, and made as merry as we could over our helpless position. We concluded to stay where we were, and, as we had a sleep-ing-car, we went to bed on the track, like a family of genuine Micawbers, waiting for something to turn up. Morning came, but no one called to claim the car or to tell us where to go. The flats were wet and muddy from the late overflow, the omnibuses would not run between the cars and the town, so we disposed of the remnant of our last evening's lunch, and patiently waited for somebody to come and put us and our baggage across the river. Once I thought I had cut the Gordian knot. I found the agent of the Transfer Company, and was about negotiating to get us across; but the treaty was suddenly terminated by the information that the Transfer Company had not breakfasted, and that nothing could be done until after that important event. I kindly proposed to breakfast with the Transfer Company; but the Transfer Company preferred to breakfast alone, so I did not breakfast at all. In the mean time, impatience was gaining supremacy in our severely-tested circle. The children were crying for want of proper food, and matrons and men were not by any means jocular, nor yet devoutly disposed, although it was Sunday. To add to the discomfort, the wind was sweeping across the river most furiously, and it was keenly cold. A muskrat enlivened the party by swimming up alongside of our car, and sailing around us as if he wanted to be sociable. Soon after bang went a rifle from the front car; but the muskrat sailed on leisurely as the bullet struck the water two rods ahead of him. The ice once broken, rifles gleamed from every car, and half a score of balls were sent after the now retreating rat; but I was glad to notice that all were harmless. It was to me an unusual Sunday service; but, under the circumstances, no one complained of the irreverent break of the monotony of starvation and vexatious delay.

At last the Transfer Company managed to get breakfast, and by eleven o'clock there were coaches brought up to take us to the river, and thence across on the boat. We put the ladies inside, and fourteen gentlemen got on outside, filling the boot, the top, the driver's seat; and hanging on all around. We had four miles of staging before reaching the river, and when we did get there, the wind

was so high that the boat could not be forced from the
shore for nearly half an hour, notwithstanding the puffing
of her engines and the splashing of her wheels. But
patience and perseverance overcame all, and by noon yesterday we were safe at the Herndon House; a house equal
to a first-class city hotel in size and charges,—further
deponent saith not.

Such was our trip across the two great rivers of the
West to the eastern terminus of what is called the Plains.
Upon the whole, it was as pleasant as we could expect,
and we have all enjoyed it, notwithstanding its privations
and delays. I have not been here over twenty-four hours,
and everybody knows me, and I know pretty much everybody. People don't wait for introductions. Your name
is read on the register, and you are at once addressed by
name, your journey and business inquired into, and information freely given you. The man is to be pitied who
cannot at once like the Western business people; they are
generous, frank, kind, and clever, and make you feel at
home at once. I had not been an hour at the hotel, before
the landlord, to whom I had never spoken, came up to me
where I was standing on the porch, threw his arm over
my shoulder, helped himself to my tobacco, named me,
and told me where I was going, how long I expected to be
away, and gave me all the good advice about the plains
he had to spare. He is but a type of the enterprise and
go-ahead-ativeness of the Great West — the people who
will, in a quarter of a century more, change our great commercial centres, and make the seat of Empire west of the
Father of Waters.

LETTER IV.

OMAHA, May 7, 1867.

COUNCIL BLUFFS was once the City of Promise on this line, and is still a most active and growing place, with two daily papers, many fine buildings, and a most enterprising people. But the perfection of Western enterprise and thrift, of Western styles and manners, of Western hazard and progress, is to be found on this side of the Missouri, in Omaha. It has over ten thousand of a population, and more carriages than any town of the same size east of the Alleghanies; sells more goods and at higher prices; deals out town lots by the foot at more fabulous rates; has more hotels, which are better patronized, dirtier, and dearer; builds more houses in a day, and rents them for more money; plays poker with a higher ante, faro and keno with a more liberal limit; runs horses oftener and for higher stakes, than any other city of ten thousand people I have ever read of. It expects to surpass Chicago and St. Louis in a few years, and talks of being the national capital by the time our sons go to Congress. The poor Pawnee Indian wanders through the streets bewildered at

(37)

this high carnival of progress; for a week's absence trans-
forms streets and rears structures where was vacancy before. One gentleman told me that while at supper a house
was reared and greeted him on his return to his office.
The houses are framed in Chicago and sent here ready to
put up, and it is done with marvelous speed. A new and
much-needed hotel is just under contract. It is to be one
hundred and three by ninety-five feet, three stories high,
and is to be completed in sixty-six days from the date of
the articles. More than that, it will be done; on the sixty-
seventh day it will be full of guests, and likely the sixty-
eighth will witness a grand ball. Fractions of a hundred
dollars seem to be unknown as rents. An ordinary store-
room, such as would rent for two hundred dollars or
thereabouts in a good location in one of our Eastern
towns, has scores of applicants for it here at from $1800
to $2000 per annum. They are generally one and a half
or two stories high, built in the cheapest manner of wood,
and in any New York village would not cost more than
one-fourth of one year's rent in Omaha. Everybody be-
lieves that the already fabulous prices will advance steadily.
I think differently, but have not ventured to set the whole
city into commotion by saying so. I doubt whether any
one would be excused for expressing the opinion that there
might possibly be a returning tide of sweeping disaster
in the headlong business and feverish speculation of this
city.

I found the "Tribune" of the 1st instant to-day, and was
not a little annoyed at the startling dispatches from St.
Louis about the so-called Indian war. I see that the
"Herald" has had dispatches from Leavenworth stating
that General Augur was about to move west from Fort
Phil. Kearney with six thousand troops, and that eleven
thousand hostile Indians were encamped on the line of his

march between Forts Phil. Kearney and C. F. Smith. I
had just returned from a protracted interview with General
Augur when I saw a dispatch in the "Tribune" correcting
the "Herald's" sensation dispatch. The truth is that there
are not five thousand troops in all, and there are not the
half of eleven thousand Indian warriors who are hostile
or doubtful in the whole of General Augur's department;
and so far from being about to march from Fort Phil.
Kearney west, he will not get his troops to Fort Laramie
before the 1st of June, will not start from there on his
expedition before the 10th or 15th of the same month,
and cannot reach Fort Phil. Kearney before the middle
of July. When he does start from Fort Laramie, his force
will consist, as I am officially informed, of the Second
Cavalry, the Thirtieth Infantry, a battalion of the Eigh-
teenth Infantry, and a battalion of Pawnee scouts numbering about two hundred—giving him an effective force of
about two thousand men, nearly one-half of them mounted.
It seems to be a small force to move against the Indians,
according to the general conceptions of Eastern people
about the Indian war. The impression prevails generally
that the campaigns of General Hancock south of the Platte,
of General Augur north of the Platte to the Yellowstone,
and of General Terry up the Missouri, are intended as a
war of extermination against the Indians. Such is not the
expectation of the commanders. If this were their purpose, the general criticism of the Eastern press on the folly
of hunting Indians with infantry and artillery would be
just. If the Indians were now engaged in a general war,
as is persistently represented by speculators and other interested parties, they could drive all the troops east of the
Missouri in sixty days, or scalp two-thirds of them if they
preferred. Not a coach or train could pass across the
mountains; and yet the overland coach runs daily, and

trains pass over all but the Powder River route with comparative safety. Occasionally a weak train is captured on the Smoky Hill route, through Kansas, and north of Fort Laramie travel is not allowed, while the massacre of Fort Phil. Kearney indicates a savage, implacable hostility in the Powder River region; but as yet the Indians have made no hostile demonstrations looking like general war, such as is anticipated in the East.

General Augur is an old Indian-fighter, and understands the Indian character well. He spent some ten years before the rebellion in fighting steadily with the Indians on the Pacific slopes—a race equally as valorous as our Sioux and Cheyennes. He is an accomplished officer, will command his expedition in person—with Brevet Major-General Gibbon second in command—and understands well that he is neither expected nor prepared to wage a successful offensive war against the red men. He will go upon the Powder River route, garrison it, fight when necessary, either on the offensive or the defensive, and punish with relentless severity all cruelties committed by his foes. When it is considered that to us, even at the headquarters of the department, the actual position of half the tribes of Nebraska and Dakota is unknown, save by conjecture, the Eastern public can judge how wild are their calculations as to the results of the Indian expeditions. There are in General Augur's department but four or five tribes which are known to be hostile, and some of them are what might be termed semi-hostile; for, while they are dissatisfied and unfriendly, they have not marshaled their warriors, as yet, for the war-path. In this list may be classed the Arrapahoes, the Lower Brulés, the Yanctonnais, and the Sans Arcs. The tribes in this Military Department either wholly or partially hostile, or whose position is not definitely known, are as follows, viz., the Ogalallas

and Brulés of the Platte, numbering seven thousand eight
hundred, mostly friendly, living on the Republican River;
the Cheyennes, north of the Platte, numbering eighteen
hundred, all hostile; the Arrapahoes, seven hundred and
fifty strong; the Lower Brulés, twelve hundred strong,
accepted as hostile, but not certainly known to be so; the
Blackfeet Sioux (a roving offshoot of the regular Blackfeet), thirteen hundred strong, thriving and hostile; the Min-
neconjous, numbering two thousand two hundred, mostly
hostile, but divided; the Uncopapas, eighteen hundred
strong, and the Ogalallas of the north, two thousand four
hundred strong, known as hostile; and the Yanetonnais,
two thousand four hundred strong, and the Sans Ares, sixteen hundred strong, inclined to be hostile, but divided.
The Two Kettles are friendly on their reservation; and the
Crows, four thousand strong, have always been friends,
and are the deadly enemies of the Sioux. The Pawnees,
the Utes, and other lesser tribes in this Department (Iowa,
Nebraska, Dakota, and Utah) are all friendly. The numbers given above are the entire population of the several
tribes, and it is a safe estimate that if all not known to be
friendly should unite on the war-path they could not marshal five thousand warriors, while it is reasonably certain
that, by treaties now in process, fully half of the warriors
regarded as hostile or unfriendly will be made neutral or
effective allies against the Indians persisting in warfare.
Already two hundred Pawnees are enlisted as scouts by
General Augur, and fifteen hundred Crows have formally
proposed to him, through the Indian Commission, to join his
forces against the Sioux, on the condition that the Yellowstone country (from which the Crows were driven by the
Sioux) shall be restored to them. Just what General Augur
will do when he moves west from Laramie, a month hence,
cannot now be even calculated. General Sully's commission,

5

now well on to Fort Phil. Kearney, will have exhausted
its powers to make peace, and to combine the friendly Indians against the unfriendly, if the shock of savage warfare must come; and his letters quite recently received by
General Augur are very hopeful of peace, or rather that a
general war can be averted. If war must come, then we
are entirely unprepared for it, for there are not one-fifth
the number of troops here necessary even to keep open
the overland route and the Missouri River—the two great
thoroughfares—much less to exterminate the Indians.
That the red man must fade away, and that during the
present century, I do not doubt; but his contact with civilization will do the fatal work more rapidly than a hundred thousand soldiers. He accepts all the vices and a
few of the virtues of the pale-faces, and disease and dissipation are fast diminishing the numbers and degrading
still lower in the scale of creation the once proud inhabitant of the wilderness. That he has little sympathy, and
that nine-tenths of the people look to his extermination
either approvingly or anxiously, is not to be questioned;
but it is remarkable that most military officers and government agents who have maintained an unsullied reputation
in dealing with the Indians, cling to the conviction that
the red men are deeply wronged, and that if fairly treated
they would, as a rule, maintain faith and friendship with
the whites. General Augur informed me that he has not
been able to learn of a single chief who signed the treaty
at Savanne last spring engaging in hostilities. Red Cloud,
the leader of the present difficulties, refused to sign the
treaty, as did some others who were present and are now
at war. This is directly at variance with the generally
received opinion among the whites, who believe that the
treaties were made to get ammunition to capture trains
and emigrants. Ninety-nine out of every hundred Western

men believe that the sooner the Indians are killed off the
better, and they insist that it is a humane work to kill them
off whenever and wherever found. How much the prevailing sentiment, and its logical results displayed in the
actions of Western people and traders and miners, have
had to do with our present Indian difficulties, I leave
others to judge. When I shall have passed through the
Indian country, I may have more decided convictions on
the subject than now.

But for the white tents which dot the bluffs near this
place, the crowd of officers that throng the streets, and the
hurried moving of military stores, with an occasional
hearty curse you hear hurled at the Indian, no one here
would suppose that there were any troubles on the Plains.
The trains and coaches run regularly. Passengers come
through on their way East, and laugh when interrogated
as to the danger of Indians. They had not heard or
thought of them, is the usual reply. Crowds go westward daily, and all things seem to be considered but the
danger of assault or capture by the Indians. All are well
armed, and the men going westward, especially those who
have been there, all consider themselves able to whip any
number of Indians single-handed if they should cross their
path. Families, embracing mothers and daughters, start
out by every train, and the Far-Western ladies make the
trip unattended without any fear as to their safety. General Potter will leave his head-quarters at Fort Sedgwick
(Julesburg), with ten companies of troops, to protect the
stage route and the construction of the railroads, and no
apprehensions are felt about the interruption of travel on
the Plains. True, a roving band of Indians may attack a
small party at any time, but it is evident that no considerable body of hostile Indians can endanger the overland
route for any length of time. Yesterday a band of them

struck one of the stage-stations between Julesburg and Denver, capturing the horses and burning the station, but did not attempt to kill or capture any of the men. They are just now in search of horses, and will be likely to trouble the overland stations—much more likely to raid upon the stations than upon the stages, for they have no love for uncertain warfare, and they can never calculate the armed force in a stage until they draw its fire. They have met with several severe defeats by attacking stages, and they call them the "fire-wagons."

LETTER V.

NORTH PLATTE, May 8, 1867.

I LEFT Omaha last evening at six o'clock, by the Union
Pacific Railroad, and must confess that I did not leave regretfully. There are few persons, not actually bound there
by the tide of business that is sweeping in and about the
place, who will spend any time needlessly in what the
Omahaians regard as the coming city of the West. They
boast greatly of the rare variety of climate—having had
snow-storms, thunder-storms, hurricanes, impassable mud,
choking dust, earthquakes, floods, hard freezes, and burning suns all in the space of three weeks. I must concede
all they claim in the way of variety, but I found most of them
differed with me when I told them that nothing but a first-
class earthquake or a general fire to batter or burn down
these miserable buildings will ever make Omaha what I
doubt not it must yet be—a substantial, thrifty, growing
town.

The Union Pacific Railroad is now completed to this
point, a distance of two hundred and ninety-five miles, and

5*   (45)

the trains run with comparative regularity. It is a good Western road,—tenfold better than the Iowa part of the Chicago and Northwestern,—and makes the two hundred and ninety-five miles in fifteen hours. It suffered considerably by the late flood, but is now completely repaired. The inundation of the Platte Valley must have been fearful. I saw as much as half a mile of railroad-track, the ties and rails still connected, swept away from the bed, and strong, new rails bent nearly double by the violence of the water. But such floods are not frequent, and I presume that it is safe to calculate that this road will not be more subject to interruption by floods than are first-class Eastern roads. After passing out through Nebraska for a few miles, the evidence of progress is not marked. There are but few settlers on the line of the road, and after we enter what is called the Platte Plains, about Fort Kearney, there seems to be little that can ever invite the husbandman. The valley, or vast plain, is bounded on every side by vast bluffs, ranging from twenty to thirty miles apart, and the bluffs seem to be terribly sterile and repulsive. The Platte River rolls lazily along south of the railroad, hugging the southern bluffs at times, and again striking out near the centre of the valley; but it tires the eye to look at it and its surroundings. It is a murky, shallow, treacherous stream, with shifting sands for its bed, and naked banks skirting it all the way. I have looked for miles along its course without seeing so much as a shrub, much less a tree; but at times, when it nears the bluffs, it puts out along its banks a stunted, miserable growth of cottonwood. I have not seen a tree off the stream in the great Platte Valley thus far, and not one even on the stream that would make a good rail or a telegraph-pole. The valley is a miserable waste, and I fear ever must be. I have not found a single stream in it but the Platte River—the whole plain thus far, north of the river, not furnishing a single tributary. In addition to this, there are but few rains during the summer, and no possible means of irrigation. The grass is now covered with a white coat of alkali, and all the water, even from the wells, is strongly impregnated with it. The ox-trains going west by this route keep south of the Platte, between the river and the bluffs, and I learn that there is better grass there, and an occasional stream running to the river. There is not a habitation on the route for nearly two hundred miles but such as are necessary to accommodate the railroad and travel. Here and there are miserable adobe shanties, with signs out, offering whisky and other luxuries to the weary sojourner; but I have not seen so much as the sign of a farm, or a fold, or even a patch, for fully one hundred miles. The antelopes would come up close to the train and gaze at it with boundless curiosity, until some ambitious sport would send a bullet after them. They would look for a moment at the dust raised by the bullet, and then fly off with bewitching grace. The buffalo grazed quietly eight miles north of us at one place on the Plains, and the prairie-dog and owl occasionally peeped out at us as we passed along.

We are beginning to realize that there is something of an Indian war going on. We are advised here that a band of Cheyennes (pronounced Shi-en') had made a raid on our stage line sixty miles in advance of us, captured all the hor.es at the American Ranch, and burned the Fairview Station beyond. I had an inkling of it from General Augur yesterday, before I left Omaha, but his advices were indefinite, and he did not fully credit them. He therefore withheld the information from the public press, but communicated it to me just as he had received it, inasmuch as I was about to travel the route. He had been advised of a probable raid on the overland line, between Julesburg and Denver, by Spotted Tail and Swift Bear, two chiefs of the Ogalallas and Brulés, who have been temporarily quartered on the Republican Fork by General ·Sully. About fifteen hundred from those tribes are, for the present, allowed to occupy the region from the Smoky Hill to the Platte, where there are good hunting grounds. They have interpreters and scouts with them, employed by General Augur, and are under pledge to keep the peace themselves, and not to allow hostile tribes to move across their grounds without sending messages to the nearest military post. A few days ago Spotted Tail sent a messenger to General Augur with word that two hundred and fifty lodges of Cheyennes and sixty lodges of Sioux, all hostile, had moved up to the Republican Fork from the Smoky Hill, and that they were offering every inducement to get Spotted Tail's young warriors to join them in a war upon the whites. He was offered one hundred horses if he would join the hostile tribes. He refused, and asked to be removed from that region, with his lodges, to some place where the hostile tribes would not harass his people and seduce his young warriors from him. The lodges of the Indians average about five persons to each, so that there are about fifteen hundred hostile Indians on the Republican Fork, within sixty miles of the Union Pacific Railroad, and near enough to both stage and railroad lines to raid upon either or both. With these hostile tribes are their families, so that, all told, there are not over three hundred and fifty warriors; but that number, near enough to strike a great thoroughfare any place in a stretch of one hundred miles, may prove a serious impediment to travel. These are represented by Spotted Tail to be the same Indians that General Hancock met in the Smoky Hill region, and which General Custer was supposed to be driving far south. One thing is certain,—that General Custer has found no hostile Indians south of Smoky Hill as far as he has been heard from, and it is equally certain that a hostile party turns up several hundred miles in his rear, that did not cross the Platte from the north. So much for the results of the expedition south. The troops sweep down toward the Arkansas, while the Indians make the plains resound with their war-whoop upon the Republican, and the belligerents are each pursuing their hostile purposes at the unusual range of three hundred miles. In this we have but a foretaste of our offensive Indian campaigns. It will be no fault of the commanders that these expeditions, generally regarded East as offensive movements, will prove ludicrous failures. They are doing the best they can. They are obeying orders, and will do much good in their way; but the practical results will not be palpable to the masses of the people who are patiently waiting for General Hancock or General Augur or General Terry to carve the epitaph of the last Red Man with his sword. It has been ascertained by calculation that every Indian warrior of the Plains killed by the military has cost the government about $115,000. Rather expensive first-class funerals, it must be confessed, to lavish on barbarians; but I do not look for the Indian funeral market to decline materially in price during any of the present campaigns.

The defeat of the bill, proposed recently in Congress, to transfer the Indian Bureau to the War Department, was a gigantic mistake, and it will cost the government hundreds of thousands of dollars, worse than wasted, this summer. General Augur commands a large Indian department, controls its armies, projects its campaigns, and fights its battles; but he can do nothing more. Some Indian agent, but too often an unscrupulous speculator or a downright thief, is supreme in all matters but actual hostilities. The Ogalallas and Brulés, now temporarily on

the Republican, ask to be transferred from the perils and
the influence of the hostile Cheyennes and Sioux, who have
broken into their hunting grounds.   One reason given by
the friendly chiefs is that their young warriors cannot be
controlled when appealed to and offered tempting bribes
to join in hostilities.   The young brave has but one hope
of distinction.   He can become great only by warfare.   He
can be honored only by wearing the rude wreath of victory known to the barbarian ; and his dusky bride or sweet-
heart ever prompts him to deeds of blood.   With good
reason, therefore, do Spotted Tail and Swift Bear, two veteran and faithful chiefs, advise that their followers be removed from the baleful influences of the hostile tribes.
But who is to remove them?   General Augur dare not,
and there is no Indian agent nearer than Fort Laramie
who has any power over the question.   The Pawnees have
their agent here, but his jurisdiction ends with the Pawnees.   When Indians are to be removed, they must be fed ;
and red tape demands, even in the midst of war, that they
eat none but rations properly issued and labeled by the
Indian Department.   If the whole management of Indian
affairs had been transferred to the War Department, we
should have started in this war with half the battle gained,
by at once sweeping from position the swarms of civil
agents who are the authors of so much of our Indian
troubles, and our military commanders would now be em-
powered to treat, transfer, feed, or fight them, as circumstances might require.   It is just possible that, at the rate
the government has been learning the management of Indians, in the course of forty years or so we may attain
something approaching common sense in this business, and
it is about equally probable that by that time there will be
no Indians left to experiment on in a sensible way.   If
the government does not solve this problem at an early

day, the settlers and miners will solve it themselves, and
some new Cooper may write "The Last of the Cheyennes," or "The Last of the Sioux," with the truth of its
bloody history making all Indian romance pale before it.
How the settlers and miners will end Indian depredations,
the Chivington massacre at Sand Creek correctly fore-
shadows. Colonel Chivington's command was composed
of Colorado volunteers—men who had felt or seen the
cruel savagery of the Red Man in resenting his real or
imaginary wrongs; and, although a dispassionate examination of the whole case must force the conviction that White
Antelope and his followers were peaceable, with perhaps
rare exceptions, he and his whole band, squaws and papooses, were put to death—not one received as a prisoner;
and yet nine out of ten of the Western people either com-
mend or excuse the act. They feel that the Indian is in
their way; that they cannot fraternize; that he will not
work, and must rob, and to rob must often kill; and they
look hopefully to the day when he shall have offered the
last of his race as a sacrifice to the progress of civilization.

But the stage is loaded. We have had a dinner of boiled
antelope and vegetables—all excellent but the water,—and
start in a few minutes for Denver, distant two hundred and
ninety miles, and will have an opportunity of crossing the
path of the hostile Indians who struck the stations sixty
miles west. We will have three stages, all well filled and
passengers well armed, and an attack is not probable unless
a powerful party of warriors should happen to strike us.
They want horses more than scalps or trunks and bonnets,
and they may attack twenty stations and allow the stage to
pass safely. The people here, passengers and proprietors,
seem to take no account of the Indians beyond a careful
examination of their repeating rifles; and if one stage-load
should be murdered to-day, another would start out to-

morrow, just as usual. Passengers would not wait merely because half a dozen persons had been butchered, and the proprietors would not think of stopping their line for even a day while there were horses enough to take the coach through. The movement toward the setting sun is accepted as inevitable, and, although many may find nameless and forgotten graves, still the restless, swelling, irresistible tide will move on, until the savage lives only in history, and his once favorite hunting grounds shall be known only as the beautiful and bountiful fields of the mighty West.

LETTER VI.

DENVER, COLORADO, May 11, 1867.

WE reached the city last night about nine o'clock, just
three days and three hours from Omaha. It is six hundred miles, of which two hundred and ninety-five is by
rail,—the rest of the journey by coach. When the roads
are good, the trip is made in two and a half days; but the
railroad is still a little shaky from the late floods, and between Indian depredations, floods, and quicksands, the
trip is generally extended twenty hours over time. From
Omaha, on the Missouri River, to the North Platte, the
country is beautiful prairie; but after leaving the river it
soon becomes dry, rains seldom fall, dews grow lighter
and more rare, until they finally disappear altogether, about
Fort Kearney, and thence westward there is but one continued plain, parched, whitened with alkali, without shrubbery or trees, almost entirely without small streams, and

6   (53)

altogether inhospitable, bleak, and desolate. From Fort
Kearney west to near this place, a distance of four hundred miles, I did not see a single acre in cultivation,—not
a single fence, garden, patch, field, or anything that indicated thrift or productiveness. The river Platte rolls its
turbid waters through the Platte Valley, and makes no
sign of life along its borders. It is wide, shallow, muddy,
broken by innumerable islands, treacherous, and apparently useless. It does not even skirt its own banks with
shrubs or timber. All along its banks is the same weary
waste that the plains present for miles on either side of it.
Occasionally it presents a petty growth of cottonwood for
a few miles, but they are mere apologies for trees, and
make the general view, if possible, more cheerless by their
deformed and stinted growth. From Kearney west I did
not notice a tree any place on the route, nor so much as
even a temporary tributary to the Platte River. One
station on the railroad is called "Lone Tree" station. I
looked carefully for the tree, and would have welcomed
such an evidence of life in that unbroken waste, but I
found no sign of it. Upon inquiry, I was informed that
the tree existed only in tradition. It is positively asserted
that there once was a tree there, a brave but rather unsightly cedar, that had successfully resisted the unwhole-
some waters and burning suns of the plain, but it fell before the march of civilization. Every traveler plucked a
twig from its branches, until the branches were gone, and
then the trunk was chipped away, as relics of the Lone
Tree of the Platte plain. Equally delusive was the title
of another railroad station called "Plum Creek." At last,
I supposed, we would find a tributary to the Platte—at
least a little rivulet winding through the sands to nourish
some vegetation along its path. But Plum Creek station
had everything but the creek. It had not even the bed or

semblance of a stream, of water. It seems that a little stream empties into the Platte on the south side, some ten miles from the station, and the railroad company did the best it could, in the absence of all babbling brooks, by honoring the name of one ten miles away to grace their titles in the railroad guide. So the country continues until the Platte divides, and in the peninsula is located Platte City, better known as North Platte. The North Fork is bridged for the railroad, and at the end of the bridge the railroad round-house and repair-shops have made a Western city. It consists of one fair hotel, several one-story boarding-houses for operatives, several warehouses, as many stores, and about forty "whisky-mills," or small groceries, where whisky, tobacco, and portable eatables are sold at fabulous prices.

The North Fork of the Platte has its course considerably north of west of Fort Laramie, nearly three hundred miles distant from the junction, and from Laramie it sweeps up northward to the Red Buttes, when it wheels around south again, and finally heads in North Park, Colorado. The South Platte has a southwestern course from the junction to this city, and from here its course is to the South Park, where it heads. Both forks start in the Rocky Range, and not fifty miles apart, but they separate as much as six hundred miles in their course to reach the junction at Platte City. The North Fork has many tributaries as it nears the mountains, but the South Fork continues for three hundred miles without any important tributaries, and its width and general appearance are just the same during all that distance, while the country is but a continuation of the dry alkali plain we had traversed by rail east of the junction.

We started from Platte City about two P.M. on Wednesday. The beginning of Western staging was anything but soothing to our expectations. A large baggage-wagon, without springs, containing a box guiltless of any sort of seats, was driven up to the door, and half a ton of mail-bags and our baggage first thrown in. These filled the bed more than full, and upon the baggage and mail-bags we were to ride for eight miles, including the fording of the river, before we could get to the coaches. It would have been in vain to protest against compelling passengers, and especially ladies, to travel in that way. We had paid our fare, we had to go, and to have complained would have provoked perhaps still harsher treatment. The ladies, three in number, were piled upon the trunks, and the gentlemen hung on and around the wagon as best they could. Between keeping themselves and the ladies from falling off, as the team went at a rapid gait over a rough road, often invisible amid the clouds of dust that swept over us, they had more on hands than men should bargain for. But we got over the river, and finally landed at the coach-station in tolerable order, considering all things. In a short time a regular Concord coach was driven up, with an elegant four-horse team, and one ton of mails and baggage and nine passengers were crowded in and on it ready for the plains. Two of the passengers took outside seats, or we should have had a sorry time of it. The coaches here are fully a foot shorter in the bed than our old Eastern coaches, and when nine persons are in one of them, they are so completely wedged together that it is next to impossible to change position. But, by dividing with the driver and the stage-top, we got fixed rather comfortably, the driver cracked his whip, and off we started for what is at least a thirty-six hours' continuous journey over the Platte Valley.

The first station we reached was about ten miles from our starting-place. The stations along the route vary from eight to fourteen miles, and are distinguished as "swing" and "home" stations. The swing stations furnish a change of horses only ; while the home stations furnish new teams and "square meals" to the passenger. As the Indians had cleaned out one station on the route but a few nights before, I need not say that the Indian question became one of especial interest to all the passengers. I walked into the stable while the change of horses was being made, and inquired of the man in charge whether he had any information of Indian movements. I found him greatly excited on the subject, and apprehensive of an attack any hour. He said that there were not less than seventy-five hundred hostile Sioux and Cheyennes just south of the bluffs,—not more than from ten to fifteen miles distant,— or between that and the Republican River, and that they would certainly sweep the stage-line with scalping-knife and torch, as they did in the winter of 1865. I got but little comfort from him, and I kept his information to my-self. He was evidently frightened out of all judgment on the subject ; and, while his fears were not entirely ground-less, I was satisfied that there was no large force of sav-ages so near. But he doubtless felt as I did—that fifty would settle the business with a station or a stage-coach just as effectually as five thousand. At the second station I made the same inquiry, and found the station-keepers— usually from two to four men—greatly alarmed, but much more rational than the others. One of them told me that he had ridden out over the hills near at hand and seen two Indians quite distinctly. He supposed them to be spies, looking out for the best method and time to attack the station. The driver evidently believed the report of the station-keeper, and considered an attack upon the coach as probable. He said that he would do the best he could for himself in case of an attack—that he had a good knife

6*

and a good leader, and they would be smart if they caught him. I asked him whether he would desert the stage and passengers in that manner; to which he replied that he would take care of himself. I told him I thought that no man would get away with the leader should the Indians attack us. "Why not?" was his quick and somewhat excited response. "Because," said I, "we shall watch that our leader *don't* get away." We had a fearless Canadian Frenchman on the outside, who has spent many years in the Indian country. I handed him a good revolver; and, although no explanations passed, there were at least three men, including the driver, who understood that the lead-horse would *not* leave the team in case of trouble. At the next station we found a squad of soldiers, protecting and patronizing a whisky-mill, and apparently proving themselves a most effective force in the last part. They had no reports of Indians, and pronounced the route to be clear. When we reached the next station, the men were busy tunneling from the stable far enough off to be safe in case of fire, and they were panic-stricken about the expected Indian raid. They were indeed to be pitied, for they are entirely without protection,—most of them not even armed, —and, as the Indians want horses badly, they are more exposed than any other class of people. On the entire route I found but three stations where there were any arms. They say that they are not furnished with arms, that they cannot afford to buy them; and that even if they were armed they could not defend themselves in stables, where the Indian has but to apply the torch to the hay roof and burn them out. About ten o'clock P.M. we reached the first "home-station," known as Alkali Station, and we were there to try our first "square meal." The station-house is, like all others on the route, one story high, and covered with sod. The sod is cut in the lowlands about

six inches thick, and probably eighteen inches square.
These are piled upon each other to the height of eight
feet, wide rafters are thrown across, and another course of
sod for a roof completes the building. All ranches, stables,
and residences on the line are built in the same way. The
lady of the house set to work at once to get supper, and,
while it was being prepared, we were invited to be seated
and make ourselves at home. Her shanty bore many evidences of neatness, and looked as heartsome as such a
hovel could be made. In a short time, supper was ready,
and we were all most agreeably surprised by the repast
spread for us. We had excellent warm rolls, canned tomatoes, peas, blackberries, peach-pie, fried ham, stewed
veal, and fried potatoes, with tolerable butter and coffee
and tea. It was, in fact, the best meal I had met with
since leaving Chicago. We were all hungry as well as
tired, and did ample justice to the supper. The price was
one dollar and fifty cents, which we all paid most cheerfully. We found the station-keeper and his wife both
much concerned about the Indians, and they talked about
closing out at an early day.

The late supper, and the liberal patronage we all extended
to it, made sound sleep rather difficult in a stage-coach.
We had by this time become used to Indian reports ; and,
as there was no place so safe as in the stage, we all got
our shawls about us, looked well to the loading of our
rifles, and to their position, so as to be of easy access in
case they should be wanted, and devoted ourselves to rest.
Most of the passengers dozed more or less ; but I could
not sleep. My long legs placed me at a great disadvantage, as they became so painful from the interruption of circulation by being squeezed together in one position all the
time, that I could not rest. I looked anxiously for the
stations, just to give me a few minutes to straighten myself

out and get up a little motion of the blood. The night passed without any event of interest, and soon after sunrise we arrived at Julesburg—a little town of three buildings, all rude frame shanties. At Fort Sedgwick there were over one thousand troops stationed; but they were unfitted for any service that could give protection to the route. The men were unmounted, and, beyond protecting themselves and their officers, they are of no possible use in the West. I called on the commanding officer of the fort, to ascertain whether he had any authentic information relative to Indian depredations on the route. Colonel Dodge (formerly Assistant Provost Marshal at Harrisburg) was in command; but, as it was only eight o'clock, he had not yet made his toilet. In answer to an inquiry sent him by an officer, he answered that the Indians had broken the telegraph-line the day before, some fifteen miles west, but he considered it safe for the stage to proceed. I did not ask for an escort,—although by an official letter I bore I could have commanded it,—for the reason that the practical men on the route, the drivers and passengers who were familiar with both soldiers and Indians, preferred not to have an escort. A large escort cannot be given; a small one would be useless under any circumstances; and the Indians, I learn, don't care much for ordinary escorts, whether large or small. After breakfast we passed on until we came to the second station, at a ranch kept by "Buffalo John," where we met the telegraph operator and his escort, consisting of a squad of cavalry. He had been out repairing the line supposed to have been broken by the Indians, and reported that he had seen a large body of them, probably a hundred; and the officer who commanded the squad added that he had seen fully a hundred, and had been fired upon and chased into the ranch. They said that these hostile demonstrations

had been made about two miles ahead on our road. I
asked the officer whether he considered it safe for the
stage to proceed. "All safe; they won't attack the stage,"
he answered. He deemed it unsafe for a body of armed
and mounted troops to be there, but considered it safe for
three ladies and six gentlemen to go over the route. I
suggested that probably we had better detail a mixed
guard of ladies and gentlemen from the stage to protect
the troops ; but he walked off as if he really considered me
insolent.

With the cavalry skulking in and about the whisky-mill,
we all decided to proceed, as the driver insisted that the
soldiers were not to be believed, and that the telegraphic
operator was never known to tell the truth. He probably
put his point a little strong, but he certainly did not believe the report, positive and circumstantial as it was, and
so on we went. The driver was a cool, intelligent, determined man, an old resident of the Indian country, and
he was very positive that we should proceed ; and as to an
escort, he didn't want to have it about him. He suggested,
however, that it was barely possible we might meet with
Indians, and if so, he named the place where they would
attack. At his request, four of us, with repeating rifles,
took the top of the coach. I sat beside him on the driver's
boot, and three others, with well-loaded rifles, lay on the
baggage. About three miles west of the station, the road
runs close to the river, in a low, narrow flat, and a series
of broken bluffs come close to the road. The driver held his
lines with perfect steadiness, but did not wholly conceal
the apprehension he felt that, after all, there might be Indians about. "Watch well for their heads, front and rear,
and don't let them get the first fire," was his advice; and
we did watch well. Every rifle in and about the stage
was cocked and pointed toward the bluffs, and fifty balls

could have been fired without stopping to reload. The
driver showed his appreciation of strategy by keeping as
close to the river as possible, thus giving the bluffs a wide
berth. There was scarcely a word spoken by any while
passing the bluffs, a distance of a quarter of a mile; and
all breathed freely again when they receded behind us.
"I knowed he was a d——d liar," was the brief but expressive remark of the driver as he whirled his long lash
over his six gay horses and made his silken cracker
rend out its sharp, keen music. About three o'clock
we stopped at "Riverside Ranch," and did justice to a
good dinner. Here we came into the sandy region.
For twenty-five miles the road is mostly over a bed of
deep quicksand, and three miles an hour with a heavily-
loaded coach is good time. It is a much greater impediment than mud, and is, besides, very oppressive upon passengers. The fine sand keeps a perpetual cloud about the
coach, and penetrates the eyes, ears, nose, mouth, hair, and
clothes, and, impregnated as it is with alkali, it makes
every one most uncomfortable. Nor do its torments stop
with itself. It has an ally of innumerable little sand-
gnats, so small as to be hardly perceptible, and they get
in the hair and under the clothing, and bite much worse
than even Western mosquitoes. We bore all, however,
with commendable fortitude and patience, and finally got
out again on good road, only to find the ruins of the
"American Station," burnt by the Indians but a few nights
before. It was not by any means a pleasant reminder of
the perils of the trip. But it is wonderful how people can
become used to almost anything. Even the old woman's
traditionary eels got used to skinning; and we had certainly become used to Indian rumors. The ladies were
not the least heroic of the party, and had their revolvers
ready to aid in the common defense in case the war should

come to close quarters. From the gravest apprehensions felt by all at first, the Indian question became one fruitful of jokes, although there were some grim smiles at times as the loss of a scalp was made the theme of wit. At last we ceased to borrow trouble about the Indians, and as night drew her sable curtains about us, most of the party were ready for sleep.

About half-past eleven we drove up before the ranch of " Old Wicked," one of the home stations of the route. We were due there for supper about six, but a heavy load and bad roads had detained us. No one wanted supper at that late hour, but we concluded that " Old Wicked " was entitled to a benefit, and seven of us answered to the call for supper. We had to wait for it to be cooked, and I was glad to have an hour with the proprietor. His name is Hollen Godfrey, and he is the most noted Indian-fighter on the Plains. He was the only man on the Platte Plains who defended and saved his ranch in the raid of 1865. He and three others defended it against one hundred and sixty Indians for half a day, killed over a dozen of them, and finally compelled them to raise the siege. The Indians named him " Old Wicked," and by that name he has since been known. He has a sod fortification connected with his ranch, and defending it at all points, and he proposes to do his own fighting in his own way. He *hopes* to have a brush with them this summer; but the general judgment of all along the line is that if an Indian raid is made, " Old Wicked " will *not* be honored with a call. He gave us a good supper; and I was so entertained by his modest but intelligent history of our Indian difficulties, that not until the driver's whip cracked after several calls of "all aboard " did I bid him good-by and get into the coach. I must tell more of him at another time.

We had nothing of special interest after leaving " Old

Wicked" until we came near "Living Spring" station, within forty-five miles of this city. One of the station-keepers informed us that he had seen ten Indians that day, evidently spies, who were planning the capture of the station and horses, and he said that he would remain no longer. We had become so used to frightened station-men and military reports that we did not even take the trouble to discuss the probable correctness of the story. Dinner was just ahead of us at "Living Spring"—the only spring I have heard of during a journey of nearly six hundred miles; and I was glad to find one oasis in this parched plain where fresh water gave life to vegetation. From thence to Denver the scenery is grand indeed. The Rocky Mountains are in full view, with their eternal snow-clad peaks, the prairie is broken by gentle undulations, habitations begin to show some of the signs of civilization, and here and there are irrigated gardens which are beginning to bloom with life and beauty. It was a grateful change from the flat, hot, monotonous valley of the Platte, and we were all more than rejoiced when, stiff and sore, we were landed at the Pacific Hotel in Denver. Of Denver and Colorado I will write hereafter. I find the road through the mountains almost impassable, and while it is improving I will spend a week in the mining regions of Colorado. I go to Central City, Idaho, and Empire, on Monday and Tuesday.

LETTER VII.

Efforts to understand the Indian Question.—The Western Demand for Chivington or Conner.—Western Contempt for the Regular Army.—Why Regulars do not fight Indians successfully.—Advantages of the Indians in a Summer Campaign.—The Monuments of Indian Warfare.—The Platte Valley Raid of 1865.—Horrible Cruelties of the Savages.—Hollon Godfrey, or "Old Wicked."—His Defense of his Ranch.—A Supper with him, and his Story of his Fight.—His Solution of the Indian Problem.—He regards Indians as Peaceable when they are Dead.—How Indians conduct Campaigns.—Their Signals and Spies.—There must be Peace.—It will be the Peace of Death to the Indian.—The Harney and Chivington Wars.

Denver, Colorado, May 13, 1867.

Ever since I reached the Missouri, at Omaha, I have been laboring most industriously to get something like a correct understanding of the causes, progress, and probable results of the present Indian war. It would seem natural that the officer commanding a department should be best informed, and two days with General Augur, who kindly allowed me access to his maps, data of the various tribes, reports of the Indian Commission and of scouts, gave me, as I supposed, a reasonably accurate idea of the condition of affairs. After leaving Omaha, I made it a point to gather all the information I could from every available source, without regard to the prejudices which might partially or wholly neutralize the truth. Ranchmen, drivers, station-keepers, train-men, and freighters have, after all, the best practical ideas of Indians, and it is remarkable

7 (65)

how universal is their contempt for military campaigns. "Give us Chivington or Conner" is the answer to all questions as to how peace may be attained; and I have not found one resident or habitual traveler of the plains who does not demand extermination. Their testimony is fearfully concurrent that there can be no peace while the government negotiates with the Indians and treats prisoners in accordance with the usage of civilized warfare. Next to the Indians, the residents and sojourners of the Platte Valley west of the railroad have the greatest contempt for soldiers of the regular army. They say that such troops fear the Indians, and will not fight them. They have no private wrongs to avenge. They have had no friends butchered, no wives or children scalped or tortured, and they know that they are exposed to all the atrocities practiced by the Indians, while they are compelled to fight them as if they were humane and chivalrous. Is it not natural that soldiers of the regular army, who fight mechanically, should be inefficient in a campaign against Indians? However extravagant may be the views of the Platte Valley residents as to the folly of regular military campaigns, it must be confessed that their logic is more easy to overrule than to answer. No one here doubts that Generals Augur and Hancock are doing, and will do, all that is in their power under their orders; but the conviction is just as universal that they cannot even protect the great thoroughfares to the West, much less bring the savages to peace, by military success. They might protect the two great routes across the continent if they were instructed to do nothing else; but when they are directed to divide their forces, and make offensive movements north and south of the Platte, they must fail to protect the routes behind them, and also fail to gain any decided success in the field. Every day I have spent in the Indian country

has but confirmed the opinion I expressed in my first letter from Omaha—that there will not be a decisive battle
fought this season by either General Augur or General
Hancock, and that the so-called Indian war will be but a
war, on the side of the Indians, by fleet bands of warriors
against weak posts and isolated commands; and I do not
hesitate to add that there will be ten or, more likely,
twenty whites butchered for every Indian killed by the
troops.

Do not understand me as intending to reflect upon the
capacity or efforts of our military commanders. They cannot do impossible things; and I assure your readers that
what is expected of them generally in the East, and I presume by the government, is as impossible, under existing
circumstances, as would be a campaign against the denizens of the moon. It is conceded that there are some hundreds, and probably over a thousand, hostile Indians on the
Republican Fork. It is the central line between the
Smoky Hill and the Platte routes, and an excellent base to
operate in every direction against the lines of travel and
against the settlers. They can strike the Platte route for
several hundred miles in one day's ride, and the Smoky
Hill is equally accessible. Of their movements no one
can be advised. They will burn a station on Smoky Hill
one day, and the next strike the Platte. Within the last
week they have made two raids on the Platte, and two or
more on the Smoky Hill. The country they occupy is
held solely by hostile tribes. Spotted Tail and Swift Bear,
with their followers, crossed the Platte northward on Friday, a few miles below Julesburg, so that the Republican
region is now entirely in possession of the hostile Cheyennes and Sioux. Spotted Tail and his followers were
located there but a month ago by General Sully, but the
incursion of the hostile tribes compelled him to leave, as

he reports, or allow half his young warriors to be seduced into war. He has, therefore, left for the north, and not entirely pleased because the government agents or commanders would not allow his young warriors to fight the Pawnees a little occasionally, "for fun." I find that the residents all along the route, as well as the people of Denver, have no faith whatever in Spotted Tail, and they predict he will be on the war-path, or at least part of his tribe with his consent, before another month. It is not questioned that in his lodges are quite a number who were concerned in the Fort Phil. Kearney massacre; and yet no effort has been made to have them surrendered to justice, lest it might force all of them into war. I must agree with the Western people, so far, at least, as to demand the summary and relentless punishment of all Indians who have countenanced or participated in the butchery of captives; and, if it should make a thousand more warriors for a time, hundreds of lives would be saved in the end.

The evidences of the necessity of a change in our system of warfare against Indians are not confined to the opinions and prejudices of the settlers. I saw for three hundred miles along the route, from North Platte to Denver, the mute but terribly eloquent monuments of savage warfare. But a little more than two years ago, in January, 1865, the Indians raided the entire Platte line, from Denver almost to Atchison, and spared neither age, sex, nor condition. There were not three ranches between this and North Platte that escaped—indeed, I know of but one. A portion of the ranchmen and station-keepers escaped, but not one man who fell into the hands of the savages lived to tell the story of his capture. His scalp graced the belt of some brave, and was carried home to win the favor of some dusky daughter of the forest. Every ranch and station between this and Julesburg was captured and burned, with a single exception; the men, women, and children who did not escape were inhumanly butchered, and nothing was left to show that the country had ever been inhabited but the charred walls of the mud hovels. At Julesburg they burned the station and warehouse, within range of the guns of Fort Sedgwick, in open day, and not a gun was fired, nor an effort made to arrest the appalling atrocities which traced their line of march. How much the garrison of the fort could have effected, had they tried, I do not pretend to say; but that they did not try, lest they might provoke an attack by largely superior numbers on the fort, is the truth of history. In sublime contrast with the action of the military was the heroism of several ranchmen some fifty miles east of Julesburg. The Indians had passed all the military on the route without losing a man, and had left no habitation or resident behind them except the troops, until they encircled the ranch of Hollen Godfrey, a native of Western New York, but an old resident of the Indian country. I supped with him a few nights ago, and had his story from himself. He gave it with a degree of modesty and candor that stripped the popular history of the affair of some of its romance; but that he gave it truthfully there could be no doubt. He is an intelligent, keen-eyed and brawny-armed man of over fifty, and makes no pretensions to the heroic; but he does pretend to protect his little store of whisky, tobacco, canned fruits, and notions, and his wife and children; and, more than that, he does it. He has a sod fortification running along the south and west sides of his ranch, and extending out some six feet front and rear, so as to protect two sides of the building and command the other two. His fort is but a sod wall, six feet high, with loop-holes, but it is an infinitely better fortification than the scientific officers of Fort Sedgwick have to protect that post. One hundred and sixty warriors

attacked the Godfrey Ranch, but, as it was defended, they
exhausted Indian strategy to reduce it. There were but
four men and two women in the ranch, but they had several guns each, and plenty of ammunition. The Indians
first formed a circle about the ranch, at a distance of four
hundred yards, and endeavored to draw Godfrey's fire, so
as to get his range; but he never pulled a trigger until he
had an Indian within two hundred yards. " My favorite
double-barrel ain't sure at over two hundred yards," he informed me, " and I had no ammunition to waste." Judging
that they could not accomplish anything without a direct
attack, they selected thirty of their fleetest riders, and
charged to within thirty yards of the ranch, in single file,
each one firing, and wheeling at the nearest point. They
made several such charges, each time selecting different
loop-holes for their fire; but they harmed no one, and one
or more of the charging thirty fell in each attack. Finally
they abandoned the direct attack, and fired the grass at
various points, hoping to set the ranch on fire. At one
point they had forced the fire close to the stable; but
Godfrey could reach the endangered corner under cover,
to extinguish the fire. Sixty balls struck the corner of the
stable where he was working; but he managed to protect
himself, and escaped unharmed. The siege was maintained,
with occasional charges, until night, when they were glad
to abandon the ranch and leave their dead behind them.
Wherever a dead Indian lay, Godfrey kept special watch,
knowing that they would make every effort to get their
dead off the field, and shot several who attempted to remove their fallen comrades, until they finally surrendered
their dead braves as trophies for the victor. They gave
Godfrey the euphonious sobriquet of " Old Wicked," and
since then he is known only by that name. His ranch is
called " Fort Wicked," and his actual name of Hollen God-

frey is almost forgotten. He is now expecting another
raid, as do all ranchmen on the line, and he is the only
man I have found whose face seems to brighten as he
speaks of the probability of " another brush" with them,
as he calls it. I made a careful examination of his armory.
It contains eighteen rifles, from the old hunter's to the most
improved Spencer and Sharpe. All are loaded, and ready
for the combat at a moment's warning. When we arrived.
it was nearly midnight, and the old man was on guard himself, in front of his ranch, armed with a Spencer rifle.
Night or day his ranch is never without a sentinel, and
surprise is impossible. The general belief of the ranchmen is, that when the Indians do come, they will not mo-
lest " Old Wicked." At the American Ranch, two miles
east of Godfrey's, five men, one woman, and a child were
residing, who fought the Indians until they had killed
eleven ; but they were finally overpowered, the five men
were scalped, and the woman was carried off to suffer worse
than a thousand deaths from Indian violence and torture.
At the Wisconsin Ranch, the next on the line east, two
men defended it successfully until night, killing half a
score of their savage assailants ; but their ammunition was
nearly exhausted, and they escaped to the river under cover
of darkness, and passed down safely on the ice. These
three ranches are famed in the Platte Valley as the only
places where Indian assaults were made bloody victories
or disastrous defeats in the winter of 1865. From the
Wisconsin Ranch east, clear down below Fort Kearney,
there was not a living man or woman left, excepting the
few who made miraculous escapes by flight. The stage
did not run through for six weeks ; but the tide of emigration set in as usual in the spring, and now ranchmen and
station-men occupied the line, rebuilt their sod hovels and
stables, gave the ghastly, mutilated dead decent sepulture,

and from that time until now have lived in comparative
safety.

At present the signs of an early and fearful outbreak on
this line are unmistakable, unless General Hancock can
dislodge the hostile tribes from the Republican River.
That they occupy the country from the Republican north
to the Platte Valley is evident to all. They can see every
.train, and every military movement in the valley, without
exposing themselves even to discovery. The unbroken
range of bluffs which skirt the valley on the south command a complete view of the entire Platte region. Their
spies occupy the bluffs constantly, and, as they have good
field-glasses, which they purchase from the traders, they
can distinguish every movement for twenty miles. It
seems impossible to Eastern readers that they can so
readily ascertain every movement; but when it is considered that a train can be seen distinctly on the plain ten
miles distant with the naked eye, it needs no argument to
prove that the Indians, with good glasses, know every
military movement as soon as it is commenced. During
all of last week they were signaling from the Southern
Bluffs southward toward the Republican. They signal
easily for twenty miles with a lighted arrow, which they
shoot into the air, and they can give any communication
from bluff to bluff in that way. During the day they
signal by various methods. Sometimes they do so with a
pocket looking-glass. They get the focus of the sun, make
the reflection visible for miles, and thus direct the movements of various parties to such points as they may wish.

I have thus minutely described the position and action
of the Indians to show how utterly fruitless must be Indian campaigns. Suppose General Hancock should move
north toward the Republican. They can keep twenty
miles in advance of him, and learn his whereabouts every

hour in the twenty-four. If they find his command divided and part of it vulnerable, they will assail and overwhelm it. If not, they will retreat toward the Platte, and perhaps by the time he gets to the Platte they will be in his rear on the Republican again, and no one but themselves cognizant of their whereabouts. Equally futile would be a movement from north of the Platte. They know to-day within fifty of the number of troops at Fort Sedgwick (Julesburg), and those troops cannot be moved in any direction without the spies on the bluffs signaling their numbers and direction, every hour in the day and night, clear to the Republican if necessary; and, should General Potter (in command at Sedgwick) move south to the Republican, the foe would retreat before him, keeping out of sight, and, when necessary, they would flank him east or west, and could capture the entire Platte route and be hid again before he could bring back his command. I have given the facts relative to our Indian campaign, and I leave it to your intelligent readers to determine how much the military are likely to do this season toward re-establishing peace on our great thoroughfares.

But there must be peace at any price on the Plains; and how is it to be attained? This is the great vexed question which the government is laboring to solve. Throughout the West, the ready answer is on every tongue. Recall General Conner, give Chivington a command, and let them assail the Indians wherever they can be found. The preference expressed for Conner and Chivington has its existence in the fact that they fought Indians as Indians fight white men—attack all they meet, and don't encumber themselves with prisoners. "Old Wicked" assured me that five hundred Colorado volunteers, under an acceptable commander, would not leave a hostile Cheyenne or Sioux between the Platte and Smoky Hill in two

months' time. "Where would they be?" I asked him.
"In hell," was the characteristic reply. "But are there
none of them peaceable?" I ventured to ask. "Yes, when
they're dead," was the significant answer. And yet he
confesses that the difficulties do not rest wholly with the
Indians. "They have been greatly wronged," he said;
"robbed by agents, killed without cause by thieves and
settlers; but the white man or the Indian must now be
driven out, and we can best spare the Indian." Whatever
may be the views of the government, the policy of the
Western settlers will, in the end, make peace; but it will
be the peace of death. The government will not, cannot,
assume to exterminate the Indian. It cannot make war
upon squaws and papooses; but such war will come, and
it will be effectual. The government may protest; it may
even exercise its power to shield the Indian and the fame
of the nation from savage warfare; but in the mean time
every centre of Indian hostilities will have its Sand Creek,
and every section will have its Chivington. A single
massacre now, in any of the mining regions, would result
in the destruction of every Indian within range of the
miners. They would organize independent rangers, select
their own leaders, arm and provision themselves, and their
trophies would be only Indian skeletons bleaching on their
path. Thus is Montana moving now since the murder of
Bozeman, and so will Colorado act whenever the provocation comes. The military will come after the rangers,
and keep up the semblance of civilized warfare; but the
Indian will wade through the blood of his race to entire
submission and peace, or he will finally end his history as
he falls before the pursuit of the outraged and merciless
settler.

I speak of what will be, and not of what should be. It
will be a fearful chapter when read from the opening to

the close; but the white man will know only of the necessity for relentless warfare against the red man, while his
wrongs to the savage will be without a faithful historian.
We find that these lands have gold or timber, and we want
great thoroughfares through them. The whites pass on
without treaties, with their rifles in their hands, and they
make might right. The Indian is indolent, thriftless, and
naturally a thief. He steals a horse or a cow, and they
are paid for by a war upon his tribe by the settlers or
miners. He takes the war-path, spares neither innocent
nor guilty, and the government is obliged to recognize an
Indian war. Campaigns ensue, usually without important
military results, and end in treaties made to be mutually
violated by agents on the part of the government and by
equally debauched Indians. Mr. Hooper, Delegate from
Utah, who has been with me most of the trip thus far,
assured me that the Harney war was the result of the
stealing of a cow from a train of Mormon emigrants. The
owner complained to the officer at the nearest post, and a
detail was made to recapture the cow; but the Indian
chief could not restore her, because she had been killed
and eaten. He could not surrender the guilty parties,
because he did not know them; but he proposed to pay
for the cow in horses. The officer planted a gun to command the camp, and required the restoration of the already
butchered and eaten cow in fifteen minutes. Of course it
could not be done, and he opened on the camp, killing the
chief and many others. The Indians rallied, and killed
and scalped the officer and every man of his command.
The Harney campaign followed; and thus a cow worth
about $17.50 cost us $1,000,000, or more, and many hundreds of lives. The Colorado war, which culminated in
the Sandy Creek butchery of a whole Indian camp, including women and children, had, I am credibly informed,

not even so good an excuse for its origin as the loss of a cow.* That honesty would have arrested it I do not doubt; but when once started it had to reach its logical conclusion, as must all Indian wars be decided, in meeting the savage with his own shocking savagery. It ended Indian depredations in Sandy Creek by exterminating the Indians in that section, and therefore is justified or excused. Thus will the Indian problem solve itself in time, and I think speedily; and while he may live in future story and song to gild the romance of some tale or sonnet, there will be few to stop and lament his sad fate, as the resistless march of progress appropriates his home and hunting grounds to his pale-faced oppressor.

Of Denver, Central City, and the mining regions of Colorado, I will speak in my next. I start for the mines to-morrow.

---

* I give these statements as I received them from one who warmly espoused the cause of the Indians in all our wars. At the time the above letter was written, I had more faith in the Indian than subsequent observation and experience sustained. Still, I prefer to give the letters on this subject as originally written.

LETTER VIII.

DENVER, COLORADO, May 14, 1867.

THERE is so much here that is entirely novel and intensely interesting, that I scarcely know where to begin to write and where to stop. With all the jolting, wedging, bruising, and blistering of the trip, I have written seven long letters already, and it seems to me that I have not told half of what I would wish to record. Here are gold-fields, vast prairies, fruitful farms systematically irrigated, a city that has grown from nothing in less than a decade, the Rocky Mountains presenting their colossal magnificence to the eye for one hundred and fifty miles, and a thousand and one things and incidents which crowd upon my pen; but time and space demand that they shall be sparingly touched.

I have now had several days in Denver, have tried their horse-races, their theatre, their drives, their churches, their reading-rooms, their stores, and had a gratifying trial of

8 (77)

their hospitality, and all seem to be first-class. It is true that I was not nearly so much crowded at church as I was at the race-course and at the theatre; but it is possible that most of the people were at the other churches. On Saturday a friend drove up to the hotel and invited Mrs. McClure and myself to accept a seat in his carriage for the races. His wife accompanied him, and on every side the youth and beauty of the city might have been seen driving in the same direction. Wishing to see Denver as it is, we concluded to go, and soon found ourselves on a splendid course belonging to the Agricultural Society, inclosed by a concrete wall, and cleverly filled with as fine turn-outs as could be displayed in any of the inland cities of Pennsylvania. Nor was the crowd confined to the elegant and fashionable. Here was a rude mountaineer on an Indian pony, with spurs something after the fashion of a cogged cart-wheel; there was one on an obstinate mustang, with blanket and buffalo coat; and there were hundreds of others, from regular sports, boys and men, to the staidest the city can afford. Deacons and vestrymen act as judges, and elders time the horses and make clever side bets on their favorites. The ladies have their watches, time the horses, and are most enthusiastic over the result. This may seem odd enough far East; but they tell me out here that they *don't* raffle, as the churches do East, and they thank the Lord that they are not as other men. I had never seen a horse-race, and have no love for a fast horse. I consider a 2.40 horse a nuisance; and I went to the course mechanically, because the politeness of my friend required it. I hoped that it would be brief, but in this I was disappointed. The course was fixed up for a regular afternoon's entertainment. The irrepressible lager beer was dispensed from licensed booths within the inclosure, by a regular Reading Dutchman, and ladies and gentlemen

washed down the clouds of dust occasionally by taking a
draught of the cooling stimulant.

At last time was called, and we drove up to the course
along with hundreds of others, and prepared ourselves to
enjoy the sport as much as possible. It was, as I understand it, an entirely original sort of a race. The best horse
did not run, nor did the fleetest trotter win. The purse
was offered to the horse that could trot or pace a mile the
nearest to three minutes. "Lady Alice," for instance,
trotted it in 2.44 and lost, because another horse trotted it
in 3.1$\frac{1}{2}$. After several rounds had been made, I found
myself pulling out my watch, because it seemed the custom, and, to my surprise, I found that I had been carrying
for several years the best watch for the purpose to be found
on the ground. I could time to the one-fifth of a second,
and in a little while my watch became the centre of interest
for all the amateur sports around me, of both sexes. One
heat there was a variance between the report of the judge
and the report of my watch—his making the time 3.1$\frac{1}{2}$,
while mine made it 3.1$\frac{3}{5}$; and, as another horse had been
timed at 3.1$\frac{1}{5}$, the discrepancy between the two watches
led to the repetition of the race between the two horses,
when one made time one-half second better than the other.
My excellent sporting watch, of whose valuable qualities
I had been in blissful ignorance until then, at once stamped
me as a first-class sport, and I was recognized by most of
the attendants as if I had been an old acquaintance. Indeed, I found the sport by no means hard to take, and, after
I got into it, no one watched the runs with more interest
than I did. I was fascinated with "Lady Alice,"—certainly the most graceful trotter and most amiable, winning
little pony I have ever seen. She went her mile without
the slightest break, and would have made it in 2.30 but
for the sly admonition of bystanders, who kept the time,

that she was going too fast. She is perfectly white, not larger than a good-sized Indian pony, and is the favorite of men, women, and children in Denver, and well knows and highly appreciates it. Ladies stop to caress her on the streets, and children fondle her as they would a household pet. In spite of myself, I wanted her to win, and grieved when her splendid time made her lose.

Denver is a clever place, and has clever, substantial, thrifty people. I have seen no place west of the Mississippi that equals it in the elements of positive prosperity. They have gone through the severest ordeal, and have come out purified in the crucible of sad experience. They have seen the day when gamblers, cut-throats, and thieves controlled everything—elected their municipal officers, possessed the wealth of the city, intimidated the officers of the law, and held high carnival in their work of robbery and death. But crime culminated, as it ever does, and gave birth to vigilance committees, which made a number of the most desperate outlaws dance jigs upon nothing on the hill hard by. Sometimes they would give them the form of a trial by an improvised court; but the poor devil who was ever brought before that court knew that his time had come. At other times they would determine upon the death of some notorious outlaw, and a select party, chosen for the task, would "go for him," as they all say out here, and a hasty funeral was sure to follow. One fellow, named Steel, took offense, several years ago, at an editorial in the *News*, and rode up to the editorial office and fired several shots at Mr. Byers, the editor, while another man stood off some distance to protect the assassin. A simultaneous hunt was made for Steel, and in less than half an hour he lay on the pavement dead, having been shot as he turned a corner in his effort to escape. Steel had a brother who resolved to take the life of the man who had killed him, and for two years they kept a lookout for each other. Once they met on a highway, both armed with rifles, but Steel was not the first to recognize his foe, and, when he did recognize him, the rifle of the latter was leveled. He did not fire, however, but told Steel to pass, which he did in safety, with a "dead bead" drawn on him until he was out of range. Subsequently they met in New Mexico, and the recognition was simultaneous; both attempted to fire, but the "drop" was got on Steel, and he shared the fate of his brother, and from the same hands. The man is now a quiet, respected citizen of Denver, and is generally beloved for exterminating the Steels. Another murderer was hunted by the vigilants among the Indians, captured, brought back, and hung; and a man named Ford was taken from the coach a few miles east of the city, by a company of the vigilants, shot by the roadside, and buried. Who did it, no one has ever inquired. Many doubtless could guess, while some certainly know; but it is a forbidden topic. Ford had to die to give peace and security to Denver, and he was therefore shot like a dog. It is worthy of note that the people of new Territories, who are annoyed by the usual incursion of desperadoes, make it a point of honor not to banish them to other countries. They consider it in the highest degree dishonorable, and they never allow it. One citizen of this Territory, otherwise highly respected, has lost the confidence of the people for a lifetime, for saving the life of a bad man on condition that he should leave the country forever. "It's a pity," they say—"he's a clever man, but he didn't do the fair thing in getting that fellow off." Two years ago they had pretty well banished the characters dangerous to the peace and safety of the citizens; but the orderly gamblers still controlled the municipality, had vast wealth, and pursued their shameless vocation in open day. They had their

8*

gambling-houses in some of the best buildings and business localities of the city, conducted them in view of every passer-by, just like merchants and tradesmen, had bands of music playing in front of the doors to entice the stranger, and were most prosperous. Indeed, so powerful were they at one time, that they controlled the legislature—something after the Pennsylvania fashion, I doubt not—to pass a bill legalizing gambling; and it is the chief blot on Governor Evans's official record that he approved the measure. Last winter a year the growing morality of Denver rose up against the gamblers, and drove them out. They still doubtless remain in some numbers, but they dare not expose their business to the public gaze, and they are under as wholesome restraint as in our best-governed cities. It was this early history of Denver that made Dixon blunder so fearfully as to its present social condition. To-day it is as free from open outrages upon public morals as any other Western place of the same size. Indeed, I regard it as far in advance of most of them. In Omaha the two most attractive and courted ladies at the most fashionable hotel in the place were, when I was there, known only as "Mrs. Faro" and "Mrs. Keno." Here they would not be tolerated in any circle outside of a church-pew or a horse-race. On Sunday the city was as quiet and orderly as is Chambersburg, and the number of elegant churches, seminaries, schools, including a convent, reading-rooms, etc., leaves no room to doubt that Denver has a moral tone controlling • its social life quite above the average of new cities. Dixon seems to have fallen into queer hands when he was here. His hero of the city is Bob Wilson, who, like the prophets, perhaps, is unknown as a hero at home; and his statement that from three to five persons were usually killed during the night, and sometimes in open day, has not the shadow of truth to justify it. Upon the whole, I have found no place in the Far West that appears to me so pleasant socially, and so substantial in its business, as is Denver. True, it discounts its future development of the precious metals, but not more than is fully warranted.

The general character of the Western settlers is strikingly peculiar. They cannot be judged by any prevalent rules in the densely populated agricultural regions of the East. They are here solely because they differ from those they leave behind them. Many of them may be directed to the isolated life of a pioneer by circumstances ; but the fact that they have the energy and determination to defy adversity and brave the perils and privations of the plains, shows that they are made of sterner material than those who bow to the storm. The "ranch" is the home of the Western settler. Whether of the farmer, station-keeper, or retailer of the scant necessaries which command a sale to the emigrants and travelers, all are called ranches. For six hundred miles east—from Denver to the Missouri River—there are scarcely any buildings but sod hovels, a single low story in height, and covered with sod or prairie grass. In these miserable holes they live, without a shrub or tree to shield them from the bleak storms of winter or the scorching suns of summer. Around them there are no signs of vegetable life but what is presented by the vast prairie that reaches from bluff to bluff, north and south and east and west, until the vision is lost in the hazy distance. Not a plant is cultivated; not a single growth is known that affords sustenance for man. If they should plough and sow, they would be denied their harvest-time. The dry summers, usually without rain from May until fall, parch everything that is green, and only the tough grasses of the prairie preserve a sickly, shriveled life. These settlers produce nothing. They brave the perils of the scalping-knife for a time, to gather enough money to enable them to remove east or still farther west and get a fruitful home. None of them, except those at important points like Julesburg, dream of spending a lifetime where they are. If they drive a prosperous trade for a few years, they save a considerable amount of money from the sale, at fabulous prices, of whisky, tobacco, canned fruits, bread, etc. But few of them, however, live thus until their ambition is satisfied. Every few years the Indians make a clean sweep of their ranches—the last in 1865, leaving scarcely a habitation or a settler from the Mountains to the Blue River—and if the squatters save their scalps they are glad to sacrifice their accumulated property. If they fall victims to the merciless savages, others are ever ready to take their places, and thus a continued line of settlers is kept up throughout the dreary plain.

As yet I have not seen a blossom west of Ohio, save an occasional prairie-flower, that seemed to have flung its shrinking beauty untimely upon the wide-spread waste. Nor have I heard a song except the short, sweet warble of the lark, which has been ever on our path, and merry as if surrounded with the fragrance and dews of the East. The buffalo has at times gazed at us from his retreats along the bluffs, and the elegant antelope has often paused to gratify its curiosity by viewing the intrusion of its deadly enemy upon its grounds; but whenever we got within long rifle-range it would bound off with grace and beauty that made me ever wish for its escape from the bullets sent whizzing after it. Only the jolly little prairie-dog and his inseparable companion, the owl, seemed to welcome us to their homes. In places there would be hundreds of them on an acre of ground alongside of the road, and they seemed to take especial pride in displaying themselves in their most graceful attitudes. The sober, solemn owl keeps guard at the door of their earthen house, while his dogship suns himself on the grass or gathers his meals, and sometimes both sit in fraternal peace upon the common hearth. At times the owl will fly away as the coach approaches, but usually he sits in sullen composure and merely greets us with an occasional blink as we pass. The dog, more jolly and curious, will sit up on his hind legs and chatter away until we get close to him, when he usually utters a low bark, and disappears head-foremost in his little cavern home. The tradition that the rattlesnake shares the hospitality of the dog and owl, I very much question.* I have watched carefully for such a happy family, but never saw it, and the weather we have had after leaving North Platte was just the kind that would have brought his snakeship to the surface to sun himself with his reputed companions. I doubt not that he often enters the joint abode of the dog and owl, but as an intruder and spoiler, and not as a welcome associate. I can understand why he should want to visit a nest of young prairie-dogs, for they would make a most delicate meal for him.

The Indian question is becoming one of unpleasant interest. I just escaped three incursions on the Platte route made while I was on it; and two raids have been made on it since I reached this city. The Smoky Hill route (there are two routes from the river to this point) has been raided daily since I started west from the Missouri;

---

* I notice that Mr. Greeley and some other writers insist that the rattlesnake shares the home of the owl and prairie-dog as friendly tenants in common. After writing the foregoing, I made very particular inquiries among the oldest and most observing settlers, and their testimony is generally concurrent that the snake visits the home of the prairie-dog only to forage on the little dogs. In all my observations, I never saw a snake in any of the hundreds of prairie-dog towns I passed.

and now the Indians have taken possession of the route
between this and Salt Lake. The transportation company
have refused to carry passengers westward since yesterday; and when I can get off at all, and whether it can be
traveled with safety this season, are problems I cannot
now solve. The coach company have appealed to the
military authorities for prompt protection; but when it
will be had, and, when had, whether it will be ample, are
questions the future must decide. The coach that left
Sunday for Salt Lake is stopped at a fort about one hundred and fifty miles west, and will not proceed until a
force can be had to escort it safely. Mr. Hooper, the
Mormon Delegate to Congress, and Harry Black, son of
Judge J. S. Black, of Pennsylvania, are among the passengers. Since they left, no passengers have been permitted to go, and none will start until there is a largely
increased military force on the line. Is it not most remarkable that, with fifteen thousand troops in the different departments east of the Mountains, not one of the great
thoroughfares is protected at all? There were five thousand troops in General Augur's department when I traveled
from Omaha to Denver, and yet the coach passed the ruins
of one burnt ranch, and where another had been plundered
by Indians, but two days before, without any effort to protect it. At one point the military were clustered about a
whisky-mill, because, as they said, they had been chased
in by Indians but two miles ahead, and they enjoyed their
retreat while the coach passed over the very line they reported unsafe for them to occupy. There are enough
troops in the West to guard the three great thoroughfares,
if they were detailed for the purpose, and, if that were
done, the tide of emigration would settle the Indian question more speedily and effectually than regular troops will
ever settle it. Look at the record of the last week. The

Smoky Hill route is raided daily. That of the Platte every other day. The Sauta Fé route has its tales of Indian horrors. The Missouri River route, from Benton to Helena, has its fresh graves of cruelly murdered settlers and travelers; and the Salt Lake route is confessedly impassable. Most justly do the Western settlers complain of the neglect of the government. They do not ask for troops. Their appeal is that they may be authorized to engage a force to protect themselves, to be armed, equipped, and paid; but it is persistently denied. No one doubts that one thousand Colorado volunteers would do more to suppress Indian hostilities than will the whole force under Generals Augur and Hancock. The well-known fact that they would do their work mercilessly, as do their cruel foes, would make the Indians glad to abandon their thoroughfares. They have no fear of regular troops, but they have a most wholesome dread of Western volunteers. There have never been renewed hostilities where Western men have suppressed them.

LETTER IX.

Colorado and her Progress.—The Substantial Progress of Denver.
—Its Depression and Prospects.—The Evils of Selfish Politi-
cians.—Colorado a Gigantic Suicide in the Management of her
Rich Mines.—The Rage of Speculation, and consequent Bank-
ruptcy.—The City of Abandoned Quartz-Mills.—Twenty Mil-
lions of Capital wasted in Feverish Speculation.—Legitimate
Development retarded.—The Prospect of Restoration to Pros-
perous Business. — The Trip through the Mountains. — Their
Matchless Grandeur. — The Storm-King in Conflict with the
Snow-Capped Peaks.

IDAHO CITY, COLORADO, May 17, 1867.

I HAVE now spent a week in Colorado—mingled freely
with her ever kind and generous people of all classes;
visited her vast and rich but sadly unproductive mines;
shared the proverbial hospitality of her thrifty farmers;
attended her horse-races and reading-rooms, her churches
and theatres; witnessed her variable climate—from the
chilling snow-storm to the hurricane that illumines its
path with the lightning's flash; perspired under her scorching noonday sun, and spent the evenings of the same days
around the cheerful, welcome fires of her own coal-fields,
and seen her hopeful, expanding business centres in the
tide of prosperity, and her deserted villages, created by
feverish speculation, now the unsightly monuments of
decay.   All these pass before the inquiring tourist like
some swift-revolving panorama, and each day leaves him
bewildered with its shifting scenes and its impressive
lessons.

(88)

. Of all the Western cities I have visited, Denver seems to me the most inviting and substantial. It has had the usual schooling of prosperous cities in mining regions; its history has been blotted by the supremacy of thieves and desperadoes; its vigilance committee has been compelled to usurp the functions of law in behalf of morality and public safety; its gamblers have even, until within two years, occupied its choicest places, where the victim was lured to ruin in open day by bands of music; but a sturdy, earnest, faithful people have steadily warred upon defiant crime, until it has surrendered the contest and left Denver a city of commendable order and morals. It now numbers probably eight thousand inhabitants; has seminaries and schools, nearly half a score of churches, three daily newspapers, an excellent reading-room, the finest stores I have seen west of Chicago, and a class of business men unsurpassed in character and attainments in any of our Eastern towns of the same size. It has the common fault of all Western cities. While they grow at all, they grow with feverish, unhealthy pace. Instead of systematically laboring to cheapen homes, business places, and products, they all struggle to swell the tide of inflation. In a few instances, it may be sustained by fortuitous circumstances; but as a rule it results in financial disaster and in prostrating prices, business, and growth below their proper level. Denver was the creation of the mines. It now is floating on the waves of hope, and discounting all its prospects. If the mineral wealth of Colorado shall be mastered at an early day, then must Denver even surpass the expectations of its citizens; but if successive years of doubt and hope deferred should be the fate of Colorado, then must its decline be fearful and to very many fatal. I share fully the hope of the business men of Denver, that they have reached nearly or quite the depth of misfortune,

9

and, while lots and rents are still at fabulous prices, I look for them to advance rather than decline. There is wealth enough to maintain the struggle until science shall pour into its lap the untold riches of the surrounding mountains, and the busy husbandman is yearly making the parched plains about the city to bloom and ripen with the golden fruits of the field.

Colorado has been sadly wounded in the house of her friends. She has been the football for contending cliques of selfish and corrupt politicians, and is ever convulsed by their ceaseless machinations. It would seem that Cæsar has a party, and Antony a party, but that Colorado has none. Badly as most of our Territories have been and are still governed, I know of none that has been so played upon and bedeviled by ambitious tricksters as Colorado. Her policy is unsettled, her future uncertain, and doubt, disappointment, and humiliation constitute the experience of her people. Governor Hunt would doubtless make her a State to-morrow, if he and his friends could hold the winning cards ; but whether many of the present State leaders would not, in that event, recede in favor of a continued territorial government, certainly admits of argument. This struggle, ever injurious to Colorado, must continue thus, it would seem, until she is admitted ; and for that reason alone, if for no other, I trust Congress will speedily end the contest in that way. The fact that those who ask her admission are in sympathy with the loyal men of the nation, while those who resist it are in harmony with and sustained by the faithless here and elsewhere, is an additional argument in favor of ending this bitter and disastrous strife, that should be conclusive. I firmly believe that the material interests of Colorado would be more advanced in one year under a State organization than in five years of territorial misgovernment and acrimonious political warfare.

But also in her business prosperity has Colorado been a gigantic suicide. In 1862 her mines yielded not less than eight millions of gold. In 1866 they yielded less than one million; although her mines to-day present ten times the number of rich leads they had developed when the product was greatest. True, gulch-mining has passed away—it has done its work; and the free gold of the surface-ores has changed, as the shafts have descended, into a combination with the refractory metals. But still Colorado should now be producing five millions of gold and silver annually. The rage for speculation in the East made some of the shrewder owners of the mines put them into huge corporations at bewildering prices; and the miners were not long in learning that it was easier to make a hundred thousand or so by a single sale to verdant capitalists than to earn it by pan and shovel or by rude stamps, however rich the yield. Thus the infection reached the mines, and thousands who were once content to earn treble wages at mining, became mere proprietors, speculators, and often swindlers. Legitimate mining was almost entirely abandoned, and the whole industrial wealth of Colorado was paralyzed. As soon as one good lead was sold, a hundred others, in the same locality, would be forced on to the market successfully by a regular system of jeremy-diddling, and "salted" lodes and hired certificates were used to tempt the insatiable appetite for sudden wealth.

It is a startling fact, but nevertheless true, that there has been nearly as much money invested in Colorado by corporations as the entire product of the mines from their discovery until now. I have seen the fruits of twenty millions of capital in one day's ride from Denver to this place. The Clear Creek gulch, for several miles east of Central City, until we leave it to ascend the range west of Central, is almost one continued city of idle mills and

machinery. Some are rotting down and their machinery
falling to pieces ; others give unmistakable signs of abandonment and decay. Still others are closed up in tolerable preservation, but evidently have served their purpose
in the hands of their present owners. A few—not one in
ten—are in operation ; but all, or nearly all, are guiltless
of dividends to their stockholders. Many of the finest
mills have been built by companies who were cheated in
their mines, and who found, when they were ready to run,
that they had no gold ore to reduce. Others found their
ores so charged with sulphurets that they could not amalgamate ; but perhaps the larger class were swindled and
bankrupted in their management. None seem to have had
practical ideas of the successful development of gold.
They had been promised easy dividends by those who
sold them their mines, and they all rushed up their mills,
at enormous expense, before they had opened their leads
or had any proper preparation for getting out their ore.
The result was delay, wasteful extravagance, and, usually,
bankruptcy. I saw fully a score of mills erected by Eastern companies which had not one good mine, put them all
together. One excellent stone mill, built by General Fitz-
John Porter, is now used as a stable, and it serves a better
purpose than do most of the others. Many of them have
good mines ; but they never can work them profitably as
at present organized. They must, as a rule, begin again,
procure new machinery adapted to the peculiar ores of
Colorado, bring their inflated capital down to something
like a rational figure, and enforce the same system of
economy in their management that their owners practice
in their private business affairs.

It was a painful spectacle to see miles after miles of abandoned mills standing as grim monuments of the folly of
disappointed or ruined stockholders. Their owners have

paid out their millions of money without stint, and built up a continuous city along the gulch. Black Hawk City, Mountain City, and Central City have no visible lines of separation. A single narrow street winds along the stream, with compactly-built lines of houses on either side; and even in the midst of the general prostration and ruin which surround the cities, they are keeping up the semblance of business in the very depths of despair. They are waiting and struggling to live until the new order of things shall dawn upon them—until the dead corporations shall be decently buried, and strong arms and practical minds shall drag forth the slumbering wealth. Missouri City stands in melancholy solitude upon the hill west of Central, with its tenantless houses, idle mills, and empty flumes, and Nevada City, winding off to the northwest, in continued decay, completes this colossal tomb of buried hopes.

Think not that this gloomy picture is to be perpetual. This almost universal desolation is in the midst of enough gold to pay half our national debt. The mountain-ranges along Clear Creek, and thence westward to and beyond this place, are studded with gold. The gulches have all been dug over, and have well rewarded the heroes of the pan and spade. Russell Gulch, just above Central City, had five thousand miners in it seven years ago; and from the top of the hill near by, wherever the eye turns, it meets the ridged surface that tells of the wealth given up to the industrious laborer. From where I write, I can see the same evidences of the rich deposits from the range beyond; and Empire and Georgetown are new centres of mining success. Georgetown has silver-mines which, for vastness and richness, are hardly surpassed on the continent. Like the gold-mines, they are not yet mastered; but they will soon yield to the progress of science, and then must Colorado once more send forth her millions of treasure annually. How soon this can be done, I do not pretend to say; but I hope and believe that another year will nearly, if not quite, achieve this great result. I have visited every accessible place where it is pretended to master the Colorado ores; and, while a number claim to have conquered them, I doubt whether any of the different methods now being tried combine all the essential requisites. Some of them, doubtless, save the gold; but they have not been able to work large quantities at a moderate cost. The Reese process, now in operation below Central City by the California Reduction Company, seems to have attained the highest measure of success. They are producing from $100 to $150 per ton from ores which yield no results on the ordinary mill; but they require a large cylinder, five feet in diameter and probably ten feet long, to reduce a ton per day. This process is the best effort at simplicity and the complete separation of the gold from the base metals ever yet put in operation. They can save from eighty to ninety per cent. from the obstinate ores of Clear Creek region. The Keith process is more complicated and, I learn, more expensive, but works more ore with the same power, without saving so large a percentage of the precious metal. The smelting-works of the Consolidated Gregory may or may not be successful. Of their operations and results the public have no knowledge, and stockholders generally but little, if any, more. The practical men here call them the Wall Street Works. Their stock is depressed and inflated at will by a circle of controlling owners, and of its actual value none but the initiated can judge correctly, as there are no dividends to determine the question. I do not, of course, pretend to express an intelligent judgment about these different processes. I welcome all of them, and would be glad to see ten times the number in actual operation; for only by persistent, patient, practical efforts, and the combination of the successful features of each system, can the Colorado ores be made to give up their countless wealth. The day cannot be far distant when they must yield to complete mastery, as the New and Old Worlds are both directing their best scientific and practical efforts to solve this great problem. I do not hope that any process will ever be discovered to save the corporations now scattered all over the mining regions of the Territory, as they are now organized; and the sooner this fact is appreciated, the better it will be for all parties interested. The inflated capital and cumbrous managements must be abandoned, and new organizations effected, based upon actual capital and confided to practical miners or scientific mill-men. Mining and the reduction of the ores will become separate and distinct enterprises; both will command the most skilled labor in their respective branches, and both will thus prosper. I believe that one year hence no owner of mines will think of reducing his own ores, and few owners of mills will trouble themselves about the purchase of mines. When this fearful rubbish of decayed corporations—now holding many valuable, but to them useless, mines in their clutches—shall have been cleared away, mining in Colorado will again become a legitimate business, and the miner will need no more than his own industry to develop his claim. Then, and not till then, will mining be profitable to any parties in Colorado; and when that time shall come, this rich but sorely-depressed Territory will rival California and Montana in the production of the precious metals.

I should be glad to say something about the magnificent scenery presented by the trip from Denver here, but I have neither time nor space. From the base of the mountains, some thirteen miles west of Denver, we were whirled through the narrow cañons, over the steep declivities, and along the mountain-sides, over the best stage-road I ever traveled, until we landed in this lovely little village, hemmed in by a circle of ranges. Its celebrated hot soda-springs made me tarry a day to enjoy them; and I hazard nothing in predicting that in a very few years they will attract thousands annually from the Eastern coast in search of rest and of nature's sublimest beauties. Go where you will in this section, the prospect is most charming; but all is dwarfed by the indescribable grandeur of the mountains. Volumes have been written about the grandeur of the Alps; but the world has only one such view as is presented from the rolling prairie east of Denver. In bewildering sublimity it is without parallel. There may be isolated views of the Alps as beautiful as any twenty miles of the Rocky range, and the icy land of Russian America has its St. Elias, that towers higher toward the heavens than the highest of these; but here is presented, in one grand view, nearly two hundred miles of the Rocky Mountains, from beyond Pike's Peak far off to the south, thence by the Spanish Peaks, to Long's Peak, and still on toward the north, until the range is lost in the dimness of distance. Black, threatening clouds hung about them when first I saw them, and added to the peerless beauty of the scene. Around Long's Peak the storm-king seemed to be spellbound or held an easy captive, for he had no deliverance until his heavy clouds had been discharged and broken and his thunderbolts drawn in harmless violence. Far behind the struggling tempest the setting sun was casting his evening rays through the tossing clouds. On either side of the storm he was reaching out his light, flinging the silver lining around the raging elements, breaking in refulgent splendor on the distant peaks, and flashing in

almost dazzling brilliancy upon their eternal snows. To
the north the sweeping snows, falling and flitting in graceful waves, seemed to defy the lightning's erratic flash,
while on the south the bow of promise illumined the
heavens. It was the very sublimity of moral and material
grandeur—a panorama that God alone could have fashioned. The great Snowy Range is the first to meet the
eye, and the vision insensibly wanders along its vast,
ridged, and broken sweep, which loses itself in the deep-blue
vaulted dome on either side. It has no two points alike, as
if the Great Architect meant to confuse the very conceptions of men in this colossal masterpiece of His creation.
Yonder is a cluster of peaks which look as if made up of
huge inverted icicles, and beside them it would seem that
gigantic snowdrifts, with their unique and countless forms,
had fallen in. Here is a hillock of spotless white, whose
clothing changes not with the revolving seasons, regular,
graceful, rounding with apparent mathematical precision
until it finishes with its tapered cap of snow. There are
deep ravines, vast gorges, and rude, scraggy peaks, as if
the earthquake had taken the Western world in its frenzied
arms and tossed its mightiest rocks in wild disorder across
the plains. Thus, north and south, as far as the eye can
see, and for five hundred miles toward the setting sun,
these vast, snow-clad monuments of omnipotent power present their varied beauties and surpassing grandeur, and I
turn from them only when the last ray of the receding sun
has parted with their topmost crowns, and the mellow
moonlight takes up the grateful task of displaying, through
night's weary shadows, this mute but most impressive
tribute which an all-wise God has reared to Himself.

LETTER X.

Indian-bound in Denver.—The Savages controlling the Overland
Route East and West.—General Augur's Use of Troops.—In-
teresting Telegraphic Correspondence with Him.—His "Upper
Country" Campaign.—No Earnest Effort to protect the Great
Overland Routes.—A Pleasant Time with the Coloradans.—
New Treatment of Strangers.—Why Dixon was fooled.—The
Variety of Character in the West.—The Stage-Driver.—His
Skill, Intelligence, and Courtesy.—Staging about Denver.—The
"Square Meals" of the West.—High Prices of Labor.—House-
Servants and Wives wanted.—Judge Eyster.—Colonel Wash.
Lee.

DENVER, COLORADO, May 20, 1867.

STILL in Denver, with no prospect of an early departure.
If I had the time to spare, I would not regret the detention; but, anxious as I am to get to the north by Utah, the
days hang heavily on my hands. I dare not leave for any
of the many distant points of interest in the Territory, lest
I forfeit my title to the first coach that starts out with passengers for Salt Lake, and I am putting in the time as best
I can, between devouring the exchanges of the several
newspaper offices, boring the coach-agents, complaining of
the military, and discussing the Indian question with the
people generally. It is the question of all others that the
Far-Western people prefer to elucidate; and they seem to
thrust it upon every visitor, morning, noon, and night,
until they consider that their policy of prompt and merciless extermination has been adopted.

The stage company has declined passengers since the
12th instant. On that day, Mr. Hooper, Delegate to Con-

(98)

gress from Utah, and others, started west; but they have enjoyed the luxury of rusticating for a week at Cooper's Creek, without accommodations, and living on provisions sent them daily from this place by coach. From that point west, for fifty miles, there is no stock, and, of course, no transit for passengers. The horses not captured by the Indians have been "bunched" at either end of the hostile country, and I doubt whether there will be regular coaches through for a month to come, if indeed they get into operation at all this season. The universal impression of the people is that the Indians are now stealing stock to mount their warriors, with the intention of inaugurating general hostilities as soon as the grass is sufficiently grown to feed their horses, on the war-path; and, if this be true, the Indian troubles are just beginning, and a month hence there will be no coaches at all west of this point, and very few regular trips between this and the terminus of the railroad.

I have exhausted every means I could devise to get off, but without in any degree facilitating my passage westward. Knowing as I do that General Augur has nearly or quite five thousand troops in his department, that over one thousand of them are at Fort Sedgwick, less than two hundred miles east of this point, and that he has but this one great thoroughfare to protect, the Smoky Hill route being in Hancock's department, I at once appealed to him, by telegraph, to hasten forward a sufficient number of troops to protect the stations and the travel. I was amazed to find less than three hundred troops on the entire line between this and Salt Lake—a distance of six hundred miles,—and of that number less than one-third mounted, or in any way fitted to protect the route. I took it for granted that General Augur would at once open the line, as it seemed to be entirely in his power to do so; but he telegraphed me a speech in reply, at the cost of $18.06, the material portion of which was that the route didn't need protection, and that if it did he couldn't protect it. He also favored me with the luxury of a disquisition on the obstinacy of army contractors, who were preventing him from moving his army into the "upper country." I need not say that I ceased telegraphic communication with military head-quarters. I may, if detained at Big Laramie, get General Augur to telegraph me the 119th Psalm, if the time passes wearily; but I do not think it likely that I shall make any further telegraphic efforts to get the Indians out of the way.

The "upper country," of which General Augur speaks as the destination of his army, is where not a solitary traveler nor private train has ventured this season, and where none will venture while there are any Indian disturbances. There are forts to supply, and government trains must be protected in supplying them; but beyond that any military movements in that direction will be disastrous failures. Here is a great thoroughfare, over which thousands of people wish to travel this season, and it should be made safe first of all; but it seems to be the last point looked after by our military commanders. They insist that the Indians are not. at war,—that they are simply stealing stock. Granted, for the sake of argument, that they are now simply stealing, what are they stealing horses for? It is done by Indians who have openly declared war; and when they have the horses, what will they do? I may be stupid on this point, but I cannot resist the conviction that if the Indians were to try their peculiar system of thieving upon General Augur, he would use different terms to express his idea of their acts, as long as he could use any terms at all. In the same raid by which they interrupted the coach-line west, they killed and scalped one railroad engineer, and severely wounded and imperfectly scalped another ; and on the Smoky Hill route they have killed three station-keepers since I have been here, scalped them, cut them in pieces, and burned their remains. This is called "thieving" in military parlance out West; and I presume that if the Indians should scalp me, and have a war-dance over my mutilated corpse, the commanding officer would report a case of petty larceny on the part of the savages.

Judge Carter, of Bridger, has been among the detained passengers here for several days, but he got together a party of half a dozen frontier-men and started off in the coach yesterday for Cooper's Creek, intending to do the best they could thence westward. They will join Hooper's party at Cooper's, and may manage to "bunch" (as they call it here) two coaches, and proceed slowly, traveling in the dangerous country only at night. In this way they may get through ; and Judge Carter proposes to do the work of the government by sending back friendly Indians to protect the coaches. So far as concerns the opening and protecting of the stage-line, I would not exchange Judge Carter for a score of major-generals, even with a lieutenant-general thrown in.

Save my disappointment in not getting west, as I hoped, my stay among the people of Colorado has been exceedingly pleasant. They do not cultivate the ornamental very much in the reception of pretentious strangers, but they do welcome, with genuine kindness and hospitality, all who behave themselves properly. Those who come here overflowing with knowledge, and the grace to dispense it in a patronizing way to the denizens of the plains and mountains, generally go wooling and come home shorn; but those who come as gentlemen, and prove themselves worthy of the title, meet with gentlemen and receive the treatment due. The people here judge quite as

well of the merits of a gentleman as do the more assuming
circles of the East—perhaps a little better. They do not
lay much stress on the color of a man's gloves, the cut of
his coat, or the elegance and grace with which he swings
his cane; but they appreciate good manners, intelligence,
and fair repute, and welcome them to their firesides. He
who comes here, expecting to judge men by appearances
and get his information from the outward signs of gentility,
will, as a rule, spend his money and time in vain, besides
making a fool of himself. You will often find some graduate of Yale "bull-whacking" his own team from the river
to his mines, looking as if he had seldom seen soap and
water, and had pitched his clothes on at some second-hand
shop; while if you want a first-class loafer you will find him
in seedy gentility, sponging upon strangers and visitors
about public houses, ever ready with startling tales, such
as were played off upon Dixon. Had that gentleman met
the people as a student rather than as a teacher, leaving
the "Athenæum" behind him, he would have been spared
the fantastic figure he cuts in his history of these settlers.
Even Bob Wilson, his galvanized hero of Colorado, admits
only to having casually met Mr. Dixon, and, beyond Bob,
no one confesses to his acquaintance.

There is here, as elsewhere, every variety of character ;
but of all classes the sojourner can learn much, if he so
chooses. The jolly, self-complaisant, semi-comic whittler
who described to me the nature of the cottonwood by
saying that he had built a shanty of it and found it
warped, in one day and night, so that it stood "*square* on
the roof," and who described the perpendicular heights of
Pike's Peak by declaring, in the most positive manner,
that it required a man to look four times, and chalk the
places, before he could see to the top, was neither fool nor
knave, nor did he leave, without giving me, in his own

extravagant way, much information that I desired. But the stage-driver is the institution of the Far West, and I have enjoyed his acquaintance iu no common degree. The driver of the plains and mountains is an expert with the lines and whip, and has no charge of horses except-ing when they are on the road. He is an educated man in his line. He usually drives from forty-five to fifty miles, while the teams are changed every ten miles. When he arrives at a "swing station" (where the teams are changed), he drops the lines, and chats with the land-lord or the passengers while his team is unhitched and another attached. He then walks, with becoming dignity and conscious responsibility, about the newly-hitched team, sees that the traces, lines, etc. are all in perfect order, then gathers up his lines and, with the majesty of a legislative presiding officer, calls out, "All 'board," and away he goes. I have made the acquaintance of every one I have traveled with, and never yet found one that even approached loqua-city. They will talk freely, and always intelligently, but you never get more than a hasty glance of their eyes from their gay and fleet teams. Some, indeed, I found unpleas-antly reticent, but all, without exception, were courteous. I doubt not that they are often bored until their patience is sorely tried, and perhaps I repeated, in some instances, that particular feature of their experience; but, as a rule, I found them highly entertaining. They usually drive six horses, and aim to be, as they doubtless are, the best drivers in the world. I rode outside with them frequently, and was charmed with the caution and precision they display in the narrow, steep, and sharply-curved roads of the mountains. With a single hand they will sweep their horses around a short turn, or pass another team, with a grace and elegance that are perfectly artistic; and, while they almost fly down the steep mountain declivities, they insure safety by never

losing for a moment the complete control of a single horse
in the team. A word from the driver is expected to be
obeyed by the horse to which it is addressed; and woe to
the luckless animal that does not heed! The long lash of
the whip will whirl in the air, and its keen, silken cracker
will bring the blood from the flank of the obstinate animal.
The teams are all matched, with the gayest of leaders, and
it is not uncommon for them to make ten miles an hour on
the plains, or descending the mountains. Distance in staging seems to be dwarfed, out here. I now consider fifty
miles of staging, over these excellent roads, but a pleasant
little morning ride. Last week I breakfasted at Idaho, drove
six miles over one of the steep spurs of the mountains,
and was in Denver for two o'clock dinner—having traveled
nearly sixty miles over harder hills than separate Chambersburg from Bedford. I tire, of course, of being cramped
up in a crowded stage ; but a little walk at each station, in
this region, makes one feel as fresh as if resting for an
hour. The air is so pure that it seems to strengthen not
only the lungs, but the blood, the brain, the very bones,
and it is a luxury to breathe in its sweet invigoration.

I had read so much of the "square meals" of the Far
West, that I expected to find eating anything but a luxury
in this country. In this I have been agreeably surprised.
I have traveled the plains for three hundred miles by
stage, and the mountains for over one hundred miles,
and the meals have been quite as good as the average
of hotel meals in the East. At the Alkali Station, fifty
miles west of the railroad, with not a cultivated field or
even a garden within two hundred miles of it, I had the
best meal set before me since I left Chicago ; and all along
the plains, and far up in the heart of the mountains, I have
found good bread and butter, fresh eggs, tolerable ham and
beef, and often the most delicious antelope or venison

broils, and I have had canned fruits and vegetables at
every meal, whether breakfast, dinner, or supper. Corn,
tomatoes, beans, oysters, and all kinds of fruits are
scarcely luxuries in this far-off region, for they tempt the
appetite of the traveler every day. The uniform price of
meals for travelers is $1.50, and they are usually paid for
most cheerfully. By fall the Pacific Railroad will have
passed Denver one hundred miles to the north ; and the
Eastern Division, from Leavenworth by Smoky Hill, will
run direct to Denver in the spring of 1868. Prices must
then diminish, as the cost of transportation has heretofore
been enormous, and living will be nearly as cheap in Colorado as in Pennsylvania.

The high cost of the necessaries of life makes the wages
of labor very high, and the development of the country
has thus been greatly retarded. Ordinary farm-hands
command from forty-five to sixty dollars per month, with
boarding, and in the mining regions five dollars per day is
a moderate price. But the highest rates, comparatively,
are paid to domestics, for the reason that female servants
are exceedingly scarce. But few laboring women can afford to come to the Territories, and those who happen here
get fabulous wages. The most ordinary female house-ser-
vants get fifty dollars per month, and board, and good
female cooks command from seventy-five to one hundred
dollars per month. One hundred ordinarily good female
servants could now find permanent employment in pleasant
homes in Denver, at an average of twelve dollars per week
and boarding ; and three months' wages would pay their
fare from the East to this city. Besides the high wages they
can get, they are in equal demand in the matrimonial
market. The adult unmarried population of the Territory
is probably ten males to one female, and here, as elsewhere,
people continue to be given in marriage. The importation

10*

of several hundred virtuous, industrious, single females into Colorado would be a great benefaction both to the females themselves and to the people of the Territory.

I had hoped to meet Judge C. S. Eyster here by this time, but he is not even reported on the route as yet. He is the most popular official in the Territory, and is anxiously inquired for daily. It will be gratifying to his many friends in the East to know that he is deservedly esteemed here both as a citizen and as a judge; and whether Colorado shall be a State or a Territory, Judge Eyster *will share her honors.*

I send my kindest regards to Colonel Wash. Lee, of Luzerne, for the *magnificent glass* he sent me before starting on my trip. With it I can bring the distant ranges alongside of the coach-wheels as I travel along, and can fringe the green grass of the prairie with the far-off mountain snows. I have not yet tried it on Indians, as I have not lost any, and therefore do not hunt for them; but, if they should come around the edges, unless all appearances are deceptive, I could kill them ten miles off with a common rifle and Lee's glass. I trust that he will take my word for this, as I prefer not to practice shooting at redskin targets during this journey.

Still Indian-bound in Colorado.—End of Hancock's Expedition.—
Another Peace-Talk to be had with the Savages.—The Indians
raid the Overland Routes, while the Troops are ordered to hunt
Indians where they are not to be found.—General Sherman's
Policy.—Great Injustice to the West.—The Tide of Emigration
arrested.—The Necessity of protecting One Route.—Contrac-
tors said to be encouraging War.—The Sad Failure of Mining
Companies in Colorado.—Their Hopeless Future.—Legitimate
Enterprise the only Way to Success in the Mines.—The Varia-
tions of Colorado Climate.—The Crops.

DENVER, COLORADO, May 21, 1867.

I AM still Indian-bound in this city, and when I can go
on westward with reasonable safety depends entirely upon
the enemy, rather than upon friends. With nearly ten
thousand troops in the departments of Generals Hancock
and Augur, there are not any ten miles of the two great
thoroughfares, from the Missouri River to this place, that
twenty Indians could not "clean out" any day. Hancock
has made one campaign against the red-skins, and with
what result your readers well know. It is now officially
announced that his expedition is at an end, and General
Sherman has joined Hancock to go down and have a
peace-talk with the same Indians who talked peace with
him at Fort Zarah and immediately proved their pacific
intentions by fresh atrocities. In the mean time, while the
troops are "bunched" in forts, the Smoky Hill route is
the scene of a fresh raid or murder almost daily, and the
coach passes solely because the Indians thus far have

(107)

allowed it to do so. Since I have been detained here, three station-keepers on that route have been murdered by the Indians, scalped, their bodies cut to pieces and burned, and several stations have been robbed of stock, and ranches have been destroyed. There are enough idle troops in the department to station fifty on every mile of the road; but they seem to be used for every other purpose than that for which they should be employed. On the Platte route five distinct raids have been made since I have been on it, one station burned, and but two days ago a stock-keeper was killed and scalped within a mile of Fort Sedgwick. West, the Indians have cleared the stage-route of stock for eighty miles,—stealing part of it and compelling the withdrawal of the balance,—and two men have been scalped. The stage company have declined to forward passengers west from this point since the 12th instant, when Mr. Hooper and others started and got as far as Cooper's Creek, where they still remain. Judge Carter picked a party of frontier-men and started, determined to fight their way through and organize a force of the Indians to escort the stage. All these things have occurred in a department where there are five thousand troops, with nearly the same number in Hancock's department, immediately south. Instead of protecting the thoroughfares, they are planning grand campaigns north and south of the lines of travel, leaving them to be raided, ravaged, and crimsoned with the blood of the emigrant and traveler whenever the Indians take a fancy that way. The stage-line of six hundred miles from here to Salt Lake, traversing all the passes of the mountains, where the best ambuscades in the world are to be found, has less than three hundred soldiers on it—two companies of infantry at Fort Bridger, just where the Indians are friendly, and one company of cavalry, reduced by desertions and demoralized generally. Instead of posting troops on the line to protect emigration, transportation, and travel, General Augur (doubtless acting under specific orders) is busy preparing for a campaign into the "upper couutry," just where nobody thinks of going, and where there is nothing to protect but the troops in the forts. Last year the Reno and Phil. Kearney route was pronounced open for emigration; and hundreds of graves along its entire length, with the Phil. Kearney massacre as the central figure, attest how the promise was kept with the emigrants. This year it is accepted as hostile and impassable, and two thousand troops are about to march along it, strengthen its posts, and play the farce of protecting a route that is a stranger to the tread of the white man, while the great thoroughfare is practically abandoned by the military, excepting as troops are huddled in huts here and there to mock the sojourner.

I do not hope to accomplish anything by stating the facts. Out here no one expects sensible action on the part of the military, and they have to bow to perpetual imbecility and wrong. General Sherman is presumed to have more common sense than usually falls to the lot of commanders; but should it be necessary to say to him that his first duty to emigration, to the West, and to the country is to determine upon some route or routes to the Far West, and give adequate, complete protection? Colorado, Montana, Idaho, and Nebraska are inviting fields for thousands upon thousands of the enterprising and industrious people of the East; and the right way to make the West self-protecting is to maintain safe routes for emigration, so that settlements may spring up in this distant world of wealth. When the settlers once rear their homes or the miners open their claims, the Iudian is doomed to peace or death. He well knows that red tape and the circumlocution of government warfare do not obtain in the summary adjust-

ment of difficulties between him and them, and he therefore emigrates, or smokes the pipe of peace in their ranches.
I doubt not that ten thousand people will be prevented
from emigrating to the Far West this season by the Indian
troubles on the great thoroughfares, and this, too, when
there are more than enough troops already here to afford
the amplest protection. Is the government wise in this
policy? If it is, I must confess that the whole West, and
all who visit it, are most fearfully deluded. I know that
the popular impression in the East, and perhaps the prevalent conviction in official circles, is that Indian wars are
mere speculations. I am not prepared to deny this as a
general proposition. I cannot resist the belief that most,
if not all, Indian troubles have their origin in frauds, or
contemplated frauds, alike upon the Indians and the
government. I hear it charged that government contractors, agents, and officers have much to do with the
creation of Indian wars; and the suspension of travel
West is imputed to a deliberate purpose of certain contractors who wish to compel modified terms from the
government. These grave suspicions may or may not be
so; I have not means of ascertaining whether they are
wholly or partially true; but I do know that if the
government would throw its troops upon the routes of
travel and make them safe for the contractors, there could
be no pretext whatever for attempting to create Indian
troubles. It would seem that the surest policy for the
government to pursue would be to open the lines, fight, or
beat the Indians away from them, and then say to contractors, "The way is open: perform your duty."

But enough of grumbling: it will do no good. I am but
repeating the earnest protests of the Western people for
years against the costly and terrible mismanagement of
Indian affairs; and, as they have thus far been disregarded,

I need not cherish the hope that now, when silly campaigns have been deliberately planned and the troops disposed to carry them out, the observations of an humble tourist will be heeded. I will get away West as soon as I can, and have some faint hope that to-morrow will see me on the way to Fort Saunders, to take my chance with the rest in passing the gauntlet of the savages.

There is much I would like to say about Colorado; but time and space compel me to be brief. I have visited her gold and silver mines, and seen the fearful waste Eastern speculation has scattered in fatal profusion among them. With countless wealth in the mountains, there are palpable decline and distress in every mining region I have seen. Let me entreat Eastern companies to learn at once the utter hopelessness of their enterprises as now organized and managed. Their mills are almost wholly worthless, because they are not adapted to the successful reduction of the obstinate combinations to be found everywhere in the Colorado ores. Many companies now on the very verge of bankruptcy, or actually in its embrace, have valuable mines, and they cling to the hope that they may yet make their enterprises successful. It is folly; it is madness. It would be a blessing to both Eastern capitalists and Colorado if one vast fire should sweep the mills of Clear Creek from existence. Their charred walls would not impede progress, as do vast buildings with engines and mills unemployed, and never to be employed, as at present constituted. Equally foolish, wasteful, and disastrous must be every effort of amateurs to reduce the ores by experiments with the various processes, flooding the market, and tempting the disappointed stockholder to make another effort to save his investment. Let every Eastern company wait until the problem is fully and practically solved here among the mines, and then they may hope to get more returns.

They could profitably employ some capital, in the mean time, by thoroughly testing their lodes and bringing to the surface large quantities of ore. When the time comes for the successful reduction of these ores, the work of reducing them will be as distinct from mining as is milling from farming. Where there are good mines, therefore, the companies which early accept the inevitable revolution in the production of the precious metals will yet attain success; but let them understand that these mills are, as a rule, valueless, and the cost of their construction an irretrievable waste. I firmly believe that this year will nearly, if not entirely, master these ores, so that every good mine can be worked profitably; but stockholders might as well attempt to change the fashion of the Snowy Range as to persist in the effort to mine and reduce these ores with their present machinery. I know that this will be unwelcome information to thousands of your readers; but its truth is fearfully attested by the sacrifice of $20,000,000 in fruitless efforts to refute it.

I have seen almost every feature of the variegated climate of Colorado. I entered Denver through a regular old-fashioned thunder-storm. Next day I braved its scorching sun and parching winds. I next spent a day in the mountains, starting with a clear morning and a hot sun, soon to be exchanged for a thunder-shower, and that soon to give way to a driving snow-storm—giving me sunshine, rain, thunder, and snow in a distance of thirty miles. Since then we have had what would pass for regular Pennsylvania March storms of sleet and snow. Yesterday the snow fell all the day, and now the mountain-ranges are clad in white, while the plains have been cleared of their snowy garb. Each year seems to increase the number of showers, and I doubt not that both Colorado and Utah will soon be farmed with very little, if any, resort to irrigation. It seems that as the water is conducted over the plains by ditches, and spread over the fields, it creates clouds and rains, and as irrigation is extended its neces sity is gradually diminished. Last year, Utah could have grown all its field-crops without any resort to irrigation, and even in Colorado, where irrigation is in its infancy, but little was needed in the settled regions. But for the grasshoppers, the agricultural interests of the Territory would be enjoying a high degree of prosperity. Last year they did but little harm, and the crop of wheat is more than equal to the wants of the people. It is now sold cheaper here than in Philadelphia; but oats, barley, and corn command the same price as wheat—five cents per pound. Should the mines be conquered by another year, the population of Colorado would double in six months, and agricultural products would command a still higher price ; but, in any event, farming seems to be one of the certain channels to success in Colorado.

I hope to get away to-morrow. If not, I may go down to Pike's Peak to visit the Garden of the Gods, the Boiling Spring, etc., and may write again of Colorado.

11

LETTER XII.*

A Journey to Colorado City.—Crossing the Divide.—Thunder- and
Snow-Storms.—The Pines.—Bierstadt and the Colorado Rocks.
—Storm-staid at "The Dirty Woman's Ranch."—A Western
Cabin.—A Pleasant and Hospitable Hostess.—A Bright Fire
and Excellent Supper.—The Guests chat away the Evening.—
The "Garden of the Gods."—Grandeur of the Monuments.—
Natural Pillars from Three to Five Hundred Feet High.—They
appear like Ruins of Colossal Statuary.—The Mineral Springs.
—Camp Creek Cañon.—A Severe Snow-Storm.—Vain Attempt
to procure Shelter from a Fugitive Mormoness.—Petrifactions
on the Platte.

DENVER, May 26, 1867.

THURSDAY, the 23d, trunks packed, bills paid. Coach
drove up at seven for Salt Lake, and we were all at the door,
expecting to bid farewell to Colorado and its beautiful
mountains, possibly forever. Agent comes along, and in-
forms us we can only go to Fort Saunders, one hundred and
thirty miles, and will have to remain there over Sunday,
on account of the great accumulation of mails caused by
the Indians stealing Wells, Fargo & Co.'s horses. "Uncle
Sam" makes the drivers take an oath that they will see
the mails through safe, giving the passengers the widest
liberty of looking out for themselves in case of attacks

---

* This letter was written by Mrs. McClure to a friend, who furnished it for publication in the Chambersburg "Repository." As it
gives an account of a very interesting portion of Colorado that I
did not see, and as the letter has already been given to the public,
I embrace it in this collection of letters, to complete the description
of the many points of peculiar interest on the overland route.

(114)

from the noble red men, danger from high waters, or any of the other difficulties which are liable to beset one's path on a journey "Across the Continent." Much disappointed, we had our baggage moved again to our rooms, and I at once made up my mind to see Colorado's greatest wonders, "The Monuments," "Soda Springs," and the magnificent rocks called by the pretentious name of the "Garden of the Gods."

Hired a livery "turn-out," with a boy driver, and, with W. and Mrs. C. for companions, was on the road to the classical ground in less than an hour. The weather was not promising, and the mountains, especially the Snowy Range, were hidden from sight by clouds threatening and sullen in aspect. We had not proceeded far when rain set in. The road was generally fine across the plain, with a gradual ascent of fifty or sixty miles to the Divide, a high piece of ground separating the head-waters of the Arkansas from those of the Platte, and famous for its thunder- and snow-storms, both of which we encountered. The country is diversified with groves of beautiful spruce pines, so refresh- ing to an Eastern eye after the long stretches of treeless prairie on the Platte; and the hills on each side are full of white sandstone rocks, in broken, irregular lines, looking precisely like ruins of Hindoo or Egyptian temples, with their broken arches, columns, porticos, and overhanging towers in endless confusion. Bierstadt, it is said, made some beautiful drawings of these rocks, but refused to paint them, giving as his reason that few people would be- lieve they were real rocks of this continent, and would say he had taken some foreign ruins and tried to palm them off on the public as specimens of Colorado rock-scenery. Since seeing them, I am not surprised at his conclusion.

The distance from Denver to Colorado City is seventy miles. We drove fifty by six o'clock; the last twelve through a furious thunder-storm. Jove hurled his bolts around us in a manner terrifying to mortal ears, and the winds were not gentle breezes, but blew what a sailor would call "great guns," the carriage rocking at times in the blast. There are three ranches on the road, known by the euphonious names of the "Red-Headed Woman's Ranch," "Pretty Woman's Ranch," and the "Dirty Woman's Ranch." After a most tedious and anxious drive, we arrived at the last-named, so called from the untidy person and habits of the divinity who once presided over it, and who, as the legend runs, finally died of dirt. The place was not inviting; but, as the gods seemed determined not to be propitious, we concluded any sort of shelter was preferable to a farther drive in the pelting storm with a tired team. The house was a low one-story hut, divided into four small rooms, devoid of almost all comfort. One ordinary-sized pane of glass constituted the window in the "room," as it was called. The furniture consisted of a round pine table, covered with an old white muslin cloth; three chairs (one wooden, one split-bottom, and one with seat composed of strips of calf- or cow-skin plaited across), a small looking-glass, half broken away, the remainder, from familiar marks upon it, looking as if it had not seen water since the previous summer, and indicating clearly that the flies were the sole possessors and the only vain members of the family; a small trough, in which was a wooden bucket with ladle; a tin wash-basin; and on a nail opposite hung a homespun towel. The walls were papered with "Harper's Weekly," leaves from the "Atlantic Monthly," etc., which served us for reading-matter for a half-hour or so, and struck us as "useful as well as ornamental." The sole occupant was a little girl, five or six years of age, who sat shivering over a scanty fire in a cook-stove in the kitchen. On inquiry for the mistress, she informed us she was milking. She soon made her appearance; a tall, pleasant-faced woman, with a pair of beautiful brown eyes. I knew at a glance that a kind heart had written the lines so easily read there, and, in spite of ill health, advancing age, and poverty, they had maintained their sway. She made many apologies for her rude home, but said she would make us as comfortable as possible. In a few minutes pine chunks and sticks were placed endways (no andirons) in the rudely-built chimney, and soon a roaring fire lighted up the bare walls and floor with a glow peculiarly its own. We were soon cosey and comfortable, drying our clothes and wondering what the "folks at home" would say could they take a peep at our experience of frontier life. In a little time supper was announced. As we had only lunched instead of dined that day, we did ample justice to the fare, which was excellent,—much better than we had expected from the appearance of the hovel. Delicious soda-biscuit, poached eggs, ham, honey, coffee, butter, and cream, constituted the bill of fare. The pasture is so fine that butter and milk are unusually good—much better than we had tasted since leaving home. The dining-room furniture consisted of an old pine sideboard, and a long table with a bench on each side for seats. One pane of glass served for a window. Two storm-beaten travelers of the bifurcated species were added to our party,—one an old frontiersman from the San Luis Valley, an eighteen-year resident of the country. After supper, "we formed around the ingle a circle wide," the old pioneer leading in the conversation, giving us many interesting accounts of the settling of the Territory and of the Indians. The latter he hates most intensely, and, like all the other settlers, thinks Chivington and Conner the only two men who can keep the Indians at peace with the white men. We each chatted our favorite hobby; mine, of course, was border-warfare in the nineteenth century, and

11*

our experience with the chivalry. About nine o'clock our hostess made her appearance with a tallow candle, in the most primitive of tin candlesticks, and offered to show us to bed. Bidding "good-night" to the pioneer who had entertained us so pleasantly, we followed the "brown eyes." Our room—about six by ten or twelve, no window, not even a crevice for fresh air—looked like a huge store-box. In this were two clean-looking beds, with just room for one to stand between them. The bedsteads consisted of two posts or pine logs fastened in each side of the wall, and the beds were made on them. The only furniture was a small stool on which to set the candle. After retiring, being really very comfortable, we were soon made oblivious by "tired nature's sweet restorer, balmy sleep," and did not wake until called to breakfast.

After that very important meal, we paid our bill ($10), hitched up our horses, found them gay as ourselves after the night's rest, bade good-by to our kind hostess and the guests (the old pioneer hoping "it would burn out"—meaning clear off—before we had gone far), and started for the remaining drive of twenty miles. The clouds were threatening, and in a little time poured torrents of rain upon us. The mountains were completely veiled in the mist; had it not been for the sandstone rocks in their picturesque ruin the ride would have been a dreary one. We passed Monument Creek, eight miles this side of Colorado City, in the rain, and concluded to visit it on our return. As we approached the "Garden of the Gods," the clouds lifted a little, and the sun gave us a few dreary smiles as we entered. And such an entrance! Here my pen fails to give any correct idea of the grandeur of the rocks. On either side towers a sandstone rock of bright brick color, from three to five hundred feet in height, and seventy-five to a hundred or more in length; at a little distance in front, directly in the pathway, stands another, of grotesque form, looking like some colossal sentinel placed there to guard the sacred inclosure. After passing his majesty, numbers of these bright-red rocks meet the eye on every side, looking like ruins of colossal statuary, their sides marked and seamed with the snows and rains of ages. We spent an hour wandering among these stupendous monuments of the Creator's power, gathered a few wild flowers, broke some pieces of rock, to take with us as souvenirs, looked again and again, and could scarcely tear ourselves away. But the clouds gave ominous signs, and, with many regrets, we took our seats in the carriage and finished our drive of one and a half miles to Colorado City.

Here our patience was sorely tried. The hotel had changed proprietors, the new one having moved the day before, and everything was "confusion worse confounded." The Soda Springs, three miles north, being the next on the list of curiosities, we hoped after dinner to be able to drive there and spend the afternoon; but it rained incessantly, and we were obliged to give it up for that day. Retired early, and, in spite of bedbugs and other luxuries too numerous to mention, slept soundly. By our own request, we were called at half-past five. The sun had just risen over the mountains, lighting up the snowy crest of Pike's Peak (fifteen miles away) with the rosiest hues, lifting the vapory clouds from the foot-hills and the middle range and sending them in myriads of graceful forms up the mountain-sides, striking the immense white and red sandstone rocks near the "Garden of the Gods," and making altogether a most gorgeous and never-to-be-forgotten picture. These beautiful red rocks extended along most of our way to the springs. One in particular attracted us from its resemblance to the pictures we see of the Coliseum. The

springs are three in number, and bubble up out of the
ground in the merriest way, emptying into the "fontaine
qui bouille" (boiling fountain), named, I suppose, from the
swiftness of the current and the noise it makes in rushing
over the rocks and pebbles in its bed. The water is very
strongly impregnated with soda, and with lemon or other
syrups makes a most delicious drink. The water, as it
runs from the springs into the stream, deposits a calca-
reous tufa, white and in waves, looking almost like snow-
drifts. I should have been glad to bring away specimens,
but had not room in my valise. There are no fish in the
"fontaine qui bouille;" they don't like the soda-water, it
is said, although the stream looks like our trout streams.
Near one of the soda springs is a small iron spring; and
doubtless when the place is prospected, as it will be, there
will be other springs found of valuable medicinal proper-
ties. Many persons visit these springs now for rheumatism, scrofula, etc., and are always much benefited. A
hotel is talked of; and, should it be built, the place will be
very attractive. We had an hour there, and then the clouds
gathered.

We drove home through the "Garden of the Gods;"
stopped at Camp Creek Cañon to see the rocks there, and
found them equal in grandeur to their brothers. I slipped
into the creek and got my feet wet. We rode eight miles
to Monument Creek; raining and very disagreeable. Here
we found a still more wonderful rock-formation. At a little
distance some groups, hidden as they are by pine-trees,
look like a huge cemetery, the rocks running up in columns
land single shafts from six to fifty feet in height; others
look precisely like groups of Shakers in capes and broad
brims. By moonlight they must have a weird, wild look;·
and one could imagine them the ghosts of giantesses sent
back to hold some special conclave on material subjects.

Our ride home was through one of the most severe snow-storms I have ever been in. Once the road was so drifted that we were fearful we had missed it and were driving at random on the prairies. The snow blew in our faces, covering the blankets to the depth of three or four inches. A hut looming in sight, we drove to it. Such squalor and poverty I never saw before, and hope I shall never see again. The hut was floorless, and leaking in every part; the children were put to bed to keep warm, and I really believe the mother was insane. She had a wild look about the eyes, and her dress was very eccentric. She had run away from the Mormons, and had been in this hut only four days; the storm coming on, she could not look for food, work, or anything else. I was heart-sick, and determined that a night on the plains was preferable to staying there. Finding we were not lost yet, and hoping to be able to keep the road, I slipped some money in her hand, and started again in the frightful storm. We reached Denver at half-past four o'clock, wet to the skin and perfectly benumbed with cold, and did not have an ache or pain after. One peculiarity of this climate is, that, however drenched and cold you may be, you rarely ever suffer from it, particularly if you have flannel next the skin. The snow was two feet deep in the mountains.

This is Sunday. I have been interrupted all the time; and, as we expect to leave for Salt Lake to-morrow morning, have concluded to finish to-day. Yesterday I spent the day on the banks of the Platte, sixteen and a half miles from here, in search of petrified fish and other curiosities. I saw fish almost a foot long imbedded in the rocks, with a pearly case around them, which on exposure to the sun reflects all the colors of the rainbow. They are, however, so brittle that we could only get pieces of them. The specimens of petrified wood are beautiful. I will have quite a nice cabinet if all reach home in good condition.

Storm-bound in Denver.—An Old-fashioned Eastern Settled Rain.—The "Oldest Inhabitant" cannot explain it.—Rapid Rise of the Mountain-Streams.—The Stage stopped by the Flood.—Peril of Passengers in crossing a Little Stream.—Prospects of Indian Raids.—No "Friendlies" visible but the Utes.—The First Settlers of Colorado.—Legislation to defeat Foreign Creditors.—Summary Execution of Part of Quantrell's Band.—Agricultural Productions of Colorado.

DENVER, COLORADO, June 1, 1867.

STILL in Colorado. The snow-clad ranges of the Rocky Mountains, which awakened such enthusiasm when I first beheld them, have become common and uninteresting in my anxiety to get out from this Indian and weather imprisonment. Think of it, in this usually sun-parched land, where vegetation gasps for the artificial stream and withers in its absence—a regular storm of eight days' duration. Just a regular, old-fashioned, Eastern settled rain, much to the surprise of the oldest inhabitant, and defying all the weather-wise of the city to explain the order of its coming. And what was rain in Denver was snow and rain on the first and second ranges, and a regular driving winter snow-storm on the Snowy Range. But gradually the frosty breath of winter reached out from the mountains to the plains, until it chilled the storm eastward two hundred miles, and robed the eastern prairies in spotless white. Just as we were about to enter the threshold of summer, Old Winter crowned himself in his proudest attire, and bade the blossoms and verdure of the plains and mountain-forests wait

(122)

for a more convenient season. For eight days the sun did not appear. At times the clouds would lift up along the mountains and give us the faint promise of a ray of sunshine; but soon the storm-king would assert his imperious sway again, and the flitting snow-storm would frolic with the mountain-peaks, hurled hither and thither in fantastic forms and flights, while the lightning kissed the plains and rocked them with its thunders.

In this country, where the mountains shed the rains and melting snows so speedily, the streams rise and fall with marvelous rapidity. The road to Salt Lake was utterly impassable for several days, and is now unfit to be traveled. The little rivulets, which are dry most of the time, and usually can be stepped without wetting the feet, rose from ten to fifteen feet in a few hours, when the temperature moderated so as to turn the falling snow to rain and add the melting snow to the current of the water. The rude bridges were swept away, and the coaches were brought to a stand. One coach coming in from the west was swept down the stream in Thompson's Creek, the lead-horses drowned, the stage whirled over by the resistless current, and the passengers saved only after almost superhuman efforts to get out of a stream but twenty feet in width. But they fall as rapidly as they rise, and in three days of good weather the results of an eight days' storm will scarcely be perceptible on the roads. To-day the sun dawned upon us almost without a cloud to shadow his splendor, and by Monday we hope to start for Salt Lake with a reasonable prospect of a safe and pleasant journey. True, the Indians may return with the return of good weather; but that is a chance all travelers on the Plains must take, and they do it without borrowing trouble on account of it. It is not doubted by the oldest settlers, who understand the habits and can judge of the temper of the Indians, that there will be a general outbreak in some portion of the overland route as soon as the Indians have stolen enough horses to mount their warriors and the grass is sufficiently grown to sustain their stock on the march.   Just where they will strike, no one pretends to guess, as they can assail the great line of travel anywhere for six hundred miles with equal facility.   Among the many signs of a general Indian outbreak, the most signifi-cant is the entire absence of friendly Indians on the line. When they are at peace, they crowd around the stations and ranches with their squaws and papooses, begging and stealing everything they can get; but this spring I did not see an Indian on the road from the Missouri to Denver. Here the Utes wander through the streets daily; but they are now, and ever have been, peaceable.

The history of the peopling of a new Territory like Colorado is a most interesting study.   It had no tide of emigration until rich gold diggings had been discovered, and nine-tenths of those who came at first were either fugitives or adventurers.   In one mingled mass came the honest bankrupt, the fugitive from justice, the gambler, and the loafer, all trusting to some new turn in the capri-cious smiles of fortune.   One of the first acts of the Terri-torial legislature prohibited the collection of claims against any of the residents of Colorado, for the benefit of non-resident creditors, for the period of five years; and no one was brave enough to test the infamy and impotency of the statute in the courts.   It would have been just worth an attorney's life, in the early days of Colorado, to have at-tempted the collection of foreign claims by process; and none dared to do it.   In such a mass of reckless residents, of course the desperate soon gained the mastery, and mur-ders were of such frequent occurrence, without any pretense of justice, that finally the Vigilance Committee was forced into existence, and executed thieves and murderers and gamblers relentlessly, until they were either driven away or subordinated to the safety of society.

But, while the Vigilance Committee has served its purpose and disbanded, it has left its impress indelibly stamped upon the character of the settlers. There remains a recklessness of life that would appall any old settlement in the East. If a bad man is discovered in any of the mining regions, the law is considered too slow and too doubtful in the administration of justice. After the sacking of Lawrence, Kansas, by Quantrell, thirty-one of his gang came to Colorado in a body, and scattered through the Territory. Numerous thefts and several murders followed, and they were charged—justly, I believe—to these rebel desperadoes. The miners at once organized parties and commenced a hunt for them. They were overtaken several times, several killed each time, and finally all the survivors were captured, with a single exception. Their captors returned, but they were without prisoners, and the explanation given was that they had tied the prisoners to a tree and they had killed themselves pulling at the ropes to get away. No inquiry was made by any one beyond ascertaining the fact that there would be no more disturbances by Quantrell's men. Gradually, however, the majesty of the law is gaining ground in every part of the Territory, and the supremacy of order will be maintained by all classes.

When Colorado shall have recovered from the terrible incubus of bankrupt corporations, now holding the most valuable mines without the ability to develop them successfully, her destiny must be a great and prosperous one. There are no insuperable barriers to the growth of all the cereals, fruits, vegetables, etc. of the Eastern States, and some of them are produced in matchless perfection. With the climate and soil to produce bread and every kind of

12

food for treble the population of Pennsylvania, and with the boundless mineral wealth of her mountains, Colorado must some day become one of the mightiest and wealthiest commonwealths of the Union.

But again I bid adieu to Colorado, and hope next to write you from the now green pastures and fragrant flowers of the Saints, six hundred miles farther toward the setting sun.

LETTER XIV.

SULPHUR SPRING STATION,
ROCKY MOUNTAINS, June 7, 1867.

ON the 3d instant we bade good-by to Denver, but not without serious misgivings as to our success in getting through the favorite retreats of the "friendlies," as the Indians are termed by the Western people. Our party consisted of seven, all going clear through,—viz., Mr. Perry, of Missouri, an old freighter of fifteen years' experience, intelligent, and brave as he is unassuming; Dr. Cass, of

(127)

Denver, who had crossed the Plains over a dozen times; Mr. Phelps, of New York, who was making his third trip; and our Pennsylvania party, consisting of McKibben, Mrs. McC., W., and myself. We were all well armed—had three repeating rifles, three of the best breech-loaders, and from one to two first-class revolvers each. Had the eastern route been safe, we would all have willingly retraced our steps to the Missouri River and proceeded to Montana by boat, and taken the chances to return overland in the fall; but the Indians seemed to be more numerous and quite as hostile and savage on the Platte and Smoky Hill routes from Denver to the Missouri, as on the route to Salt Lake. We were thus between two Indian fires, as it were, and without apparent choice as to safety: so we finally resolved that we would go through the mountains, and take the chances of coming out with whole scalps. Our route once determined upon, the greatest obstacle was removed; and, after many ominous shakes of the head by friends, and much cheap advice, as they bade us farewell, we started out on as bright a morning as the East could have furnished.

The streams were still high from the recent storms, and we apprehended some trouble with them for the first hundred and fifty miles; but, as we supposed so much of the road to be clear of the Indians, we did not complain of extra jolts, or frequent walks up hills and over deep mud-holes. We considered a stick in the mud, an upset, a walk or wade through a rebellious stream, or anything of that sort, a luxury, if not mixed up with the war-whoop of the son of the forest. When we came to Boulder, a stream that ordinarily can be stepped over in the dry season, it had appropriated several acres of contiguous territory, and made bogs which would have swallowed up the team, coach, driver, passengers, and baggage. Fortunately, it ran through an agricultural settlement, and there was a fence across it, made of pine poles, neither trimmed nor barked, and the gentlemen passengers were invited to walk the pole fence for a distance of forty rods. We strung out on it, and crawled or climbed along, sometimes walking, at other times creeping, now astride, and again hanging on to the side, or calling to our aid the profoundest strategy to flank a rough, knotty post, until the boisterous mountain Rubicon was passed. Most of us came out with numerous scratches on the hands and various unpoetical rents in our breeches; but as they were invisible under ordinary circumstances, and as none of us have had any of our clothing off as yet, since we started, but our hats, we have not taken a careful account of damages. When we get to the land of the Saints,—if we ever do,—we may have time to look up the necessary improvements in our garments.

Excepting an occasional tussle with a creek or a bog, we got along quite well until we reached Virginia Dale the next morning, about ten o'clock, for breakfast. We had made ninety-nine miles in a little more than twenty-four hours, and were congratulating ourselves that a week might land us among the long-wished-for Mormons. At Virginia Dale we had an excellent breakfast of antelope-steak, with fresh eggs and fine potatoes and coffee; but they would hash up the Indian with it. The first news we heard was that the Indians had just cleaned the place of a mule-team, and that the Black Hills, just beyond on our route, were full of Indians—their spies having been seen for several days, and their signals at night. The Black Hills are a series of spurs from the Rocky Range, and are a wild confusion of rude bluffs and ravines, with interminable windings and occasional thickets of stunted growth—all peculiarly adapted to Indian attacks. The landlord at the station, and the drivers, agreed that we

stood a fair chance for a brush with the Indians, and they
posted us as fully as possible as to the proper precautions
and best system of defense. We had expected when we
started from Denver to find Indians some sixty miles
ahead, from Cooper's Creek to the North Platte, as they
had been operating on that line but a short time before;
but here we had the savage on our path at least a day
before we had contracted for his society. There was but
one remedy, however; and that was, to go ahead, keeping
our heads steady and our powder dry.

We passed the Black Hills in safety, notwithstanding
the alarming prophecies of our Virginia Dale friends; but
we allowed the Indians no particular chances on us that
we could prevent. We sent out a skirmish-line at every
dangerous pass or bluff, and exercised every possible caution. Our guns were never out of our hands. · When
sleeping, they were kept loaded and resting on our knees,
with the muzzles projecting a little out at the sides of the
coach; and when eating, they were stacked within reach.
The tactics of the Indians is ever to surprise and confuse
travelers or soldiers by their fiendish war-whoop; and if
they fail in their attempted surprise they will flee from
one-fourth their number of resolute men. At Big Laramie
we had dinner about four in the afternoon, and there
learned that the Indians were along the line, swooping
down upon stock wherever an opportunity presented, and
scalping the herders. During the evening we had a
pleasant road to go over, free of bluffs and ravines, and
night came before we had reached any localities where
Indians could conceal themselves. It is a remarkable fact
that the Indians always select either evening or morning,
just after sunset or before sunrise, to attack, when they
can; and they will rarely attack at night. They do not
attack at night, because they never risk the danger of

meeting unexpected numbers; and they select evening and morning, because travelers are generally weary in the evening, and in the morning they are drowsy or sleeping. They never attack a train or a coach without first accurately counting every man and gun in the party. This they can do from the bluffs during the day, and then follow up the party or signal to others of their band on the line ahead.

About three in the morning we reached Cooper's Creek, and found no horses to take us on. The Indians had captured the stock but a few days before, scalped one of the herders, and there would be no team for us until the coach arrived from the west and the horses had been rested and fed. As usual, there was but one rude bed in the shanty, and that was occupied by the station-keeper, his wife, and two children. He was gallant enough, however, to give his share of the bed to Mrs. McC., and the rest of us formed a circle around the stove, rolled ourselves up in our robes and blankets on the ground-floor, and soon were sound asleep. At seven we were waked for breakfast, and had a good "square meal" on elk-steak and potatoes. No western coach having arrived, we started on with our old team about eleven o'clock, and had a cavalry escort of three men to protect us. Colonel Mizner, of Fort Saunders, is charged with the protection of the route from Denver to Fort Bridger, a distance of five hundred miles, and has to protect a corps of railroad engineers in addition. To do this, he has sixty cavalry and sixty infantry—just about enough to protect twenty miles of the road. He has appealed for an additional force; but the authorities are still waiting to see whether we are to have war or not, and they leave the whole overland route unprotected, to tempt Indians to steal and murder, while the problem of war or peace is being solved. The management of the Indian war, with ample troops to protect the route perfectly, would disgrace a corporal; and the sooner the policy is changed upon the Plains, the sooner will wanton murders and robberies and the wasteful expenditure of millions of money cease.

From Cooper's Creek to the North Platte, a distance of sixty miles, was regarded as the only really dangerous part of our route; and as three troopers accompanied us all the way, changing at the stations, we felt tolerably comfortable. We found an infantry guard of six at each station, and Rock Creek, Medicine Bow, and Wagonhound stations had all protected their stock for several days, although occasionally attacked. At Elk Mountain (Old Fort Halleck) we found a serious condition of affairs. The Indians were encamped but a few miles over the bluff, in strong force; they had stolen the horses the evening before, and an attack to destroy the station was hourly expected. The most dreary place on the entire route was Elk Mountain. The fort has been abandoned, and its buildings are crumbling to ruins. Close by is Elk Mountain, covered with snow. On the opposite side are wild, irregular cliffs, with frequent ravines, and ahead is a narrow cañon for miles, with a dozen chances for Indian ambuscades in every mile. Near the station is a burial-ground, where, for a number of years, the emigrant or the settler who yielded up his life to the savage was brought for a resting-place. I noticed some thirty graves; and the rude inscriptions told how merciless is the hand of the red man in his warfare against the encroachment of the whites.

As the Indian camp was ahead on our route, and but a short distance from the road over the cliffs, we regarded an attack as more than probable. The soldiers assured us that we could not expect to escape it; and our escort started out with us fully satisfied that they would have a brush before they got three miles away. They behaved

most manfully. Never were saddles and trappings put on
with greater care, arms were all carefully examined, and,
although it was very cold, they took with them nothing
that could embarrass them in a fight. Our driver was a
regular Western "brick." He said but little, but always
to the point, whistled merrily while he looked to the
charges of his rifle and pistols, and took an extra quid of
tobacco as he mounted his box with the dignity of an
emperor. In the quaintest Western vernacular, he told us
how to act in case of an attack, in the mean time whirling
his long whip mechanically over his head; and at the end
of every direction on any particular point he would add,
with an extra jerk of his whip, "But never scar'; never
scar'—they're lightnin' when you scar'!" It was nearly
sunset, just the favorite time for Indian attacks, as we
passed through the cañon, and everything seemed just
then and there to conspire to make an attack inevitable.
Every gun was put in position, with muzzle projecting
from the coach so as to be visible, and, when all was ready,
the driver's long lash was flung out as only a Western
driver can fling it, and we dashed into the ravine at full
gallop. There were occasional ruts and bogs, but the
sharp report of the whip told both team and passengers
that we had not time to slacken our speed for such trifles.
Occasionally, as the front wheels would plunge into a
deep water-course, the middle and hind passengers would
land in most ungraceful attitudes on the laps of the front
ones, and as the hind wheels would drop in, the whole
load would sweep back in a pile on the back seat; but
soon all would be right again, and on we whirled, until
darkness and an open country gave reasonable assurance
of safety.

We reached the North Platte about three in the morn
ing, in the midst of a drenching rain; but, as we supposed

it to be the end of our Indian troubles, we welcomed anything and every sort of weather that put us there. Judge
of our surprise when told that the Indians had just broken
out on the road for fifty miles west, that there was not an
occupied station on the line, that a number of station-men
and emigrants had been killed within a few days, and that
all travel was suspended! How long we should have to
stay, no one pretended to say. " The line cannot be run
any longer without troops," was the reply of the agent;
and, as there were no troops within four hundred miles, the
prospect was by no means flattering. We had by this
time, however, learned not to borrow trouble on any account; and we concluded to turn in for a sleep and talk
about traveling in the morning. Here, as usual, there was
but a single bed in the ranch, and that was a pile of straw
on two poles fastened into the wall. Mrs. M. was favored
with a place on the soft side of the floor near the cooking-
stove, and the rest of us took the dining-room, where, by
lying on, under, and all around the table, we managed to
find room for a snooze. Our beds consisted of our robes
and blankets, with our carpet-bags for pillows; but never
did anybody sleep more soundly. The stage that had preceded us from Denver was stopped at the Platte also: so
that there were eleven passengers there.

After a hearty breakfast on elk-steak, we held a council
of war and transportation, and found that all were well
armed but two itinerant speculators of the Hebrew faith.
We resolved unanimously that they must arm themselves,
if arms were to be had, and a committee soon after reported that arms could be had at a ranch a mile distant.
They sullenly obeyed, at last, by purchasing two old mus-
kets at fifteen dollars each (worth about two dollars and a
half), and twenty rounds of ammunition. There were two
broken-down teams at the station, and the agent of the

division (Mr. Stewart, of Indiana, Pennsylvania) proposed to go through the Indian break with two mud-wagons, if the passengers would go along and stand together in case of an attack. All promptly assented. Mr. Stewart for some time refused to allow Mrs. M. to go; but she insisted that the party must not be stopped on her account, and declared herself perfectly willing to share the fortune of the rest. Finally, we made up seats in the wagons out of mail-bags and trunks, and started on a journey of fifty miles through a region where the Indians had driven every man and horse away. It was a pleasant morning, and we had the promise of a delightful day to cross the summit of Bridger's Pass on the Rocky Range; but how deceptive were all such indications the sequel will show. The first station (Sage Creek) we reached was not disturbed; but when we came to the top of the hill, near the second station (Pine Grove), it was in ruins, and the remains still burning. The thicket close to it was an admirable retreat for Indians, and we stopped and surrounded it with a skirmish-line, but found no foe there. We then drove by to a hill beyond, where we stopped to lunch and feed the jaded horses. The Indians had captured the stock the day before, and the station-men had escaped at night. A large brindled dog first told of the presence of the savages, after the stock had been stolen, by coming in with three arrows sticking in his body; and when they destroyed the station they vented their spite on the dog by running a pitchfork through him, and pinioning him where his head was burnt entirely off. The literature of the station was scattered around the ruins. Our driver picked up a book that the Indians had flung out on the road, and, after turning it over several times to be sure that he had it right side up, he said it was called "Triumphs." After another prodigious effort at spelling, he said it was by

Curtis. It turned out to be a copy of Curtis's " Trumps," and was given Mrs. M. as a relic of Pine Creek Station.

Before we left Pine Creek, a heavy rain set in, and we lunched under our wagons on our robes. It was a dreary day for all. We had twenty-five miles to go to reach Sulphur Spring Station, our teams were exhausted, and there was neither shelter nor food on the route, while every hour we were exposed to attacks from the savages. We got down on the bottom of the wagon-beds, and covered ourselves, all but our heads, with our blankets. The storm was extremely cold, and before we had gone two miles it turned into snow, accompanied by a pitiless northwestern gale. The snow blew into our faces and froze stiff on our whiskers and clothes. If we could have covered ourselves entirely, we might have been comparatively comfortable; but every man had to keep his rifle dry and in constant readiness, and a sharp lookout for the Indians. As we ascended the summit of the pass, we saw abundant evidences of the presence of the savages. At one place two wagons were standing, and their contents scattered on the bluffs on either side. They had evidently been captured the day before, the horses taken and the goods destroyed. When we reached the summit, we saw the Bridger's Pass Station in flames. It has an open country for a mile around it: so we could see that the savages had gone; and we drove down to it without delay. It had evidently been fired but a few hours before, as it was still burning and the tracks of the Indians in the snow were fresh. We got out and warmed ourselves by the fire, while the fierce snowstorm raged with fury around us. Our situation was now manifestly most critical. The tracks of the ponies showed that the Indians had gone toward Sulphur Spring, the place we were striving to reach, and it seemed more than probable that they would destroy that place before we

could reach it. If so, we would be left on the top of the
Rocky Range, without food or shelter, in a terrible snow-
storm, with teams unable to travel, and surrounded by the
fiends of the Plains. It was a sad prospect; but every one
seemed animated with the resolve to yield only when it
was no longer possible to save ourselves. We determined
to proceed after the Indians, if possible reach Sulphur
Spring, fifteen miles distant, and there stop whether the
station was destroyed or not. "Big Dick" was our mas-
ter-driver—that is, the two teams were under his direction;
and he was fully equal to the task. He stood six feet three
in his stockings, had a giant frame, had been educated on
the driver's boot, in the stable, and among the Indians,
and he was perfectly familiar with their habits. He seemed
insensible to fear, and insisted that our party could make
Sulphur in spite of all the red devils this side of the hottest
place he could name. He also seemed almost insensible
to the terrible storm that was raging, and faced its cruel
blasts as he would the gentle, balmy breeze of spring.
After warming ourselves thoroughly around the burning
station, we got in again to start on our journey. It was
then nearly night, our teams were entirely worn out, and
on any sort of a hill we had to stop every five minutes to
let them rest. About five miles from the station, Dick
pulled up, and said, "Fresh pony-tracks, gentlemen—lots
of 'em—they're not half a mile ahead of us." The snow
and the moon made it tolerably light, and the tracks were
plainly visible as just fresh, when closely examined. At
the word, a dozen men jumped out from under the blankets
and robes, with guns in hands, and a brief council was
held as to how Mrs. M. could be best protected. "Kiver
her up in the bottom of the wagon, pile the baggage around
her, and leave her to me," was Dick's order; and it was
obeyed. In less than a minute she was snugly covered

13

over in such a manner as to leave no sign of anything in
the wagon but mails and baggage. She had a brace of
well-charged revolvers in her hands, and her purpose was
firmly fixed to take her own life, in case of the capture of
the teams, rather than suffer the unspeakable horrors of
Indian captivity. To most of the party she was an entire
stranger; but all seemed to forget their own peril in their
anxiety for her safety. Dick's profoundest admiration was
won because, as he said, "she didn't take on and screech,
as most of 'em would." Our party scattered out, some
considerably in advance of the teams to follow the trail in
the snow, while the others were in a circle around the
teams, which were kept close together. The road was
through a narrow cañon (can'-yun, the term applied to
narrow ravines between spurs of the mountains), and the
broken bluffs and frequent sharp turns, together with the
snow, made it impossible for us to see any considerable
distance ahead. We followed the tracks for about a
mile, when they turned off to the left toward a cañon
running at right angles with the road. The bluffs terminated abruptly where the Indians had left the road, and
soon a bright light was visible in a deserted ranch
"There's the cusses!" exclaimed Dick,—and there they
were; but, instead of surprising and attacking us, as we
apprehended, they were the surprised party and apprehensive of an attack. The moment the wagons came out of the
cañon in hearing of the Indians, their light went out. We
were not over one hundred and fifty yards from them; but
a swollen stream divided us, so that they could not make
a dash upon us. We knew that their numbers were not
greater than ours, from the tracks of their ponies, and we
felt safe from attack where it had to be done on open
ground. Their ponies were plainly visible picketed around
the ranch, and we could have killed or crippled half of

them by a single fire; but Dick would not allow the experiment to be made. "We've not lost any," said he, "and we are not hunting 'em." In obedience to his orders, we moved on, all of the men walking through snow and sometimes in mud six inches deep. We had still four miles to the station, but our teams could scarcely draw the wagons, and we had to wade along the best way we could. When within a mile of Sulphur, one of our horses dropped down, and had to be unhitched and abandoned. As we supposed that we were beyond the Indians, one wagon, with most of the men, went on to the station, leaving the other with the driver and several of the party to remain with it until we could send back a fresh team. When we reached the station, we found the men on guard, expecting an attack, and learned that the Indians had made two attacks in the afternoon and captured some sixteen horses and mules. This startling information developed the fact that the Indians were in front of us as well as behind us, and that they could unite their bands in an hour and greatly outnumber us. No lights were allowed about the stable, and all possible haste was made to send a well-armed party with fresh horses to get in the party left behind. When they reached the wagon, the deserted ranch, where we had left our band of Indians, was in flames, showing that they had fired and deserted it as soon as we got out of range of attack; and the station-men concluded that their united force would attempt to destroy the station at daylight the next morning.

We found things about the station by no means calculated to quiet our apprehensions. The station- and ranch-men had gathered in there for safety, and there were over thirty armed men when we joined them. One of them, the division agent, had his arm in a sling. He had come through with the last stage a day before us, and was at-

tacked near Bridger's Pass. He was first wounded in the
arm; next, the driver, who sat beside him on the boot, was
killed instantly; next, a ranchman, who was along, was
killed, and his body put in the coach; and another ranchman was killed, and his body captured by the savages.
The agent drove the stage in, some fifteen miles, through
an Indian attack of two hours, and landed at Sulphur,
driving with one arm, a dead comrade lying under his
feet, and another in the coach. Two emigrant-wagons
were with him, making a party of eight to resist the attacks; and they brought their teams safely through. The
same evening they attacked Bridger's Pass Station, in
which there were but two men—Captain Wilson, of Philadelphia, and another man—and they repulsed the assailants, killing one and wounding two others. Four Indians
had also been killed by the party with the coach; but they
always carry the bodies of their dead from the field. An
Indian will brave the greatest danger to get off a dead or
wounded comrade. Captain Wilson, however, brought in
the pony, blanket (a new government, evidently recently
issued), robe, and battle-flag. The battle-flag was a light
pole, about eight feet long, with a fork at the end. Each
prong of the stick was decorated with a feather at the
extreme tip, and near the base of the prong two long
streamers, made of beaver-skin, were attached. Captain
Wilson begged me to apologize to General Sherman for
killing the Indian, as he understood it to be against the
regulations; but, he said, as the Indian insisted upon his
scalp, he had to kill the Indian even at the risk of incurring
the displeasure of the lieutenant-general and becoming
liable to the grave charge of provoking an Indian war.

A strong guard was put out around the station, and
kept up all night, with reliefs every three hours, and the
rest of us tried to find some sort of a bed. We were all

drenched to the skin, and so bespattered with mud that we could scarcely recognize each other. No one pretended even to draw off his boots, but in our wet clothes we rolled ourselves up in wet blankets and piled into every corner of the shanty, with our rifles and ammunition close at hand. Mrs. M. had a part of the only bed in the house— one belonging to an emigrant-wagon, which the good lady kindly invited her to share. It was a thin straw mattress, and blankets and a borrowed robe served the purpose of sheets, pillows, and cover. All slept soundly: indeed, I never slept better; and, but for an alarm about four o'clock, I would have nearly got square with sleep for the loss of several previous nights. About daybreak, a wild Indian yell rang out from the cliffs, not far from the station. The guard accepted it as the signal for an attack, and hastily aroused the slumbering warriors. There were no toilets to make. In a twinkling, each man had kicked off his blanket, grasped his gun, and was ready for action. The port-holes were opened, parties stationed at the proper places, and all was in readiness in an incredibly short time. We were all ripe for a brush. We had been chased, fretted, and bedeviled by the Indians for several days; some had lost their property, others their ranches, and still others their friends; and there was a universal desire to have the thing settled by a square fight. We had the advantage, and felt strong enough to repel five times our number; and that fact, doubtless, had much to do with our general desire for a fight. But the alarm proved groundless. The Indians did not come; and in the course of an hour we ventured out and restationed our guards; but no man left the door without his rifle in hand. Immediately in the rear of the station-house was a high cliff, the top of which was within short rifle-range, so that the Indians could approach close enough to fire upon us before they could be seen. A fine sulphur

13*

spring rises within five yards of the building, near the foot
of the bluffs. I started to get a drink, but was promptly
stopped until some one could cover my movement with a
rifle, by standing in the door. Usually, when water was
wanted, a boy was sent, and a man stood in the door with
his cocked rifle leveled toward the cliff. As an Indian
could not fire without uncovering himself to some extent,
they did not interfere with our bringing in water when a
rifle guarded the carrier.

The morning was cold and cheerless, and altogether
everything seemed most unpropitious. The snow still fell
in fitful gusts, the roads were almost impassable, but little
stage-stock remained, and that was worn out, and, to
crown all, the Indians were around us, and in such numbers that the party could not divide with safety. We had
a hearty breakfast of elk-steak, bread, and coffee, and then
began to devise ways and means to get forward. We
could not remain there, for provisions were becoming
scarce, and hunting (upon which the station depended entirely for meat) was impossible: so we resolved to move
ahead, if at all possible. The agent finally concluded to
send out two stage-loads of passengers westward, and our
same party that had braved the storm and Indians the
day before, unanimously agreed to go. By noon we are
to start; and of our experience on the rest of the route the
next letter will tell—provided, always, that the Indians do
not capture the writing-materials and the writer.

LETTER XV.

SALT LAKE CITY, June 12, 1867.

WE left Sulphur Spring Station on Friday, near noon, all glad to get away and ready to brave new dangers with the red-skins if necessary. We started out with two coaches, containing the same party we had from North Platte to Sulphur Spring, and all, of course, well armed. When we reached the top of a bluff a mile west of the station, we saw the Indians on the bluff behind the station, making an accurate observation of our numbers and movements. They were all mounted, and seemed ready for a dash; but we felt satisfied that they would not try their hands on us in daylight, in a comparatively open country. There were occasional bluffs and ravines for some miles west of Sulphur, but the country gradually opens out until it becomes a wide plain, for fifteen miles. With a little precaution, and

(143)

going in advance of the coaches here and there to guard
against surprise, we felt tolerably safe. At the first station (Waskie) we found that no Indians had appeared
there as yet. The old station-keeper had the hind carriage
of a stage-wagon mounted with a section of large stove-
pipe, a caisson improvised out of a wheelbarrow, and the
letters " U. S." painted on them in the largest possible
style. While the team was grazing, we had a pleasant
chat with the old fellow, and heard him tell some thrill-
ing stories of the early trials on the plains and in the
mountains.

The stations were ever places of interest to me. They
are isolated, generally located in a hollow beside a stream,
and the occupants have no companions except their horses
and such other animals as they gather about them. The
"swing-stations," where the teams are changed, and no
meals furnished passengers, consist of a rude stable, built of
logs or mud and invariably covered with earth. In a little
corner is a small room partitioned off, in which the station-
men cook, eat, sleep, tell stories, read yellow-covered literature, and caress their pets. In every instance I was
first greeted by one or more cats. They are the inseparable companions of the stable-men, and usually answer to
the tenderest names. They always come stepping out as
soon as the stage stops, and approach the passengers,
giving the most cordial welcome, and rubbing themselves
against them to get a kind stroking in return. Sometimes
one large Tom has the monopoly of the establishment,
but generally Tabby follows with her litter, and directs
attention, with maternal pride, to her jewels. The little
ones will spring into your lap, climb on your shoulders,
and purr in your very ears to win a little notice. The
Newfoundland or St. Bernard dog is also the invariable
companion of the stable-man, and they, too, greet the pas-

sengers with every evidence of hospitality. Frequently
the Creole chickens are part of the family, and they are
as tame as the rest of the pets. The rooster steps out in
front of the stable when the passengers get out, and gives
them a touching reminder of home as he rises in his conscious dignity and makes the bluffs ring with his shrill,
defiant crow. With him come the biddies, sometimes with
their broods, meekly presenting their claims to a kind word
or a crumb from the passers-by. The men, animals, and
birds constitute one family. When meals are ready, puss,
Jowler, and the chickens all are present, and are trained to
earn a liberal share by practicing cunning tricks which
they have been taught. At the "home-stations," where
meals are furnished to passengers, there is always a log or
mud shanty in addition to the stable, and usually the landlord has a family. I did not find one of the home-stations
without a landlady. Frequently there were other household pets, such as obtain in most well-regulated families;
but babies did not appear in the assortment. I cannot recall a station, in the trip of six hundred miles from Denver
here, where the cats and dogs did not come out in the most
friendly manner to welcome us, and always persisted in
pressing their acquaintance until they were recognized
kindly. At Sulphur Spring the station-keeper of Bridger's
Pass was one of our party, and his keenest grief was because of the brutal murder of his favorite cat. Had she been
burned or shot, he would not have complained; but I gave
him the profoundest sorrow by telling him that the Indians
had skinned his cat, cut the head off, and set the carcass out
in the road on a tin plate. The Indians well knew that next
to scalping the station-keeper himself, they could not have
inflicted upon him a deeper wound. "They've skinned her
alive, the devils of hell," was his exclamation, and, with
gritting teeth, he vowed vengeance. For horses, ranch,

elothing, traps, ete. he eared not; but that the Indians should wreak their atroeities upon the pet of his little family, was more than his nature eould endure with equanimity.

When we got out some twenty miles west of Sulphur, we had a beautiful open prairie, and the sun was struggling with the elouds to give us a pleasant day. At times he would seem to triumph, and the green grass, and the ponds just filled by the storm, seemed to give us a grateful weleome; but again the heavens would blaeken, and the spiteful snow make us close up our coach and gather about us our blankets and robes. We met a large mixed train of mules and oxen just as we had gained the wide prairie, and gave the master the details of our trials. He informed us that there was another train some miles behind him, and that he would wait for·it to go through with him. He had sixty armed men, and felt pretty safe—so safe, indeed, that at the next home-station the telegraph informed us that the Indians had, that very day, eaptured all his mules and killed one of his men.

About eleven o'eloek at night we reaehed Laelede, and stopped for supper, rather to have a little rest and get warmed up, than to satisfy hunger. There we found ourselves fairly in the eelebrated Bitter Creek region of the Rocky Mountains. For a distaneo of about one hundred miles, there is no water fit to drink. Bitter Creek, whieh drains the eountry, is so impregnated with alkali that neither man nor beast ean driuk it without injury; and the wells at the stations are almost equally bad. The water, if drunk in the usual quantities, produees violent nausea, and does not satisfy thirst. Even in eoffee and tea it is tasted, and the "square meals" seem throughout as if alkali had been spilled profusely on everything. Fortunately for us, we entered it about dark, and the reeent storm prevented dust, and the eontinued cold weather did not provoke thirst. When the weather is warm and the roads are dry, the dust of this section is almost intolerable. We had but a small installment of it the last few hours we were on it, and it parched the lips and irritated the nose with a keenness almost equal to that of quicklime. It is the most desolate section between the Atlantic and Salt Lake. Even the sage-brush and grease-wood, the only growth it can boast, are stunted, and seem to eke out a miserable existence. There is no grass to protect the traveler or trains from the widest sweep of its almost impalpable sands, and when the season is dry it envelops everything in its burning clouds. It is a portion of the desolate route that every tourist hurries over with the utmost speed, and usually the most delightful view of the trip is the fresh water of Green River. It is hailed as an oasis in the desert, as it furnishes clear, sweet water and invites the traveler to continued fresh waters beyond.

We ferried Green River just before dark, and supped at the station on potatoes, dry bread, and coffee. The general derangement of the stage-stock by the Indians left us without horses to proceed farther with our two coaches, and it became a nice question who should get the preference. There being no agent there, the driver was the supreme power in the case. The rule of the line is to send on the first coach that comes. As we came together, each claimed precedence—we because our party had the oldest tickets, and the others because they started from Denver a day before us. Just here our old freighter (Mr. Perry) came in excellent play. The driver was obstinately non-committal, and a brief council decided that even rights were marketable in the Far West. The driver was called behind the baggage-boot on pretense of locking up a valise. There were a few words said, a very slight rustling of fine paper in his vest-pocket, and he promptly decided that we

were entitled to the first team. One of A. J.'s appointees
was in the other party, and he demonstrated the fitness of
his appointment by such an Executive, by swinging his
pistol and demanding to be forwarded at once because he
was a government official. While he was swearing, the
driver coolly handed him his baggage and told him that
he should have the first passage "after the gentlemen and
lady had gone." He rushed to the telegraph and sent a
message to the stage-officer at Denver, at a cost of $7.20,
while $10 had settled the whole question against him but
a few minutes before. As nobody paid any attention to
him, he finally subsided, and in a short time was asleep
with the rest of us in the little room around the stove.
Mrs. M. had been favored with a corner in the kitchen,
where there was a good fire, and the rest of us had a comfortable bed on our blankets and robes in the dining-room.
We had to wait for the arrival of a western coach before
we could proceed, and we were allowed to sleep until
one in the morning before we were called to pursue our
journey.

From Green River to Fort Bridger, a distance of about
sixty miles, there are the finest springs, and a continuous,
broad, green valley. The day was beautiful—the first
pleasant weather we had been favored with since entering
the mountains. The Church Buttes are the special object
of interest to the traveler in this valley. They consist of
immense rocks situated on abrupt cliffs, presenting the appearance of vast churches with altars, pulpits, and domes.
Some of them tower up three hundred feet above the top
of the bluffs, with almost perpendicular walls, and present
every variety of architecture. The roads being fine in this
region, we had some original teams. At Millersville,
twelve miles from Bridger, they hitch up six raw bronchos
(wild California horses). It required a man to each horse

to get them into the harness, and then each one had to be held until all was ready. They reared, plunged, kicked, pulled back, lay down, and played all manner of fantastic antics; but the driver finally mounted his box with a coolness that showed him to be perfect master of the situation, and, as he yelled to them to "git," his keen silken cracker flashed about their flanks and kept flashing until all started on a run. They don't take time to break horses on the plains, but where there is a level country they harness them with a pitchfork and drive them under the whip until they are glad to be docile. Bogs and washes in the roads are of no consequence—they dash through them as if they did not exist, and, with a yell and a sharp crack of the whip, they rear out on the other side. The strange feature of these horses is that they are never broken until they are worn out. They seem to be by nature intractable, and as long as they are able for the road they yield to harness only after an exhaustive struggle.

We reached Fort Bridger about the middle of the afternoon (Sunday), and were met at the station by Judge Carter, and made to share his proverbial hospitality. I had met him at Denver when we were all blockaded there, and was glad to be welcomed to the abode of civilization after a full week of unpleasant adventure among Indians and ranchmen. He has a comfortable house, an estimable wife, several daughters (most of them East at school), a fine piano, library, and everything that is to be found in Eastern residences. He came to Bridger with General A. Sidney Johnston, in 1857, as a sutler, and remained after the so-called Mormon war was ended. He is a Virginian by birth, a tall, spare, flaxen-haired gentleman, with white flowing beard and moustache, and evidently a gentleman of much more than ordinary character and culture. He has expended some $10,000 in building on the military

14

reservation lands, and has an immense store. He deals largely with the friendly Indians, and emigrants, and supplies the garrison with sutler's stores. As is usual in the exercise of Western hospitality, he took us into his well-filled cellar, and, as I declined whisky, brandy, gin, rum, etc., he went on to something else, until he turned up a bottle of what he called favorite bitters, and that, he said, I *must* drink. Being under military rule, I, of course, complied. Before I had the glass empty, he had a bottle in my overcoat-pocket; and, as I was starting, he insisted that I didn't balance properly, and he crammed one into the pocket on the other side. To resist would have seemed to be affectation, and I submitted. In case of accident they may, as Mrs. Toodles would say, be handy to have about the house.

Judge Carter and Colonel Miles, the post-commandant, favored me with a general inspection of the works and buildings. The position was first chosen by the Mormons to resist Johnston's advance, and their cobble-stone fortification still stands, and serves as a stable for the garrison. It is most beautifully situated in what seems to be nearly the centre of a vast plain. A number of rapid mountain-streams flow through and around the works, and a heart-some growth of cottonwood breaks the monotony of the prairie. It was there that General Johnston was overtaken by winter, and compelled to go into winter quarters; while the Mormons retreated west and wintered in Echo Cañon. The next year the regular fort-quarters were erected; and it is now an admirable military post. As we had no change of horses, we were glad to remain with Judge Carter until late in the day. There were swarms of Indians around the buildings, begging, trading, and stealing. The chief of the Bannocks, a northern tribe, was there to confer with Judge Carter about peace and supplies, and

Waskie's tribe always stay close to the fort. They wander about in squads, the "bucks" and "squaws," as they are designated, always separate. The males have the profoundest contempt for the squaws. They will never recognize or speak to them before the whites, unless to order them away. One bedizened warrior, glorying in beaded buckskin pants, and silken streamers elaborately embroidered flying from his feet, was mounted on his pony before the door. Mrs. M. approached to examine his finery, and he looked at her for a moment with intense disgust, when, yelling out, " Pooh, pooh—squaw !" he galloped off. Some of the Bannocks came in front without any trappings, and their squaws came meekly after, sitting astride of their tent-covers, with their papooses tied to their backs and their lodge-poles trailing behind them. When they arrive at the place where the tent is to be pitched, the dusky lord lies down on the grass, while his bride builds their shelter and prepares their meal.

We left Fort Bridger a little before sunset, but could not make rapid progress, as our old team had to be taken. Toward midnight we crossed the Quaking Asp Summit. It is about nine thousand feet above the level of the sea, and is the greatest altitude attained on the route across the Rocky Mountains. The road across was very rough, and when we reached Bear River, about midnight, the driver refused to go farther until his teams were rested. Accordingly, we turned in at the station, and made up our beds, as usual, with robes and blankets, giving Mrs. M. the kitchen floor and the benefit of the stove. It will doubtless seem strange that the stove was ever in demand at the stations; but for five hundred miles we did not have a single day or night that a stove was not desirable. After a sound sleep and a hearty breakfast, we started out with a bright morning, and soon came to the head of Echo Cañon

—one of the most remarkable ravines in the mountains, where the echoes can be heard for miles. It is a continuous narrow passage through the broken mountains for twenty miles, at times so narrow that there is not room for both the little creek and the road; and it is usually driven by one of the famous drivers of the overland journey. Hank Conner, a fancy and decidedly fast hero of the whip and lines, is the regular driver; but he was off his beat by the general derangement. We had one, however, who was determined to sustain Hank's reputation. Mrs. M. sat out with him on the driver's boot, to get the full benefit of the wild scenery, and he could not miss the opportunity to display his art to the best advantage. We had reached a region where grain and hay were plenty, and we had excellent horses. One of our teams was so wild that it took all of us to get them into the harness, and when in, " Ginger" and " Lantern" well-nigh defied the power of the lines; but the road was good most of the way and all down hill, and we whirled along in the liveliest manner until we emerged at Weber's Station, near the foot of the Wasatch Range, and but fifty miles from Salt Lake City. After an excellent Mormon dinner, we started off again through the first settlement we had seen since we left the streams near Denver. For some fifteen miles we passed through a thick settlement of Mormons and one or two considerable villages. They have good fences, and seem to be most thrifty farmers. About every house there was shrubbery and shade, grown by irrigation, and all had gardens in bloom. At the eastern foot of the Wasatch Range we stopped with Wm. Kimball, son of Heber Kimball, second president of the Mormon Church. He keeps a hotel, and has the first regular two-storied house I had seen within five hundred miles. He had three wives to shower blessings upon his domestic hearth, and quite an assortment of children. The favorite wife was in the parlor, with two small children, and entertained us while the others prepared supper. We had some music on the piano, and spent an hour most pleasantly. How it would have been had the three wives and their latest editions of little Kimballs all been with us, I cannot guess; but I doubt whether there would not have been some clouds mingled with the sunshine.

About ten o'clock we started to climb the Wasatch. We were but twenty-five miles from this place, and were most impatient to get through. It was a beautiful night, the moon more than half full, and the road passably good. Near the summit we all got out to walk, and had to pass over five feet of beaten snow in the road on the tenth day of June. We had a magnificent team of six grays, and expected to whirl into Salt Lake City handsomely as soon as we crossed the summit. After we had got fairly over, we got in, and off we started ; but in less than twenty minutes the stage plunged into a deep rut and upset instantly. Fortunately, the team stopped, and we directed our efforts to get the passengers out. I was on the upper side, and soon got out through the side door, and as each passenger was hurriedly called the answer came that no serious damage was done. They presented a strange mixture. Rifles, traveling-bags, satchels, lunch-baskets, bottles, etc. were all in admirable confusion among the passengers ; but luckily no material harm was done to either passengers or property. We soon righted up again, and had a delightful moonlight drive down through Parley Cañon to this place, where we arrived about three o'clock on Tuesday morning, after a most tedious and eventful journey of eight days from Denver.

14*

MAIN STREET, SALT LAKE CITY.

LETTER XVI.

SALT LAKE CITY, June 18, 1867.

I HAVE seen Mormonism in its best garments only. Its
dignitaries have made me welcome. Its hospitality encompassed me. Its fruits and flowers, its bright spots
and pleasant recreations, were all before me. With its
humble followers and its shadowed household circles I
must repeat the experience of all other gentile visitors,
and go, as I came, a stranger. But on every hand, on the
streets, in the homes where crime wears its richest gilding,
in the tabernacle, and even in the very fountain of the pol-
luted stream, are plainly visible the melancholy evidence
of mingled fraud and infatuation, of cunning wrong-doers
and deluded wrong-sufferers.

The world elsewhere may be sought in vain for a des-
potism so relentless and pitiless as is Mormonism. Kings

and emperors rule millions of willing or unwilling subjects, but there is no people in such utter, abject servility to their monarch. There are churches wherein infallibility is accorded to the head, or limited power of an absolute character conceded; but in none could any spiritual potentate rise up, as did Brigham Young on Sunday last, before twenty-five hundred people, and prescribe their worldly actions, their ordinary daily dealings, with the penalty of eternal damnation proclaimed for disobedience. At first glance, the arrogant exercise of power by the Mormon leaders, and the willing submission of their followers, bewilder the observer; but when the whole theory of this stupendous fraud is unraveled, the character of its subjects studied, the thousand channels through which absolute power reaches out and ramifies into almost every household, it ceases to be incomprehensible. A very large majority of the Mormon people are the rescued serfs of the Old World—not so perhaps in name in most cases, but so in fact. They are ignorant, superstitious, fanatical, and ready victims for a new doctrine that promises to bring them into immediate communion with God. When once brought to the home of the Saints, often by the generous aid of the Emigration Society, their temporal condition is readily bettered, their social status is elevated to recognition by even the inspired teachers, and they never learn aught else but submission to the dogmas of the Church and the mandates of its apostles. They, as a rule, remain aliens to the government; and no claim upon the citizen is tolerated that in any degree antagonizes the claims or doctrines of the Church.

I regard Brigham Young as a man greatly underestimated by most persons in the East. They all judge him mainly by his ribald and often blasphemous harangues from the pulpit, and do not appreciate him as a great ad-

ministrator and a leader of surpassing attainments. I
first saw him in his own business-room. He was nearly
or perhaps quite alone when I entered, but almost instantly
several side doors opened, and half a dozen brothers, sons,
secretaries, etc. were seated around the little office. I learn
that he never sees any person alone, unless he knows perfectly the character of the visitor, and that when strangers
call on him his person is guarded from possible assassination
by the apparently casual but doubtless systematic appearance of his immediate friends. He greets the visitor with
serene dignity and faultless courtesy, and converses freely
and quite intelligently on all agreeable topics. He was
evidently in no mood for a talk about the inside workings
of Mormonism; and an inquiry as to the number of his
wives and children, and their health, would doubtless have
terminated the interview most abruptly. He is a well-pre-
served man of sixty-six years, of medium height, rather
corpulent, with an abundant growth of light, auburn hair,
and a heavy crop of sandy whiskers, excepting on his
upper and lower lips. His eyes are of a very light, dull
blue, and wanting in expression, his nose sharp and prominent, his lips thick and firmly set, and the whole gives
him the appearance of a man of obstinate will and cold,
calculating purpose. His head is of unusual shape. The
face is quite broad just across the centre, and gradually
narrows up to the top of the forehead and down to the
point of the chin, while his neck is of uncommon thick-
ness, and describes a semi-oval line from the base of the
head to the top, tapering gradually to the crown, giving it
a sugar-loaf finish. He is evidently a man of the keenest
perception, of great self-reliance and will, of the subtlest
cunning, and possesses a physical organization capable of
the highest measure of endurance. In his manner and
movements he is quite graceful, indicating considerable

culture, but really the fruit of his varied experience and
intercourse with all classes of men. No man could acquire
any needed quality more readily than Brigham Young.
He is eminent as a mimic, and often resorts to mimicry as
his most powerful weapon in hurling his anathemas against
the gentiles or apostates in his sermons. In short, I would
put him down, after meeting him in his office and hearing him in the pulpit, as a finished impostor, singularly
able, versatile, and unscrupulous, and as one who seeks
to hide his revolting licentiousness by deliberate blasphemy.

I do not pretend to know the number of wives and children Brigham Young can boast. I believe that no two
writers have estimated them alike; and I have found no
Mormon, in the scores with whom I have conversed on
the subject, who professed to know. It is conceded, however, that he has some twenty who are members of his
household, and probably a score of others who are simply
sealed to him as spiritual wives, to share his high crown
in the future world. Even the dead have been wedded to
him by proxy, to satisfy the anxiety of deluded parents
who wished their departed daughters to wear starry robes
around the prophet in heaven. Of his living wives, who
are subject to his domestic laws, the first, who was his
lawful wife before polygamy was thought of as part of the
Mormon faith, now lives in a pleasant, spacious cottage by
herself, some distance from the harem that is peopled with
the fairer and more tender acquisitions to his family circle.
She is said to be a firm believer in the faith, and accepts
her situation as a cross imposed upon her to enhance her
reward hereafter. I saw her in the theatre, along with
five junior wives, who had succeeded each other in the
favor of the prophet and had given way in time to younger
and fresher charms. Of all the so-called Mrs. Youngs I

have seen, the lawful wife seems much the most intelligent
and refined.   The last one, and of course for the present
the favorite, had a private box in the theatre, sported gay
ribbons and furbelows, and seemed to look down upon her
faded predecessors with the contempt they deserved.   She
is a niece of the first wife, and defies even Brigham's boasted
domestic government.   She was tried in the harem, but her
rebellious spirit threatened the subversion of all law and
order there, and she is now quartered in a house of her own,
beyond range of the others.   I do not, of course, credit all
the stories of revolting scenes detailed as occurring in the
extensive family of the Prophet; but it is well known that
the last addition to the wives hectors her anointed fraction of a husband in the most irreverent style, and storms
the holy inner circle of inspired power with profane speech
and violent pugilistic gestures.   Although each one after
the first has usurped the place of another, not one has
been discarded for a successor without the keenest sorrow,
and often only after frenzied but fruitless resistance.

Polygamy was not a part of the Mormon creed as pro-
mulgated by Smith.   On the contrary, he expressly denounced it, and his widow and sons have discarded the
Salt Lake Mormons because of the adulterous practices
committed in the name of the Church.   Brigham Young
is the founder of the polygamic feature of the faith of the
Latter-Day Saints.   While I doubt not that lust had much
to do with its adoption, yet, as a means of attaining despotic power, it has served an important purpose.   Mr.
Young has four brothers, all adhering to the Church in
this city, and all with a plurality of wives.   His sons
imitate his example with filial fidelity; and his daughters
are married only into harems of the more intelligent and
influential members of the Church.   By this system he is
directly related to every family of importance in Zion, and

his power is perpetuated. By thus binding the more intelligent to his cause by marriage ties, he is enabled to
command the complete submission of the unlearned, by
declaring polygamy to be the duty of the faithful, and
promising the heart-broken wives that their crosses are
but creating for them brighter crowns above.

I had much anxiety to see polygamy in the household,
but have failed. Not only are strangers practically denied
acquaintance with plural wives, but the subject is never a
welcome one in conversation. I have talked with many
Mormons who are polygamists, and in every instance
when I asked respecting their wives, they responded as if
I had introduced to them some painful and delicate scandal
about their families. I found but one who claimed, and I
learn justly, to have two wives in one house, and both
happy. In most instances each wife must have a separate house, to hide herself from humiliation and shame.
Of all who introduced the subject to me, I asked the
question, "Did your first wife cheerfully consent to
your marriage to another?" and in not a single instance
was an affirmative answer given. Mormon or gentile,
with one accord the women revolt against it. They
must cease to be women, and descend into the scale of
brutes, before the wives of Salt Lake can voluntarily
consent to such appalling degradation. One-third of the
entire adult male population of Utah is now practicing
polygamy, and in Salt Lake City the proportion is larger.
It hangs like a terrible pall upon the mothers, wives, and
daughters of the Saints. Not only those who have been
enfolded in its slimy embrace mourn from day to day their
hard lot, but those who have thus far escaped its pollution know not how soon the spoiler may enter their firesides, and harrowing anxiety dims the lustre of their eyes
and traces its shadows upon their faces.

Not only is licentiousness ever pleading the cause of polygamy, but the Church demands it of all men who can afford more than one wife, and women are taught to consent to it on pain of eternal damnation. I heard four Mormon sermons on Sunday—two by fools and two by knaves. The one, for instance, who declared that he had seen Joseph Smith perfectly personated in Brigham Young when he thrust Rigdon out and assumed the presidency himself, even to a broken front tooth, was simply a lunatic. In the course of his sermon he gave the particulars of his conversion. He proposed to the Lord that if He would appear in person to him he would believe, and the Lord appeared to him, and he thenceforth became a Saint. He was followed by one of the shrewdest of the elders, who argued with some plausibility that the original Church of Christ had strayed and broken into discordant branches, and that it had been founded again by Smith and Young and was separate from the world and united in its great work. In the afternoon, we had an incoherent and senseless harangue from a Cockney; but Brigham pulled him down by the coat-tail in a short time, and took the pulpit himself. His speech would read, away in the East, like the foolish vaporing of a conceited blackguard; but never were remarks more timely or better adapted to the people he addressed. He argued for twenty minutes, that not one person in forty knew how to take care of himself in either temporal or spiritual matters; that all must have leaders experienced in temporal, and inspired in religious affairs; that they must live submissively to those who are competent to lead them, or be cut off with the wicked. He complained of the selfishness of some of the Saints. Said he, " People I brought here from serfdom, who could not own a chicken before they came, and who were glad to take a spade from me to get a crust of bread, now have lands, and houses, and cattle, and greenbacks, and carriages; and they want to dictate to me; they want to sap the foundation of Zion; but I will not be dictated to. I am called of the Lord, and it is mine to teach, and yours to obey. I say what I please; I put up this pulpit with the crimson covering, and paid for it myself, expressly to go into it and say what I please. I will take it away if I like, and stand on a table or. chair; for the Lord's will can be declared in one way as well as another." And thus he rambled on, but always with evident method. After pleading for unity, he told the young ladies of the Church that they had no capacity for taking care of themselves and their honor, and that the Church, with its ceremonies and covenants, was their only safety. He closed by demanding that gentiles and apostates be shunned in all dealings, even although it costs more to purchase from a Saint. "You may answer," said he, "that is none of my d——d business. Perhaps it is not, just now; but the time will soon come when it will be my business to testify respecting this people, and I pledge you that those who disobey this command shall *not* enter into the strait gate. I will not speak hard of you if you don't stop wasting your dollars with gentiles and apostates, nor will I think hard of you; but I will say, in the name of the Lord Jesus Christ, let the righteous be saved, and the wicked go their way to everlasting punishment." I saw poor infatuated Mormons shudder at this terrible anathema from one they supposed to be an inspired oracle of God; and the fear of his malediction is one of the strongest elements of cohesiveness with the deluded masses of his followers. In the foregoing quotations I have given his language almost literally, and preserved the sentiments faithfully, without the least embellishment.

Brigham Young is the supreme temporal as well as

spiritual head of the Church, and he is no more responsible to his fellows in temporal than in spiritual matters. The Church property is all in his name in fee, the titles are received by him, and he accounts to no one, nor will he tolerate inquiry as to the expenditures. A prominent Mormon merchant here, whose tithes amounted to a very large sum of money, demanded a statement of the receipts and disbursements, and he was cut off from the Saints here and from the Saints in heaven. When it is considered that all Mormons are required to give to the Church one-tenth of all they raise in kind and one-tenth of all they make in any business, the magnitude of tho fund intrusted to Young without question or check of any sort is startling. First of all he supplies his harem and numerous progeny; then he builds at the tabernacle and temple; then mills, theatres, factories, etc., all in his own name, receiving the proceeds ostensibly for the Church, and no one daring to question his judgment or demand a balance-sheet. His annual income now cannot be less than half a million dollars. The humble, deluded followers believe that it is wisely and faithfully expended; but do not the licentious leaders know better?

There are palpable signs of dissolution in the Mormon Church. The Josephites (the followers of Smith) pronounce polygamy a sin, and they claim to be the true Mormon Church and entitled to the Church property. When Brigham was South, this spring, he had to "cut off" several hundred members for heresy, because they adhered to Smith; and over one hundred wagon-loads of emigrants are now in the mountains on their way East to escape his fearful vengeance. The Morrisites are another class of dissenters, and have no fellowship with the Salt Lake Church. They denounce polygamy, and are constantly receiving acquisitions to their numbers. They have a strong settlement in Utah, at Soda Springs, under the very shadow of the Prophet. Every sermon I heard from the Mormons betrayed nervous fears as to divisions; some appealed, some unfolded the duty of submission, and Brigham thundered his fierce anathemas against the faithless. Gentile dealings and associations are forbidden, because Mormonism cannot bear contact with virtue and truth, nor can its crowning crime of polygamy bear contact even with vice. Virtue and vice are alike its foes and equally fatal to its perpetuity. Thus is the Mormonism of Young beset by schisms, periled by growing intercourse with gentiles; and soon the Pacific Railroad will pour thousands of population into all the fruitful valleys of the West, and in but a few years the distinctiveness of this people must fade away. While the government has been shamefully remiss in tolerating the habitual, insolent defiance of one of its soundest laws, it seems that natural causes are fast converging to the overthrow of this foulest blot upon the American name. One gentile family in a community of polygamists is better than a thousand sermons against this colossal crime. One happy, cheerful wife, confident of the undivided affection of her husband, is like an angel of light in the region of despair; and even the deepest-seated superstition gradually yields, as it sees the gentile wife worship with her husband and household gods, read from a common Bible, plead the atonement of the same Saviour, and supplicate the same God. Secret discontent, positive dissatisfaction, or open rebellion has its place around every fireside, and each year develops in bolder tones and more defiant actions the restless cancer that is preying upon the vitals of this monstrous vice. It must soon die. Its own enormity must give it the grave of a suicide, if no other great causes were tending to its destruction; but it is a blistering shame that, in this noontide of the nineteenth century,

BRIGHAM YOUNG.

just laws forbidding this wholesale prostitution, practiced in appalling mockery and blasphemy of all that is pure and holy, stand as dead letters upon our national statute-books. With the strong arm of the government firmly maintaining virtue, order, and law—ever careful to encroach upon no rights of conscieuce cr freedom of worship —this wrong would soon hide itself from the scorn of society, instead of boasting of its social supremacy, and linger out its future existence in shame. As an institution, it would at once cease to have a habitation or a name, and this twin-sister of human bondage, equally fruitful of treason and of crime, would perish from the fair land of freedom and justice.

LETTER XVII.

SALT LAKE CITY, June 19, 1867.

I HAVE now spent a week with the Latter-Day Saints,
admired their green shades, beautiful artificial streams,
pleasant homes, and the innumerable evidences of industry and prosperity which appear on every hand. Their
markets are filled with the choicest vegetables, and the
finest strawberries of the continent are offered every hour
of the day, at reasonable prices. Stores equal to those of
the cities of the Western States are numerous, and business of all branches has an air of system, capital, and
thrift that is delightful. This is a city of twenty thousand
population, without paupers, brothels, or gambling-hells.
Among the Mormons, who constitute over ninety per cent.
of the people, there are none idle, and they claim that none
suffer. The bee-hive is found on the dome of the Prophet's
house, and frequently on rude business signs, as typical
of the habits of the faithful. All must work; and, while
each owns his property gained by industry, there is still a
common store where the distressed and children of want
repair. And industry is brightened in every possible way.

In the evening the merry dance is to be heard in almost
every ward; the theatre is never closed for any length of
time, and recreation is devised in every conceivable manner
to lighten the burdens of toil.

Salt Lake City is in what is called the Great Basin of
the West. A section of country, nearly a circle, with a
radius of about three hundred miles from the centre, is
walled in by the Wasatch Mountains on the east, the
Sierra Nevada on the west, and their broken spurs north
and south. This great valley has no outlet for its waters.
The Jordan, Ogden, Bear, and Weber Rivers, with many
lesser streams, empty into the Great Salt Lake, distant
about twelve miles from this city. It is ninety miles long,
and averages about thirty in width, and is the most briny
body of water in the world. So strongly is it impregnated
with salt, that its shores are but a bed of salt, and a man
in the lake will float like a cork. Sink he cannot; but the
head must be kept carefully uppermost, for in whatever
position he lands in the water he is likely to remain. If
head down, down the head will stay, and it requires
almost a superhuman effort to reverse the position of the
body. In the lake are vast islands and high, rugged
mountains, some of them covered with nutritious grass and
abounding in fresh springs. Cattle and horses are grazed
there, and thrive better than anywhere else in the Territory. South of this the river Sevier empties into Lake
Sevier, which is also without an outlet; but the waters
sink, and do not become salt. In the western portion of
the Great Basin (now the State of Nevada) there are a
number of large rivers, and all sink into the earth at different points in the valley and doubtless find subterranean
passages to the sea. The Humboldt, Walker, Carson,
Truckee, and other rivers drain Nevada, and all are without
an open channel to the ocean. Some of them empty into

lakes, but none of them are salt, and all doubtless have invisible outlets.

This great basin was once regarded as a vast desert. The Mormons accepted it as their home to escape the antagonism of the Christians, and supposed that here they could remain unmolested for centuries. When they arrived here, there was not so much as a trail across the mountains. This valley, as well as all west to the Pacific and south to the Gulf, belonged to Mexico; and one of the chief motives for the Mormon pilgrimage to this place was to escape the hated jurisdiction of the United States. But, within a year after they located here, the territory was acquired from Mexico, and they again became unwilling and disloyal subjects of our government. When they arrived here, there was nothing to promise them requited labor and plentiful harvests. The soil was sterile, acrid, full of alkali, and refused to produce anything but the dreary sage and grease-wood; but Mormon industry flooded it with artificial rains, tamed it with corn and buckwheat, and now raises as fine wheat, oats, barley, etc. as are grown in the Union. Not a shrub or tree shaded this vast desert plain when they made it their home; but they had with them the seeds of the locust, and they gathered the little cottonwoods along the streams, and now the city is one forest of the most heartsome shades, and the gardens are covered with the green foliage of every species of fruit trees. They seem to have aimed to make this as nearly a paradise for the stranger as human effort could make it, and they have succeeded better than do most Christians in surrounding their homes, from the most humble to the most spacious, with the beauty, fragrance, and fruitfulness of nature.

But the peculiar religion, or professed religion, of the Mormons, is the most marvelous problem of the age. Here are one hundred thousand people, the most industrious, as a class, on the face of the earth,—sober, neighborly, of good repute as a rule, and most of them sincerely and devoutly pious in their way,—who tolerate and sustain in their leaders the most arrant swindling and revolting licentiousness, and call it making sacrifices to the Lord. Of the one hundred thousand Mormons, nine-tenths are ignorant aliens, who were the slaves of the mines or the serfs of the proprietors in the old countries. They need but little here to improve their condition, and, as a rule, they have been made owners of their homes. All they ever did learn, they have learned from the Mormons; and it is not so surprising, therefore, that they bow implicitly to the teachings of those they believed to be inspired from on high. If I were going to analyze the Mormon population, I would set down nineteen of every twenty as pitiable dupes, and the remaining one-twentieth as the most expert and successful knaves on the earth.

Brigham Young is the spiritual and temporal head of the Church. He assumes to be the successor of Christ, and is esteemed by his deluded followers as of equal power and glory with the Saviour. They hold that Jesus was the first Messiah, Joseph Smith the second, and Brigham Young the third ; and I heard it distinctly taught in the tabernacle that Christ, Smith, and Young would come back to the earth together, in the fullness of time, to reign with the people of God. Accepted as of divine anointment— indeed, as being in immediate communication with the Almighty, as the oracle through whom God speaks to his chosen people,—it is not wonderful that he can riot in wealth, pick the fairest and tenderest lambs from the flock to gratify his beastly lusts, and have the streets filled with his children who are fed, clothed, and schooled by the labor of his followers.

I spent half an hour with him in his inner sanctuary;

but it was a mere show,—like going to see any other monstrosity. Some half a dozen others were with me, including Mrs. M., and the Prophet was courteous, but reticent. He did not know who we might be, and his never-failing sagacity made him self-poised and diplomatic in an eminent degree. He most adroitly warded off several neat strategic movements to get an insight of Mormonism, and kept the party to glittering generalities with masterly skill. Whenever the conversation became unpleasant for him, he would turn to Mrs M. and address her with great elegance and fluency on commonplace topics. I had a seat beside his oldest son, who was not so prudent as the father, and I had his view of true Mormonism. " Religion," said he, " without plurality of wives in the Lord, is the play of Hamlet with Hamlet left out;" and he gave me a patronizing look, as if he pitied my unbelief. I did not venture on a discussion, as we had merely called to see the lions, and could not, in a general conversation, learn much worth knowing. Around the house, or rather houses, of Mr. Young, there were a score of children, from three to ten years of age, most of them girls, with different mothers, but all owning Brigham as father. He has some twenty wives who are named to him in the flesh, and perhaps twice as many who are sealed to him merely to become his spiritual wives in heaven. I need not say that these, as a class, are long-neglected spinsters and unsightly widows, who have failed to gain a union in the flesh. I saw several of them stowed away in one corner of the theatre ; and it was not difficult to determine why they were merely sealed as wives for the spirit-land. I notice that in no instance do the Prophet and Elders seal the young and beautiful daughters of the church as spiritual wives. Severe as they profess the cross to be, they accept them in the flesh, usually to the neglect and sorrow of their older partners. In the theatre were

six of Brigham's wives in a row, the original wife occupy-
ing a comfortable rocking-chair as the honored mother in
Israel. She looks like a woman of intelligence and refine-
ment; but rude furrows have been plowed in her face by
ever-visible grief. She lives in a cottage by herself, and
seldom is favored with visits from her lord. The others
are all women beneath mediocrity, all more or less faded,
and none bearing the traces of early beauty. They are the
sobered and practically discarded mistresses of the Prophet,
and have served their purpose, while other and fairer faces
usurp the favor they each in turn enjoyed. They are
relics of the past, and seem to have quietly resigned themselves to their fate. And why should they not? Each
one, as she became the favorite so-called wife, pushed others
aside; and they accepted their degraded position with the
full knowledge that the passions which were sated with
their predecessors would in time demand others to take
their places. The favorite is, of course, the last wife; and
while the venerable, unsightly spiritual wives were huddled in a corner in plainest garb, and those discarded in
the flesh crowded each other in a row near the centre of
the parquette, the richly gilded and curtained private box,
and softly cushioned chair, held the last fair flower trans-
planted to the harem. She is still gay and festive, has a
queenly step, sports her elegant opera-glass and the best
of ribbons and laces. She is the niece of the first wife, and,
like most babes in large families, is the spoiled child of the
establishment. Notwithstanding the holy sphere in which
she moves, she occasionally combs the head of the Prophet
with a three-legged stool, raises Hail Columbia in the very
sanctuary of the holies, and smashes a chair over the
piano to prove her devout affection for the sacred calling
she has accepted. So revolutionary has she been, in spite
of divine commands from the very oracles of Heaven, that

she had to be "corraled" in a house by herself; and there she rules in her own boisterous, obstinate way, and makes the Prophet bow at her feet, instead of becoming the meek, submissive wife the Church demands of all on pain of eternal punishment.

According to the Mormon faith, women have no status in heaven excepting such as is given them by their husbands; and, as they cannot be given in marriage there, it is of the first importance to all women to become wives. If they become the wife of a man who has many others, and sad crosses and trials result therefrom, they thus lay up for themselves bright crowns in heaven. In accordance with this belief, it is not uncommon for dying damsels to send for high officials in the Church and be sealed to them before death, so as to gain a high seat with their spiritual husbands; and even the dead are sometimes married by proxy, near friends representing them, to lift them up to a level with their spiritual lords in the future world. This doctrine is preached daily to the women by men who claim, and are believed, to be inspired by God, and as a rule it is accepted religiously by the Mormon women. Yet each one struggles to avert the pollution of her own domestic circle, and prays that the bitter cup may pass from her. I hear of one man who married two wives together who has a peaceful household; but no wife in all Utah has received another to divide or rather to usurp the love of her husband, without consuming sorrows. They bow in submission to it, but, in spite of their religious infatuation and the promise of a brighter crown above, their womanly instincts revolt at it, and they go in grief the remainder of their days.

I wished to learn of Mormonism from its votaries, and of polygamy from its advocates and victims. I have met its advocates, a class confined to husbands, and heard the

best defense of that peculiar feature of their faith; but its
victims are not accessible to the stranger. I met a few
Mormon ladies who are wives without presiding over a
brothel, and the saddest shadow is brought to their faces
by the slightest reference to the plurality of wives. One
most intelligent and accomplished wife, who with her husband professes the Mormon faith and has increased in
worldly prosperity thereby, advocated the claims of the
Mormon people to the generous support of the government, with much earnestness. I was about to ask her
whether she would be willing for her husband to bring another so-called wife into her house; but it would have been
too cruel, and I was silent. It would have ended the conversation, and been regarded as a wanton indignity from a
guest to a hostess. I have seen one man who has five wives,
—three of them a mother and two daughters; others who
have brought to their homes children of fourteen years and
made them the reigning queens of their firesides, while
their lawful wives, often with children older than their
associates, or rather successors, bow in shame with broken
hearts. Old men of sixty, dignitaries in the Church, have
half a dozen or more, from the aged partners of their
youth, down to the latest fancy, always of the tenderest
years; and young girls are thus freely sacrificed, by infatuated parents, to decrepit, lecherous beasts, with the
firm belief that it is a religious duty and will be rewarded
in heaven. After a careful observation of this polygamic
people, I must accept the conviction that the leaders teach
and practice it simply to gratify their unbridled licentiousness, and they deliberately blaspheme God and his holy
precepts to maintain their polluting doctrines. Bear in
mind that polygamy is not general among the Mormon
people. Not over one-third of the married men have a
plurality of wives, and they are, as a rule, the bishops,

elders, councilors, and other dignitaries, who handle the tithings and fatten on the toil of their miserable dupes.

On Sunday I attended Mormon service in the tabernacle, morning and evening, and heard four sermons. The high officials do not attend in the morning, and I was surprised at the low grade of faces almost uniformly presented. There were over one thousand women present, and there was scarcely a bright, intelligent, happy face among them. In the afternoon the élite of the Church attended with the others, the sacrament was administered (as it is every Sunday) and Brigham Young preached. There were fifteen hundred women present, and among them were very many bright, pretty faces, with lustrous eyes, rosy cheeks, and pouting lips that might tempt even a gentile kiss. The choir looked like a jolly May-party,—filled with pretty girls, with jaunty hats and feathers, and all most tastefully clad. A crazy Cockney opened the service by a rambling harangue demanding equal division of property and wives, and cautioning, with peculiar fervor, the "ewes and lambs" of the Church against gentile unions. Brigham sat behind him, and wearied of his erratic doctrines. He first tried to stop him by crying out "amen" at an appropriate moment; but the inspired minister rushed on. Finally Brigham's patience was exhausted, and he seized the Cockney by the coat-tail and jerked him down, when the Prophet ascended the sacred desk and spoke an hour with rare adroitness and perfect fluency. He at once took issue with the man who had preceded him, and declared against an equal division of property. "Equalize to-morrow," said he, "and how long will it remain equal? Not a month, not a week, not an hour. It is folly to talk about it. Not one in forty of you can take care of yourselves, and you must be dictated to by some one who has experience in temporal matters and is inspired on spiritual matters."

16

After he had shown them that they could not manage their own affairs, he declared that he was their leader by divine appointment; he would dictate to them, and they must obey. He appealed to the women to be true to the faith, and proclaimed it as the will, even the command, of the Lord, received directly from Him, that they must not trade with gentiles or apostates, who refuse to give tithings to the Church. His arrogance, profanity, and frequent assumption of omnipotent power were shocking; but a careful survey of the audience clearly demonstrated that he spoke with much worldly wisdom to maintain the infatuation and abject submission of his people. After church, Sunday was devoted to recreation, and the delightful gardens of Salt Lake were filled with pleasure-parties.

How long is this blot on the American name to last? It is in open violation of law, and yet the law seems powerless to vindicate its majesty. Congress has enacted that this monstrous crime must cease to pollute the fairest homes of the Far West. Why does it not enforce its own solemn law? It needs but one season of stern justice to scatter it to the winds and drive the bloated impostors from their sore oppression of a deluded people ; and morality and public decency demand that it be speedily done.

LETTER XVIII.

Continued Interruption of Travel.—The Indian Campaigns.—The Injustice done the Western People.—Desire of the West for Peace.—The Inefficiency of the Military.—Wells, Fargo & Co.—Their Horses exposed to Indians for Want of Feed.—No Valuable Horses on the Mountain Divisions.—Passengers exposed to Danger for Want of Stock.—The Stables undefended. —No Horses stolen from Defended Stables.—Mr. Holliday.—He deranges the Line, and then falls back.—Kindness of the Employés of the Company.

SALT LAKE CITY, June 20, 1867.

As yet we have no mail-communication from the East since the interruption of travel by the Indians west of the North Platte ; and, judging from the telegraphic reports, it may be a month before there can be anything like regular mails again from the terminus of the Pacific Railroad. If military matters shall be directed as bunglingly henceforth as heretofore, then may the people East and West at once abandon all hope of maintaining the overland route this season. If General Sherman, with nearly ten thousand troops in the departments of Augur and Hancock, and fully two thousand of them mounted, could not, in sixty days after reaching the Smoky Hill and Platte, protect any fifty miles of either of these routes, how long must it require, under the same military direction, to protect three hundred miles from Platte City to Denver, some three hundred miles of the direct line of railroad from Platte City west to the mountains, now being located and constructed, and six hundred miles from Denver to this city ? Until all these

(175)

lines are under military protection, the overland mail cannot be run; and the people of the East can judge as well as I can, from the facts stated, how soon our present military system will accomplish this work.

There is no excuse for the failure of the military commanders to protect the overland route, other than that they don't know or won't discharge their duty. General Sherman has wasted fully two months in petty quibbling with the Western people, and must have known that nearly every day lives of settlers and emigrants were wantonly sacrificed to Indian savagery, and stock and property stolen or destroyed, until they now amount to millions in value. I doubt not that he was harassed by speculators, contractors, and thieves, as he justly complains, and that they were most anxious for a general Indian war; but had he covered his glittering stars and spent a few hours in plain conversation with intelligent stage-drivers and ranchmen on the line—the men who have most to fear from war, and who of all others want peace—he might have learned in a few hours not only the actual situation, but also the true way to meet the peculiar foe that never confronts him and yet is ever attacking him. When General Sherman declared that "the people could have an Indian war or not, as they chose," not less than fifty people had been butchered within his department since the opening of spring, and in not a single instance had the victims sought to provoke war, unless traveling the great thoroughfare to the West, supposed to be under his protection, was an act of hostility against the red man. I have been on the plains since the 6th of May, and I deem it as due to truth to say that to the obstinacy or imbecility of military management we are indebted for the crimsoned record the overland route presents this year. The government did everything that could have been asked in furnishing men, but to this day there has been no practical use made of the thousands of troops, now nearly as long on the Plains as Sherman required to march against a powerful and well-commanded foe from Chattanooga to Atlanta.

I do not know who is to blame for the wasteful expenditure of money in the character of troops sent to contend with Indians. I believe that not more than one-fourth of the force west of the Missouri is cavalry; while fully one-half of it should be mounted in the West. First of all, the troops should be taken from the Far West, as the people of the Territories understand the Indian character, cherish the intensest hatred toward them, and will fight them "until they can't rest," to use a favorite Western saying. On the other hand, the regulars prefer any other sort of warfare to Indian warfare. They both despise and fear the savages, and fight them only when they cannot avoid it. They have deserted until many regiments are reduced thirty per cent., and in some instances, it is believed, have joined the Indians in plundering trains. Certain it is that the marks of white men have been detected in a number of the raids made upon the ranches and stations. Our American horses, on which the cavalrymen are mounted, are utterly unfit for Indian campaigns. They are heavy, sluggish, and cannot march a week without grain; while the Indian pony and broncho will travel all the summer on prairie-grass, and outstrip even a well-fed American charger. One thousand men from Colorado, Nebraska, or Montana, mounted on such horses as they would select, would be worth double their number of regular troops mounted as is our regular cavalry. It seems to me impossible that these facts, which are so patent to every Western man, have not been pressed upon the military authorities; and, if so, upon whom does this costly, bloody blunder rest?

Since I have been on the overland line, probably not less

16*

than five hundred horses have been stolen by the Indians
from Wells, Fargo & Co., who run the line and carry the
Pacific mails. I understand that for this mail service the
Company are paid some $900,000, and the government en-
gages to protect the route. After the contract was made, a
special act of Congress was procured prohibiting the transmission of transient newspapers, books, or pamphlets, except upon payment of letter-postage. A single copy of the
"Tribune" cannot be mailed to any point west of Denver
without the payment of letter-postage, and publishers cannot mail books without paying the same rates. The express
rate for such articles is one dollar per pound, about the same
as letter-postage. Congress has thus practically given up
to Wells, Fargo & Co. a monopoly of the mails, exclusive of
letters, at enormous rates, as the responsibility of a company of common carriers gives them a positive preference
over the Post-Office Department.

Hitherto every horse taken by the Indians, and all
property destroyed on this line, has been paid for by Congress, in accordance with the terms of the contract. As
I have no knowledge of the facts, I do not question the
honesty of the claims thus made and paid, but of the claims
to be made for the losses of stock this spring, while I was
traversing the route, I feel constrained to say a word. As
we had rumors of Indians and Indian depredations from the
first station at the western terminus of the railroad to Denver, three hundred miles, and also from Laporte to Green
River on the mountains, a distance of three hundred and
fifty miles, I made it a point to look into every station, and
learn the actual condition of affairs, and the measures taken
to protect the lives of the station-keepers and the stock. Not
one-half of the "swing-stations" (stables where the teams
are changed) had so much as a single gun of any kind, and
not one-fourth of them had taken any measures whatever

to defend the stock. At the ranches owned by individuals, there were always rifles in readiness, often tunnels to outer fortifications, and invariably some sort of defensive lines. "Old Wicked," of whom I wrote in a former letter, with three men to aid him, repulsed a regular attack upon his ranche made by one hundred and fifty savages, and saved his goods and stock, two years ago, while every stage-station was cleared and most of the horses stolen. Nine-tenths of the raids made upon the Platte stations this spring could have been repulsed by three well-armed men, always on the alert to prevent a surprise; and there are not less than that number at a station. Had the precaution been taken by Wells, Fargo & Co. (the ordinary diligence and care that the law requires of every individual), more than half the horses stolen on the Platte would have been protected and saved. The Indians are proverbial cowards, and will never fight at a disadvantage, however sure of success, and they have rarely raided the stations in numbers so large that several well-armed men, protected by stables or ranches, could not have repulsed them. We read daily of their capture of trains and the murder of train-men; but they never attack excepting where the train is scattered and portions can be cut off, or when they can be surprised and the stock stampeded. Such a thing as a square, stand-up fight for a train has not occurred in all the Indian depre-dations this year.

But west of Denver, where probably three hundred horses have been captured from the stage-line within the last month, the carelessness of the Company has been so marked that I cannot resist the conviction that it was delib-erately planned to have them captured. Let me give you a simple statement of facts as they came under my own per-sonal observation. A company using thousands of horses must necessarily always have a large number nearly or quite worn out. I found none such between Platte City and Denver, and none from Denver west until I reached the country infested by the Indians, and there I found none fit for service. From Big Laramie to Laclede, a distance of two hundred miles, where the Indians were troublesome, there was not a team of horses fit to drive, and the Company took no measures whatever to save them from capture. In all the raids made upon this part of the line—most of which were made while I was traveling west—there was not a single occupied station captured, and not a single horse stolen that was stabled. Bear in mind that, although early in June, we waded through snow-storms daily, and vegetation was so late that stock could scarcely live on the grass, and yet for more than one hundred miles of this part of the line there was not a pound of grain for the stock, and there had not been any for a month, and not one station in five had had hay to feed for six weeks, some having been out as much as two months. The broken-down horses have been placed on this part of the line; there was no grain or hay to feed them, and every horse captured, so far as I could learn, was taken while out grazing his scanty meal, when he should have been in the stable feeding on grain and hay. I stated these facts to Mr. Tracy, the General Superintendent, who passed me west of Fort Bridger, and he gave as an excuse for Wells, Fargo & Co. that they came into possession of the line too late last fall to supply it properly with forage. This may be so, and is something in extenuation of the total neglect to have proper food for the stock; but when hundreds of horses are stolen because the predecessor of Mr. Tracy failed to do his duty, does the government become responsible? But the excuse offered was not wholly true. At Cooper's Creek we found, as a rule, the end of grain and hay on the line. But one hundred miles southeast, at Laporte, grain and hay are abundant in market at reasonable prices, and they could have been supplied without difficulty. At North Platte there was but a single bag of grain, and that belonged to the station-keeper. After much bargaining, we got it for our two four-horse teams intended to take us through to Sulphur Spring; and even with that, and a liberal time for the horses to graze at noon, the horses in one of our teams had to be taken out on the way and were abandoned on the road, in a trip of forty-five miles, with but six persons to a wagon. At Pine Grove and Bridger Pass stations the horses had been stolen the day before we arrived, because they were out grazing on grass insufficient to satisfy their hunger. Bridger Pass station was attacked at the same time, and successfully defended by the men ; but, as the stock was gone, they abandoned it, as did the occupants of Pine Grove, because they had nothing to defend that was worth risking their lives for. At Sulphur Spring station, where there were twenty men, six-teen head of horses and mules were captured the day I ar-rived there. The stock was out browsing under the snow, because of the want of grain and hay, and no ordinary number of men could defend them. No attempt was made to capture the stable. At Waskie, in view of Indians seen by our party on the bluffs as we left Sulphur, the stock was grazing out of sight, because there was no feed, and two days after it was captured. At Laclede I found eighty-three head of horses, seventy-three of which belonged to the Company, and but a few herders, and not a single gun to defend them. Even the few men there, without arms, make the stable and building safe ; but the miserable stock had to be turned out to hunt up a scanty subsistence on the prairies, and the Indians watched their opportunity and bagged sixty-five of them. The next Congress will doubt-less be applied to for restitution for some three hundred good horses stolen on this part of the line, when in fact I did

not see a single good horse, or more than a half-priced
horse, on the two hundred miles raided by the Indians, and
not one was taken that was stabled as ordinary care required. The traveling public must bear the inconvenience
of disabled teams in the mountains; but when they are so
placed as to invite the raids of the savage, and the government expected to pay the Company double or treble value
for practically handing their stock over to the Indians, it
is cutting it rather fat!

We had practical evidence of Mr. Ben Holliday's appreciation of the condition of things on the line. He is a Di-
rector of the Company, one of its largest stockholders, and
was on his way East as I was journeying West. He was
about to start from Salt Lake as I started from North
Platte; and as we dragged our way through the Indian
country we were delayed and badgered from place to place,
because the horses able to travel had to be saved up to put
Mr. Holliday through. We found one team at a number
of stations resting up for his benefit, while the crippled
stock, as was usual, were out grazing when we arrived at
the stations, and we had to wait until it was driven in
(not a difficult operation), harnessed, and hitched to the
coach. He had orders all along the line for resting the
best horses, and for an escort of the employés from station
to station, while he left the poor station-keepers at the mercy
of the savages, three or four at a stable, and often without
a gun to defend themselves from the scalping-knife. After
thus deranging the line for two hundred miles, he arrived
at Weber, fifty miles east of this city, and then concluded that discretion was the better part of valor, and
retraced his steps to California, to return by steamer. With
command of the entire stock and employés of the line, after
periling the lives of all on the route by holding the best
drivers and teams, and deranging the stock not given over

to the Indians by systematic neglect, he would not venture
to pass over the thoroughfare that he invites the public to
travel daily at the liberal rate of twenty cents per mile.

It is due to the employés, and indeed all the ranchmen
and other persons on the line, to say that they were
uniformly courteous and kind; and our party will ever
cherish most grateful recollections of their efforts to contribute to our comfort and safety. I cannot recall a single
instance of neglect or discourtesy on the part of any one
on the route from Denver to this place—a distance of six
hundred miles. Their rude shelter and often scanty stores
were ever freely given us; and they were tireless in their
efforts to smooth the many rough places of the journey.

A Delightful Journey through Mormondom.—How Brigham
"dictates" to the Faithful.—The Bishops and their Revenues.
—How they assist the Poor.—The Mormon Industrial System
a Success.—Ogden City.—Bishop West and his Eight Wives.—
How a Mormon Bishop luxuriates.—The Prairie-Flowers.—
Bear River.—Countless Mosquitoes and Gnats.—Passengers
and Driver veiled.—Idaho.—Appropriate Names of Stations.—
Climbing the Rocky Range again.

SNAKE RIVER, IDAHO TERR., June 21, 1867.

WE had a delightful journey from Salt Lake northward
to this point. The weather was pleasant, the roads good,
the teams spirited, and the country beautiful. The tourist
never wearies of the study of the industrial system of the
Mormons. I doubt whether any other association ever
attained such a degree of perfection in the division, government, and success of labor. In the remotest parts of
Utah the same system, industry, and thrift prevail, and,
whether scattered in settlements or crowded in cities, the
Mormons are subject to the same peculiar laws, and they
are enforced with scrupulous care. No Mormon is in any
sense his own master, unless he is one of the very few who
belong to the governing class. I heard Brigham Young
say to three thousand of his people, in a sermon, that without some one to "dictate" to them how to manage their
affairs, both temporal and spiritual, they would soon be
scattered to the four winds of heaven; and he did not forget to add that " we, the chosen oracles of the Lord,"

(184)

must "dictate" to the faithful. This doctrine he enforces relentlessly. In Salt Lake City the Saints dare not sell their own houses without the consent of the President, and in the rural settlements the rule has no exception, save when the iron yoke becomes intolerable and apostasy is preferred to submission.

When emigrants are landed in Utah, they are brought to Salt Lake, an inventory of their cash, stock, and worldly goods in general is taken, and the men are examined as to the particular branch of industry for which they are best fitted. The church bishop has a record of the condition of every settlement, of the number of acres still uncultivated that can be irrigated, and of the wants of each community respecting all kinds of labor. The emigrants are then directed where to go and what to do. If they have means, they are instructed how and where to invest; and if they are destitute, they are directed to the proper bishop for a start in the world. Each ward in every city, and each settlement, however small, has a bishop, whose duty it is to "dictate" to the saints in all things, spiritual and temporal, and especially to see that no one withholds any part of his tithings from the Church. When an emigrant reaches the place to which he is assigned, he reports to the bishop and obeys orders. If destitute, the bishop assigns him two, five, or ten acres of Uncle Sam's land, sells him a yoke of cattle, wagon, and seeds, takes his note, and puts him to ditching and planting. Each year the new settler reports his products to the bishop, and they are disposed of as he directs. First of all, one-tenth is taken for the Church, a portion is allowed for the family, another portion for seed, and the residue is appropriated on account of the debt for the outfit, until all is paid with interest. Over this fund, into which the tithing is gathered, the bishops have immediate control,

17

but report regularly to the President. They give to the poor when the necessity is imperative, but never fail to demand restitution if it can be recovered even years afterward. One of the first duties required, when a new farm is opened, is the planting of all kinds of fruits; and the result is that in every settlement the houses are first recognized by the clusters of green foliage or fragrant blossoms which surround them.

As an industrial system the Mormon Church is a positive success, and challenges the admiration of the most embittered foes of this peculiar religious faith. I did not see a single home of a Mormon where there were signs of dilapidation or decay. It is forbidden by their faith, and the bishops see that no sluggards bring reproach upon their religion. For nearly one hundred miles north of Salt Lake City there are numerous Mormon settlements nestling between the Great Lake and the Wasatch range, and they dot the earth with fruitfulness and beauty. The wild flowers are thick on every side, and climb over every home, however humble. At one place I saw a beautiful hedge of the wild rose, carefully trimmed, and blooming in profusion. On the route there are several towns or cities of note. Ogden contains a population of over two thousand, and has excellent buildings, stores, and gardens. Two of Bishop West's eight wives (the second and eighth) keep the hotel in the city in a most creditable manner. His other six live on his farms, at his mills, etc., while he rotates around generally among them. He supplies the faithful with bitters by the small at his bar, manufactures their grain into flour and whisky, preaches on Sunday, and sees that every tenth egg the Ogden chickens lay is properly returned to his tithing-house. Brigham City is another Mormon village, of over one thousand inhabitants, and bears the many evidences of well-directed industry which characterize all the residences of the Saints. The strip of land between the Lake and the Wasatch, prairies from five to twenty miles in width, is one of the most beautiful sections of Utah. From every settlement the lake is visible, and, while the prairie and the fields are green with verdure and variegated with every hue of the rose, the Wasatch and the Lake Mountains are capped with snow. Some of the mountain-islands seem to be entirely bare of grass or timber, and the sun gives them a pale pink color, which is reflected in the shadows of the lake, and, with the deep lines of blue which encircle the island, and the white crowns of the waves, represent the various colors of the rainbow. As we came near to Bear River the land became more sterile, and the settlements were not so frequent. But, even where the soil seemed to repel the settler, the prairie abounded in every variety of wild flowers. The cactus was in full bloom, presenting almost every shade in its flower, from its favorite pale yellow to the brightest pink; and mingled with it were countless varieties of Nature's offerings to beautify the plain, from the huge sunflower down to the modest little daisy that shelters its delicate tints among the sage and grass.

Bear River is the end of Mormon settlements. It cuts its way through the Wasatch range, leaving almost perpendicular walls, hundreds of feet in height, on each side, and has washed out a deep bed in the prairie. It is quite a large stream, and the most northern of the leading tributaries of Salt Lake. I found it most remarkable for the size, quantity, and vigor of its mosquitoes. We took a square meal down under its high banks, and the mosquitoes and gnats were so thick that we could scarcely see each other across the table. The gnats literally darkened the windows in their persistent efforts to get inside and devour us while we were taking tea. I need not say that we broke bread

as briefly as possible with the hostess of Bear River, and
rejoiced to get out on the prairie again.   But north of the
river I found that we had only escaped from several billions
of the winged varmints to meet with a million or so; and
there was but little iu favor of the plains. Fortunately, we
were all provided with coarse veils—an article that no
traveler pretends to dispense with on the northern route
—and we all veiled ourselves closely, including the driver.
The poor horses suffered intensely, for the mosquitoes and
gnats literally covered them, and they had to be driven at
a gallop to keep them manageable.   Twelve miles distant
we reached Mound Springs, on high ground, and a stiff,
chilling breeze settled nature's blood-letters for the night.

Some fifteen miles north of Bear River is the line between Utah and Idaho; and thenceforth there are no more
orchards or cultivated fields.   At Malade City I saw the
last field for five hundred miles.   It is a settlement of the
Josephites (anti-polygamy or Smithite branch of the Mormon Church).   They crossed the line to get away from the
dominion of the Brighamites, and, but for the higher altitude and colder climate, would compare favorably with
the Brighamites in the fruits of their industry.   They
have two settlements in Idaho, one at Malade City, and
another at Soda Springs.   From Malade north there is
nothing that can ever invite the settler, unless the precious
metals should be discovered in the bluffs and gulches.
" Devil's Creek," " Robbers' Retreat," "Desert Wells,"
" Rattlesnake," and " Stinking Water" are the euphonious
titles of as many stations ; and no one who travels the
route will deny their appropriateness. " Robbers' Retreat"
is memorable as the place where the stage was robbed
some two years ago, and seven passengers murdered.   It is
in Port Neuf Cañon, one of the most repulsive, dreary passes
I found in the mountain-trip of one thousand miles.   The

weather in the region between the northern and southern
lines of Idaho is universally described as consisting of
nine months of a hard winter and three months of a very
cold spell. In the entire two hundred miles across Idaho
I saw nothing but the most sterile prairies, wild mountain-
passes, and the bleakest of bluffs.

This evening we reached Snake River before sunset,
and had several hours' rest. It is a large river, and at
this place, known as Eagle Rock, the main channel is over
sixty feet in depth, and the current very swift. It is
unusually high, and great fears are entertained for the
rude bridge that spans it, as the coaches could not be
ferried over it at any point at this time. It is one of the
main tributaries of the Columbia River, and heads at the
base of the Rocky range, near the Montana line, and has
many tributaries from the east, but none from the west.
Some seventy miles north of this the summit of the Rocky
range is reached, and there the waters divide between the
Missouri and the Columbia: the two great rivers which
drain the Far Northwest, and course their ways respect-
ively to the Pacific and the Gulf, there have their sources
within a stone's throw of each other.

But the coach is about to start; and I must make my
second effort to climb the Rocky range to-night. I hope
to find it at least more agreeable than was Bridger's Pass,
where I warmed myself by the fire of burning stations
with the fresh tracks of the Sioux thick around me in the
snow.

17*

A Night-Ride on the Summit of the Rocky Range.—The Mos-
quitoes again.—Pleasant Valley Station a Fraud.—Parting of the
Waters on the Summit to the Eastern and Western Seas.—The
Source of the Missouri and Columbia Rivers.—The Snake River.
—Its Tortuous Course through the Mountains.—The Stinking-
Water River.—Virginia City.—Its First Settlers.—Alder Gulch.
—Its Wonderful Yield of Gold.—Belt of Rich Mines.—The Pre-
cious Metals of Montana.—Agricultural Resources of the Terri-
tory.—Irregularity of the Mails.—Wells, Fargo & Co.'s Special
Mails.—A Premium paid for Neglect to convey the Mails.—
How to test the Safety of the Overland Route.

VIRGINIA CITY, MONTANA TERR., June 27, 1867.

AFTER a pleasant evening at Snake River, we crossed
the frail bridge, then swaying to and fro before the violence
of the current (and since swept away), and started for a
night-ride toward the summit of the Rocky range. The
mosquitoes were eminently sociable, and forbade sleep in
the coach. Our coarse veils were of little use; for they
would touch the face at some points, and just there our
tormentors would settle, like a swarm of bees lighting on
the green, and present their inexorable demand for blood.
Even toward midnight, when it was so cold that I had to
wrap my thick blanket around over my great-coat, the mosquitoes wearied not in their efforts to forage upon us. They
seem to be perfectly acclimated in this region, and defy the
chilling blasts of the snow-clad mountains hard by. As we
reached the higher bluffs, a most welcome breeze greeted
us, and cleared our path of the buzzing and biting pests.

(190)

Early in the morning we reached Pleasant Valley station for breakfast. I had noticed its enticing name on the little guide-book, and had grateful anticipations of a delightful mountain-home, but was doomed to disappointment. Of all the filthy, repulsive stations on the route, Pleasant Valley is the worst. It consists of a narrow gulch between two high bluffs, and we could not get out of the coach into the station without plunging into mud ankle-deep. It furnishes us one of the regular "square meals" of the most primitive life in this primitive land. A miserable apology for coffee, no butter or milk, stale eggs and bacon, and bread almost as gritty as the mountain boulders, constituted our breakfast. I need not say that we partook most sparingly, paid our two dollars each, and waded out as speedily as possible. Let me say, however, for the "home-stations," that, in fifteen hundred miles of staging on the plains and through the mountains, I can recall but two meals that. were not inviting, and, upon the whole, no better fare would be found traveling in the States.

Nine miles from Pleasant Valley we reached the summit, the dividing line between Idaho and Montana, and the grand divide of the great waters of the Northwest. Just on the summit numerous little springs start, and soon unite, to form Red Butte Creek, the southernmost source of the Father of Waters. Black Tail Deer and Stinking Water rising farther east on the range, and Horse Plain and Big Hole on the west, form Jefferson River, the main source of the Missouri ; while, still farther east, the Madison and Gallatin rise in the mountains, drain and irrigate fruitful valleys, and unite at Gallatin City, some sixty miles north of this place, to form the Missouri. The Snake River courses southwest from the summit until it reaches close to the southern line of Idaho, when it describes a semi-circle northward, thence runs nearly due north to Lewistown, on the Idaho and Washington line, within one hundred miles of the British boundary, when it sweeps around southwest again, and unites with the Columbia at Walla-Walla.   It is to the Columbia what the Missouri is to the Mississippi—a tributary greater than the river that receives its waters and ends its history and name.   It drains Idaho, and all of Oregon west of the Cascade range, and a large portion of Washington.   I have no data before me to make an accurate estimate of the distance this remarkable stream traverses in reaching the ocean, but it must be fully fifteen hundred miles in its tortuous windings to find a water-grade from the top of the Rocky range to the Pacific coast.   I crossed it at Eagle Rock, not one hundred miles from its source, and there it was over sixty feet deep in the main channel, and nearly one hundred yards from shore to shore.   Like the Platte and the Green, however, it will ever defy the navigators, lending no assistance to the march of commerce.

From the summit, the overland line traverses the same bleak, sterile, and broken country we left on the other side, in Idaho, and no sign of cultivation is visible until Virginia City is reached, and here there is no pretense of rearing more than sickly flowers and some vegetables in the gardens.   Some distance from the city we struck the headwaters of Stinking River, and followed it for some miles. It gained its repulsive title from the fact that it was once the favorite deposit for the Indian dead.   Instead of burying their deceased comrades in the earth, they wrapped them in their blankets and robes, and gave them sepulchres in the forks of trees or on elevated poles, causing, as the miners say, the most "flagrant fragrance."   The stream has a rapid descent, and is admirably located for irrigation, but it has no valley of sufficient width to be productive.

Virginia City, the capital of the Territory, was founded

in 1863, and was originally called Varina, in honor of the wife of Jefferson Davis. The first settlers were mainly rebels, and to this day they have maintained their supremacy in this portion of Montana. Alder Gulch, of which Virginia was originally but the mining camp, was the richest gulch of the size ever found in any of our gold regions. It first built up a considerable mining town a mile below Virginia, called Nevada; but it has gone into dilapidation, and is practically abandoned. Out of this gulch millions of gold have been taken. For ten miles it has been worked, some places as much as five hundred yards in width, and at its head are now found the richest quartz leads. Although every bushel of earth in the gulch has already been panned, still, it is lined with miners, who are now bringing the more improved systems to work it over again profitably. Ditches have been brought from lakes ten miles distant, and the hydraulic process is at present washing down the hard banks and sluicing the once-worked earth. A number of quartz-mills have already been erected on the leads at the head of this gulch, and, when brought down to proper management and legitimate enterprise, must make immense returns to mill-owners. It is admitted, I believe, that no better-defined or richer leads are to be found on the continent than in the summit district. Imperfect machinery, worse direction, and impatient, ill-advised, and wasteful efforts at development have made failures on mines where practical men would gather fortunes.

This whole belt, or rather the entire mass of broken and confused ranges, seems to be studded with the precious metals. Helena has taken a sudden start, and now distances this city in population and enterprise. Most productive gulches are being worked there, and very rich gold and silver mines have been developed and tested by mills.

Argenta, forty miles distant, has silver mines which yield from $100 to $400 per ton, and the lead, or litharge, is worth $250 per ton at the furnace. The litharge is eighty per cent. pure lead, and lead is now worth thirty cents per pound wholesale. It will in a short time become cheaper, and supplant wood for roofing. I learn that one company will shortly turn out sheet-lead for that purpose. Deer Lodge, west from here of a high mountain range, has also developed very valuable gold and silver mines, and rich gulches are being worked there; and Edgerton and Jefferson, directly north of this, are yielding largely of both silver and gold. As yet, the Montana miners have not had to contend with the base metals, as in Colorado; but, as they descend in their mines, they will meet with them more or less. Their leads are yet in the infancy of development, and at no point that I have been able to hear from have they reached a depth sufficient to prove the measure of richness of the Montana gold leads. While in California they must sink down a considerable depth to get paying ore, here they work ore from the grass-roots at a profit, with labor and all expenses thrice as high. Laborers command $5 per day; miners, engineers, etc., from $6 to $8; and most of the ore is raised by shafts, to hasten operations, instead of tunneling and waiting until proper systematic development is attained. I have seen ore worked profitably that costs $25 per ton to deliver it from the mines, while in California the same ore would be delivered at about $3. The hills in which the valuable leads are found are singularly adapted to the cheap delivery of ore by tunnels. Most of the mines I have seen could be reached by tunnels of a few hundred feet, and then be struck at a great depth from the surface. In a few years the mines will be worked as they should be. Speculative companies will die out in bankruptcy, and practical men will make the mountains yield fabulous quantities of gold and silver.

When it is considered that these mines have not been known more than four years, that they have been almost inaccessible for machinery until one year ago, and then only by the perilous overland route or the almost equally perilous waters of the Missouri, it is wonderful indeed that human energy could have accomplished what it has accomplished here. It is not strange that its quartz mining is most imperfect in both machinery and management, and thereby rendered comparatively unproductive. Notwithstanding all these obstacles, Montana is second only to California in her yield of gold, and will this year go up to fully twenty millions of treasure, with a gradual increase from year to year, as legitimate enterprise is displayed in her mines of almost boundless extent and bewildering wealth. I doubt whether any part of the world will yield such large returns on the same capital and labor as will Montana, in time. Just now the best scientific talent is directed to the mastery of our Rocky Mountain ores; each year will simplify and cheapen their reduction; capital and energy will come armed with the improvements science may offer, and make Montana, now with but four years of history, the great centre of the production of the precious metals on this continent. It has the experience of the older mining Territories to profit by, and its almost impassable mountains have been a wall of protection against mad speculation and the waste of millions to paralyze legitimate corporations. Colorado is cursed by speculative corporations, which have not vitality enough to live and not sense enough to die, and they sit in idleness and bankruptcy upon valuable mines; but Montana is open to practical business enterprise, and will well repay those who thus come to develop her surpassing richness.

In addition to the vast mineral wealth of Montana, the production of breadstuffs is now quite equal to the consumption. Wheat, barley, oats, rye, and most vegetables, are raised here in the valleys in wonderful perfection. It will startle Eastern farmers to read that wheat-fields in Montana have produced eighty bushels to the acre; but it is certainly true. Corn cannot be grown here, as the season is too short. Cattle graze out all the winter in the valleys, and usually keep in excellent order. Last winter, however, many were lost from the uncommon severity of the weather; but during any ordinary winter the cattle will sustain themselves comfortably on the grass. Even as far north as Fort Benton they graze their stock all the year. The finest agricultural portion of the Territory is still un-inhabited, save by the savages. The Yellowstone region has the most salubrious climate north of the Platte; and it must soon be surrendered by the red man, and blossom with beauty and plenty to reward the husbandman.

The irregularity of the mails to this Territory is terrible. Of the "Tribune," thirty copies of the daily are now due me here, and I have received but two. Of the "Times," sent me semi-weekly since the 1st of May, I have received but one number. Letters or papers mailed in Wells, Fargo & Co.'s mail-bags come promptly. At Salt Lake I received papers and letters through that channel before the same dates had reached Denver by mail. The government pays Wells, Fargo & Co. $1,000,000 or so to carry the mails; but they lose so much mail-matter that business men are glad to pay them treble postage, in addition to the government postage, to insure prompt transmission of papers and letters. They carry more than half the letters from Salt Lake to California in their special mails, and have government envelopes, with Wells, Fargo & Co.'s stamp on, which are bought and used to guard against the loss or delay of mail-matter. While Wells, Fargo & Co. are permitted to have special mails, carried at a large extra profit, they have every inducement to confuse, delay, and lose the regular mails, so as to compel correspondents to pay them, in addition to their government compensation, twice or thrice established postal rates; and they have not been slow to avail themselves of this advantage. If they can carry letters and papers through in regular time in their own special mails, why cannot they bring the regular mails through in the same time? They have contracted to deliver them promptly, and, save when stopped by a public enemy, their failure to do so must be the result of carelessness or a want of the necessary coach-room and teams, all of which they have obligated themselves to furnish. I found at different stations on the way tons of mails piled up; and sometimes mail-bags are scattered along the road, apparently dropped off and carelessly abandoned. If Congress would have the Far West supplied promptly with mails, for which an ample sum is paid now, the right to compete with the mails must be taken from the Company, and the contract enforced rigidly. But one coach has been captured by the Indians on the plains this spring, and yet tons of mail-matter have been lost. Where is it? Will the government make the inquiry in earnest?

I have, as yet, no means of knowing the condition of things on the mountain-line between Denver and Salt Lake; but I beg leave to suggest to the military and stage authorities that they test the safety of the route before they expose travelers hereafter, as heretofore. Let Mr. Ben Holliday, for instance, take passage in a coach at Julesburg, or Junction, for Salt Lake, with Lieutenant-General Sherman as escort. Let them have the best of horses for changes along the line, and invite visits from the "friend-

18

lies" by turning the advance teams out to graze, so that Sherman, Holliday & Co. may exercise themselves, as I did, in helping to catch their teams at the stations. They would doubtless need some hair restoratives before they got through; but, as it is their business to protect and carry passengers, it would be equally their business if they should part with any of their hair. The route once thus traveled and officially reported upon could thereafter be held out to the public as a thoroughfare meriting patronage. Until then, passengers who do not prefer to be scalped had better stay at home, or select some other route.

LETTER XXI.

VIRGINIA CITY, June 28, 1867.

WITH all their faults, I left the land of the Saints reluctantly.   We had pleasant quarters at the Revere House—
the best hotel west of Chicago, and kept by a gentile who
seems to have no fear of the Mormons before his eyes—and
the heartsome shades, fresh vegetables, delicious strawberries, together with the thousand novelties to be seen,
all conspired to make the visit a delightful one.   The Mormon theatre is one of the best structures inside that is devoted to public amusements in the Union.   It is quite large,
most tastefully finished, has three galleries besides a large
parquette (where only the Saints are admitted excepting
by special permission), an excellent orchestra, and the
acting was above the average, although almost entirely by
amateurs.   The Mormon services at the tabernacle on Sunday are also decidedly amusing, and partake largely of
comedy.   Some of Brigham's best profanity repeatedly
"brought down the house," and his sallies of wit and
sarcasm often made the vast building echo with the merry

(199)

peals of laughter which followed. In short, Salt Lake City
is a jolly place for the tourist, and as it is always reached
after a tedious journey over the bleak ranges and often
sterile plains of the mountains, its pleasant features are the
more keenly appreciated. But more than ten days could
not be spared to enjoy the good things and curiosities of
the Saints, and on the 19th I had to bid farewell to Brigham
and his harem and the enticing shades, sweet fruits, and
rippling streams of the City of the Saints. But, although
taking leave of the great centre of Mormondom, we did not
get away from Mormon thrift and beauty for nearly one
hundred miles on our northward trip toward the mountains.
A little valley bounded on the east by the Wasatch range
and on the West by the Great Salt Lake, ranging in width
from five to twenty-five miles, is thickly dotted with Mormon settlements, and has several cities of from one thousand to two thousand population. The homes of the Saints
all along the route have the same peculiarities which mark
their residences in their chief city. Every house is in a
cluster of fruit-trees, and every garden is green and beautiful with fruits and flowers. It would seem to be a part
of their religion to beautify every home, however humble,
and in no single instance did I see the signs of dilapidation
about their little farms. Their farms are assigned to them
by the bishop of the settlement, and all of them are quite
small—ranging from two to twenty acres, as the new
farmer may be able to cultivate it well. Let no one suppose that because the homes and gardens and fields of the
Mormons are ever beautiful and fruitful they are easily
made so. In no part of the entire Union, where agriculture is the main dependence of the settlers, must the farmer
toil so long and so untiringly to make the earth produce.
Naturally it is sterile, and boasts of only the sage and
grease-wood as its products. It has to be cleared, broken

up by powerful teams, and even then denies a harvest to the sower unless he is prepared to supply it with artificial rains during the entire summer season. He must have a main ditch for every patch, level the inequalities of the surface, so that water will flow over it regularly, and then have numerous small ditches to carry moisture to every tree or plant he aims to grow. None but Mormons, most of whom were the slaves in the Old World who labored for the titled classes, could have made the Salt Lake Valley thus cast off its natural sterility and clothe itself in the rich verdure of plenty.

At Ogden, a beautiful Mormon town of two thousand people, we stopped for dinner, and were well entertained in a large modern hotel, presided over by two wives (second and eighth) of Bishop West, and surrounded by a garden blooming with flowers and most luxuriant in its growth of vegetables. One of the eight wives waited on the table, and the other did the honors in the parlor, proving herself as agreeable in her part as the other was expert in the culinary art. The master of the harem was not visible, and probably dined with some one of the other six of his fair partners. In addition to retailing whisky to the faithful, it is his business to gather the tithing for that rich settlement; and he seems not to lose in worldly goods in the performance of his office. He owns valuable mills and farms in and about the city, maintains eight families, and gradually increases in his basket and store, as well as in his already numerous progeny; and all this is done in the name of religion; and the deluded followers of Brigham Young and his apostles sweat and toil from day to day and year to year, and live often in poverty, to enable them to deliver their tenth dozen of eggs, quart of strawberries, ton of hay, bushel of grain, and every tenth of the increase of their herds, to maintain the leaders of the

Church in their licentious debauchery. They seem to like it, however, and if they don't complain, I presume that I should not; but I can't help thinking that most of the humble members of the Saints, who are but hewers of wood and drawers of water for the dignitaries, come under Brigham Young's class of "poor devils." In his sermon that I heard, he divided the world into three classes, viz.: God's poor, the devil's poor, and poor devils; and in the last class I would place two-thirds of his infatuated serfs, who toil and sow and reap while he and his favorites enjoy the fruits.

But enough of the Mormons for this journey. I must leave them and their fairest valley of the West, to trace a journey over the Rocky range again. The Rocky Mountains form nearly a semicircle from the western part of Montana to the heart of Colorado, and in an overland journey to this place the main range has to be crossed twice—once into Salt Lake, and again northward into Montana. After leaving the Mormons near Bear River there are no signs of agriculture until the valleys in this Territory are reached. All is a dreary, cold, sterile waste, with broken and generally abrupt mountain-bluffs, deep cañons still visited by snow-storms, or open plains which seem as if shrouded in perpetual winter. The snow passes off the plains; but no flowers or fruits can withstand the fearful blasts which sweep over them, and nothing but a sickly, frost-stricken coat of grass keeps up the semblance of vegetation. Strange as it may seem, this region is the renowned home of the mosquitoes; and they descend upon the luckless traveler in myriads, with a pluck that is truly appalling. They seem to an Eastern tourist more like some fiends of the feathered tribe than like insects. It would require half a dozen of our Eastern mosquitoes to make an average one in the Bear River region, and their songs are

more like the music of a brass band, bass drum included, than
the modest strains of the insect tribe. We all wore veils, as
travelers must in that region; but some of them seemed to
have bills equal to pipe-stems, and could penetrate anything
but a regular iron-clad. Even when we were almost frozen
in the coach, the winged devils were active as ever; and
only when we attained high ground and a friendly breeze
came to our aid, did we escape these merciless tormentors.

The country from Bear River to the summit presents
nothing novel. All is a perpetual waste, without anything
to vary the monotony of a tedious journey but the new faces
to be greeted at the stations, and their inevitable pets. Until within fifty miles of Virginia City, I did not find a station where puss did not answer to a call for her and come
out in the most friendly manner to receive the caresses of
the strangers. One huge cat welcomed me at one of the
stable-doors, cheerfully accepted my introduction, and escorted me to the coach again, purring gayly and rubbing
her head against my leg, until I got into the stage, when
she mewed me a kind farewell and walked off majestically
to her stall. At some of the stations I found a variety of
pets. Dogs are common, and always welcome the passengers with every manifestation of delight. Occasionally
chickens and pigeons are added to the family of pets, and
at one stable I met with a brace of solemn owls, who ventured upon a friendly wink when I patted them, but maintained their proverbial stoicism in all other respects. They,
with a dog, a cat, and a half-score of pigeons, make up the
happy family of the stable-man, and they share his room,
divide his frugal meals, and most of them claim a portion
of his bed. At one station I missed the cat, and inquired
of the stable-man why he was so singular as to be without
his feline companion. "I've more and jollier pets than
she be," was the reply; and he took me into his little cor-

ner partitioned off from the horses for a kitchen and chamber, and pointed me to a score of mice, rollicking in his
dishes, over his bed, playing hide-and-seek in his clothes,
and industriously trying to force a passage into his sugar-
can. At the sound of his voice they gathered around him,
scampered up the legs of his pants, prospected his ears,
hair, and pockets, and turned upon me their sauciest
glances. " That's not half of 'em," he said, as he turned
to the first stall, where his bacon and other stores were
deposited. And, true enough, there were scores of them,
enjoying his provisions and ready to welcome him as their
benefactor and friend. It was not hard to understand why
that stable-man has no cat or dog.

We took our last square breakfast at Pleasant Valley
station, for which we each paid two dollars, and threw the
victuals in. It was the only meal I attempted on the entire route that was utterly unmanageable. Some were
evidently filthy, but they were made to look passable on
the table, and, with a little forgetfulness, enough could be
worried down to satisfy the demands of hunger. But the
Pleasant Valley breakfast was a "dead beat" on all of us.
The coffee was nothing but water made bitter by some
nauseous ingredient, the fat bacon was stale, the eggs
rather worse than stale, the butter worse than the eggs, the
bread worse than the butter, and the potatoes were fried
in the fat of the bacon. It would have required a first-
class quartz-mill to masticate the bread ; and nothing more
dainty than a buzzard could have eaten the other articles.
The cook was an Irishman, who was filthy enough himself
to sell as real estate. We all politely paid our money, and
hastened away to escape the fragrance of our meal. Our
last meal on the stage-route was at Black Tail Deer station ;
and it presented a most delightful contrast with Pleasant
Valley. We were then within fifty miles of the end of our

long journey; and, as we found a clean, bountiful, and well-prepared meal, and a pleasant landlady, the driver acceded to my request and gave us two hours to rest. The people of the East, who think a day's travel on a railroad-car a great task, have no appreciation of a few hours' rest at a clean station in the Rocky Mountains, after three days and nights of continuous staging. The softest and most grateful bed I have ever tried was the bunk of a stage-driver in a tidy adobe cabin after having been cramped up in a coach for several days. It was the greatest luxury to find a place to stretch my limbs and steal a few minutes of quiet sleep. It seemed to me that I had scarcely got my head on the blanket pillow until the driver shook me and informed me that the time I had asked for was up, and the coach at the door.

We were soon aboard again, and started on our last drive—to me the longest fifty miles of the whole trip. I could not at any time sleep in the coach. Occasionally, the second or third night, weary nature would give way, and I would fall into fitful dozes, but soon to be startled out of them by an imaginary upset, an Indian attack, or some other horrible spectre of troubled sleep. As we started, the clear starlight was dimmed in the east, and rays of the mellowest tints threw their soft lustre above the mountain-tops. The moon was struggling to brighten our dreary path, and gradually she climbed the Rocky range, five miles above the Eastern Sea, on which her meridian brilliancy was then lavished, and reflected her welcome crown, in matchless splendor, from the peaks of eternal snows which stood in her course. In my far-off home she had greeted old friends three hours before; had heard love's tender story from smitten swains; had witnessed reluctant partings as midnight stole unconsciously upon them; and across the deep-blue ocean she was gilding the starry vaulted dome above as she fled from approaching day to bless the night of the Western World. Faster and faster her lines of light and beauty spread, the shadows receded from the mountain-sides, and soon her full effulgence flung its grandeur over the dreamy stillness of the towering cliffs or sullen plains. She brought mute but swift messages from home,—from distant but unforgotten, and I trust unforgetful, friends : had just brightened their evening strolls, inspired their social minglings, and then hurried off to proclaim from sea to sea, to Christian and heathen, the omnipotent power of Him who fixes the stars in their spheres and notes the falling of the sparrow. In a few hours the east was again lit up, as the god of Day was coming to obey the immutable laws of Heaven. Gently he lifted up the silvered shadows of night and rolled them back to the far, far west ; and, as he wove his golden lining about the frosted rocky domes, one of the loveliest of mornings witnessed the end of my long and eventful journey, at Virginia City.

LETTER XXII.

Union City.—Its Architecture and Population.—Its Sobriety.—
The Single Monument of its Mortality.—The Bluebird and
Robin.—The Natal Day of the Republic.—How it was not cel-
ebrated.—The Western People.—Their Cordial Hospitality and
Kindness.—How People are "corraled."—Western Terms and
their Significance.—How they live.—The Bountiful Boards of
the Miners.—How Sunday is observed.—Sunday Auctions.—
Gambling-Hells licensed by Law.—The Charms of Western
Life.

UNION CITY, MONTANA TERR., July 4, 1867.

UNION CITY, the place where I am celebrating the natal
day of the Republic, although bearing the dignified title of
city, has not, as yet, found a place on the map of the country, and it is quite probable that the urchins of future gene-
rations will be flogged through schools in blissful ignorance
of its existence. It consists of five gigantic mountain-spurs,
or bluffs, forming a complete circle, with the exception of
the narrow passage of Spring Gulch, and in the bottom of
the hopper, but a few hundred feet in width, nestle a quartz-
mill and a dozen of the rudest pole cabins. Winding
ravines are plowed down through the steep cliffs which
almost hang over the city, and the clearest, purest, sweetest of mountain-springs come dashing and splashing down
to find the walled and sinuous outlet of the gulch below.
The snow still whitens the tops and depressions of the
mountains all around us, and, while the people of the East
are panting and sweltering under scorching suns, we wear
our woolens with comfort, and demand double blankets for

pleasant sleep. Green pines adorn the slopes of the almost perpendicular hills; wild flowers crop out in magnificent profusion, and even decorate the very edges of the stubborn snow-banks. The little daisy presents its modest tribute to the beautiful of earth on every hand, and the cactus flings out its variegated hues, iu happy contrast with the repulsive sage-brush that claims the mastery in our vegetation. We have no bristling guns, to make the mountains around us re-echo our rejoicing that the Republic still lives, redeemed to unstained Freedom and omnipotent in the majesty of justice; nor can we have the measured tread of processions, marching to hear sophomoric eloquence and inspire their patriotism with dubious beer. Our little mountain-city has no hotel, no restaurant, no sideboards, no flasks, to tempt the patriotic from the path of sobriety. Beyond the innocent game of quoits, it has no amusements to break in upon the industry of the staid inhabitants. Forty men, four ladies, three children, five cats, three dogs, four pigeons, three horses, six oxen, and densely crowded suburbs of gophers (a species of the ground-squirrel) make up the living population of this modest city of the mountains; and one green grave, on the hill-side, of a loved and lamented wife, tells the story of its mortality. Visitors now and then add to our various circles. Spring has just spread her lovely verdure on the mountains, and the blue-bird comes with plaintive song, and the robin with merry chirp, to make the air sweet with their melody. They come, with their morning warbles, after they have blessed the bright sundown in the valleys hours before, and leave us, as the early shadows of evening gather, to enjoy the lingering day of the cliffs and plains. Two donkeys thrust their solemn but friendly faces into our doors thrice a week, and beg a dainty morsel of old cloth or paper by the most awkward manifestations of affection, while their burdens

of meat, butter, eggs, and vegetables are emptied to supply
our wants. Not even the anniversary of a nation's birth
can turn this people from their steady, tread-mill course of
life. The dull click of the miner's pick may be heard far
down in the bowels of the earth, as if freedom had never
been born in the Western World; the ladies sew and
sweep and gossip and spread their tables with accus-
tomed regularity; the babies crow and scream and tumble as if they repelled all patriotic teachings; the patient ox-teams wind up and down the almost perpendicular
steeps as usual; the shrill but home-like sound of the
engine-whistle calls the sons of toil to their daily routine of duty; the busy hum of machinery goes on in
ceaseless murmuring; puss claims her passing caress, and
purrs her everyday song; the mother pigeon struts upon
my table as I write, bristles her feathers, and cooes her
demand for recognition; the horses browse on the tender
grasses of the bluffs; the dogs bask lazily in the welcome
sun, and the squirrels chatter their morning and evening
chorus all around us, and purloin from our frugal larders,
as if stealing had no holidays with them. Thus in peaceful, sober industry has our Fourth been honored, and its
flight will mark no unusual record for the steady, plodding
inhabitants of Union City. Nearly every leading nation
of the world is here represented. The sturdy Cornish-
man, the imperturbable Welshman, the impetuous son of
France, the quiet Swede, the wandering Swiss, and the
brawny Russian, all mingle their broken accents in their
evening gatherings, as they smoke their pipes in the wealth
of contentment.

Not only the renowned mountains of the Far West, but
also the peculiar people who inhabit them, present endless
novelties to the tourist. Of the bewildering beauty of
these ranges—whose cliffs and cañons and plains have

19

been ever present through a journey of over a thousand
miles, and still seem to be endless—I have written before;
but of the people with whom I have mingled so pleasantly
I have not had time to speak until now.   The whole civilized world does not furnish a more cordial, frank, and hospitable class of citizens.   Mutually dependent upon each
other, they cultivate the highest measure of true neighborly kindness; their humble homes and frugal boards
ever offer shelter and bread to the stranger, and the children of want are not turned away in sorrow from their
doors.   With them came crime, armed with power and
wealth and defiant of order and authority; but there are
many nameless graves to attest the stern retribution of the
honest settler, as he cleared the path of the bullet and dag-
ger and made his treasure safe from the incursions of the
robber.   They are eminently social; and their peculiar expressions have a significance of which the more cultivated
East have no knowledge.   In all classes, from the most
learned to the least favored in letters, the same expressive
Westernisms are in common use.   If a man is embarrassed
in any way, he is "corraled."   The Indians "corral" men
on the plains; the storms "corral" tourists in the mountains; the criminal is "corraled" in prison; the tender
swain is "corraled" by crinoline; the business-man is
"corraled" by debt or more enterprising and successful
competitors; the unfortunate politician is "corraled" by
the mountaineers, the gulchmen, or the settlers; the minister is "corraled" when he is called to become the pastor
of a congregation; and the gambler "corrals" the dust of
the miner.   Indeed, the application of the term is almost
as indefinite as it is universal.   "Git" is another of the
favorite and most expressive of Western terms.   It is the
invariable word by which the hero of the whip and lines
starts his teams; and they understand it well.   "You git,"

is the most emphatic notice that can be given to any luck-less chap to leave the room or ranch, or to escape a re-volver; and "You bet" is the most positive manner of affirmation. Everything is an "outfit," from a train on the plains to a pocket-knife. It is applied almost indis-criminately,—to a wife, a horse, a dog, a cat, or a row of pins. A "lay-out" is any proposed enterprise, from organ-izing a State to digging out a prairie-dog. Anything that has been tried, from running for Congress to bumming a drink, has been "prospected" or "panned out;" and "he didn't get a color," expresses the saddest of failures. When a Western man declines any proposition, he "ain't on it," he "don't go a cent on that," or "none of that in mine," is his answer. When he wants to deal or fight with a man, he proceeds to "go for him;" and "I'll bet my bottom dollar" is his strongest backing to his expressed opinion. "The man in the wagon" is the author of all sayings and doings which can find no visible or responsible source. When the miner goes for the savages, he "cleans 'em out to the bed-rock;" and when a braggart is to be silenced, he is informed that "nobody's holding you," or "there's no weights on your coat-tails." When one gets the de-cided advantage of another, whether in deadly conflict or in business, he "has the drop on him." The universal term for eatables is "grub;" and the most degrading epi-thet that one can apply to another is to pronounce him "a bilk." No Western man of pluck will fail to resent such concentrated vituperation. The term was entirely novel to me, and I first asked its meaning of a landlord, who ex-plained by saying that "a 'bilk' is a man who never misses a meal and never pays a cent." There are many others, equally original and expressive, which I have heard often, but cannot now recall. Used as they are by all classes, in business and social circles, and by both sexes, they have become part of the language of the country; and a stranger's fitness for Western life is judged by his readiness in acquiring the use of them.

The first settlers of the mining regions are proverbially improvident. As a rule, they earn to-day and spend to-morrow, and often discount their earnings to gratify their appetites or have a frolic. They live well—better, as a class, than do the laboring people of the East, where all articles of food are attainable. They never plant or beautify. Their home, as a rule, remains the same rude pole cabin, without regard to the smiles of fortune; but their plain tables will be loaded with the delicacies of the market. Oyster-soup or -pie, sardines, fresh tomatoes, corn, peas, beans, pineapples, whortleberries, blackberries, raspberries, strawberries, plums, cherries, pears, peaches, etc., are no luxuries in these mountains, thousands of miles distant from where most of them can be produced. They may be seen in the miner's camp every day, and the most juicy beef and the sweetest butter grace his bountiful board. They labor hard in their gulches or mines, but are ever ready for a change, whether it be to hunt down some thief or murderer for hundreds of miles, or attend a ball or a "hurdy-gurdy." They love the semi-civilized condition of society, and rarely ever can content themselves in the East after having spent a year or two in the mines. The conventionalities and the restraints of established communities are painful to them, and they long for the freedom of their huts and Western life. As a rule, they are good citizens,—honest, scrupulous in maintaining their plighted word, and just, even generous, between man and man; but they don't cramp themselves with the religious ideas of the Puritans. Their Sundays are but holidays, if even that. Generally they refrain from their regular work on that day; but they will do odd jobs, attend street-auctions,

in places like Virginia City, and sell or buy, as their wants
may dictate; while those who have a taste that way will
take a small spree, or amuse themselves with a game
of poker or monte, generally at the cost of all their ready
cash. In Virginia City, gambling-hells are licensed by
authority of law, and the games are carried on in the most
public places. On Sunday, the streets are crowded with
miners; the loud yells of half a score of auctioneers drown
your own voice in conversation; and most of the stores
and places of business are open, and drive their most
profitable trade. Gradually this condition of things will
wear away; the missionaries will come and rear churches,
to which the gamblers and miners will contribute liberally;
a higher moral tone will steadily infuse itself into society
as families become settled among them, and the better
class of the early citizens will conform to the new order of
things, while the lower strata will seek new homes, where
the exactions of civilization will not confront them for a
time. Such is Far-Western life in the mines. With all its
privations, it has its charms, which, to most men here, are
stronger than the love of home or family; and they thus
live through "life's fitful fever," wandering from one El
Dorado to another, until fresh graves, marked by hard
hands but tender hearts, tell the story that the rugged
journey is ended.

19*

LETTER XXIII.

Mining in Montana.—The Failures of Quartz-Mills in the Midst of Rich Mines.—Hundreds of Mills should be paying in the Territory.—The Cost of Mining and Working Ores.—Prices in Montana.—The Money paid for Freights.—Fluctuations in Business.—Why Mining Companies fail.—The Best Mines owned in Small Fractions.—Economical Development impossible.—The "Freeze-out" Game.—How Companies should test Mines before purchasing.—Mills not needed until Mines are fully developed.—Character of Ores to determine Character of Machinery.—Montana as a Field for Successful Investments.

UNION CITY, MONTANA TERR., July 6, 1867.

I FIND in Montana the same ill-conceived, badly-managed, and, of course, unsuccessful mining enterprises that the gold-fields of Colorado present, only on a much smaller scale. The failures are not so nearly universal here as there, for the reason that the ores are richer, of easier access, and as yet they have not presented the combination of refractory metals which have defied all ordinary processes in Colorado. Some companies have succeeded in Montana, and are now doing well, with flattering prospects ahead; but in every instance, so far as I have been able to learn, they have been successful rather in spite of the management than because of economy and skill in their direction. There are from twenty-five to thirty quartz-mills in this Territory all completed and supposed to be in order for running. Some of them are total failures and hopelessly bankrupt; others are partially defective in their

(214)

machinery, and must await modification or repairs; still others have the machinery and the power, but have been defrauded or disappointed in their mines; and a very few are more than paying expenses. All these failures are in the midst of the richest gold and silver mines on the continent, or probably in the world, and where the gold is more easily obtained than in California—the Montana quartz, as a rule, paying from the surface down, while in California, and most other mines of the precious metals, shafts must be sunk hundreds of feet before "pay-rock" can be obtained.

Unfortunate Eastern stockholders in gold companies, doubtless, are at a loss to understand why their enterprises, embarked in with such confident hopes, drag along in wasteful expenditure and finally end in serious or total loss; but any one of them, possessing ordinary business sagacity, need but glance at the actual condition of things here to appreciate that their failures are the legitimate, inevitable results of their own follies, and not the fault of the mines, which teem with boundless and available wealth. There ought to be hundreds of quartz-mills in operation in Montana to-day, paying the stockholders their entire cash investment each year in the shape of dividends; but there must be a radical change in the prevalent system of purchasing mines, selecting, freighting, and constructing mills, and in their general management, before success will crown the efforts to develop the wonderful wealth of these mountains. There are leads enough opened in this Territory proffering ore that will yield from thirty to one hundred and fifty dollars per ton, to employ five hundred or more stamp-mills indefinitely; and by the exercise of a sound judgment in the purchase and opening of the mines the ore could be reduced at a total cost, including mining and delivery, of from ten to twenty dollars per ton. While in California they work ore profitably that yields from fifteen to eighteen dollars per ton, here no ore can be reduced to pay expenses on a yield of less than thirty dollars per ton, and in many instances it must yield fifty dollars to pay any profit.

It is true that wages are much higher here than in California, and must remain so for years to come. The Territory produces nothing but gold, silver, grain, vegetables, and a little stock. It has no manufactures, and will have none to supply the present generation. Machinery, clothing, groceries, prints, iron, coffee, lead, etc. must be purchased at fabulous prices. Old iron is worth fifty cents per pound; sheet iron is worth seventy cents; copper sheets command two dollars per pound; lead ranges from forty to seventy cents per pound; and the necessaries of life are so costly that five dollars per day is not more than living wages for ordinary laborers, while experienced miners, engineers, and all classes of skilled labor command. from twenty to fifty per cent. more. This cannot soon be remedied, even in a country where wheat is sometimes fed to stock, as it was last winter in some of the bountiful valleys, because there was no market for it. Two years before, flour was worth as high as one hundred and ten dollars per sack of one hundred pounds, in gold, and the large profits realized by those who exported it from Salt Lake stimulated them to repeat the operation last year, and they were met with an abundant supply—indeed, a surplus—of home-grown flour, and had to sell out at less than freight. Beyond the agricultural portion of the citizens of Montana, none seek to produce anything but what they expect to yield a speedy fortune, and no systematic efforts are made to lay the foundations of rich and prosperous communities. The settlers are mostly miners, who count on but a temporary residence here, and the traders and speculators who ever follow in their track to gather the lion's share of the precious metals after they have been produced. Just now the Territory is drained of one million of greenbacks to pay freights, and money commands from ten per cent. a month up to six per cent. a week. Business ebbs and flows to a degree unknown in old centres of trade, and sudden wealth and as sudden bankruptcy sweep close upon each other. Two years ago, when the gulches were producing many millions, in the leading settlements the scant supplies of goods sold readily at prices regulated merely by the usually elastic consciences of the merchants. Last year business was still brisk, and this year an immense surplus of goods has been shipped, the market is perfectly glutted, and very many articles are sold at St. Louis prices. Some merchants have been compelled to borrow money at from ten to twenty per cent. per month to pay freight at Fort Benton and then sell their goods at a loss of fifty to seventy-five per cent. to meet their obligations. One year presents no data for the business of the next, and everything goes by surges or waves to fortune or disaster. Even the mining has been done in the most reckless, wasteful manner. The richest gold-beds are hastily and imperfectly hurried over, leaving more in them than is gathered from them, and new prospects or diggings call the heroes of the pick and spade from Alder to Helena, from thence to Deer Lodge, thence to Salmon River, and so on through the hundreds of placers where the incalculable wealth of the mountains is developed.

By-and-by, system, patience, and practical enterprise will come to this great work, and the wealth of Montana will startle the world. Just how soon the new order will arise, I cannot pretend to judge. If I had not gone through the desolation and wasted millions of the mining

regions of Colorado, I would predict the speedy advent
of most successful enterprise in Montana; but if good
business-men in the East will persist in wasting fortunes
in Colorado, I cannot assume that they will not continue
to repeat the same insane profligacy in Montana,—soon
encircle its hundreds of millions of accessible gold with
bankrupt coporations, and paralyze this peerless fountain
of riches. It is not too late to save Montana from this
terrible curse, and save the many millions which I fear
may be wasted, or worse than wasted, in the most inviting
field for legitimate enterprise the whole world presents.

The chief cause of the failure of most mining associations organized in the East is the loose, hap-hazard, and
careless manner in which they are started and prosecuted.
Even the most judicious and careful men in their regular
business at home seem to lose sight of all sound princi-
cles in projecting and directing mining operations three
thousand miles distant. In nine cases out of ten the buyers
are imposed upon in the sale of mines, not that they are
wanting in gold, perhaps, but because they are so scattered
that they cannot work them to advantage. The best mines
in Montana are still held in a manner that precludes successful development. One man will own the whole or a
fraction of "discovery claim" (the one hundred feet on
which the lead was discovered), and there will be different
owners for Nos. 1, 2, 3, 4, and so on each way from discovery; and most likely no one man will own more than
a half or fourth of the one or two hundred feet of each
claim. Take the "Dakota," the "Ora Cache," the "Golden
Era," the "Whitlach," the "Boaz," the "New York Belle,"
the "Pony," and the hundreds of other first-class leads
already partially developed, and the claims, or fractions of
claims, are generally owned on the same leads so promiscuously and adversely that economical mining is impossi-

ble. Most of the owners, as a rule, are men who have no means to develop their claims, and, if they had the means, they could not afford to do so. Each would have to sink an expensive shaft in his claim or fraction to reach say from twenty-five to one hundred feet; and that is impossible. All believe that the lead is valuable; but each waits for the others to prove the richness of their whole property; and when some one does venture to make the costly and hazardous experiment, and this establishes the value of the lead, he must then pay the others fabulous prices for having developed their wealth. Development is not the rule among the miners who own most of the valuable mines, or at least fractions of them. The "freeze-out" game is much more common. One cannot succeed without securing additional claims, so as to justify shafts or tunnels, and his necessities are fully appreciated by the other owners, and they get up a most expensive "lay-out" for him. I have seen several parties sinking separate shafts in the same lead, producing ore at from fifteen to twenty-five dollars per ton, because of the small space worked by each shaft, where a tunnel would deliver all the ore of the lead at a cost not exceeding five dollars per ton. In this way companies are often involved in disastrous expenditure to procure their ore from first-class mines. They believe certain leads to be good; they buy two, five, or ten hundred feet on them, without knowing how their claims are located or how the lead can best be worked; they invest thousands of dollars to purchase, ship, and erect machinery, and when they want their ores they discover that, while they have plenty of good ores under ground, several others own intervening claims, and compel them to buy them out at ruinous prices or work their claims of good leads at a positive loss. No company should ever purchase a lead for the purpose of working it, without an accurate map showing the location of every claim on the lead, the streams of water accessible to mills, the formation of the ground traversed by the mine, its altitude and grade, its timber, and satisfactory points for shafts or tunnels which will command the ore at the least cost. When companies announce in their prospectuses that they own claims on a dozen different leads whose names are in good repute as valuable mines, unless they own connected claims on some one or more well-tested leads which can be worked by one shaft or tunnel, rest assured that the projectors of the companies either have been fearfully cheated, or they are seeking to defraud the public by the sale of stock that can never be valuable unless by accident. I have explained in detail this feature of mining claims, because it is the rock on which very many have wrecked the most sanguine hopes, and it is alike the interest of the country at large and of stockholders that they look well in the start to this peril. A mill once erected, whose success depends upon the control of adjoining claims, is certain to suffer extortion to a degree often fatal, or make its bed in bankruptcy beside untold wealth.

Another fundamental error committed by nearly all companies is the expenditure of hundreds of thousands of dollars to start mills before their leads are developed. This is the common disease that has spread hopeless failure throughout the mountains; and, strange to say, the most stupendous failures have been made by the most trusted scientific men. It will doubtless startle thousands of your readers, but it is nevertheless true, that there is not a single gold-mine in Montana that is developed, and few, if any, in Colorado. Good "pay-rock" has been found here in the surface ores, and they have been worked with tolerable success; but the character and value of the leads, down where they are clearly defined, no one has as yet ascertained. Experienced miners judge of them by the walls, clay, pockets, and streaks, and pronounce them the most valuable and trustworthy in the world; but one claim of two hundred feet on a lead may be of surpassing richness, while another may cap, or pinch, or narrow to almost nothing. One claim will present free gold, while the adjoining claim will be so strongly impregnated with iron as to defy reduction by the ordinary stamp-mill. I have seen free gold and heavy sulphurets at the same depth, on the same lead, and within one hundred feet of each other. When these facts are considered, sensible men will see the folly of rushing up mills on undeveloped leads, where they have to run the risk of striking barren mines or a character of ores that their mills will not reduce. No mining company in Colorado or Montana should entertain the idea of purchasing machinery for at least one year after they have secured their mines. When they have purchased their leads,— always being careful to have their claims in a body or bodies sufficiently large for the most economical mining,— they should employ a trustworthy, experienced, and practical miner to develop their mines. Ten or twenty thousand dollars thus expended will prove beyond all doubt the character and value of the ore ; and until at least one thousand tons of ore are on the bank, its value proven, its cost calculated, and its peculiarities ascertained, nothing else should be considered. If the mines refuse to yield good ore at a reasonable cost, the loss is comparatively slight, and the project can be abandoned without involving the sacrifice of the whole capital of the company and the embarrassment of many of its founders. Companies thus foiled, with the expensive mills erected, are naturally tempted to borrow and assess additional sums, with the faint hope that they may succeed by mistaken persever-

20

ance, until finally hope and means fade out together, and
the enterprise is abandoned in despair.

If the mines prove valuable, and an abundance of good
ore can be produced at a reasonable cost, the character of
the ore is next to be considered, and the selection of the
proper machinery and power to reduce it and save the
largest percentage of the gold or silver. For crushing
all kinds of free-gold quartz, the ordinary stamp-mill is
the best, while for slight mixtures of the pyrites of
iron the Chilian mills and barrel amalgamators are preferable. The stamp-mill is the simplest and most wasteful machinery used in the reduction of ores. It requires
less skill, and is less expensive. The Chilian mill does
better work, and, with the barrels, will often take more
gold out of the ore after it has been reduced by the
stamps and ordinary amalgamation, than the stamp process yields. When the ore is largely mixed with the base
metals, as in Colorado, there is no process yet perfected
that will reduce it profitably. The best scientific talent of
this country and of Europe is now directed to master
these refractory ores, and is steadily attaining a higher
measure of success; but, until entirely successful, amateurs have no business experimenting with any of the
various patents which flood the markets. Companies
which develop such ores will save money by waiting for
science to overtake them; and they can do it with entire
confidence that they will ultimately make their mines
profitable. When companies have thus fairly developed
their mines and ascertained the character of their ores,
they can readily determine what kind of machinery is
best adapted to their wants, and they can then wisely proceed to ship it. First, however, they cannot be too careful
in looking to the quality and completeness of their mills.
There are mills now erected in this Territory which were

worn out in a month. This is no country for defective machinery. It cannot be repaired, and missing pieces cannot be supplied. Every part of a mill likely to break should be duplicated, and a forge outfit is essential to success. There is, as yet, no foundry in the Territory. I learn that one is about to be established in Helena; but the stoppage of a profitable mill for days to get repairs done one hundred miles or more distant, is attended with fearful loss, not to count the exorbitant charges for work and transportation. If anything important is found wanting in the machinery when it arrives, it requires another season to supply it, as no trains or boats leave the East for Montana, the same year, after a mill is delivered on the ground, and its defects discovered by its erection. One company here lost a year by the omission to send some essential portion of the mill. If they are improving the lost time in developing their mines, it was a fortunate accident; but they can claim much above the average of good management, if they thus made their supposed mishaps a blessing.

The mill selected and started by the river, a first-class, industrious business-man is wanted for superintendent. In most cases, some son or friend of one of the leading officers of the company, having no fitness for business, and entirely inexperienced, is sent out to enjoy fast horses, good liquors, and cigars, and speedily mismanage the company into debt and failure. Sound, practical, experienced, and frugal men only can conduct such operations properly. With wages from five dollars to eight dollars per day, and everything else in proportion, mismanagement tells upon profits and capital here with a rapidity that Eastern men can scarcely appreciate. In no ordinary business in the East is judicious supervision so essential, and the dividing line between success and failure so narrow.

I have, for obvious reasons consistent with truth and fairness, given the dark side of mining operations in Montana. It is one vast field of bewildering wealth, and I most earnestly hope to see it speedily and most successfully developed. Twenty millions of capital could be more profitably invested here than in any other locality; and, by simply observing the same sound business principles which govern capitalists in other enterprises, not one dollar in twenty should be lost, while a very large majority of the investments would pay fabulous returns. In no other mining region are the leads so uniformly good and so easily tested; and they can, as a rule, be developed by tunnels, and the ore delivered at a very low rate. Not only the mountains, but the gulches are of incomparable richness. Alder Gulch, that has already produced more gold than any other single gulch in the world (so I am informed), will soon be worked over again and repeat its previous yield. It was once worked for ten consecutive miles, in claims of one hundred feet, and each claim yielded from two hundred dollars to two thousand dollars every twenty-four hours. Clear-headed business-men are now gathering up the claims, and will, by one central flume traversing the rock-bottom, work over the whole gulch with vast profit, while others will wash down the rich hill-sides by the hydraulic process. In the mean time, the rich bluffs whence the gold of the gulch has been washed will be disemboweled, and their leads, studded with gold quartz, worth from thirty dollars to one thousand dollars per ton, will be worked, and boundless fortunes amassed. There is no part of this continent where Eastern capital is so much wanted, and where it will so well reward its judicious investment, as in Montana; and I entreat men to discard "professors," jobbers in claims, inflated speculative concerns, and lend a helping hand in the legitimate development of this slumbering wealth. Send practical men to secure leads properly located for development, and then, above all things, "make haste slowly." Test all things, and failure is hardly possible. Different degrees of success will be attained; but, upon the whole, there must be incalculable profits, and the colossal fortunes of the next decade will have their birth in this long-unknown but richest offering of our national creation.

20*

LETTER XXIV.

VIROINIA CITY, MONTANA TERR., July 9, 1867.

THE term "Vigilance Committee" is familiar to all Eastern readers; but there are few who have just conceptions of crime as it compassed the isolated mountain mining regions, or of its merciless retribution. California tolerated the rule of murderers and desperadoes for years, but finally effected an organization founded on the maxim *salus populi suprema lex*, and the leaders of disorder and lawlessness were executed or banished. But California then had large cities, vast commerce, easy access to the great business centres of trade, and a social bulwark to strengthen the harsh but imperative reformation. Not so with the Territories of the Rocky Mountains. Their wealth was discovered just when the golden slopes of the Pacific had become intolerable for those who preferred any crime

(226)

in the decalogue to honest industry. Colorado, Idaho, and Montana were isolated from the civilized world. Hundreds or thousands of miles had to be traveled over, mountain-passes and almost trackless plains, unpeopled save by the pitiless savage; and the population was of necessity rude, without social restraints, and naturally tended to semi-barbarism. There was no government, no law, no access to the protecting power of the national authority for years, and here were most inviting fields for the banished desperadoes of other lands, and every incentive to lead the upright down through the tempting but ultimately fatal labyrinths of crime. Few families were among the early settlers, and the happy influences of faithful wives and virtuous daughters were unknown. The influence of woman, so far as felt, came from the hopelessly fallen, and, like all perverted angels of light, they but hastened the mastery of wrong and led the way. Gamblers plied their vocation, without blush or restraint, on the most public places. Murderers infested every locality where there was the least inducement to take life for gold; and organized thieves ramified into every settlement. It is a tradition of Denver that Mr. Greeley was so highly respected when visiting that place in 1859, that, as he mounted a box to address the citizens near the "Elephant Corral," the dealer of three-card monte on the sidewalk close by suspended his game until the speech was concluded. This was considered a most marked deference to the public appreciation of the man, and a tribute that few bishops could have won. So common was this fearful vice there, and in all the other Territories as they were first settled, that every public place on the streets and sidewalks, but two, successfully invited the minor to be defrauded of his earnings.

I have in a previous letter referred in general terms to the reign and decline of crime in Colorado, and the stern retribution the Denver Vigilanters visited upon some of the most desperate leaders in lawlessness; but it was reserved for Montana to organize and maintain the most efficient combination of order-loving men that this country has ever witnessed. Just as Colorado had become strong enough to enforce some measure of public order and safety, the richest gulches of the continent were discovered in Idaho and Montana, and there was a general exodus of thieves and murderers from all the other mining regions, and also from the haunts of evil in the Eastern cities, to inaugurate the supremacy of crime in this new El Dorado. Four years ago (in June, 1863) the surpassing richness of Alder Gulch was discovered. With the lucky adventurers who opened its glittering wealth, came

> " The first low wash of waves, where soon
> Shall roll a human sea. "

Nevada was the first mining camp established. It is down near the extremity of the gulch; but, as its wonderful deposits of the precious metals were opened up the stream, Virginia City was founded. It was called Varina, in honor of the then rebel chieftain's wife, and two-thirds of its inhabitants were jubilant with the hope soon to be subjects of the notorious heroes of treason. Antietam, Gettysburg, Vicksburg, Atlanta, Nashville, Five Forks, and Appomattox were then unknown, and the fitting representatives of unholy rebellion in these mountain-fastnesses had forgotten that there is One high over all, whose justice sleeps not. Little did they dream that, like the name they so fondly cherished as to rear thereto a city, they must soon live only in the history of the overthrow of wrong in Montana. Judge Bissel indignantly and arbitrarily expunged the name, and substituted Virginia, in his first legal record, informing the bewildered audience, in language more emphatic than polite, that no such blot should mar the records of justice in his court.

A year before the settlement of Virginia, the rich placers of Beaver Head and Deer Lodge had been discovered, and it was in these localities that the most perfectly organized and best appointed band of desperadoes ever known on the continent had its origin. Its system was perfect, its plans devised and executed with consummate skill, and it reached into every camp close upon the footsteps of the miners. While Bannock City was its original centre, as Virginia grew in importance and surpassed all other camps in wealth and population, it promptly extended its operations until its chief field was here. It was no loose aggregation of independent thieves and cut-throats. It had a commander, subordinate executive officers, secretaries, agents, stool-pigeons, signs, and by hieroglyphics could so mark a man, a coach, or a train as to make them innocently invite their own destruction on the way. Certain of the leaders even wore their neck-ties in a peculiar knot, and by day or night, whether visible or shrouded in darkness, they could communicate with and aid each other. They were not, as in California and Colorado, the shunned and abandoned men of the communities in which they lived; they were the most wealthy, influential, and by many at first believed to be useful citizens. The leader of the band, Henry Plummer, was one of the most accomplished of villains, and a master-mind in the application and government of men. So shrewdly did he direct his operations that he was chosen sheriff of both Madison and Beaver Head counties, and his deputies were selected from the most trusted and expert of his band. The counties had no legal organization; no authority was known other than the regulations adopted by the settlers, and might made right. With the power of the people in the two richest and most populous counties in his keeping, it is not wonderful that for nearly two years the band prospered and defied detection. So completely did the organization compass everything relating to their interests that every placer was watched, its yield traced to the time of shipment, and it was rarely indeed that any man could get safely to the States with treasure. They were, as a rule, lucky if they lost only their gold and saved their lives. If they started in a coach or with a train, unerring signs were marked upon them, or upon something about them, to notify the predatory bands to strike and secure the plunder; or if vengeance was to be glutted, as was often the case, the traveler would unconsciously notify the skulking foe that his life-blood was to be theirs. Hundreds of thousands of dollars were thus plundered from miners and business-men, and, if arrests were made, the prisoners were delivered to Sheriff Plummer, the chief of the robbers. They thus escaped punishment, and were soon off again to operate for the band in some new field, where recognition was improbable. This organization became known as "Road-Agents," from the fact that they committed most of their depredations on the routes of travel; and to this day no other term is applied to highway-robbery in the Far West. They numbered over fifty desperate men, all well armed and most skilled in the use of weapons, and had, besides, probably a hundred or more outside allies and dependents. They would scatter in every direction, and simultaneously rob coaches, trains, or travelers hundreds of miles apart. They had stations all through the country, where they could stop in safety, as the keepers were pimps of the band and received small shares of the common booty. Thus these thousand sinews of crime extended throughout all the settlements and highways of Montana, held the law paralyzed in their clutches, and were supreme everywhere in the Territory. Even when the civil law pretended to assume its prerogatives, this band either furnished or corrupted its officers, and no jury could be sworn that did not contain enough of their own members to control the verdict. Not only did they murder when necessary to rob, but they gradually became so bold that, upon the slightest provocation, they would deliberately shoot down men on the streets of Virginia, Nevada, or Bannock, and none dared to call them to account. Encouraged by habitual success, and confident that there was no power equal to the task of bringing them to punishment, they finally flung over Montana a reign of the most appalling terror, and men were compelled to defer to Plummer, obey his authority as an officer, and submit in silence to his atrocities to save their own lives.

But, though "the mills of the gods grind slowly, they grind exceeding small." Many prominent citizens had been murdered or robbed, and the depredations of the band on the routes to the States were so frequent that no one ventured to return with treasure. Every good citizen felt that there must soon be a terrible remedy applied, or all legitimate pursuits abandoned. Strange to say, the murder of one of the humblest residents of Montana—a simple, friendless German—was the feather that broke down public forbearance and called into existence a power that has executed nearly one hundred men, banished hundreds of others, and restored order, safety, and peace in Montana without a single stain of injustice upon its fame. The German was murdered to obtain some mules he had sold, and was on his way to deliver to the purchaser, who had already paid him for them. He had been in the employ of Mr. Clark, an old resident of California and a member of the Vigilanters. The lifeless body had been secreted in a thicket of sage-brush, and the story circulated that the

German had left for unknown parts with the mules and
money. For some time there were no data to controvert
the explanation made by the murderers; but finally a
hunter brought down a grouse, which fell in the very
thicket in which the body of the German was concealed,
and told the story of another murder by the "Road-
Agents." The body was taken to the city, and Mr. Clark
was the first man, I believe, to give form to the ripened
resolution against the desperadoes. The effort was generally and promptly seconded, and, once started, its sweep was
boundless and merciless. It was a perilous undertaking.
A single failure would have been fatal to all concerned in it;
and it was not doubted that the lawless were in a decided
majority. Had any ten or even fifty men been suspected
of such a purpose before the organization was effected, not
one could have lived to see their plans succeed; but they
were discreet as resolute; their vengeance was unseen and
unfeared until it took the murderer from his bed and the
light of morning dawned upon his lifeless body suspended
from a tree. There was no muttering thunder before the
bolt fell with pitiless destruction upon the wrong-doers.

Of the many brave men who inaugurated and openly
sustained this movement, no one can justly be awarded
exclusive praise; but there is one who figures as conspicu-
ously in the history of the Vigilantes as did Plummer in
the reign of terror. Some twelve years ago I was accus-
tomed to meeting, on the streets of Chambersburg, Pa., a
young man named John X. Beidler. His frugal wants
were supplied by the manufacture of brooms, and finally
he mixed the best of cock-tails and juleps at a neighboring
summer resort. He was as amiable and unoffending a lad
as the community could furnish, and his jolly, genial humor made him a favorite with all who knew him. Although
he had attained his majority, he was scarcely five feet six

inches in height, and was far below the average of men in physical power. He finally wandered West in search of fortune, and soon after the advent of Plummer came "X," the name by which he is universally known in Montana. Thus the bane and the antidote were close upon each other. Strong in his inherent love of honesty, a stranger to fear, not powerful, but quick as thought in his actions, and firm in his purpose as the eternal mountains around him, he naturally entered promptly and earnestly into the effort to restore order and safety to society. That little was expected of him when he first cast in his lot with the stern reformers is not surprising; but his tireless perseverance, unfaltering courage, and singular skill in thwarting the plans of the common enemy soon made him the chief pillar of the organization, and the unspeakable terror of every desperado. This diminutive man, without family or property to defend, has himself arrested scores of the most powerful villains, and has executed, in open day, an equal number under the direction of that wonderful, dreaded, unseen power that surrounded the hasty scaffold. So expert is he with his faithful pistol that the most scientific of rogues have repeatedly attempted in vain to get "the drop" on him. Quick as a flash his pistol is drawn, cocked in the drawing, and presented at the doomed man, with the stern demand, "Hands up, sir," and the work is done. At one time, without aid, he arrested six of the most desperate thieves in a body, all well armed, and marched them before him to prison. "Hands up, gents!" was the first intimation they had from him that he had business with them, and submission was the only course of safety. Had any one of them attempted to reach toward his belt, he would have fallen that moment. There were citizens close by; and how many of them, if any, were sworn to protect and ready to aid Beidler, he

21

know, while the prisoners did not. This indefinite, unseen, immeasurable power seems to have ever stricken the most courageous thieves and murderers nerveless when its sudden and fatal grasp was thrown around them. They would fight scores of men for their lives in any ordinary attempt to arrest them, but they seemed weakened when the citizen confronted them in the name of public safety. No formalities were known. No process was read bearing the high seal of the courts. When or where the dread summons of the great unseen tribunal would come, none could conjecture. The sleeping companion of the desperado in some distant ranch would probably drink and breakfast with him, and then paralyze him by the notice, " You're wanted—business at Virginia !" In no instance did any of the many lawless characters arrested by the Vigilants ever fire a pistol in their own defense, even when they knew that death was inevitable. In most cases the opportunity to do so was but slight; but, under ordinary circumstances, the closest chances would be taken to effect escape. From " X " no criminal ever got away. To have attempted it would have been to hasten death. So much did the desperadoes respect as well as fear him, that most of them, when condemned to die by his hand, committed their last requests to him, and with him they have been sacred. Order and public safety have been restored, but he still has employment in his favorite line. He comes and goes, and none but himself know his errand. "What's up, X ?" is a query that is generally answered, "After tracks;" and " Don't know" is his usual reply to all questions as to his route or time of departure. He has traversed alone every highway and settlement of Montana, prospected many of the unexplored regions, and is always ready, without escort or aid, to pursue a criminal wherever he may seek refuge. His career has, indeed, been most remarkable, and his escape unharmed, through his innumerable conflicts with the worst of men, seems almost wholly miraculous. He has recently been appointed Collector of Customs for the port of Helena ; but, while there is a thief, a defaulter, a murderer, or a savage to disturb the peace of Montana, he will remain the most efficient messenger of justice known in the mountain gold-regions. He has lost none of his genial, kindly nature by his long service as the minister of vengeance upon the lawless, and wherever he goes he is welcomed by every lover of order and government. When he is upon the war-path "it's no for naething the gled whistles," and crime has no escape but in timely retreat. Fully three thousand perfectly organized men are at his back. They have their companies, officers, minute-men, and messengers in every settlement, and he can rally in an instant scores or hundreds of true men to his side.

The first execution was that of George Ives, and he was condemned by a court of the people. It was the turning-point of order or anarchy. The outlaws were numerically the strongest, and the rescue of the prisoner was among the probable results; but brave men were braver than before, and the cloud of crime that encompassed the court to control the verdict or save the accused by fresh murder was dissipated by the stern integrity and unblenching courage of the lovers of order. Colonel Sanders, a young advocate, small in stature, but large in soul and manhood, conducted the prosecution, and for the first time the advancing column of wrong recoiled as the verdict was announced, "That George Ives be forthwith hung by the neck until he is dead." Fifty-eight minutes thereafter, but ten yards distant from the place where he had been tried, the fatal drop fell, and justice had a foothold in Montana. This was on the 21st of December, 1863. Soon after, Sheriff Plummer and two of his band were executed together at

Bannock. He swung from a gallows he had erected for the execution of another, and he maintained his wonderful self-possession to the end. His last act was a deliberate examination of the rope and drop, to be sure that his neck should be broken by the fall, and he was launched into eternity without a prayer. Five of his followers sleep in unmarked graves on the hill close by this city: they died together, on one of the street-corners, and then the resistless course of justice ran on, until, at last, near the head of the murmuring waters of the Gallatin, a lifeless body, suspended from a tree, bore this inscription: "Bill Hunter, the last of Henry Plummer's band." Several of those first arrested and executed confessed upon the gallows, and revealed the names of the whole organization, and with this information the Vigilants rested not until there was not one of the original Plummer band among the living. Not one remains of that once omnipotent organization to tell its crimsoned and fatal history. After the leaders had been executed—three at Bannock and five at Virginia—one by one, the scattered fugitives were hunted down and sent suddenly to their long homes. All of them died without even the profession of penitence, and many of them blasphemed until utterance was choked by the death-noose. Two of them leaped high in the air from the gallows, to hasten their presence before an unreconciled and avenging God. For the crimes of these men self-banishment was considered no atonement. Thousands of dollars were expended in the pursuit of those who fled hundreds of miles to escape this merciless and inevitable retribution. When they felt safe in their isolated retreats, the hand of the Vigilants would fall upon them, and they would find graves, unshrived and unmourned, wherever the ministers of justice crossed their path. Some had climbed the narrow passes to Idaho and Oregon, others had sought for refuge in California, and even South America was tried as a retreat from this resistless current of vengeance. All, all was fruitless. The solemn judgment of the unseen tribunal must be executed, though the ends of the earth had to be searched for the guilty victim. Not only justice inflexibly demanded it, but common safety was equally imperative in exacting that none, once condemned, should escape. They could infest the thousand miles of unpeopled plains and mountain-cañons between here and the States, where the ministers of justice must sometimes travel; but not one was left to renew the vengeance of crime. They made themselves and the public safe by ceaseless pursuit, until the murderer lived only where all are judged in righteousness. Nor is their work wholly of the past Although unseen and unknown, their sleepless eyes guard the Far West with tireless vigilance. No desperado can ascend the Missouri without his name, description, and antecedents either preceding or coming with him, and every settlement will have its faithful sentinels to challenge him on his arrival. There is no pomp or parade in their proceedings, and most who would fear them naturally suppose that they have disbanded as an organization; but the hapless rogue who lands in Montana will have the ardor of his hopes speedily chilled by some unknown friend bidding him good-by and suggesting that he depart without delay. No explanation is given, none is needed, and Montana loses a citizen she can better spare than keep. Many miles from this place I saw a doomed man—doomed to death by this matchless human agency, and conscious of it. He was a prisoner in the hands of the law. He could have escaped, but dared not, for around him were the silent and unknown sentinels of a tribune that has no technicalities in its trials. He may escape the cobwebs of the civil law, but the world is too

small to afford him an asylum, and he lives from day to
day in hopeless despair. Ere long he will surely go un-
wept to his final resting-place, and none will inquire why
he has made an untimely exit.

Such is a brief, and necessarily imperfect, history of the
triumph of justice in Montana. The civil courts are now
in operation, but, without the power of the Vigilanters,
crime would soon regain the ascendency. Their organization is maintained as an auxiliary to the courts, and to
reach out the arms of justice where the civil power is unequal to the task. Should the law ever prove too feeble
for the support of order, then will three thousand men
guard the public safety. So inflexible have they been,
that no means, no ties, no circumstances, could shield
the guilty. One of their own number was found to have
sought shelter from just punishment in their "circle,"
and he was summarily executed. In another instance the
friends of the condemned proposed to make restitution
of stolen property, if the sentence could be changed from
death to banishment; but the criminal was one of the
robbers' band, and the restitution was made by the Vigilanters, and the robber sent to his grave. In three years of
operations, covering nearly one hundred executions, this
organization is not to-day charged, by friend or foe, with
partiality or prejudice, or with a single unjust punishment.
Sternly, patiently, untiringly, it has prosecuted its unwelcome labor, and its history is but the history of the supremacy of virtue, order, and justice in Montana.

LETTER XXV.

A Political Mandamus.—Opening of a Mountain Political Campaign.—Western People.—Their Generosity and Prodigality.
—Extravagance of Prosperous Times.—The Restless Prospecter.
—Sunday in Virginia City.—Street-Auctions.—Cheap John on Eastern Notions.—Shepherds get astray.—Sunday in Union City.—The Children of the Village.—Departure of Little Eva.
—Her Affecting Farewell.—Little Alice.—Her Theological Disputation.—Corraled in the Mountains by Indians and Low Water.

UNION CITY, MONTANA TERR., Aug. 12, 1867.

As I have been absent from our little mountain-city of cabins but twice since I arrived here, and then less than a day each time, I cannot be expected to write about general affairs in the Territory. During the six weeks I have been in Montana I have not rotated outside of a circle of eight miles from this place; but the Union Territorial Committee have issued a peremptory mandamus directing me to put on the political harness again; and by the late papers I find that I am to speak once a day, commencing on Thursday next, until the election on the first Monday of September, and must often travel from forty to sixty miles each day. I have not the remotest idea where most of the appointments are, as many of the names of the cities (three cabins constitute a city here) I had never so much as heard of before. As it was my purpose some time this summer to visit the leading mining-districts of the Territory, I shall do so while the political campaign is in progress, as it will afford the best possible opportunity to

(239)

mingle with the people and acquire reliable information
relative to the wondrous mineral wealth of Montana.   I
made my first appearance before a mountain-audience on
Thursday last, and during the whole of the speaking
there was a degree of order and attention that Eastern
audiences could often imitate with profit.

I have seen the Far-Western people in almost every
phase of life, and I have never, in a single instance, found
respectful conduct on the part of a stranger met in any
other way than with a just, if not a generous, measure of
respect.   I have already written of their horse-races, their
theatres, their churches, their reading-rooms, and their
proverbial hospitality.   That they are merciless on "bilks"
and pretenders generally, is true; but no matter how
humble the straightforward visitor may be, he is received
with the warmest cordiality, and will meet with generous
hearts and welcome boards wherever he may find the
camp of the miner.   Every settlement in Montana, and
every city as well, is but a mining-camp.   Virginia City
is but the centre of the great Alder camp; and Helena is
the same for the various gulches which surround it.   They
are sustained solely by the mining-interests about them,
and the cities advance or recede with feverish haste just as
the mines improve or degenerate.   There are agricultural
settlements in Deer Lodge, Jefferson, Madison, and Gallatin; but there is not a farmer—or ranchman, as they are
called—who has not his claims, or fractions of claims, on
various gulches and leads, and he is merely farming to
live until his slumbering wealth is developed by others
more able than himself.

As a rule, the successful gulch-miners are most improvident; and of the scores of men who came here without a
dollar and made from ten to fifty thousand dollars of gold
out of Alder Gulch, there are very few indeed who could

to-day command one thousand dollars, while most of them are utterly "broke." Their necessary expenses were very heavy, but 'their needless expenses were usually much heavier. A newspaper would bring from one to two dollars in gold in the days of gulch-mining, but three years ago. A letter usually cost five dollars. Flour cost from fifty cents to one dollar a pound; and everything else in proportion. A cat would sell very readily in the days of gulch-mining for one hundred dollars in gold, and the display of pets of any kind was one of the easiest means of reaching the miner's well-filled buckskin bag. Then came the gambler's claim, and the fever of speculation, and what the indulgence of the appetites left was mostly sure to be swept into the faro-bank 'or frittered away in some fancy purchase.

This restless, profligate, and heterogeneous mass has long since departed from Alder Gulch. Many of their rude and now tenantless cabins remain; and the continuous ridges through the gulch for more than ten miles tell of the thousands of sturdy men who here delved for the precious metal, gathered it in fabulous sums, and scattered it as lavishly as they found it. Now most of them are spending their time in prospecting, and earn a precarious subsistence by resuming legitimate labor when stern necessity leaves them no other channel through which to find bread. I have already spoken of this class of men. How much they do for the world, and how little for themselves, but few can appreciate. It is to them that the nation at large, and all who profit by mining-operations, are indebted for unlocking the vast wealth of the mountains; but the fruits of their labors are in most cases gathered by strangers. They sow through merciless storms and spiteful snows, while others reap in the sunshine of golden harvest.

Although there seems to be general safety to person and property in Montana, and a leaven of healthy moral tone apparently pervades all circles, the outward signs of morality, as recognized in the East, are among the novelties of the Territory. Sunday is the main business-day of Virginia City. On that day the gambler's saloon, licensed by law, is gayest and receives its largest profits. Most of the stores are open and drive their briskest trade on that day. The streets swarm with miners, who gather in their week's wages or "clean up" in their pockets, and commerce readily accommodates itself to their wishes and wants. Every corner in the main street has an auctioneer, whose stentorian voice is raised to its utmost volume to compete with that of his rival who is bawling out his bargains on the opposite corner; and through the crowd the horse-jockey and his mounted salesman ride, John-Gilpin-like, expecting every one to look out for his own neck and limbs. "Cheap John," whose sign I have seen in every Western town, deals out heavy pepper-and-salt suits for thirty-five dollars each, and sends a score or two of the mountaineers home every Sunday in his favorite costume. He had trouble in fitting me when I called for a suit, and invited me to come on the following Sunday, when he would open his new goods. In answer to my inquiry whether Monday would not answer as well, he gave me a look of pity, as if he considered me totally unfitted for life in this region, and expressed the belief that I would soon "get over that Eastern notion." Of the six mills in this section, that of the Montana Gold and Silver Mining Company is the only one that suspends operations on Sunday.

Such a thing as a sermon I have neither heard nor heard of since I have been in Union City. Occasionally a stray shepherd comes along to look after his lost sheep wandering through the mountains; but as a rule the shepherd gets lost among the sheep, and seems to prefer glittering nuggets of gold from the gulches and mines to the promised glittering stars in his future crown for the salvation of souls. I have had bishops and divines at my frugal board; but they were merely viewing the confines of their commands, and did not tarry to expound the gospel.

There is now some show of Sunday in Union City, but by most Eastern observers it would be regarded as a microscopic view. The miners and other laborers reluctantly leave their work, and the mill stands in apparently uneasy solitude. Here may be seen an innocent game of quoits; there a pair of bronzed arms kneading the bread for the coming week; yonder the sounds of the axe tell that there will be a bountiful supply of firewood to serve through the days allotted to regular labor; and thus throughout the city the odd chores are done up to save what is regarded as the more precious time when wages can be earned. Some gather in their ponies—for many miners keep their ponies, letting them graze and roam at pleasure until wanted, when they seldom search in vain for them—and take a pleasure-ride; others, armed with pick and shovel, devote the day to prospecting for new mines. There is no Sunday-school, no church, no public observance of religious ceremonies in the city.

Two bright-faced little girls, one rollicking boy, and one infant constitute the children of the town; and one of them drew tears from eyes unused to the melting mood as she twined her little arms about our necks, from house to house, and kissed us all a long good-by. She was the fairest and most fragile flower of the mountains. When she came to gladden the little cabin on the hill-side, she was tried in the scales, and the needle quivered about the figure three, as if unwilling to fix that low standard to the little lump of mortality that filled the swaddling clothes; but in obedi-

ence to the laws of gravity it pointed to three pounds as
the "heft" of the little stranger. The pure breezes of five
brief mountain-summers had fanned her marble cheeks
when I came, and infused some strength into her still
delicate frame. Lovely and affectionate in disposition
as her finely chiseled face was beautiful, and fastidious
in her dress as her most cultivated Eastern sisters, she
was as a bright sunbeam wherever she wandered, and the
horny hand of toil would steal a fond caress as she tripped
along. Each day I claimed and received a portion of her
companionship; and I only knew how much I prized her
daily prattling when she was about to start for "the
States." She knew no home but Union City, and to her
the whole world was embraced within the five mountain-
cliffs which shut us in from even the sight of a habitation
or the evidence of fellowship. She had already passed
the severe ordeal of her "aunties" and "grandmothers"
when she reached me, and her soft blue eyes were flooded
as she gave me her last embrace and kiss and promised
as usual to come again to see me "the morrow day." I
gave her my best equipage—a brace of sober oxen and a
homely cart—for her journey to the coach-office, and there
were many longing looks and tender regrets as the slow
but steady cortège passed around "Lincoln Avenue" to disappear behind the abrupt bluff beyond. Strong men, long
used to rugged mountain-life, leaned upon their picks and
spades as little Eva passed from among them, and thought
more of "home" than they dared to tell. Alice, her only
companion, was bowed in inconsolable grief, her red dishev-
eled locks streamed in the air, and her sobs broke painfully
upon all as she followed her playmate until the last farewell was given, when she sought the child's last refuge
from grief in a hearty cry. To her it seemed as if the
sun had gone out in perpetual darkness, and the future

appeared as only a dreary, withered waste. Alice is a bright waif with more than a common share of nature's better qualities, and she floats down life's unseen current with a smile and a kind heart for all. We have a persistent difference in our theology, as she insists that her aunt Mary was her creator, while I have maintained that we have all a common and an infinite author of our being. She staggered at times in her belief, but finally relapsed hopelessly into her original conviction, because the common Creator had not created sausages—a favorite dish of hers, and of whose origin she desired to be informed. She is now the pet of the city, and each day brings her a fullness of pleasure.

It has been my fortune to get "corraled" every now and then in my journey. Between Indians and storms, I was detained three weeks in Denver; and now the elements and the Indians seem to combine again to prevent my return home. The Missouri River, which was navigable last fall until October, has been falling so rapidly that it is feared no more boats will get up to Fort Benton, and the Indians have practical possession of the overland route. As things are now, I have but one chance to get back with any show of safety this fall, and that is by pack-mules over the Rocky range to the Columbia River, thence to the Oregon coast, and around by San Francisco to New York—a journey of nearly two months. I borrow no trouble, however, on account of these mishaps. I can stand it in the mountains as long as the government and the people on the line can stand the Indians on the overland route, and hope to come out of the trial improved in health.

22

LETTER XXVI.

HOGGUM, MONTANA TERR., August 20, 1867.

THE city bearing the romantic title of Hoggum is a little
mining-camp near the Missouri River, some thirty miles
below the junction of the Madison, Jefferson, and Gallatin.
The mining-gulch in which it is situated was discovered
last spring; and it is charged that a few parties " hogged
up" the whole of the pay-claims before the usual stampede
thereto was fairly inaugurated, and the disappointed adventurers named the new camp Hoggum and turned away
from it in disgust. A little branch camp near the main

(246)

one is known only as "Cheatem;" and the whole outfit is regarded by the itinerant miners as a sort of fraud upon the profession. Some of the more poetical Montanians have endeavored to change the name of the city to Springville; but when they placard the place for public meetings they go back to the original title. I had spoken daily for nearly a week, and traveled from thirty-five to forty miles each day over hard divides, under scorching suns, and with a miserable team, and I did not regret particularly that I was behind time in reaching Hoggum, as I hoped thereby to escape a speech. It was fully eight o'clock when I arrived there, and the deserted streets of the camp plainly indicated that, if a public meeting had been thought of, the idea had been abandoned. The city was, however, crowded with brawny miners, most of them in and about the rude cabin saloons which comprise nearly one-half the buildings in the camp; and, as they had fairly set in to their favorite games of poker and all-fours, I supposed that they could not be congregated for so tame an entertainment as a political speech from a worn-out stumper. But I was not to escape in that way. A prominent Republican merchant, with whom I stopped, had a bonfire blazing before his store in a few minutes, a box was rolled out for a rostrum, and in less than ten minutes over a hundred miners had gathered around the door. Begrimed with dust, and tired, sore, and hungry, I mounted the stand and waded through a short speech, to which two-thirds of the audience listened with sullen silence, and the other portion put in occasional cheers at stated intervals, apparently as a matter of duty, and usually without reference to the fitness of the moment. The truth was that two-thirds of my audience were Missourians, or Democrats of like proclivities, and they attended the meeting merely to vary their usual evening routine of cards. It is possible,

too, that they hoped to have a row, as they had enjoyed that
"delectable pleasure" the evening before (Sunday), when
the regular Democratic meeting of the campaign had been
held there, and, as there were not enough Republicans in
the camp to get up a shindy, they got it up on their own
hook, and proceeded to mutilate each others' mugs. The
meeting being over, the audience adjourned to the different saloons, and only the excuse of indisposition exoner-
ated me creditably from imbibing Hoggum strychnine. I
hastened to the ranch of an old Pennsylvanian, two miles
distant, on the river-bank, and was welcomed with the proverbial hospitality of the Far-Western people. Mr. Vandil-
berg, from Washington county, Pennsylvania, has the finest
farm I have found in the beautiful valleys of Montana; and
his was the first modern house and furnishing I have met
with in the rural districts of the Territory. His farm lies on
the river-bottom, and his large fields waved with the most
luxuriant and bountiful crops of wheat, oats, and barley. I
felt this morning like staying a day with him, regardless
of political appointments; but I am in charge of the Central Committee, the driver is under positive orders to deliver me in Helena this morning, and soon I must start out
for another hot, dusty, and most tedious journey of thirty-
five miles, to be dumped out of the wagon and put up to
speak in the principal city of Montana. But I shall not
borrow trouble, as it will neither cool the air nor inspire
oratory.

Excepting the hard drives over parched and dusty prairies and bluffs almost blistered by the pitiless rays of the
sun, the trip has been rather a pleasant one, and abounding in interest. I left Virginia City on horseback at noon,
to reach an appointment thirty-five miles distant that evening. To escape the dust, we took an Indian trail, and
traveled twenty miles without seeing a residence. Only

the abandoned and well-nigh decayed ranch of Slade relieved the uuiform garb of nature, now withered beneath the intensely hot suns of the heated term, save where some little stream defied the drought and preserved the verdure of the dwarfed growth along its banks. The Vigilanters had summarily ended the mortal career of Slade by swinging him to a cross-beam, and his rude grave is still marked by a pile of stones close by his deserted ranch. A fine spring, carefully walled in by the hands of the desperado, refreshed my Democratic guide and myself, and from thence for ten miles we did not find cool water. The heat was fearfully intense, and even the usual welcome breeze that tempers the hot rays of the prairie was utterly forgetful of its duty. Occasionally we would get into a little cluster of alder-bushes where water had been, and stop for a few minutes to enjoy the shade, and once or twice little streams crossed our trail, but were too warm to satisfy thirst. We could refresh our dripping horses, but could not take time to rest, as, with two long, steep spurs of the mountains to cross, we had no time to spare. After twenty miles had been traveled, we came out on Meadow Creek, near to the Madison River, and found a pleasant ranchman, clear, soft mountain-water, plenty of ice, and sweet bread and butter. It was one of the most grateful entertainments I had enjoyed for a long time; and, after an hour of rest and pasturage for our horses, we started to climb the last divide into the Hot Springs district.

Meadow Creek comes from the mountain-range north of the Madison River, and empties into the river just as it turns from the Madison Valley to rush off through a deep, narrow cañon. Nearly the whole valley is visible from Meadow Creek, and just now its aspect is that of one vast field of desolation. The table-lands, which have never yet been cultivated, are parched into a pale pink color, and the only sign of life is a narrow green line that winds up the valley, following the serpentine course of the river. But even where the moisture from the river was sufficient to satisfy the wants of vegetation, the grasshoppers devastated almost every field and garden. With the first soft breath of spring they came up out of the ground —where the eggs had been deposited the year before—by millions, and marched in countless throngs wherever anything green and succulent invited them. Here and there a field or farm escaped their destructive visits, without any visible reason for their forbearance; but, as a rule, they cleaned the fields and gardens to the very earth, and as often as the roots would start out fresh stems or leaves they would renew the attack, and keep repeating it while anything grew to tempt their insatiate appetites, until wounded and exhausted vegetation gave up the unequal contest. The potato-crop alone they have spared, and it will be very large; but the Madison valley, one of the most fertile prairies of the mountains, will not harvest as much wheat, barley, and oats as were sown last spring. Nor does the terrible plague end with present destruction. The now full-grown grasshoppers have again deposited their eggs, and the ranchmen have fair notice that they may sow next season, but cannot reap. I learn that these winged pests usually disappear after the third year, but seldom sooner.

In crossing the eastern fork of Meadow Creek I found the first evidence of the work of the miner. The water was muddy and carrying the sluiced earth down to the river. Most of the leads discovered in the Hot Springs district are on the eastern slope of the divide; but I noticed during the whole journey the evidences of continuous gold-leads running in a direct northeast line from Summit to Hot Springs, a distance of nearly forty miles. Where the

belt starts on the mountains beyond Summit City, fully a
score of good leads are more or less developed, and some of
them are of wonderful richness. From that point the leads
seem to be in an unvarying line, regardless of the confused
formation of the many cliffs they cross at all angles, and
end only in the great foot-hills which divide the Gallatin
Valley from the broken mountains on the west. That the
belt ends even there, I think improbable ; for the range
dividing the Gallatin from the Yellowstone "prospects"
in almost every gulch, and undoubted evidences of the existence of rich leads are abundant, not only on the Yellowstone range, but as far beyond as the adventurous prospecter has braved the scalping-knife of the savage. I
hazard little in saying that before five years there will be
one succession of mining-camps from the Rocky range
southwest of Virginia clear through the Gallatin and Yellowstone ranges on to, or beyond, Wind River and Big
Horn Mountains. In this I do not rely upon conjecture
merely ; for hurried prospects have been made in the regions named, and in every instance satisfactory results
have been obtained.

The Montana militia are about to start out on an
offensive campaign against the Indians,* and I noticed
that every company is supplied with pans and other implements to test the quality of the diggings as they clear
the Indian from their path. There will be some five
hundred of them, and there are not enough hostile Indians in the mountains to impede the progress of that
number of mountain-volunteers. There are several thousand of the savages—enough to defy General Sherman

---

* This expedition was stopped by order of General Terry, commander of the military district. Had it been allowed to proceed,
the country would have received reliable information of the mineral and agricultural wealth of the Yellowstone region.

with over eight thousand men; but they will not raid
upon five hundred earnest men who are not cramped, as
the savages well know, by the sentimentalism of Sherman's
orders. When they first went upon the border, after the
Indians had murdered Bozeman and stolen a large amount
of stock, a professedly friendly Indian stole one of their
horses. They traced him out, surrounded the camp, and demanded the thief. He was promptly surrendered, because
the chief knew that the militia meant "business," and he
was made to dance a hasty jig on nothing under the limb
of a cotton-tree, in sight of the camp of his tribe. Interwoven in his hair they found the tresses from a white
female scalp; and the Indian was scalped to add another
to the innumerable evidences of the atrocities of the savages, who are fed, paid, and armed by the government to
murder the defenseless settlers of the West. These brave
volunteers, each of whom has a personal account to settle
with the savage, are about to prospect the Yellowstone,
Wind River, and Big Horn regions; and if they find
gold, as I doubt not they will, the Indian question north
of the Platte and east of the mountains will speedily settle
itself. How it will be settled, the bleaching skeletons or
hurried graves of the red man alone will tell.

I reached Sterling City, the central camp of the Hot
Springs district, about sunset, and was hospitably welcomed by Mr. Pratt, of the New York and Montana Mining Company. I found his experience but the old story of
inflated hopes, the most unwise direction in the outset, and
disappointment in the end. To save the cost of boiler and
engine and transportation, they erected a water-mill. The
water failed, and, between ditches, flumes, etc., they have
now expended ten thousand dollars on their power, and
can run but half the mill in the dry season, and stop entirely in severe winter weather. They are now about to

erect an engine, and then will have a good mill, at nearly double cost. Their leads developed unsatisfactorily, and they do nothing now but custom-work at fifteen dollars per ton in currency. They have numerous good leads around them, still in the hands of the miners, and they are wisely content to pay expenses now, and make fortune certain, as they can, in the future. Professor Ward is about finishing a first-class mill close by. It is conceived, manufactured, and erected on the most scientific principles, and will want only plenty of good ores to give it a high measure of success. The district has the ores, but the company has not, so far as developed; and I was sorry to see so magnificent an enterprise measurably or wholly at the mercy of others. The Clark mill was idle—cause, want of ore. These three mills are in the midst of hundreds of thousands of tons of good ore, and in a district where millions of capital will soon be profitably employed in the production of the precious metal. I saw ores from half a dozen leads, all of which have large strata of gold-bearing rock and are easily mined, which yield from forty to sixty dollars per ton, and some of them yield as high as one hundred dollars per ton. In the midst of these remarkable mines there is not, as yet, a single prosperous mill, for the reason that the mills were located, as a rule, on speculative mines, and the original discoverers still own the valuable leads. This mutual wrong to both the miner and the capitalist will soon be overcome, and there will be many most successful mining companies in the Hot Springs district.

Soon after dark, several hundred of the miners gathered in the central part of the city, and we devoted the evening to a free discussion of national politics in general and Montana politics in particular. If any ambitious Eastern orator supposes that it is an easy task to declaim to the people of the mountains, and that any sort of speech-making will be accepted as a treat, he would do well not to attempt to carry his theory into practice. I have never been before audiences in the East where political questions were better understood than by the people who compose public meetings in Montana, and I can conceive of no worse place for pretentious stumpers than just here. They not only detect the want of fitness for the task of enlightening them, but they are merciless in exposing it on the spot. Every public speaker in this region must be prepared for any questions the audience may see fit to propose; and it is deemed no breach of propriety for a Democrat to get up at a Republican meeting, after the regular speakers are through, and reply to the speeches. This was done at Sterling by a Democratic candidate, who directed his answer to Mr. Claggett, the silver-tongued orator of the mountains; and I have never listened to a more chaste, eloquent, and logical speech than was his reply. Cavanaugh and Sanders, the rival candidates for Congress, are both singularly gifted on the stump, and as skillful as able; and almost every portion of the Territory can turn out campaigners who would rank with our ablest disputants in the old-settled States. Both parties seem to attend all political meetings, and the speeches here, as a rule, are above the average of Eastern addresses in point of candor and respect for political differences.

I spent most of the next day in visiting the mills and mines of the Upper Hot Springs district, and there, as everywhere else I have been in Montana, I was bewildered by the profusion of mineral wealth. The time for its systematic and successful development seems not yet at hand, but it cannot be long delayed. The interests of capital and miners need only to be harmonized to give a very high measure of success to both. So far, they have seemed to be in antagonism—a policy mutually disastrous; but gradually they are progressing toward concerted action. Whenever it is once known here that Eastern capitalists cannot be cheated into the purchase of undeveloped leads at enormous prices, there will be a wholesome change in the management of mines. They will be developed by their owners, under the encouraging policy of the mill-men, and capital can then be invested wisely and safely, and the owners of valuable mines will realize just prices for them.

As my next appointment was in Bozeman City, forty miles distant, over two hard divides or mountain-spurs, we concluded to shorten the trip by making a portion of it in the cool of the evening. Mr. Muffly had overtaken me at Sterling with a hack, bringing his wife and Mrs. McC.: so we had a party of five, and a miserable livery team. The first evening, we went down to the Lower Hot Springs district, where the more recent, and, I believe, the richest, discoveries have been made in gold-leads. A mill is in course of erection, and three prominent leads now promise an inexhaustible supply of first-class ore to half a dozen mills. We stopped at a ranch, and by dark several other wayfarers had joined us, to lodge for the night. The landlady was a most intelligent and agreeable dame, but without a maid or cook, and herself confined to bed by a diseased limb. In addition to lodging the many travelers on the route, she keeps thirty cows—all of excellent stock, and in the best of order—and raises all the calves of the herd. Her butter is worth from sixty cents to one dollar per pound in gold, and her new milk sells readily at thirty cents per quart. Two young men milked the cows and fed the calves, and the son of the landlady came in with his team about sunset, after which he prepared us a most bountiful and delicious meal. One of the guests was a returned Salmon-River miner, who had staked and lost in that stampede; another was a Gallatin farmer, out on a four days'

journey to sell a part of his crop; and another was a prospector in search of his truant pony, who had strayed off
while the master was industriously panning for a color or
a prospect. After supper, the gentlemen were ushered
into the spare room of the house, in one end of which a
cheerful fire sparkled in the large, old-fashioned chimney;
carefully-laid ox-hides made a soft carpet for the floor, and
the robed bunks served for chairs until bedtime. The
ladies had a regular bed, in the kitchen, with the landlady, and all were comfortably provided for. After a sound
sleep and an excellent breakfast, we started for the Gallatin
Valley. For some ten miles after crossing the Madison
River we were gradually ascending the divide. The bluffs
were broken in the wildest confusion, and thrown up in the
most unique and varied fashion, running in every possible
direction, and sometimes forming the most unnatural junc-
tions. The lower or table lands were covered with the
finest growth of grass I have seen in the mountains, but it
was all withered by the continued drought, excepting occasionally where some little stream preserved the life of vegetation on its banks. But, notwithstanding its apparently
dried-up and dead condition, the grass is most nutritious,
and stock of all kinds will thrive better on it than even on
the finest green pastures of the East. On this dead grass,
oxen will winter in the valleys in ordinary winters, and
come out in the spring excellent beef. During unusually
severe winters, like the last, when the snow was so deep
that cattle could not graze, many are lost, and all come out
of winter poor; but generally they thrive well without hay.

When we reached the top of the divide, the beautiful
valley of the Gallatin presented itself in one grand view,
with clusters of large, green trees on the river-banks, the
golden wheat-fields, blooming gardens, and fresh meadows
which mark the thrift and comfort of the husbandman.

From where we entered the valley, it was fifteen miles directly across it to Bozeman City, and I had an excellent opportunity to see its bountiful crops and countless herds. We crossed the river on a substantial bridge, and a few miles beyond stopped before a neat-looking cabin to get dinner and feed our horses. None of the family were at home but a grown daughter; but she informed us that she would promptly prepare our meal. After caring for the horses, I went into the house, and soon found that one of the inevitable Missourians was our host. Thousands of them came here in the early part of the war, because they were too cowardly to fight with Price and too faithless to oppose him. I found Brick Pomeroy's paper the only literature in the house, and read his latest justification of the assassination of President Lincoln, while the gentle Missouri spinster prepared our dinner. If I had not known the fact before, the appearance the table presented, when ready for the guests, would have told that its presiding genius never had its culture farther north than Missouri. We had light warm biscuits, good coffee, butter and fruits, and a palatable dish of new potatoes and peas; but the butter-dish was a black tin pan that looked as if it served for a fat lamp in the evening, and, as there seemed to be but two cups and saucers in the house, they were divided around, each guest getting a cup or a saucer, and with it a greasy, dirty, battered tin for a cup or a lamp-pan for a saucer. With good cooking, it was made so repulsive by the marks of the slattern that half the relish was lost. In due time we reached Bozeman City, and were kindly welcomed by the citizens,—a deputation meeting us a few miles out of the little village of a dozen cabins. Comfortable quarters were provided for the ladies by an extra bed spread on the earthen kitchen floor, and I was handed over as the guest of Mr. Meredith (nephew of Hon.

23

Wm. M. Meredith, of Philadelphia), who is the only law-yer of the city, and has his office, kitchen, dining-room, etc. all in a little cabin ten feet square, with an odd wing for a spare bed. He posted me on the politics of that section, and gave my forthcoming speech the proper inclinations. In the evening the church was crowded with a mixed audience of Democrats, Republicans, ladies, and both soldiers and infants in arms, and I was introduced by the embarrassed President as "Hon. J. K. McCulloh," in terms which would have been embarrassing to me had I not been able to disclaim both the name and the compli-ments. After the meeting, the city politicians kept me up until after midnight, discussing politics and Indians,—the vital theme with all Western men. I was glad when they departed and allowed me to rest. At six in the morning my host waked me, saying that he had breakfast ready, and the bed must be taken up before the table could be set; and, by the time I got my heavy eyes open and finished a simple but sluggish toilet, he had the breakfast on the table. He had delicious Yellowstone trout, potatoes, sweet butter and bread, and excellent coffee; and I have enjoyed few meals better. Breakfast over, the dishes were hurriedly washed and put away, and the kitchen transformed into an attorney's office ready for clients.

From Bozeman City we had thirty-five miles down the Gallatin Valley to Gallatin City, where my next appoint-ment was to be filled. It is the only valley I have seen since I left home that promises to rival the beautiful and fruitful Cumberland. It is from five to twenty miles in width, has cheerful streams crossing it at frequent inter-vals, is bounded by mountain-ranges on both sides, and has the most luxuriant crops I have ever seen. I saw hundreds of acres of spring wheat, just in blossom, which will yield not less than forty bushels to the acre, and many small fields of winter wheat which will yield from fifty to seventy bushels. It is the favorite grazing valley of the Territory, and swarms with finely-bred cows and the most elegant stock-cattle. It is but a few miles from the hostile Indian tribes; but three hundred mountain-volunteers protect the entire border of fifty miles, and the savage turns from them in terror to defy the mockery of eight or ten thousand regular troops. A jolly Massachusetts Democrat made us at home for dinner, and followed us to the Gallatin meeting. When we arrived there, we found none but Democrats in the city (composed of three cabins and a flouring-mill), and Major Campbell, the veteran citizen of the place, opened his hospitable doors and made us more than welcome. Two of his highly-educated and accomplished daughters are married and settled in the neighborhood; another, just a graduate from the East, brightens the cabin with her music and smiles ; while the good old people greet the traveler with old-time cordiality. Entertaining is, I presume, their main reliance for a livelihood, but they do it with a fascination to which the East is a stranger. At the usual hour for country meetings some forty men had gathered as my audience; but there was but one Republican in the whole congregation. He could not nominate himself for President, and he could not propose any one else. The problem was finally solved by the venerable major, a sturdy Democrat, calling the meeting to order and nominating the lone-star Republican as President. I may say that I spoke with reasonable prudence, and thereby secured respectful attention in return. I doubt whether I converted more than half the audience, and don't feel at all sure that I converted any.

In the morning we made an early start, in order to have a spare hour at the junction of the Madison, Jefferson, and Gallatin Rivers, where the Missouri is formed. From a

bluff in the peninsula between the Madison and Jefferson
the three rivers are visible for miles up their respective
valleys, while the Missouri can be seen for a considerable
distance as it dashes off through a deep, narrow cañon on
its northward course. From the river we turned to the
northwest to cross the divide into Crow Creek Valley, and
had a tedious and hot journey over another long spur of
the mountains, and then across a burnt-up and desolated
valley. For fifteen miles we did not see water, and our
worn-out team seemed almost famished for drink when we
at last reached a clear, cool spring on the prairie. After
crossing Crow Creek, on which there are a number of fine
farms, we had to climb another high spur, on which I saw
for the first time in the Far West the red slate soil of the
East, covered with a low growth of pine. After reaching
the summit, we found that we had circled around to the
Missouri River again, and found it skirted with most
bountiful fields. A pleasant drive of a few miles along
the river-bank, in the cool of the evening, brought us to the
renowned city of Hoggum, whose history forms the opening chapter of this letter. I would be glad to spend a day
or two among the bright harvests and green shades of
the Missouri Valley ; but the election is only a few days
distant, and the show must go on in Helena to-night.

LETTER XXVII.

Crossing the Plains and Divides to the Madison.—Madison Valley.—Its Fertility.—Indifferent Farming.—Mormon Industry and System wanted.—Ravages of the Grasshoppers.—Swarms of Millions migrating from one Valley to another.—No Crops next Year.—The Crickets and their Ravages.—Hot Springs Mines and Mills again.—The Gallatin Valley.—Its Beautiful Streams, Bountiful Farms, and Splendid Herds.—Farming a Permanent Business in the Gallatin.—Fine Crops and Implements.—Yield and Price of Wheat.—Bozeman City.—Colonel Bozeman.—His Murder by the Savages.—The Montana Militia —Gallatin City. —Its Hasty Rise and Decline.—Its Founders ignorant of Geography.—The City Cabins now grace the Prosperous Ranches.

GALLATIN CITY, MONTANA TERR., August 21, 1867.

I STARTED on Wednesday last from Virginia City to visit the mines of the Hot Springs district, and the famed agricultural valleys of the Madison and the Gallatin. These, with Jefferson and Deer Lodge, constitute the main agricultural sections of the Territory of Montana. Leaving Virginia by an old Indian trail coursing to the northeast, I did not meet with the sign of a habitation for twenty miles, excepting the crumbling walls of the Slade ranch, which was consigned to decay by the summary execution of its owner by the Vigilants in 1864. After a tedious and hot ride over the main Madison "divide," we reached the welcome waters of Madison Creek, a pure mountain-stream that hurries down to join the Madison before it plunges into the narrow cañon at the foot of the valley. I had to make thirty miles on horseback in the

23*   (261)

afternoon to fill an appointment with the Republicans of
Sterling, and it was anything but a pleasant journey. Behind us we could see a green line winding down the Stinking Water, but, wherever else the eye would turn, nothing
but parched plains and hot bluffs were visible. Occasionally a little stream would cross our path and cheer us with
a stinted growth of cottonwoods and alder bushes; but the
heat steamed up from the prairies and swept down from
the cliffs with terrible intensity. Now and then we could
get a glimpse of the Madison Valley from some prominent
elevation, but even there the general seared and desolate
garb of the country was relieved but by a narrow, sinuous
strip of verdure that seemed to hug the low banks of the
river. On the beautiful table-lands between the river and
the mountain-range beyond, there was the broad, pale seal
of death to all vegetation; and even where the narrow flats
had been sown, the grasshoppers had bared them to the
very earth in their relentless march.

At Meadow Creek we stopped to rest and refresh ourselves and horses. The clearest and softest of mountain-
water ran by, and the brook-trout sported, with their matchless grace, in its crystal ripples. Our host had an abundance
of ice,—all that the grasshoppers had left him,—and our
party had a delightful rest, and cooling draughts from
nature's sweet fountains. At this point we were at the
lower end of the Madison Valley, and could see most of it
from the rise in the prairie. It is the smallest of the four
leading valleys now settled in the Territory, and has been
very productive. At some points the bottom-land on either
side of the river widens out for several miles, and beyond
that the ranchmen have not yet ventured to break up the
ground. Between the river and the range that divides the
Madison from the Yellowstone there is a broad table of
most beautiful and fertile land, that could be easily irrigated

by the mountain-streams, or even by the Madison, if diverted some miles above through a canal. But this would require more labor than the limited number of settlers now in the valley could afford to give to such an enterprise, and they therefore content themselves with the bottomlands, which are so wet and cold in the spring that they expose their garden and field crops to the early frosts. Vegetation of all kinds would start several weeks earlier in the higher and dryer table-lands in the spring, and add vastly to the safety and product of the crops.

The greatest obstacle to agricultural progress in Montana is that scarcely one farmer regards farming as his fixed pursuit. Most of the ranchmen came here adventurous miners, and only settled on the ranches to secure a living for the time being until others should develop their quartz-lodes, or until some regular farmer should come along and buy them out at a large advance. Flour commanded as high as one hundred and forty dollars per hundred pounds when gulch-mining was prosperous in Bannock and Virginia, and when the gulches were exhausted many rushed into the valleys to make a sudden fortune out of a single crop the next season. The next year flour was down to twenty dollars per sack, and the hope of sudden fortune vanished. Thus, most of the ranches have been improved in the most temporary and imperfect manner, and great crops have been gathered rather because of the wonderful fruitfulness of the soil than the skill or care of the farmers. In the Madison Valley there is no farming except in localities where irrigation needs little artificial aid; and then it is not attended to with the degree of care necessary to secure first-class crops. If the Mormons could leave their beastly polygamy behind them, I would be glad to see a settlement of them in one of the agricultural valleys of Montana. Immense as the crops are now, they would, upon the whole, double them, and beautify their homes as they increased the fruitfulness of their fields. Farming is their calling, and they would not put out a crop each year imperfectly, expecting that by next season they would be after some new diggings or prospecting for new lands. The cabins, fences, and all implements, as a rule, are made in the most indifferent manner by the ranchmen, because the settlers do not expect to remain and pursue agriculture for a livelihood. There are exceptions, of course, but not more than enough to prove the rule.

This year the grasshoppers have almost totally destroyed the crops of Madison Valley, and last year they committed serious depredations upon the late crops. I saw them moving in the valley, and they seemed to be in swarms of millions. In their flight, they almost shadow the sun. As far as the eye can distinguish an object the size of one of these fearfully destructive insects, they may be seen circling around, apparently in general confusion; but a careful examination shows that the countless body is steadily moving on toward some desired point. In the evening, when the eye can face the sun, they can be seen until the white specks fade out in the dimness of distance. Thus they migrate from place to place; and woe to the luckless ranchman upon whose fields they light, if the crop is still green. But their devastation does not end with the destruction of the growing crop. They deposit their eggs while desolating the fields this season, and thus give the farmer notice that their successors will be more destructive, if possible, next year. Last summer they migrated into the Madison Valley, and this spring the valley swarmed with little grasshoppers, who began their fatal work before they were half an inch in length. As fast as vegetables or field crops grew, they were eaten down, until finally the last remnant of life was destroyed,

and the fields and gardens were left as bare as the highway.   Of all vegetables, the potato alone escaped their
devouring appetite ; and, while there is general destruction
of crops and vegetation in the Madison Valley, there will
be an immense yield of potatoes.   Here and there a ranch
escaped their march ; but how or why, no one can guess.
I saw isolated fields of elegant grain, where there was
nothing but utter waste on all the ranches for miles above
and below them.   There are but few who will venture
next year to put out anything like full crops in the valley
of the Madison, and many ranches will be sold out at a
sacrifice this fall, by the ever-restless and discontented
settlers.

At Meadow Creek I left the river, as it rushes down
into a deep, narrow cañon, and ceases to aid the farmer
until it reaches near to its junction with the Jefferson at
this point.   Another long and steep "divide" had to be
crossed to reach the Hot Springs mining district, one of
the most celebrated in the Territory.   As I arrived at the
foot of the hills, I saw for the first time the crickets,
which are no less destructive to the crops than the grasshoppers.   I came suddenly upon an immense flock of them,
covering acres of the prairie, and awkwardly jumping and
lumbering along toward the Gallatin, as if they considered
the Madison "sluiced out."   They are four times as large
as the largest of Eastern house-crickets, of every color
from black to pale yellow, and have a most clumsy motion.
They are about an inch and a half long, half an inch
thick, and stumble and tumble over each other, when
frightened, in the most ludicrous style imaginable.   They
have no wings, and travel by walking or hopping, slowly
but steadily, until they reach some field or garden on
which to try their appetites.   As they cannot fly, they
are sometimes repulsed in their movements by water

ditches, when they flank the ditch and move on to the fields of some less careful or less fortunate farmer.

After reaching the top of the divide, a short distance through a narrow cañon brought me to Sterling City, the chief mining-camp of the Hot Springs district. It is a modern mining-city of probably twenty cabins, all built within eighteen months, and most of them neatly finished. There are three quartz-mills just above the city, two more in the neighborhood, and one or two new ones on the way, to be used on the Hot Springs ores. It is undoubtedly a rich quartz-district; but I was surprised to find that not a single lead had been thoroughly developed, and not a single mill able to command a certain supply of ore from its own mines. The leads are mainly owned by prospecters and miners, who will not sell at reasonable rates, and cannot develop; and they are waiting in poverty for others to dig beside them, prove the value of their property, and make them millionaires. One mill, that was started with highest hopes, is doing a more paying business by crushing custom ores at fifteen dollars per ton in currency. Its mines exhausted the capital of the company and supplied no ore; but it is wisely managed, and is content to pay expenses and wait until the time comes to secure property that will warrant development. The best stamp-mill in the Territory is nearly completed there, by Professor Ward. It will do much for the district, and I hope that it may do as well for its stockholders. It is the most improved California machinery, is being put up regardless of expense, and will doubtless test the ores of the district very thoroughly; but, like every other mill in the neighborhood, it has no certain source of supply from its own mines, and must for some time at least be measurably or wholly at the mercy of the miners, who well understand the advantage they possess over capitalists whose

money is already invested and who must have valuable
ores to secure returns. The third mill is idle for want of
ore, while there are thousands of tons of good ore in the
vicinity. One large lead, owned by three miners who discovered it, has been several times on the very verge of sheriff's sale for twelve hundred dollars of debt. It produces ore
cheaply that yields from fifty to eighty dollars per ton,
and which can be mined, hauled, and reduced for less than
twenty-five dollars per ton. It may be worth a million or
more, as its owners estimate it; but practical men do not
pretend to see into the ground, and they know that it may
cap, or pinch, or play out entirely; and so it is likely to
remain undeveloped for some years. As far as the partial
developments have been made in that district, it promises
to be most bountiful in the production of the precious
metals. It is, so far as now known, the northeastern terminus of the great gold-belt of Montana, that starts at
Summit (eight miles southwest of Virginia) and seems
to run in a direct line across the country to Hot Springs.
It is distinctly traced all the way by the discovery of leads
for a distance of thirty-five miles.

From Sterling I started for the upper end of the Gallatin Valley. I crossed the Madison River, as it swings
around to the north, on a substantial bridge, about four
miles above the crossing on the Bozeman wagon-route. It
is a beautiful stream of clear water, with pebble bottom,
less than one hundred yards in width, and abounding in
trout and other fish. It has no timber at all on its banks,
but here and there are thickets of willow bushes. As far
as I followed it there was no bottom-land of any consequence on either side of it, and the table-lands are gravelly,
broken, and not adapted to successful agriculture. The
bluffs which skirt it close by are abrupt and timberless,
and ridged by game-trails, made before the advent of the

white man. After climbing another long and most tedious divide, made up of miles of successive prairie-hills, I at last reached an abrupt descent into the celebrated Gallatin Valley, and the river was visible for twenty miles down the valley by the luxuriant growth of timber that lines its banks. Where I entered it, its breadth is about twenty miles; it continues down for thirty miles, ranging from three to twenty miles in breadth, and extends southeast, or up the river, probably ten miles; but there are few settlers along the Bozeman route. It is the most magnificent valley I have seen in the Rocky Mountains. It is one vast meadow, almost level, dotted with green lines along its numerous tributaries to the river, and its soil is as productive as any in the world. I crossed almost its entire breadth to Bozeman City, and saw its most bountiful crops of wheat, oats, barley, and buckwheat, and its tempting vegetables. The spring wheat is just in blossom, and the winter wheat is about ready for the reaper. Until two years ago the settlers sowed spring wheat entirely; but a trial of winter wheat gave such satisfactory results that last fall all that was in the valley sold for twenty-five dollars per bushel in gold, for seed. This season about one-tenth the harvest is winter wheat, and the whole crop will be sold at five dollars per bushel for seed again. I cannot question the evidence that establishes the raising of eighty bushels of winter wheat on an acre of ground in the valley. Even spring wheat usually yields forty bushels to the acre. I saw winter wheat on Saturday that is expected to yield seventy bushels to the acre; and I do not think the calculation an unreasonable one. This valley is so well watered, so easily irrigated, and so universally productive that it is being rapidly settled by men who mean to follow farming as their calling. I saw on one splendid farm a reaper and mower, grain-drill, hay-rake, thrashing-machine, etc., of the most improved Eastern pattern; and throughout the valley farming seems to be regarded as a legitimate business. The ranchmen do not fly off to every new diggings reported, but are, as a rule, content to labor in seed-time and wait for harvest for their abundant reward. There are two excellent flouring-mills in the valley,—one at Bozeman City, on the Gallatin, and the other here, on the Madison. Both have the most improved turbine wheels, run two pair of burrs, and can each turn out one hundred sacks of flour (equal to fifty barrels) in twenty-four hours. Just now there is some depression in this valley, owing to the low prices for produce; but there are vast fields of gold over the Yellowstone divide, and, I doubt not, in the mountains close by, and the day is not very distant when this section of Montana will be as prolific in the yield of the precious metals as it is now bountiful in the yield of the staff of life.

Bozeman City took its name from Colonel Bozeman, who opened the Renno or Powder River route to Montana, and who was basely murdered by the Indians last spring. He welcomed the Indians into his camp, believing them to be friendly, as they professed; and, while he was eating his dinner, he was butchered. Mr. Coover, of Bozeman City, was with him, and escaped with a wound after Bozeman was killed. I have had his statement of the affair; and a story of Train (given in a speech in Omaha after looking into the Indian question from railroad-cars), that Bozeman had been killed for insulting a squaw, is utterly false, as there were no squaws with the Indians who killed Colonel Bozeman. Although a young man, not over thirty-five years of age, he had been a long time in the mountains, was very familiar with the Indians, and exerted a great influence over them for good. His death aroused

24

the Montana borders, and it will be fearfully avenged by
the " M. M." (Montana Militia), now in the field. General
Sherman may occasionally hear of what they do when they
meet hostile Indians; but most of their operations will not
figure in official reports. One thing, however, you can
rely upon :—they will protect Montana. Bozeman City,
where I spent last Friday, is within sixteen miles of the
grounds of thousands of hostile tribes, but they have not
ventured to cross the path of three hundred mountain-volunteers. Not a man has been molested since they have been
on the border, and not a dollar's worth of property stolen
by the savages. They prefer to go hundreds of miles in
another direction, and make tilts against General Sherman's eight thousand or ten thousand regular troops. Cannot the government see why they do so? And is it so
blind as not to see the proper remedy?

I left the dozen cabins of Bozeman City on Saturday for
this place, and had a most delightful drive down the valley, skirting the river most of the way. It is the most
beautiful stream I have seen in the mountains. Its banks
have a thicket of large cotton-trees all the way,—the first
trees I have seen in the Far West that deserve the name.
Many of them are from eighteen to twenty-four inches in
diameter. Numerous springs cross the valley, each clad
in its garb of green willows; and the fruitful fields and
splendid herds of cows and stock-cattle give the valley a
home-like appearance that is seldom seen in this region.
At this place the Missouri River begins. The Jefferson
and Madison Rivers unite about half a mile above, and the
three unite a little below, where the Missouri is formed,
and it sweeps off, through a narrow cut in the bluffs, on its
sinuous course, to drain the great country northeast of the
mountains and bear its waters thousands of miles hence to
the sea. Gallatin City once had over sixty cabins, all

erected in one season, mainly by Missourians, who believed that it would be the head of navigation on the Missouri; but, after the city was built and no boats came for a whole season, some one came along and informed the enterprising residents that there were great falls in the river above Benton, which stopped the boats, and the city, once so full of promise, fell away, until a single cabin now represents it. The city cabins have been taken up from time to time and scattered over the prairie on ranches, and while a speculative city has disappeared because of the want of the proper study of geography, pleasant ranches and prosperous ranchmen have taken its place, and made the prairie blossom and ripen with the golden fruits which gladden the heart of the husbandman. I start to-day for Springville, and expect to reach Helena to-morrow.

LETTER XXVIII.

The Morning Air of the Mountains.—A Wonderful Tonic.—
Mountain-Pasturage. — How Cattle are wintered. — Bunch
Grass and Tender Beef.—The Gallatin Valley again.—Its Fer-
tility and many Advantages.—The Northern Pacific Railroad.
—The Navigation of the Upper Missouri.—The Rich Region
east of Gallatin.—The Savage resisting Civilization.—Settle-
ments extending East and West through Montana.—The In-
evitable Solution of the Indian Problem.—Prickly Pear Valley.
—Dinner and Rest.—Don Pedro and his Mistress.—Welcome
to Helena.—Dr. Cass in Command.—His Ideas of Water as a
Steady Beverage.—A Bottle of Wine his Sovereign Remedy.—
Another Political Meeting.—Speech refuted in the Newspapers.
—A Day at the Hot Springs.—Mrs. General Meagher.—Excellent Dinner and Baths.—Virtue and Vice.

HELENA HOT SPRINGS, ⎫
MONTANA TERR., August 23, 1867. ⎰

I WOKE up in the suburbs of Hoggum on Tuesday
morning, with heavy eyes and more than weary from my
daily hard drives and stumping every evening. But the
morning air of the mountains is the most wonderful tonic
in the world, and a little stroll along the clear streams
sweeping down to the Missouri, clad in their cheerful garments of green, sharpened my appetite for an excellent
breakfast, and soon thereafter we started for a drive of
thirty-five miles to Helena. Our course was rather west
of north, leaving the river to hug the mountain-range east
of us ; and we had the usual long, hard, rough divide to
cross to pass from the Missouri Valley to the Prickly Pear.

(272)

As we gradually ascended the prairie to the summit, we were soon beyond the irrigating streams, and for ten miles we had to traverse an elevated table or meadow, with a bountiful crop of loose boulders to impede our progress. The grass there, as elsewhere on the undulating lands, was parched almost white; but innumerable herds of the finest stock grazed upon it, and were fat and sleek as our Eastern stall-fed bullocks. An Eastern stock-grower, used only to the green fields of Pennsylvania, would at first sight pronounce these prairies unfit for pasturage; but in no place in the world will stock thrive better than on this same seemingly burnt-up grass. Although the stock and blades are dead, they are still nutritious; but the chief sustenance of cattle and horses is in the "bunch grass," to be found on all elevated lands in the mountains, which never loses its freshness at the roots. In the dryest seasons of summer, and the coldest winters, it preserves its perpetual greenness near the roots, and is succulent and most nourishing. No amount of hay or grain fed to cattle in the winter will bring them out in the spring in as good order as grazing on the bunch grass, if the snows do not fall so deep as to prevent them from reaching the roots; and no other feed will make the beef so sweet, juicy, and tender. Hitherto all the thousands of cattle in Montana have been sent to the valleys to shift for themselves during the winter; but last winter was so severe that many hundreds were lost, because the snow denied them access to the grass. In the winter of 1863 there was but little severe weather in Montana. The months of November, December, and January were like early autumn in the vicinity of Chambersburg, and the subsequent winter months were comparatively mild. The winters of 1864–5–6 were more severe, but still not sufficiently so to prevent stock from wintering very well on

24*

grass. Last winter, however, gave Montana three months of terrible winter, with from two to three feet of snow in the valleys; and a considerable proportion of the stock perished. Most of those that survived were reduced almost to skeletons, and came out singed of most of their hair by the fearful severity of the winter. In a few localities fat beef-cattle were turned out off the grass, but as a rule the stock wintered badly. Admonished by the experience of last winter, most of the herders in the valleys, and many of the farmers, have put up hay, and will be prepared to feed their stock if a bad spell should arrest grazing. Throughout the whole agricultural regions of Montana I have found the finest short-horn stock. I doubt not that cattle develop better here than in any other portion of the United States east of the mountains.

I cannot take leave of the beautiful valleys from Bozeman to Helena without another reference to their many advantages. The Gallatin is the most eastern of the Montana settlements, and is incomparably the finest agricultural region I have found in the Far West. I doubt whether even its settlers have any just appreciation of its future destiny. It is on the well-known Bozeman route,— the shortest and best-watered route to Montana,—and abounds with the finest pastures. The Northern Pacific Railroad will cross it, if it does not follow it a considerable distance, making it in all respects the most accessible portion of the Territory; and a few years at most will see steamers land not far from Gallatin City, the lower end of the valley. The Missouri is navigable in the dryest season, for light boats, from the junction of the Jefferson, Madison, and Gallatin to the falls above Fort Benton; and a railway of eighteen miles there would connect the upper Missouri lines with the lines now plying from Benton to St. Louis. In addition to these advantages, now certain,

I trust, soon to be realized, the route east from Gallatin Valley abounds in equally fertile valleys and even more salubrious climates. The Yellowstone is confessedly one of the most fertile regions of the Far West, and its climate invites the buffalo from the Platte, hundreds of miles south, to winter in its more genial atmosphere. Besides the vast agricultural resources of this region, it is known to abound in precious metals; and already the sturdy prospector has gone as far as Wind River and Big Horn Mountains from the Gallatin, and camps now swarm on the Musclesshell, northeast of Bozeman. The savage has most jealously guarded these sections of the West, and many prospecters have found bloody graves as their reward for pioneering civilization; but the Indian has lost all the sympathy of the pale-faces by his relentless savagery, and he must recede or die as the miner and ranchman advance with their trusty rifles and implacable hostility. Before five years there will be continuous settlements and mining-camps from the head-waters of the Missouri east, until civilization from east and west shall strike hands in the great Northern wilderness. It matters not what shall be the policy of the government with reference to the Indian. It cannot save him if it would: it will not try to divide this region for him, if it is wise in its policy. The march of progress is inexorable in its mandates, and neither troops, treaties, nor poetical commanders can reverse the logic of facts. I trust that but a few years will see the beneficent fruits of a generous policy on the part of the government in the construction of the Northern Pacific Railroad, and the removal of obstructions to the navigation of the Missouri; but, even if the government shall be penny-wise and pound-foolish enough to refuse its aid in the rapid development of this region of incalculable mineral and agricultural wealth, the current of progress will move steadily

onward. I wish indeed that our Congress could be thrown
into these blooming, fruitful valleys and mines of surpassing richness for a month, instead of sending committees
to view the mountains and Indians from railroad-cars,
usually to report in favor of the barbarous hordes whose
distinction is measured solely by the number and atrocity
of their butcheries.

When we reached the summit of the divide northwest
of Hoggum, the Prickly Pear Valley was presented in all
its beauty. We dined sumptuously at a two-story ranch
on savory elk-steak and the finest of vegetables, and had
an hour of rest among the latest Eastern periodicals. I
tried to catch up with some of my lost sleep; but a newly-
returning boarding-school miss kept up a perpetual struggle for the mastery of " Don Pedro," a wayward poodle-
dog, and between them I was forbidden sleep. Don Pedro
insisted upon being sociable with me,—prospected my
clothes, and demanded his full share of the lounge and
newspapers for his amusement. I could have managed
him; but his romantic mistress would follow him in every
few minutes and lecture Don Pedro for his rudeness to
strangers and playing truant with her. Although Don
Pedro and his simpering mistress stood sentinels against
sleep, I still had an hour of rest, and pursued my journey
much refreshed. The Prickly Pear Valley extends for
some twenty or thirty miles, ranging in width from five to
twenty miles, and nestling in a flock of mountain-spurs
stands Helena, the principal city of the Territory. The
Missouri is on the same side of the mountain-range, but
divided from the valley by high foot-hills, as it courses its
way northward, some sixteen miles east of the city. The
Prickly Pear traverses the valley, marking its sinuous line
by a luxuriant growth of shrubbery, and on either side
there are beautiful farms, with the golden wheat in shock.

The whole valley is covered with the finest pasturage, and countless herds graze on its bountiful and nutritious grasses.

When within five miles of the city, we saw a cloud of dust rise ahead of us, looking as if a troop of Indians were upon our trail; but, as we met it, my old friend and companion through the perilous Indian troubles of Bridger, Dr. Cass, surrounded us with a mounted escort of twenty-five men, and bid us welcome to the city of Helena. Among them was the postmaster of the city, who did not follow Nasby in firing salutes around the groceries in honor of A. J., but is a square-out Republican and braves every thing for the cause. We all dismounted in obedience to orders from Dr. Cass, and, after an introduction all around, he insisted that our team needed refreshing. He had a buggy, and from under the seat a willow basket temptingly projected. In its capacious quarters were many bottles, tumblers, and blocks of crystal ice; and he insisted that all must partake. The scorching rays of the sun and clouds of dust gave me earnest reminders of the luxury of ice-water, and I inquired whether we could have some. "Water!" responded the genial doctor, with a jolly grin all over his face; "water is all very well in its place,—very good for baptizing infants where they have such things, and excellent for sluicing out gulches; but it don't do for a steady beverage up here, where the air is so thin." Suiting the action to the sentiment, corks flew in every direction, and Montana and her champions were toasted with increased fervor as the work progressed. We soon started for the city, and I could not deny the theory that sparkling wine refreshes the horses when imbibed by the driver or rider. Certain it is that the horses were more spirited than before, the procession more punctilious in its military orders, if less obedient in observing them; and we rushed into the city as if the horses expected another bursting of champagne for their benefit when we should arrive there. Stray horsemen, solitary and otherwise, joined us as we neared the city, and when we entered Main Street we had quite a procession. After traversing the several principal streets, we halted, our quarters were shown us, and fifteen minutes were given me to wash and dust off, when I would be wanted. Dr. Cass suggested and supplied a bottle of wine to clear the dust out of the throat while I was brushing it off externally, and in due time he called again and invited me to enjoy the cool shade of his office, where I found a bottle of wine already opened to revive the spirits of the exhausted company. In vain I pleaded the danger of headache, disordered stomach, etc. "All very well for the hothouse plants of the East; but mountaineers are strangers to such complaints," was the reply. From there we repaired to various prominent places of the city, and at each the highly original idea seemed to have just occurred to the doctor that a bottle of wine must be smashed. Barn-door handbills confronted me at every corner, reminding me that I was to be the speaker of the evening at a mass-meeting to be congregated in a few hours, and the doctor met all my interrogatories as to the character of the audience and the direction I should give my remarks, by suggesting a bottle of wine. I "wagoned" through the whole ordeal with a clear head and steady nerves, and at the appointed hour took the stand to talk to a crowd that seemed to extend in every direction as far as I could see. I spoke the time I had allotted for the task, and supposed that I had said about what I had intended to say, until the morning paper came out with a condensed report of my speech. I recognized the words "the," "and," "but," and several others I certainly had used, but beyond that I could not recognize anything. The next day the Virginia paper came to hand with its report of the speech, and it bore no similarity to the Helena report, and neither had a complete sentence I had uttered. Dr. Cass suggested that the reporters had run out of wine, and proposed a bottle to enable us to compare the reports carefully. With all his hospitality, he indulged as sparingly as I did myself, and neither of us was any the worse for the campaign.

This is the first day of the trip I have had even an hour to myself; and I took advantage of it to rest at the celebrated Hot Springs, about four miles from Helena. As ours was but a family party, Mrs. General Meagher accompanied us. When first I saw her at a social gathering in Virginia, she was the queen of wit and beauty. To-day deep shadows dim the lustre of her eyes and sadly sober her natural sprightliness; but in the midst of it all, widowed and alone in the mountains, she is as heroic in sorrow as she was devoted in brighter days. I had a delightful rest. Some six large springs rise here, ranging in temperature from cold to almost boiling heat, and all are strongly impregnated with sulphur and other minerals. Baths are so arranged that they can be tempered just as each bather prefers; and a more refreshing, invigorating luxury I have not enjoyed for a long time. We were served with a dinner that would have been creditable at the Continental. Late in the afternoon the road from the city to the springs was lined with visitors of all classes. Social or smitten pairs from the élite of Helena were jostled on the way by the fast bloods from the mines, frail Cyprians galloped through all with the finest equipages on the road, and evening found a large crowd around us, representing almost every shade of virtue and vice. Part of the establishment is devoted to the reputable, while the others—perhaps more welcome because more profitable—have their parlor, where the fast gents and their partners toss their juleps and wine to strained wit and obscene jest. Here, in a little circle, is the Far West photographed from life, and each class is true to its profession. Crime comes not in fair disguise to mingle with and corrupt the fountains of virtue, as it does in fashionable resorts in the East, but, unmasked and with that deference that wrong ever yields to right, it sweeps along as if impatient to hasten the fullness of its sorrow and leave half its days unmeasured.

The Head of the Missouri River.—A Beautiful Prospect.—The Cliff on which Lewis and Clarke first viewed and named the Jefferson, Madison, and Gallatin Rivers.—Navigation of the Upper Missouri.—From Gallatin to Hoggum.—The Missouri and Prickly Pear Valleys.—The Fertile Soil about Helena.— Helena City.—Its Rapid Growth.—Character of its People.— Its Rich Bars and Gulches.—Water-Ditches.—The Hangman's Tree.—James W. Whitlach.—The Whitlach Union Mine.— The Reward of Earnest Development.

HELENA, MONTANA TERR., August 24, 1867.

I LEFT Gallatin City on Monday for another long drive to the chief city of the Territory. Before starting, I climbed a high bluff, of limestone formation, that towers up between the Jefferson and Gallatin Rivers, and had a magnificent view of the three rivers lazily streaming out of their respective valleys, while a few rods below their waters are united, and they are lost in the Missouri, as it passes off with fretful energy through a narrow cañon to the far north. As far as the eye can see, the Gallatin, Madison, and Jefferson Valleys present their green bottoms, luxuriant fields, and countless herds of the finest cattle ; while the lines of the rivers and their numerous tributaries are distinctly marked by the dense growth of timber on their banks. I was charmed with this beautiful prospect, and lingered more than an hour to enjoy its delightful contrast with the parched waste of the prairies distant from water. A little more than threescore years ago, Lewis and Clarke stood in the same place, and made the first record of the

25　　　　　　　(281)

source of the great river of the West, and the three rivers
above were then first named in honor of the eminent
statesmen then President and Cabinet officers of the nation.
Then the source of the Missouri was in what were regarded as inaccessible wilds and wastes, where the home
of the pale-faces would never be reared.   To-day the most
bountiful crops of the world are being gathered in the
valleys of the Upper Missouri and its tributaries, and the
vast plains are dotted with the ranches of the successful
husbandman.   But, rapid as has been the march of progress here in the past, it is only in its infancy.   It was not
a mere feverish speculation that planted a city with sixty-
four cabins at the head of the Missouri, a few years ago.
True, it was a step in advance of progress itself, and the
cabins have disappeared, with a solitary exception, to
grace the farms in the neighborhood; but I doubt not that
they will return in a few years, and to stay.   The Missouri has been navigated and carefully explored from Gallatin to the falls above Fort Benton,—a distance of two
hundred miles by the course of the river,—and there are
no obstructions whatever.   An intelligent gentleman, who
was with the exploring party last year, informed me
that light boats can navigate the Missouri in the dryest
season; and one or two years at most will see a line of
steamers plying from the Falls into the heart of the agricultural wealth of Montana.   And, while the steamers
will come up from the north, civilization will be extending
from Bozeman City eastward into the Yellowstone, and
the rich placers of the Yellowstone, Big Horn, Wind River,
and Muscleshell will make a continued line of white supremacy from the Mississippi to Puget Sound.   The won-
drously fruitful valleys will fully supply the miners, and
the savage will recede or die before this "manifest destiny."

From the head of the Missouri I started nearly westward along the banks of the Jefferson, but soon turned toward the north, across a gradual divide of fifteen miles. The day was warm, and fifteen miles of successive foot-hills, without water, tired both team and passengers. Finally we landed on Milton Creek, with clear, fresh water, and there we stopped to dine and rest. The inevitable Missourian was our host, and his photograph-album was not singular in that region for commencing with Jeff. Davis, following with General Price, and ending with Wilkes Booth. We dined on our host's fresh vegetables and palatable bread and butter, rather than on his opinions, and got along very well. For more than twenty miles on this trip there was not a field to be seen; but as we descended into Crow Creek Valley we found fruitful fields again. The valley is quite large and level, but is barely supplied with water, as Crow Creek seems to be its only source for irrigation, and that has been almost drained by the miners on the Missouri side of the bluff. It has an abundance of most nutritious grass, and many fine herds were grazing on it. From Crow Creek we had to cross another divide, nearly in an eastern direction, making a complete semicircle from Gallatin. Here for the first time I found the red shale, or slate, and on it a sickly growth of pines. Evening brought me to the eastern slope of the divide, and again I was on the banks of the Missouri. It is lined with contiguous farms, and the harvests look excellent. As we passed down the stream, the bottom widened until it spread out a mile or more on each side, with beautiful table-lands rising along the foot-hills. That night we were the guests of the city of Hoggum, a small, new mining-camp that was "hogged up" by a few miners, as is alleged, and thus it won its euphonious title. Some ten miles below is the celebrated Confederate

Gulch, the richest of the size ever discovered. Four men cleaned up and took away with them, last season, a ton of gold, the result of their own labor. Over $150,000 was cleaned up in it in two days, last year; and it is still yielding very largely. Its name is a reflex of the convictions and sympathies of its discoverers.

From Hoggum to this city is a clever day's drive over another divide between the Missouri and Prickly Pear Valleys; and the country presents the parched and desolate-looking aspect now to be seen everywhere in the absence of water. As we entered the Prickly Pear Valley, the Missouri hides itself behind a series of high foothills, and hugs the range closely as it toils on to the north, and the creek that bears the name of the valley winds around and finds a passage to the river through the cañons which break the numerous ranges of bluffs. The valley is very beautiful, and quite productive, although hundreds of acres equally so still invite the settler within a mile of Helena. I presume there is not much difference between the altitude of Prickly Pear Valley and the Gallatin; but the difference is probably in favor of the Gallatin, as vegetation is here not quite so much advanced. It is, however, susceptible of cultivation generally, and will one day be all appropriated by the husbandman. The best-improved ranches (the invariable name for a farm in the Far West) I have seen in Montana are in this valley. A number rejoice in two-storied houses,—a rare evidence of progress in this country.

Helena City nestles in between a network of mountain-cliffs on the southwest side of the valley, and, like all mining-camps, it started with two rows of cabins in the gulch, divided by a very narrow street. Its location is in Last Chance Gulch,—so called because an old miner and his son, after prospecting the whole season, tried this

gulch as their last chance for "winter grub." It proved
very rich; and soon after an adventurous prospector
pushed up the ravine beyond the pay-streak, and discovered another rich gulch. His first companion was a huge
grizzly bear, which he shot and feasted thereon: hence
the title of Grizzly Gulch above the city. Here is the
most marked evidence of progress to be found in Montana.
Virginia City has handled the forty or fifty millions of
gold from Alder Gulch, and is sobering down with the
ebbing tide into substantial, legitimate business; but
Helena has all the vim, recklessness, extravagance, and
jolly progress of a new camp. It is but little over two
years old, but it boasts of a population of seven thousand
five hundred, and of more solid men, more capital, more
handsome and well-filled stores, more fast boys and frail
women, more substance and pretense, more virtue and vice,
more preachers and groggeries, and more go-aheadative-
ness generally, than any other city in the mountain mining-
regions. It has gradually swelled beyond the narrow,
crooked gulch to the table-lands; and many beautiful cot-
tages adorn its suburbs, but still guiltless of shade, or even
of the attempt to grow trees. They have not time for that
yet, although water is accessible; and they jostle along
against and over each other in the hurried race for fortune,
leaving adornment for the future. The city is surrounded
by gulches, all more or less rich in the precious metals, and
two ditches have been made, the one five and the other fifteen miles in length, to bring water to the bars and gulches
in and about this place. One ditch carries one thousand
inches of water, and the other five hundred; but so far
they have not proved profitable to either owners or miners.
The price charged for the water is so high that many of
the flumes are idle. The only tree in the city is a short,
thick pine, known as "hangman's tree," on which many a

desperado has yielded his life to the terrible judgment of
the Vigilanters.   It has served its purpose, as the proper
authorities are now supreme : its topmost branches are
already dead, and it will soon live only in history.

The wealth in precious metals in and around Helena is
truly wonderful.   There are hundreds of acres of bars
below the city which will be worked profitably in time,
as facilities increase and labor cheapens ; and five miles
up the gulch I saw men hauling dirt from the hill-sides to
the streams below, and washing out good wages.   Here
are certainly the most extensive bars yet known in Montana ; and I share the conviction of the Helena people that
the city must progress steadily, rather than recede.   I had
time to visit only two of the many leads near this place ; and,
as one of them is the only one thoroughly developed in
the Territory, I will be pardoned for singling it out in
contrast with the stupid, suicidal policy of both owners
and speculators, of whom I have spoken in previous letters.
As the lead is not for sale, I feel warranted in using it to
illustrate what judicious, legitimate effort will accomplish
in Montana.   It is owned by James W. Whitlach, who
came to the mountain-mines some years ago from Western Pennsylvania without sufficient learning to enable him
to read or write his name.   After various smiles and frowns
of fortune in California and Nevada, he came here and discovered the "Whitlach Union" lead.   Instead of plunging it into speculation, he set about its development, without means, and he struggled on, sacrificing a large share
of his profits for want of capital, but carefully putting
every dollar realized into development, until he has taken
out over one hundred and fifty thousand dollars of bullion,
and has to-day five hundred thousand dollars within sight
in his shafts and tunnels.   His mine was not half so rich
as many others on the surface, and at times I noticed that

it narrowed down to a mere seam between the walls; but he persevered until he has it now completely opened, and will soon employ several mills in its reduction. Most of this valuable lead he owns exclusively, while some four hundred feet belongs to a mill-enterprise in which he is half-owner, giving half of the four hundred feet for half of a thirty-stamp mill erected and ready to run. After developing his lead and thoroughly testing it, he can now command any amount of machinery on it, on profitable terms. His ores yield an average of about thirty dollars per ton. Eastern speculators will tell you of better mines than this one; but practical miners who have proved the value of leads have few such stories to tell. Nineteen companies out of twenty, constituted as are most Eastern corporations, would have bankrupted themselves, where one persevering miner, without capital, has built up a colossal fortune, and one that seems illimitable. I would advise parties in the East, who contemplate embarking in mining-enterprises, to select one sensible business-man to visit and learn the lesson of the Whitlach mine before they buy their machinery. But few could fail if they would thus start right.

LETTER XXX.

The Trade and Prosperity of Helena.—The Immense Consumption of a Small Population.—Climbing the Rocky Range again.—The Mullen Wagon-Road and Old Indian Trail.—Magnificent Timber on the Northern Slopes of the Range.—Fine Blooded Cattle grazing on the Mountains.—Parting of the Waters.—Meadow Brook.—Brook-Trout.—A "Batch" Dinner.—Carpenter's Bar.—Blackfoot City.—Political Speaking.—Competition of the Gambling-Saloons and Bars.—Good Order preserved.—Democratic Meeting on Sunday.—The Salute to General Smith.—Judge Williston.

BLACKFOOT, MONTANA TERR., August 26, 1867.

I HAD a good rest in Helena, the chief city of Montana, and enjoyed its liberal hospitality and jolly people after the weary rides and nightly speeches of the previous week. Helena is a specimen of a large mining city or camp. Everybody goes on the high-pressure principle, whether to a wedding, a political meeting, to church, to a frolic, to hang a man, or to a funeral. The people are not citizens in the usual acceptation of the term. They are residents, or sojourners, usually expecting to leave long before they do, and many will probably stay the remainder of their lives, confidently hoping to get away every spring and fall. Just now the city is crowded with goods. The trains have got in from the river, and the fresh supplies of merchantable commodities fill not only the many stores, but scores of fire-proof warehouses besides. The main street of Helena seems to have everything for sale you could find in Philadelphia, although the prices vary somewhat from Eastern rates. It was to me a study, when in that city, how the people consumed the immense stores shipped to them annually. Montana has not over forty thousand population, and very many of them are poor, shifting from day to day for bread; and yet the business-men of the Territory paid out nearly a million of dollars this summer for freights alone. The agricultural valleys supply nearly if not quite all the flour consumed, and an abundance of potatoes, turnips, and many other vegetables: yet more than three millions a year are paid for dry goods, groceries, provisions, vegetables, fruits, liquors, etc., by not more than forty thousand people, most of whom live in the rudest manner and spend little for finery. It proves simply that of all classes the miners are the most improvident, and as a rule earn to-day and spend to-morrow, if indeed they do not spend before they earn. Helena is now the great centre of trade for Montana, and the supplies are immense. Besides her retail trade, a large wholesale business is done by her merchants to the small retailers in the mining-camps and agricultural settlements. A very large capital is required to carry on business, as a whole year's supply of all articles must be purchased and shipped at one time.

I left Helena on Saturday for this city,—a distance of thirty-five miles across the Rocky range. We crossed the Prickly Pear near the city, where it is lined with bountiful farms, and passed along the valley several miles before we commenced to climb the rugged foot-hills of the mountains, which throw out their huge spurs to the very edge of Helena. Soon we came to a cañon, and swung off into it to commence the ascent of not less than three thousand feet. The road is over a succession of cliffs, which are thrown in the wildest confusion along and across the valley at every angle; but it is amazing with what ease comparatively the range can be crossed. For many miles the road follows an Indian trail, still distinctly visible, which has doubtless existed for centuries. The Indians come from the Pacific slopes to the East to hunt for buffalo, and have done so from time immemorial; and their trails are beaten in the earth often as much as a foot deep. Part of the way we were on the original Mullen wagon-road, which was located mainly by the Indian trail. For fifteen miles we had little else than bleak, sterile hills, with sidling roads and steep ascents and descents, and of course without the sight of cultivation. On either side high mountains encompassed us; ahead of us was the Rocky range, and immediately around us were dozens of respectable mountains, while our road took us down one only to commence to climb another. On the north sides the mountains are all densely wooded, as the snow lies most of the year there and supplies moisture, while on all points exposed to the sun they are entirely bare of trees and have but little grass. In all this mountain-region I found the finest, fattest cattle, and in one of the ravines of the main range I met a thorough-bred short-horn bull quietly grazing on the sweet, tender grass of the forest. I walked leisurely up the range, and for the first time enjoyed a genuine, old-fashioned shade. The northeastern slope is covered with large, fine timber,—mostly yellow pine, but mingled with it is the white, and almost every variety of that wood. Here and there a quaking-asp (really a species of cotton-wood) varied the foliage; but the thick, short, bushy pines were the monarchs of the mountain, and the thin air swept through their foliage with the mellowest music. I saw many yellow pines four feet across the stump, but they do not grow more than two-thirds the height of such trees on our Eastern hills. One venerable trunk, nearly the last on the summit, measured over fifteen feet in circumference.

Whenever we reached the top, not a tree or shrub was visible, excepting on the next range a little beyond. A clear, rippling spring starts down near the summit, and within gun-shot of it another starts down the western slope. Thus they rise but a few yards apart, and dash on to the Eastern and Western Seas. The western slope of the range is covered with sickly-looking grass; but not a shrub rises to break the monotony of the scene until the foot is reached, when another range, nearly as high as the main one, presents its northwest forest of magnificent trees again. In the ravine, Meadow Brook sweeps down around the mountain, and seeks its grade to the Pacific; but we had to climb again to reach our destination. Before doing so, however, we had an excellent dinner, prepared by a ranchman who "batches it," as they say out here when the house is without a landlady. There were plenty of beautiful brook-trout sporting in the stream, but we had not time to catch them and wait to have them cooked. After dinner we passed slowly up the second range, through splendid timber, and fanned by refreshing mountain-breezes as they sighed through the dense pines. When we reached the summit again, the same barrenness suddenly began, and not a tree of any size graced the southwestern slopes. We landed at its foot in an extensive mining-region, known as Carpenter's Bar, where not less than one hundred acres have been worked by hydraulic process, besides the gulch, and very profitable returns realized. After crossing another divide, we landed in this city, which consists of two rows of cabins about forty rods in length, and a street between them. It has a temporary appearance, as it is supported solely by placer-miners, whose business may "play out" any time. Half the cabins are groggeries, about one-fifth are gambling-saloons, and a large percentage are occupied by the fair but frail ones who ever follow

the miner's camp. One hotel consisted of a restaurant and
bar on the first floor, and berths up-stairs for lodgers.
One little corner was partitioned off with rough boards, to
accommodate the few ladies who chance to travel this way.
The people are intelligent and clever, and reasonably good
order is maintained.

I was placarded to speak Saturday evening; and, as
most of the miners gather in at the close of the week for
their Sunday sports, I had a very large audience. Balls
soaked in kerosene were suspended from a post, which
brilliantly illuminated the crowd and streets. I stood on
a box in front of the hotel, with a bar doing a brisk business just behind me. Immediately on my left, with double
doors and windows open, was a gambling-saloon in full
blast, with a faro-bank, three or four poker-tables, a bil-
liard-table, and a bar, all liberally patronized. On my
right was an open front with a decorated bar, attended by
several brilliantly-painted bar-keepers of the female persuasion; and next to that was another gambling-saloon. Fortunately, there were enough people to supply all with
patrons and leave me a large audience to talk to; but,
while I cannot complain of the attention, I noticed frequent surges from the crowd to the saloons,—particularly
when the dealer on my left (who was not ten yards from
me) would call out, loud enough to drown my voice,
"Single turn, gents! who'll call the turn?" Away would
sweep a share of my hearers, and in a little while they
would gather back again,—most of them, I doubt not,
sadder men than before. With all the whisky poured
down, the audience was remarkable for its order. One enthusiastic disciple of Democracy came staggering out of a
groggery and greeted me with, "Dry up, old (hic) blos-
som-top!" but he reeled off and left me to do the remainder
of the speaking. I need hardly say, after the description

I have given of the place, that it will be likely to give a Democratic majority on Monday next.

Sunday is the great day here, as in most mining-camps, for public meetings and amusements. To the credit of the Republicans be it said, they refused to hold political meetings on Sunday. The Democrats, however, held their great meetings on that day throughout the Territory. Mr. Cavanaugh, Democratic candidate for Congress, followed me at Bozeman on Sunday, and a leading Democratic candidate preceded me at Hoggum on Sunday. Governor Green Clay Smith followed me here last night (Sunday); and I notice that the Democracy are to close the campaign with a grand mass-meeting in Virginia City next Sunday evening. Governor Smith arrived yesterday from Helena, where he had started in to follow me around to Virginia. As there are no churches, school-houses, or other decent places of public resort, and no place to read even, everybody was lounging around; and when his excellency entered the city a salute was fired from two anvils, much to the amusement of the few boys and to the consternation of the many dogs. In the evening he spoke in behalf of the Democracy, to a large audience; and the side amusements which divided my hearers from me seemed to reap a richer harvest than the evening before.

My old friend Judge Williston had met me at Helena, accompanied me here, and will go with me to Deer Lodge, where he resides. He is as fastidious, foppish, and genial as ever, but complains that somebody will persist in staining his coat and shirt with tobacco, and that Western washwomen glory in tearing buttons off one's clothes. He is confessedly an able and upright judge, and commands, as he deserves, the unbounded confidence of the people for his ability and integrity. We leave Blackfoot for Deer Lodge to-day, and without serious regrets.

26

The Forests of the Rocky Range on Mullen's Pass.—The Mountains on Fire.—Deer Lodge Valley.—Its Mining-Districts.—Promising Gold and Silver Leads.—Exorbitant Prices named in Bonds to Middle-Men.—Legitimate Mining.—Failure almost invariably due to Mismanagement. —Deer Lodge City. —Its Beautiful Streams and Vast Herds.—Its Great Mineral Spring. —Agricultural Settlements of Montana.—The Missoula Valley. —Growth of Fruit.

DEER LODGE CITY, MONTANA TERR., August 28, 1867.

I LEFT Helena on Saturday morning to fill an appointment at Blackfoot that evening, and had a pleasant trip over the Rocky range and its numerous spurs. The ascent of the range really commences at Helena; for the foot-hills surround the city on three sides. An old Indian trail, that has been traveled for centuries by the Indians of the western slopes in search of the buffalo of the plains, located the road most of the way, and Captain Mullen's wagon-road follows it until the range is crossed. The rapid succession of bare bluffs over which I climbed presented nothing novel until the base of the main range was reached, when I found thousands of acres of the finest timber shading the mountains with the darkest green. On every angle of the confused network of mountains, where the sun had not easy access, the growth of timber is magnificent, large yellow and white pines, measuring from three to four feet in diameter. But on the slopes exposed to the sun there was not so much as a shrub to be seen, unless

(294)

by the side of some little brook. Where the snow lies
most of the year, moisture is supplied to sustain a bountiful crop of timber ; but not a tree can grow on the sunny
sides. Crossing the range from the northeast, it presented
the appearance of our beautiful Alleghanies. The forest
was as dense as any Pennsylvania could produce, the tenderest of grass covered the earth beneath the plaintive
whispers of the majestic pines, and herds of splendid cattle
quietly grazed on its sweet and nutritious herbage. On the
summit the timber ends abruptly, and with a regular line
that looks as if it had been planted; while on the top, and
down the Pacific slope, nothing but the usual growth of
parched and withered grass meets the eye. Two springs
rise within a few feet of each other, and dash off toward
the rising and the setting sun to the far-distant seas.
At the foot of the range I left the old trail and Mullen
Road, which flanks the next range by "the Frenchwoman's
Ranch," and had to climb another range but little less
than the main one. The magnificent view of the mountains was greatly lessened by the dense volumes of smoke
which filled the atmosphere. Not less than five thousand
acres of the range seemed to be enveloped in fire; and on
far-distant ranges I could see that the angry element was
doing its work of destruction on every side. The second
range could scarcely be distinguished from the Rocky
range in crossing it. The same beautiful timber, fresh,
tender grass, and familiar herds were found on the northern exposure; the south and west being bare and desolate. At the foot the mining-camps appeared. Carpenter's Bar, with its hundred acres or more, washed down
by hydraulics, and a gulch turned over for miles, with a
little town crowded along the narrow passage on one side,
gave evidences that the main harvest of gold had been
gathered, and that but few of the less fortunate operators

remained. Hence over another divide lies Blackfoot City,
a brisk mining-camp, in which much has been done, and
much more remains to be done. It is the beginning of a
series of camps in Deer Lodge county, and for many miles
west and south is dotted with swarms of miners, who
are well repaid for their labors. Just now the attention
of business-men is directed to this section. Its placer
mines have been worked for several years; but its leads
are the newest in the Territory, and the surface-indications
are the best ever discovered in the mountains. They are
not yet "proven up," as the miners say, and they may not
sustain the surface-richness when they are properly developed; but the top-rock of these mines is truly wonderful. Flint Creek district abounds in silver-leads, and they
are unusually alike in the width of the crevices and the
yield per ton. It is believed by those who have spent this
season in that district, including many scientific and practical men, that it will surpass any silver-region yet discovered. Several furnaces are in course of erection, and
this winter will begin systematic developments. Within
twelve miles of the silver-mines a monster gold-lead has
been discovered,—the widest, I believe, found in the Territory,—and it prospects very handsomely. Silver Bow, east
of this city, has produced a very large return of gold ; and
Butte City, Highland, and many other districts have discovered what seem to be most valuable leads. Some of
them range from five to twenty-five feet in width; and
from the decayed surface-rock good wages have been
made by panning out the gold. In Butte City, valuable
copper-mines are found, yielding as high as forty per cent.
of copper, and some silver and gold beside. Of these leads
I can express no opinion, beyond saying that they are well
worthy the attention of capitalists. It should not be assumed that they are to continue indefinitely as fruitful as

their surface-ores indicate, and it would be folly to purchase and erect mills or furnaces on them before they are fully proven; but they are well worth the most thorough development, and most of them could be secured by capitalists for little outlay beyond opening them properly, by dividing the ownership with the miners. I learn that one of these leads has been bonded to a "middle-man" at $1,300,000, and it is probably now in the Eastern market with the bonds to show the price at which it is held. It may be worth $13,000,000 instead of $1,300,000; but one-twentieth the bonded price would buy any of these undeveloped mines, and then it would be unwise to erect machinery on them until they have been opened to well-defined and permanent leads. Every indication is favorable about these leads, and I would urge capitalists to possess them and develop them judiciously; but let not the stupendous monuments of folly which now make Colorado desolate and sickening be repeated here. I regard legitimate mining in Montana as the safest and most profitable investment men can make in any enterprise; but I have striven faithfully, through these pages, to save capitalists and Montana from common misfortune. An association that will devote a year to the development of these new mines, which promise so handsomely, could devote the second year to the erection of machinery that would return colossal fortunes; while nine out of ten of the hap-hazard companies which ship mills and then hunt for mines would fail in the same districts. I have now been through the leading mining-districts of the Territory, and I have found no failure in quartz mining that could not trace disaster to the stupidity of owners or directors. I have not found an idle or unsuccessful mill that has not an abundance of first-class quartz somewhere about it. A few mills have been sent here to run on ores from a single undeveloped lead, and with its failure the company fails; and but few, after one disaster, will invest in new leads, lest they double their loss. Let me here repeat, as a rule from which there can be no departure with safety, that no mine wants a mill for a year after its systematic development is commenced. A few thousand dollars will answer to open a lead; and, if it "bilks," the loss is not serious, and others can be secured and proven.

Deer Lodge City is a little village of probably two hundred inhabitants, situated on the river of the same name, and nearly central in the most picturesque and beautiful valley I have seen in Montana. There are no mining-camps within ten miles of the town, and it wears the quiet, sober air of an agricultural community. The valley is the largest in the Territory, and is very well watered. Numerous clear mountain-streams sweep into it from the west, and thousands of cattle graze on its bountiful growth of grass. On the west, the Bitter Root range walls the valley in from Idaho, and its spurs are thrown out like huge steps to the edge of the prairie. On the east, the Rocky range divides it from the Jefferson; and between them the valley extends from five to twenty miles in width, and fully fifty miles in length. As yet it is not extensively cultivated; but occasional fields prove that it is capable of growing grain and vegetables in vast crops. Stock-growing seems to be the principal effort of the ranchmen; but it is destined to be a great agricultural valley. Its name is derived from a peculiar hot mineral spring that rises near the centre of the valley. The mineral substance in the water has incrusted about the spring until it has reared a mound thirty feet high, and one hundred feet in diameter at the base. On the top of the mound the water rises up to the surface in a strong volume, but does not overflow. It runs off through passages in the mound, and rises again in different places at its base. I spent an hour in the examination of this curious structure, fashioned by the ceaseless efforts of the water, and left it with reluctance. In the mornings, and during all the time in winter, a mist or fog rises from the water at the base of the hill, in the shape of a large Indian lodge or tent. As it was a favorite resort for the numerous deer before the settlers drove them to the mountains, the Indians named the place Deer Lodge: whence the name of the valley and county. Game is still abundant in the hills which skirt the valley. I saw a yearling elk and a moose calf grazing about the city, both perfectly tame. The moose is most suspicious of men, and inhabits the more remote ranges; but the elk and deer still come to the outskirts of the settlements, and grace the boards of the ranchmen most of the year with their savory steaks.

Of the agricultural settlements of Montana, the Gallatin and Missoula Valleys are the most favored in climate,— the eastern and western extremes of the Territory. I learn that the Missoula grows the earliest and finest vegetables raised in the mountains, although it is the least accessible of all the agricultural districts as yet. It is the northwestern county of the Territory, and is flanked by the Bitter Root range. So favorable has the climate been since the settlers have been there, that the more hardy fruits are planted, with entire confidence that they can be grown successfully.* The whole Territory is made up of alternate mountains and valleys,—the one studded with the precious metals, and the other teeming with the most bountiful crops I have ever seen. In four years, with

---

* I noticed, in the Helena papers, that several wagon-loads of excellent apples, grown in Missoula Valley, were sold in Helena in the fall of 1868.

trackless mountains and hostile savages to confront the pioneer, this Territory has been settled for nearly two hundred miles in every direction from Helena, the central city, and, with not over forty thousand people, it is second only to California in the production of gold and silver, and rivals that State in the growth of wheat to the acre. It has been cursed with adventurers in both business and politics, as has been the experience of all new Territories; but its future will make romance pale before the swift march of progress.

LETTER XXXII.

MOOSE CREEK, MONTANA TERR., August 28, 1867.

I LEFT the famous city of Blackfoot with few regrets.
A Sunday there is anything but pleasant to one who don't
gamble, race horses, or buy at street-auctions. A sprightly
terrier, added to our family by the kindness of a friend
in Helena, was stolen and corraled under a sofa, and,
although my landlord was in the house in search of the
missing dog, the damsels who had committed the theft
denied having any knowledge of her whereabouts. After
we left he returned and captured the stolen property, and
Governor Smith, who followed me all around, restored
the dog at Deer Lodge, where we closed our campaign.

. As if some devilish infection pervaded the atmosphere
of Blackfoot, one of our horses (a kiyuse, or native pony)
took a fit of "bucking" soon after we left, and was particular to select the most dangerous portions of the road

(301)

for the display of his skill in that line. The native horses become singularly skilled in "bucking," and there are few riders who can keep the saddle or make them yield to the lines when they resort to their favorite amusement. Twice our kiyuse broke nearly out of the harness, but, after persuading him gently with a stout club dropped over his head, he finally concluded to take us along peaceably. Eastern riders know little of Western horsemanship. The kiyuse is never perfectly tamed, and he is always rode or driven so as to exercise all possible control over him. I have not seen an Eastern saddle or girth in the mountains. The army saddle, or a pattern much like it, is in universal use, and a broad hair band, with a ring in each end, serves for a girth. No buckles are used in fastening the saddle. It is set back clear of the shoulders, and the band strapped as tightly as possible over the belly, so as to completely clear the lungs. Then a sharp curb and a hair rein complete the outfit. The Western man always rides at a lope, and sometimes at a gallop, and when his pony is worn down he is turned out to grass, and a fresh one brought in, who usually "bucks" vigorously when he is called into service. They will plant their heads down between their front feet, and rear and kick, keeping the head down, until they unhorse the rider or are flogged into submission. The usual way to start them is for the rider to mount firmly and ply the spurs (with rowels never less than an inch in diameter, and I have seen them as much as three inches), and a friend stands behind and plies the raw-hide whip. Finally the kiyuse gives it up, and with a fearful bound he will break off at full speed; but he is allowed to indulge that fancy, and is even aided by vigorous spurring. Then he is safe until he is turned out again, when the same struggle is gone over, with the same result.

There is nothing remarkable in the journey from Black-foot to the Deer Lodge Valley, beyond the usual confused spurs of the Rocky Mountains over which we passed; but when we entered the valley it presented a most beautiful appearance. But little farming is done; but the cattle which swarm on the green bottoms are the finest I have met in all my journey. Their stock is better bred than are our own cattle in Pennsylvania, and they seem to thrive much better here than in our luxuriant clover in the East. At Deer Lodge City, the central village and county town of the valley, we became the guests of Judge Williston, who had met us at Helena; and I could not resist the inclination to spend an odd day with him to talk up the last several years. The city is pleasantly laid out, compared with the mining-towns, as the street is wide and kept in tolerable order. Although no mining is done nearer than a dozen miles, a large trade is carried on with the different camps. I found a young moose calf grazing along the river-bank; and when it saw me it ran up to me and manifested its friendly intentions by the most plaintive bleating. Its face looked as if Old Melancholy had fashioned it for a model of itself, but it was cheerful and even jolly as it nipped the buds and leaves from the bushes. They have been very plenty in Deer Lodge; but as the valley has become settled the moose has receded to the mountains. On the commons near the village a yearling elk was browsing, and I paid his majesty a visit. His bright eyes, neat limbs, and quick, graceful movements contrasted most favorably with the awkward step and stupid, homely face of the moose; but in his normal condition the moose is the most valiant of all the wild game, and is not a pleasant foe to encounter nearer than rifle-range. One hunter informed me that he killed one last year that weighed over seven hundred pounds dressed.

From Deer Lodge we had a pleasant journey to this place, a distance of sixty miles. We made it in a day with a single span of mules and four passengers, and crossed the Rocky range. Strange to say, this place has not been dubbed a city, although it has a large pole cabin, extensive stabling, two farm-wagons, several hay-stacks, and a trout-stream that comes down from the bluffs to swell the boisterous current of Big Hole River. The ascent to the summit is very gradual from Deer Lodge, and, without appreciating the fact that you are crossing the great backbone of the mountains, you find yourself on the top, and can look east and west for miles at the beautiful valleys below. We dined near Silver Bow, with a Canadian Frenchman who was "batching;" and we could not complain of his table. Like all frosted bachelors and damsels, he had a fine assortment of spoiled pets, for the want of something better on which to lavish his affections; and my chief trouble was to keep his pet cat out of my plate while I was dining. When we reached the summit of the range, we found the waters of Divide Creek, which rises in a cliff to the south, contributing most equally to the Eastern and Western seas. Naturally it courses to the Missouri; but there are rich bars of gold deposits six miles west without water, and the miners have made a ditch from the summit to the bars, and turned all the water, not already appropriated otherwise, to the Pacific slopes. It gushes out of the mountain-rocks and dashes down the prairie summit, where it strikes the dividing ridge, and thence half of it turns off in fretful murmurs to the setting sun. For the fourth time I stood on the summit of the Rocky range to-day, and, although I have been climbing mountains for seventeen hundred miles since June last, I have never yet wearied of their varied beauty and impressive grandeur.

From the summit we had a rapid descent into Big Hole Valley,—so called because of the rapid current and uneven bed of the river that sweeps through it close by the mountain-spur that bounds the prairie on the south. Hundreds of cattle were grazing all along the eastern slope and down in the valley; but I saw no signs of the husbandman. In a little while we parted with the river as it turned off into a deep, narrow cañon, and we climbed a steep divide, at the foot of which is Moose Creek.

Having traveled sixty miles with a light team, a heavy load, and a hot sun, we were glad to stop for the night, and we all felt that our lots had been cast in a pleasant place as we sat down to a dish of trout just taken from the brook. True, things did not look as clean as I have seen them; but we were tired and hungry, and did not inspect them too closely. The house being crowded, my couch was made up on the earthen floor in the kitchen, and consisted of a bed filled with musty hay, and I lost several hours of sleep trying to conclude what color the ticking had been when it was clean. The landlord and landlady had their bed in the opposite corner, and the children were piled in around the cook-stove as circumstances would allow. During the night I had more than visions of innumerable companions in bed, with savage appetites and unpleasant habits of locomotion. To struggle with them was vain, and I bore their fellowship with all the philosophy I could command. Weary nature gave me some sleep in spite of bedbugs; and when I awoke in the morning the landlady was making up the biscuits for breakfast. As soon as she saw I was awake, she displayed the proverbial sociability of Western people by entering into a spirited conversation, made up mainly of interrogatories on her part and monosyllables on mine. As I was lying on the floor, I had a good view of her feet,

27

and, after mature reflection, decided that she had not washed
them since spring, if even then; and, if they were to be
cleaned up for winter, I concluded that nothing short of a
grindstone run by water-power would scour them white.
"Bedbugs are *aw-ful* critters," said she, as she jammed
another biscuit into the pan.   "They *do* beat me, all I
can do, here; I hain't no beds put up in the house, jist for
that," she added.   The table-cloth was hanging over a
chair that stood between us, and just then she made a
brilliant dash at it with her doughy fingers, captured two
bugs on their morning stroll, and flung them into the
stove.   "They *do* be aw-ful," she continued, as she plunged
into the dough again and hurried up the breakfast.   In a
little while I decided that the less I saw of the baking and
cooking the more I would relish my breakfast; and, in the
midst of a running conversation with my sociable and
genial hostess, I made a hurried toilet and took a walk to
fortify myself for the coming meal.   But my fastidious
appetite got the better of me; and beyond a cup of miserable coffee and a slice of stale bread I had not seen made
up, I could not indulge.   Some of the guests enjoyed the
smoking biscuits; but I concluded that they had not seen
them baked, as I did.

We have now fifty-five miles to Virginia City, when we
shall have made a circuit of four hundred miles through
the main valleys and mines of Montana, and traveled two
thousand by stage since we left the railroad at Platte City
in Nebraska,—all but three hundred miles of it through
the Rocky Mountains.   So far, we have had but one innocent upset (on the Wasatch range), and no other accident
of any kind.   We have all steadily improved in health,
and unite in our tribute to the fine, invigorating climate,
sweet waters, and unaffected hospitality we have found in
the Far West.

LETTER XXXIII.

LORRAIN, MONTANA TERR., August 29, 1867.

FROM Deer Lodge City to the summit of the Rocky range is a gradual ascent for nearly forty miles,—so gradual, indeed, that the top is reached without any of the abrupt hills and deep chasms so common in climbing the mountains. For about twenty-five miles the road follows Deer Lodge River, crossing numerous clear mountain-streams which enter it from the west, and traversing the most beautiful valley I have found in the Territory. Its altitude is greater than that of the Gallatin or the Jefferson, and agriculture is not so generally prosecuted; but the largest herds of the finest cattle dot the prairie in every direction. No sign of mining is seen on the route until Silver Bow Creek is reached, when the murky waters tell that it is employed to aid the miners to produce the precious metals. The creek winds off from the road through a short cañon to the city of Silver Bow, nestling behind an abrupt cliff, and, as I passed up the last hill of the range, I found placer-mines being worked in a large bar on one of the benches of the summit. A creek, that rises in a bluff south

(307)

of the road on the mountain-top, has been turned from the
eastern seas to wash the placers of the Pacific slope and
then find its way to the ocean with the setting sun.   It is
carried in a ditch for some six miles, where it gurgles
through the sluices, and lodges the gold in various traps,
as it carries with it the earth shorn of its precious deposits.
In the Silver Bow district the gold is mixed more or less
with silver: hence its name.

From the summit I could see, off to the northeast, a
road, winding up over a steep bluff, apparently leading to
the high mountain-cliffs which lie beyond ; but it plunges
into another 'mining-district, hidden among the broken
sweep of ranges.   Highland, with its new leads of marvelous width, filled, as far as developed, with decayed
quartz, is there ; but no mills have yet ventured to try the
new district.   Several arastras are in operation, and very
satisfactory results have been obtained.   Still farther to the
northeast lies Butte City, almost shadowed from sunlight
by the towering mountains, and, with silver and gold, rich
copper-veins are there found.   A trial of some of the Butte
City ores, in a smelting-furnace, turned out fifty per cent. of
metal, and the metal assayed three hundred and ninety dollars of silver and gold to the ton,—the rest being copper.   I
saw four assays made from the same metal, and they did
not vary materially.   The ore was selected, of course, and I
do not pretend to say that the mines there will yield anything like such results ; but I mention the trial to show
the various combinations of metals Montana produces.   If
one-tenth such results can be obtained from leads which
have an abundant supply of ore, they will be worked with
great profit.   Neither Highland nor Butte City leads have
been tested with any degree of thoroughness ; but their
surface-indications are most flattering.

From the summit we had a short drive down to Moose

Creek, where I was glad to rest after a drive of sixty miles over the Rocky range with a light mule-team and a heavy load. From the summit, east, the road flanks Big Hole River, a rapid stream that dashes through cañons and over little plains for nearly thirty miles before it gets away from the mountains. Owing to the rapid fall, and the consequent swiftness of the current, its bed is washed in large holes, from which it derives its name. Finally it turns abruptly to the northeast, and crosses Big Hole Valley on its way to join the Jefferson. The valley is small, and covered with excellent pasturage, but I noticed no farming of any account. I crossed the river on a substantial bridge, and hundreds of wild ducks were sporting on the water as I passed, while in the clear, deep stream an abundance of large fish tempted the angler. From the Big Hole the road crosses a level plain five miles in width, when the Beaver-Head River is reached. It comes out from the mountains in nearly a due northern line, and takes its name from a rock that adorns one of the cliffs near its source, shaped like a beaver's head. I dined on the river-bank, and found it uncomfortably hot. We had descended so rapidly from the summit that in twenty miles we were on a lower altitude than the Deer Lodge Valley, and bountiful crops of vegetables were on the river-bottom; but the grasshoppers had appropriated every blade and stock of grain. From the Beaver-Head I took the southern road, between the Stinking Water and the mountains, and had a continuous and splendid view of the Stinking Water Valley,—one of the most fruitful, in proportion to its size, in the Territory. Here, and in the little valleys running southward between the mountain-spurs, are the finest retreats for cattle in the winter; and it is not uncommon to turn out poor oxen in the fall, leave them to feed themselves, and bring them back in the spring in excellent order for the butcher's stall.

27*

The improvements in this valley are the best I have found
in Montana. Good stables are erected on almost every
ranch, and the houses have an air of neatness and comfort
not usual in the new settlements. Among them I noticed
several two-storied frame buildings, and luxuriant gardens
around them; but no attempt has been made to grow shade-
or fruit-trees. It is probable that fruit-trees would not
stand the weather; but the cottonwood, if properly planted
and watered, would give a pleasant shade in a very few
years. As all the farms are on the river-bottom, none of
them have good water. The wells on the river-bank are
all more or less brackish as soon as the snow-water has
passed off, and there are very few springs. Latterly, the
settlers are beginning to renew their improvements on the
beautiful table-lands which come close to the river, and
there they find excellent water by digging from twenty to
thirty feet. I saw but one spring in a distance of twenty
miles, and it threw out a volume of water more than a foot
in diameter.

About sunset I crossed the Stinking Water at this place,
and found pleasant quarters for the night. It is known as
"Ten Mile Creek," and as "Lorrain's Ranch," as it is
called, ten miles from Virginia City, and is owned by a
Canadian Frenchman by the name of Lorrain. He is an
old mountaineer, although still on the sunny side of fifty,
and kicks the beam at two hundred and fifty pounds avoirdupois, while his wife follows the fashion of her lord, and
even excels him a few pounds in the race for the domestic
heavy-weights. He was one of the early settlers, or
rather wanderers, in Montana. Twenty-five years ago he
commenced trading here with the Indians, and has followed
it until now. His usual course in his trading operations
was from Fort Benton by Deer Lodge, through to Bridger,
and around by the Yellowstone. Thus for a quarter of a

century he has inhabited this desolate mountain-region along with Bridger and others; and it is his crowning grief now that civilization has usurped the channels of trade and is likely soon to have railroads through his favorite trails. He has been blessed in his family, and in basket and store. Until a few years ago he chose his tender partners from the dusky maidens of the forest, changing them at pleasure, according to the ceremonies of the tribes; but in 1864 the noble red men widowed a woman on the plains by butchering and scalping her husband, while she was miraculously saved, and my fat and jolly host healed the wounded heart by making her his lawful wife and discarding all entangling alliances with his Hiawathas. No children bless the new alliance; but I noticed half a dozen little half-breeds at their antics in and about the house. To whom they belong I know not; but they broke bread from the same loaf with us.

Mr. Lorrain is but one of a number of Canadian Frenchmen who have peopled this country for twenty-five years, trading with the Indians; but of all of them he has most prospered. Although unable to make an entry in his own books, he is estimated to be worth $500,000. He digs no gold, and would not give a "kiyuse" for the best gold-lead in the Territory to work it. His forte is to traffic with everybody; and the result is that he owns all the stores, bridges, and most of the ranches, cattle, horses, and mules, for fifty or one hundred miles along the valley. The Big Hole bridge alone yields him eight thousand dollars a year in gold. He owns the finest winter pastures, and each fall he exchanges sound and fat oxen, horses, and mules with those unlucky enough to have broken-down animals, and by spring they are restored, and ready to be jockeyed off again for two or three times their number of cripples. His herds are scattered over the Beaver-Head, Stinking Water,

Big Hole, and Deer Lodge valleys; and his stores are found in every settlement, with their supplies of canned fruits and vegetables, groceries, a few dry goods, a profu sion of prepared cocktails, bitters, etc., and every variety of robes and skins. He lives in modern style since his white wife has shared his fortune, and would be a contented man but for the inexorable march of progress to found new empires in the Great West. A few yards above his house, Alder Gulch joins the Stinking Water, with its muddy waters from the flumes and sluices of the miners ; but above the confluence of the streams the Stinking Water is clear, and densely peopled with the finny tribe. Here come romantic anglers and maidens from the city to tell love's tender story and whisper sweet nothings among the bushes, as they tantalize the jolly trout with their awkwardness. They mount fleet horses and gallop over the smooth prairie roads, as if the race was for the capture of partners, as in olden times. It is but a pleasant after-tea ride to sweep over twenty miles; and horses and riders seem to be invigorated rather than wearied by the exercise. Between this place and Virginia there is a succession of rolling hills, and the ranches and fields turn southward into the numerous valleys. The road to the city follows the course and grade of Alder Gulch, and there are few habitations until the miners are reached, about five miles west of Virginia. Junction is the lower village on the gulch, then comes Nevada, and Central is the connecting link between that and Virginia; but all bear the impress of decay. The gulch has been worked now for fifteen miles, and none but the patient, industrious, economical Chinamen can make wages in its deep shafts and drifts and its shapeless heaps of earth. A few regular miners linger in favorite streaks, while others are washing down the hill-sides by the hydraulic process; but only by one grand bed-rock flume can, perhaps, half the remaining millions of gold be taken from Alder. No leads are found below Virginia, and all discovered for five miles above the city have more or less of silver, and did not contribute to the forty or fifty millions already washed from the gulch. From Summit its wonderful deposits have been decaying and sweeping down for untold centuries; and their nuggets slept forty feet beneath the gathering earth, while the finer particles coursed downward until the precious metal became too fine to be saved by any ordinary process.

LETTER XXXIV.

The Mineral Wealth of Montana.—Recent Discoveries of Mines of Great Promise.—The Economical Delivery of Ores.—Causes of Failure of Mills.—Improved Machinery coming into the Territory.—Prospects of Legitimate Mining in Montana.—The "Freeze-Out Game."—Judicious Development of Mines much needed.—How Gold-Mines are discovered.—The Prospector.— His Love of Adventure.—His Dream of Gold.—His Recklessness of Life.—How much he contributes to the Nation, and how poorly rewarded himself.—Rushing from Diggings to some New Eldorado.—The Salmon River Stampede.—The Prospector's Dream of Home.

UNION CITY, MONTANA TERR., September 10, 1867.

EVERY day seems to develop new sources of wealth in Montana. There are now hundreds of good leads of gold and silver in the Territory, whose yield has been well tested, which are waiting for wisely-directed capital to make them produce most satisfactory results. I have explained in a former letter how many of the best leads are owned in small claims and fractions of claims, so as to effectually preclude successful development. But it is now understood by owners here that the time is past when Eastern capitalists will risk their money in fractions of leads, scattered so that none of them can be worked profitably. I notice that in the recent discoveries, some of which are of marvelous richness, care is taken in most instances to have a sufficient amount owned or controlled by one man, or one interest, to justify thorough developments; and this important fact will give the new leads

(314)

decided advantage over many of the older ones when companies seek for mines. Hitherto there has been no such thing as economical delivery of ores from the mines of Montana, and mills, as a rule, have been of an indifferent quality. They have been erected and started as if they had to be run but a season or two at most, and the proper development of mines was not warranted. This year some of the very best mills are arriving, both from the East and California, and in many instances the mines are being handled in the most methodical manner. Although the location of the richest leads in this mountain-region gives the best opportunities for delivering ores by tunnels at half the cost of shafting, I do not know of any company that has attempted to tunnel until this season; and I doubt whether any mill in the Territory is as yet supplied in that manner. In very many cases, companies own only fractions of leads, and cannot tunnel without doing as much for the benefit of others as for themselves. They are therefore compelled to sink shafts to work one hundred or two hundred feet; and thus the cost of mining is enormous, with wages from five to eight dollars per day. I am glad to observe, however, that most of the developments started this season have been by tunnels, and generally a degree of system and far-reaching direction is taking the place of the efforts to produce gold by mere temporary and imperfect working of leads. No company or association should undertake the mining and reduction of Montana ores without being fully assured that they are prepared to do the best work at the minimum cost. Science and skill must, as far as it is possible, economize labor, or profits will be speedily wasted. Some companies have failed in this region, because they had no earthly chance to succeed; and some have succeeded in spite of the imbecility of their direction. Mills have been erected here, as in Colorado, without testing leads; and when the leads intended to supply the mills failed, the almost boundless wealth around them has saved them from disastrous failure. No good quartz-mill should fail in Montana, even if the owners have been utterly defrauded in their mines. I believe that there is not a mill in any part of the Territory where custom-work (crushing for other parties) could not be had at a fair price to employ it; and it must be so for several years to come. Some mills are failures because the machinery is imperfect and will not crush the ores or save the gold successfully. Indifferent machinery may be used for many purposes in the States, where the business to which it is applied is well understood and repairs cheap and easily procured; but an imperfect quartz-mill in Montana is not worth erecting. I noticed one mill, owned in Pennsylvania, that has a good building, plenty of ore about it, a large lot of wood ranked up (worth seven dollars per cord in gold), and the machinery gave out hopelessly in working less than five tons of ore.

Of the mills now in course of erection in Montana, I believe that nine out of ten will be positively successful. The machinery is generally of the most improved order, and, as a rule, they are under the supervision of experienced and practical men. The sad fate of so many mining-companies in Colorado, most of which were the offspring of feverish speculation, has been of most essential service to this Territory, and I look for but few failures of the mills hereafter erected or now being erected. The mines are so numerous, and so generally rich, that good machinery and good management can scarcely fail. I have paid much attention to the mineral wealth of Montana during the month I have been here, and I must to-day repeat, with increased confidence, the invitation made in a recent letter for $20,000,000 of capital to develop the vast wealth of these mountains. True, there must be occasional disappointments by unexpected and unaccountable failure of leads which promised well, and now and then a culmination of misfortune that human foresight and energy cannot control; but the proper outlay, under judicious direction, cannot, as a rule, fail to return immense profits to the owners of mines and mills in this section. The mines have not been as fully tested as in California; but all scientific and practical experience must be at fault, if the Montana mines do not increase in richness as they are developed. In no other country in the world are the leads better defined or less capricious than here; and thus far there has been no trouble in the complete mastery of the ores by ordinary machinery. Some of the richest ores contain sulphurets; but so far the Montana miner welcomes them as evidence of increased richness, instead of accepting them as an impediment to reduction, as in Colorado. But, whatever may be the character of the ores here, when the leads have been tested to the depth attained in California, there is enough, and more than enough, of easily-mastered ores in this Territory to serve the purposes of the present generation. Those who are not especially interested in the mining-operations of posterity need not borrow any trouble about the abundance and simplicity of the gold-ores of Montana. The reduction of the rich silver-ores here has been attended with some difficulty in certain localities, and has been easy and successful in others. Quite a number of silver-leads contain the necessary amount of galena to smelt them economically, and the litharge is worth from two hundred and fifty to three hundred dollars per ton, or twelve to fifteen cents per pound. The litharge from silver-ores, adapted to smelting, contains about seventy-five to eighty-

28

five per cent. of pure lead. In the entire absence of galena in the silver-ores, they are crushed and amalgamated successfully by the process employed for the reduction of gold-ores.

Let me here throw out a timely caution to all Eastern capitalists who have invested, or may contemplate investing, in distant mining-companies. It is perilous to place money at the disposal of corporations without being fully assured of the integrity of the controlling parties. The "freeze-out" game is a common and luxuriant growth in successful mining-sections. I have seen several establishments arbitrarily closed by a few in immediate control, to depress the shares and force other owners to sell at a sacrifice. I could now chalk the hats of managers in Montana who, after using the capital of all the share-holders to prove the value of their mills and mines, have closed their, mills on various pretexts, and mean that there shall be no profits realized until the flattened-out stock can be gathered into the hands of the few who govern the inner circle of the direction. In mining-regions, I regret to say, this is but too generally considered a legitimate business transaction, and Eastern men of fair standing are often seized with the infection when they are sent out as the guardians of the interests of stockholders. There are perils enough in all enterprises so distant from capitalists, without the danger of being cheated out of the fruits of the investment after the risk has been incurred and success assured. Any good mill in Montana that does not pay wants a change of management. Money may be wasted in pursuing wild-cat mines, such as are hawked about in the Eastern cities by speculators ; but no mill-owners here should follow dubious leads to disaster, when there is an abundance of good ore offering to mill-men. I am quite sure that five hundred thousand dollars judiciously devoted to the opening of mines in Montana this season would justify the erection of one thousand first-class mills next season. There have been more valuable leads discovered in the Territory, so far, this year, than in any previous season, and the gulches clearly demonstrate that very many are yet undiscovered, while there are, doubtless, thousands of leads, of various richness, in the mountains, which have never given washings to the gulches. These will be found as others are developed.

Few persons in the East have any just conceptions of the manner in which gold-leads are discovered. They hear only of the discovery of valuable mines, but no one records the innumerable failures. For every one who is successful, fifty or more are unsuccessful. The placer "prospecter" is the pioneer in the development of the precious metals. If low in purse, he traverses the mountains on foot; but, if able to own an animal, he has a "broncho" (native or California pony), mule, or jack, on which he carries his "outfit," consisting of "grub," pan, spade, pick, blanket, and revolver; and he will thus travel hundreds of miles in search of "new diggings." He observes the mountain-cliffs which give any indication of gold. In the neighborhood of most, or perhaps all, leads, may be found "croppings" of quartz, which are readily recognized by the experienced prospecter. Guided by these, he will seek the gulch or ravine into which flow the washings from the hills. The elements decay the hardest quartz, separate the gold, and wash it down into the gulches, where it naturally gravitates, by reason of its greater weight, to the bottom or "bed-rock." Wherever gold exists on the surface of the mountain-cliffs, it has been washing down for untold centuries, and its richest deposit is in the bottom of the gulch. If the surface of a gulch shows a fair "color," it is always safe to count on an in-

crease of gold in going down through the earth to the rock.
The prospector tries the earth by digging at various points,
placing the dirt in his pan, and then carefully washing it
out until the free gold and particles of rich iron with gold
in them only remain. These gradually separate from the
earth as the pan is carefully handled and sluiced out, and
settle in the bottom, and the prospecter judges, by the
"color" he obtains, of the value of the gulch. The gold
will show in various shapes. Sometimes it is in coarse
nuggets as large as flaxseed, and at other times it is in
very fine particles or in thin flakes. If the digging shows
"pay-dirt," he stakes his claim in accordance with the
mining-laws of the Territory or district, secures the water-
privilege in the same manner, and sends for his most
trusted friends to take claims with him, so as to have the
whole gulch, as far as possible, under harmonious control.
One man can take up only two hundred feet, and by staking and recording it his title is perfect until forfeited by
palpable abandonment, which the laws clearly define.
Hasty flumes and ditches are then constructed, the gulch
is dug over as far as it will pay, and perhaps half the gold
is saved by the rude process. If eight or ten dollars can
be taken out per day to the hand, it is considered worth
working. If less than that sum is realized, it is usually
not considered good pay, and the restless pioneer fits up
and starts off again to find more prolific fields of wealth,
while the seedy and unfortunate take his place and make
a precarious living by working what he has abandoned.
His love of adventure is usually even stronger than his
love of gold, and he is easily tempted from fair diggings
to search for better, and from better, if ever found, he is
again tempted to search for the realization of fabled wealth.
Now and then he becomes reduced to the verge of beggary;
but beggars are unknown in the mining-regions, and he

yields to stern necessity, and seeks legitimate employment as a laborer or miner for a season. No sooner does he recuperate his ever-varying fortunes than he starts again upon his favorite prospecting path. Often his trips are taken in winter, when gold is believed to be in some particular locality, and he sleeps in the snow, and suffers exposure that would kill a dozen Eastern men. An Indian romance about gold-deposits, or any vague rumor, no matter whence it comes, is enough to start the prospecter any distance, regardless of weather. There is hardly a gulch or ravine in the Territories of Idaho or Montana, excepting where the Indians reside, that has not been prospected more or less by these sturdy adventurers; and scores of lives have been given to Indian savagery in efforts to find the wealth of the Yellowstone. Even the scalping-knife does not deter the prospecter, and each year furnishes new victims to the ambition to find the supposed rich deposits of Eastern Montana, where the Indians relentlessly dispute the advance of the pale-faces. Thus have these pioneers prospected the whole mountain-regions; and, while the many millions of gold produced annually in Montana is the fruit of their work, there is not one in fifty of them who could pay his way back to the States to-day. Most of them have, at one time or another, been well off, or had a fortune within their grasp; but they waste as fast as they gather, and abandon good claims to gratify the ruling passion to discover better ones.

When rich placer-diggings are found, it is clear that good quartz-leads must be in the vicinity on the hills; and if two or more different kinds of gulch-gold are found, they indicate as many different sources or leads. To find them is often a task of no common magnitude, and sometimes the effort is entirely fruitless. All the hills near to pay-gulches are dotted over with the mark of the indefati-

gable prospecter. The gulches are often miles in length,
and the character and quantity of gold found up to any
one point in the gulch indicate whether any or all the
leads are still higher up in the mountains. If a particular
quality of gulch-gold is found only to a particular point,
the lead or leads from which it comes must be in that
locality; and thus the yield of the gulches indicates with
some certainty the cliff on which the lead lies. The lead,
however, is but a narrow strip, usually from two to four
feet wide, and months are often spent by dozens of prospecters in unsuccessful efforts to find it. Every few rods
on such hills show a hole dug out from three to ten feet
deep. In order to gain title to the lead, it must be clearly
ascertained, the wall-rock found, and a specimen of the
genuine quartz deposited with the Recorder, to guard
against fraud. The place where the lead is found is called
the "discovery," and the person who found it is entitled
to the discovery claim, exclusive of his right to enter a
claim upon the mine. He stakes the discovery, placards
it, stating name and date of discovery, and selects his
friends to locate claims adjoining his. Sometimes he is
paid for the privilege of taking claims with him; but he is
eminently kind and generous to his associates, and they
are usually allowed to enter claims without charge. In
nineteen cases out of twenty the operations of the discoverer and prospecter cease with the discovery, staking, and
recording of the claims. Instead of developing what they
possess, they will start out again in search of new discoveries. They have no capital for the proper development of their mines and the erection of mills; and,
if they had, they would in most cases spend it in pursuit
of the *ignis-fatuus* that is ever luring them to imaginary
fields of wealth. In time, reverses come. Hard winters
and high prices for provisions soon waste the scanty re-

sources of the prospector. The gulches are closed, and grim want flings its appalling shadows over the owners of mines which may have millions of slumbering gold. The speculator or "middle-man" steps in, buys his claim for a song, and then sells it to Eastern capitalists at a liberal and sometimes fabulous advance. After the weary, pitiless winter has been braved out in habitual suffering and privation, the prospector starts again, and repeats the bitter experience of the past, until broken health or multiplied misfortunes make him work his way back to the land of his childhood, or consign him to an untimely grave in the bleak mountains.

We little know how much of fruitless toil every dollar of gold we coin has cost the prospector. His life is one of incessant privation, sacrifice, and labor. He dreams of gold, not so much because he loves it, as because of his controlling but ever-deceptive hopes of discovering richer and still richer deposits of the precious metal. No matter how well his labor might be requited .by devoting it to what he already possessed, he ever dreams of still more brilliant stores of wealth. In his estimation, what he produces has no value beyond supplying his wants and caprices and supporting him in his delusive dream. Swift as the winds, even in this sparsely-settled country, almost without mails and telegraphs, the rumor of new discoveries, perhaps hundreds of miles distant, seems to fly; and in an hour camps are almost depopulated, cabins untenanted, flumes and ditches abandoned to decay, and with the simplest mining-outfit thrown over their shoulders the miners stream off to the new Eldorado. . Last winter the word came, no one hardly knew how, from Salmon River, one hundred and fifty miles distant across the Rocky range, that the great gold-deposit of the mountains had been discovered. None could wait for confirmation of the news,

lest others should distance them in securing claims. Clad
in snow-shoes, they traversed the mountains in midwinter,
over a route destitute of provisions and shelter, and nearly
ten thousand hapless prospecters were huddled in the
Salmon River region, where there were not paying claims
for one thousand men.   Fearful destitution followed.
Many were frozen in their efforts to get there or return ;
and now the tide of gloomy, penniless men is passing
back, glad to find a day's labor at anything to save themselves from starvation.   Similar stampedes are made
every year, and in nine cases out of ten they result in disaster.   Thus does the prospecter ebb and flow from occasional rays of sunshine to the darkest of days.   He flits
from one delusion to another, ever tireless in his devotion
to his dream of a success he could not define if asked for
the measure of his ambition.   Disappointment seems to
have no power to direct him in wiser paths.   A few have,
in the past, attained bewildering success, but only after
mountains of faded hopes had checkered their experience;
and the adventurer still dreams and perseveres, and waits
but to recover from the shock of one defeat to invite another.   His life is spent in mingled disappointment and
toil as he marks the earth's great mines of wealth for
others to develop and enjoy.   But one affection at times
ventures to dispute the mastery of his omnipotent dream.
I have seen hundreds of these bronzed and sturdy men,
who have encountered life's rudest blasts with unflinch-
ing purpose, and each one's eyes brighten, his harsh,
furrowed lines soften, and his brave heart swells with
emotion, as he speaks of "going home." It is the silver
lining to every shadow that crosses his path, and the
crowning hope that nerves him in every trial.   To be
successful and return to old friends, perhaps to long-
separated but still fondly-cherished household gods, is

the dream whose brightness gilds even the dream of gold. But few, however, realize even a tithe of their hopes; and many, very many, after bright promises have faded in continued succession, bow to the inevitable doom of mortals, and ridge the mountain-slopes with their monumentless tombs. No class of men have done so much to swell the nation's wealth, and none have been so poorly requited. I never pass their humble graves without feeling that I could there drop a tear in sympathy with the thousands who serve the world so much,—and themselves so little; and, when exhausted nature surrenders the unequal contest, the hand of the stranger must soothe their fevered brains, and perform for them the last mournful offices of earth.

LETTER XXXV.

The Melancholy Days. — The Tide of Progress. — The Living
Reign on the Oregon.—"Old Baldy."—His Advent and His-
tory.—His Relics from his Companionship in the Deep.—His
Kind Admonition of the Coming of the Storm-King.—He
changes not with the Advance of Civilization.—"Lo" and his
Bride.—The Fate of the Red Man.—How he became peace-
able.—Another Visitor. — The Mountain-Rat. — His Original
Social Qualities.—The Reign of the Storm-King.

UNION CITY, MONTANA TERR., September 18, 1867.

ABOUT this time you would probably expect me to write
that "the melancholy days have come, the saddest of the
year;" but we have no melancholy seasons in the Rocky
Mountains, such as inspired the pen of Bryant by the sober
tints of their autumnal robes. "The century-living crow,"
to which he tuned his lyre nearly threescore years ago,
still greets the settler on the plains and turns his fledglings
from the scraggy mountain-pines; but the Oregon has
ceased to roll on in solitude, "hearing no sound save his
own dashings." The dead no longer "reign there alone."
The belching steamer splashes the waters and divides the
waves of the Oregon,—which has outgrown its poetic
title,—as the tide of commerce and travel steams upward
toward the mountain-tops; and the living now reign in
the midst of beauty and plenty where the Pale Horseman
wielded his weird sceptre in the solitude of the silent
sleepers of other ages. The mountains wear no garb but
their favorite green ; and even in the midst of Old Winter's

(326)

fiercest scowls and angriest storms they change not. The quaking asp withers before the early frosts; but it decks its funeral couch with no gaudy hues. It wears the solemn seal of death, and in pensive loneliness awaits the coming of another spring. Autumn, so full of mellowest beauties in the East, has no place in the fitful seasons of the Far West. The wild flowers which repay the brief summer suns with nature's loveliest offering, fade and die before winter skirmishes with the mountain-peaks, and the few which remain will thrust out their tinted blossoms from their snowy beds.

"Old Baldy"* is my near neighbor. He is respected here as youth respects the venerable in all civilized communities. How long he has had his habitation where he now rests in conscious dignity, I know not. The time was, perhaps ere mortal's griefs began, when he slept in the bottom of the sea, and the swimming tribes, from the leviathan to the modest crinoid, climbed his rugged sides and sported in his pockets. How he came to change his sphere the learned can only guess, while he remains silent. It may be that gradually the waters were called to the Eastern ocean, and he rose from his uneasy bed as centuries rolled back into the eternal past; or perchance the angry earthquake flung him up toward the heavens and bade him stay to chill the summer breezes as they kiss his bronzed cheek in their onward flight. However he came, he was not alone. In his huge arms he brought with him his old associates. The plant of the ocean still slumbers in his watchful keeping, perfect in all its fibres and leafy beauty; although he has chilled it into stone hard as his rocky coat of mail. The shell-fish came with him, hid in his curves and recesses, and found a tomb

---

* Bald Mountain, the highest peak near Union City.

where life only decays, while its frail tenement remains
and defies the elements of destruction. The monsters of
the deep floundered about him as he rose, gave up life as
the waters receded from his precipitous sides; and now
they nestle in his petrified mosses to teach mankind the
story of the past. Whatever his history, whether noble
or ignoble, there he stands, crowned in his matchless majesty, "grand, gloomy, and peculiar," as he holds his court
nine thousand feet above the sea. The tourists are made
welcome to his homely hospitality. They can traverse
his topmost peaks, climb around his dusky breast, make
merry on his uneven sides, and gather the little wild
flowers he shelters in his chasms and waters with his
snows. He marks the seasons as they come and go, and
gives early admonition to all the living who seek safety
from man in his fastnesses, of the advent of winter. On
Friday last he came out in his frosty robes, and gradually
he flung the snow down the mountain-steeps, until he clad
all the cliffs and foot-hills in his favorite attire. The sun
will follow and restore them to increased freshness; but the
Mountain-King will defy the enfeebled rays, and wear his
crown of white until the stubborn struggle with another
summer comes. The few pines which whisker his face
are safe from the stroke of the woodman; no fertile soils
are allowed on his undulating plains and narrow benches;
the precious metals over which he has stood sentinel for
untold decades are the gifts of the satellites which surround his throne, and he stands to-day as he has stood in
the voiceless and unrecorded past, and as he will stand for
centuries to come, in his native, unbroken solitude. Civilization may sweep through the surrounding valleys with
its beneficent trains; the iron horse may make the mountains resound with his piercing screams; commerce may
whirl along from sea to sea; golden harvests may wave

from the Yellowstone to Missoula, from the Madison to
Benton; churches may point their spires to heaven, and
schools may dot the plains to ennoble our coming men;
but until time shall be no more, and his towering cliffs,
ever defiant of man, shall dissolve with fervent heat, he
will maintain his proud, imperial grandeur.

A few days ago he blew his cold breath upon the son of
the forest, and "Lo" and his dusky bride visited me. The
lord of the wilderness came from his summer of idleness,
or worse, to beg for bread, while his menial partner led
the pack-pony, and packed herself what the pony could
not bear. He shook his head mournfully as the shrill
song of the steam-whistle called the pale-faces to their
daily toil; for it told the story of a new supremacy. "Buffalo, moose, elk, deer, antelope, sheep—all gone—all gone!
Injin starve!" was his sorrowful ejaculation. "White man
everywhere—everywhere! Injin must die!" he added, as
he looked out over the expansive valleys two thousand
feet below us, and saw them spangled with cities and
farms. He was one of the few remaining noble specimens
of his race,—tall, proud in his bearing, straight as his
unerring arrows, his blanket gathered gracefully about
him, waving feathers in his hair declaring the honors he
had won in his tribe. His well-worn Kentucky rifle lay
carelessly across his arm, and he stood for some moments
in painful reflection as he seemed to comprehend the sad
destiny of himself and his brethren. "White man at war,
—Injin must die,—must die!" was his parting expression,
as he walked off, in broken pride, toward the capital, to
share the bounty of the Great Father. While her lord
was thus tarrying to contemplate the inexorable laws of
progress and mourn over the fast-receding sun of their
existence, the tender helpmate ransacked the rubbish about
the cabins for worthless rags; and, guiltless of sentiment

29

and indifferent to fate, she plodded on in her favorite pursuit. They were Bannacks, and friendly, civilized by General Connor, who taught them the path of peace as his batteries and battalions swept half their warriors to the grave.

Another visitor has come in obedience to the warnings of the Mountain-King. The migratory mountain-rat, who rivals the Norway in his majesty, and is the most mischievous of his tribe, has fled from "Old Baldy's" chilling frowns, and taken up his abode with me. He has prospected the cabin from cellar to dome, opened his thoroughfares in the walls, and has his loop-holes to command every room for retreat or offensive movements. The merchant-prince of Union City retails fruits, groceries, tobacco, etc. in the basement; and the new visitors have entered into a compulsory partnership with him. One night they will cut a sack of peaches, soften their nests with the flax, and hide the fruit in their innumerable store-houses in the wall. Another night they turn oculists, and deposit the venerable merchant's spectacles in a corner nest; and once they turned bankers, robbed the cash-box of the proceeds of a day's commerce ($6.40), and displayed the perfection of art in the reduction of bank-note and fractional-currency paper to the softest lining for their habitations. Not content with taking cash, spectacles, and fruits, they have confiscated half the matron's wool designed for quilts; and a troop of them would have taken off bodily a woolen spread, but for the fact that they could not drag it through a hole smaller than itself. If "Old Baldy" had shipped me an army of cats with his summer friends, I would have felt grateful; but, as he has failed to do so, I am now recruiting the feline ranks. "Fanny," a tan terrier recently added to the family-circle, proffered friendship to his ratship on first meeting; but, as the friendly offer was de-

clined in a belligerent spirit, she retired under the bed-
clothes to reflect upon the future conduct of the war.
Since then she has been practicing by a score of attempts
to drive a sociable pig from the door; but his majesty of
the kinky tail will lie down, yawn, and deliberately snooze
in the midst of the attack, occasionally grunting a wish
for undisturbed repose.

So winter encompasses Union City in the middle of the
first month of autumn. The six inches of snow about us
are the prelude to the coming mountains of drift, and the
hoarse winds which play their fretful melodies through
the pines are but the advance of the grand army of the
Storm-King who is about to found his frosty empire in our
midst. For two months the struggle will be constant
between sunshine and storm. Indian summer will come
to the relief of the God of Day for a brief season; but the
contest will grow more and more unequal with each shortening day; and when merry Christmas and jolly New-
Year come, the highways hence will be trackless, the sun
will only peep over the mountain-tops to tell us noon has
come, and then slide down the whitened slopes, as the cur-
tain of night spreads the shadows over the glittering icicles
of the rocky domes.

LETTER XXXVI.

A Western Court.—The Court-Room.—Limited Powers of the
Judge.—Freedom of the Lawyers —Chief-Justice Hosmer.—
A Specimen Case.—The same Point decided Five Times, after as
many Legal Wrangles.—Disregard of Judicial Decrees.—Sleep-
ing with a Professor.—Interesting Researches into the Past.—
Imaginary Wanderings over Montana Millions of Years ago.
—Con Orem and his Prize-Fight.—Invited to be a Referee.—
A Reminiscence of the Rebellion.—General Fitz-John Porter.
—Mrs. Swisshelm and General Grant.—He will be next Presi-
dent, if living.—Future Visits to Montana.

UNION CITY, MONTANA TERR., September 30, 1867.

I HAVE recently given four days' attendance to our
Western court, where justice is judicially administered
with variations of which Blackstone never dreamed in his
philosophy. The court-room is the loft of a store, and is
devoted promiscuously to justice, dances, sermons, itinerant shows, and other useful and ornamental institutions.
It has convenient side-doors, opening directly into billiards,
cock-tails, and short cards. A long carpet-covered sofa,
elevated on four blocks, accommodates the chief-justice
who holds the district courts here, and he can assume the
horizontal or perpendicular attitude during the tedious
speeches of the lawyers without encroaching upon the dignity of his great office. Under the laws he has little power
over juries, since he does not charge them, as is the custom
in Pennsylvania. Points may be submitted to him, asking
particular instructions on the law, and he answers the requests as he affirms or negatives them. Here his power

(332)

over the trial of a case ends. Of the facts the jurors are the sole judges, without judicial explanation or any suggestions whatever from the court, and cases go hap-hazard to the juries, and are kicked from post to pillar by windy advocates. Chief-Justice Hosmer seems to have started wrong in the outset,—like a timid driver failing to wield the reins with vim in his first drive of a vicious team; and the team has measurably driven the driver ever since. Stern in his integrity, and well versed in the law, he does his part creditably in all things, save in exercising with a firm purpose the high prerogatives of a court of justice. Half a dozen lawyers will speak at once, wrangling over silly technicalities, hurl disgraceful personalities at each other, play at stupid badinage to bring down the house, and talk almost endlessly, with boundless latitude, in advocating causes before juries. The judge tolerates it complacently, and usually lets the show go on in its own way, unless they undertake, as they do once in awhile, to explain away the court itself, when he bristles up, clears the board, and lets them take a fresh start. One case, in which I was incidentally interested, required four days of skirmishing, every morning and noon, to get all parties to understand what disposition was to be made of it. It was an action of ejectment. The court decided that the record-title was the best evidence in the case, and must govern it,—a principle that would not have required a written opinion to establish it in most places, as it seems to require here. The record evidence being against the plaintiff, he found himself without any evidence at all. Some question —I could not understand what it was—engaged several lawyers on each side in a protracted discussion, to which the court listened, sometimes serenely and sometimes restlessly. The jury was sworn, the plaintiff had no evidence to present, and, instead of ending it, a free fight followed

29*

as to the status of the respective parties in the case, and
the effect of the ruling of the court. Finally all got confused, and the case was postponed until the next morning.
Then the plaintiff took a non-suit, whereupon the defendant's counsel asked judgment, and another row followed,
between six lawyers, never less than two speaking at a
time; and, finally, another postponement until noon restored peace. Next the plaintiff moved to take off the
non-suit for error in the ruling of the court, and another
free fight followed, until confusion reigned again, and the
decision was postponed. When it next came up, a written opinion was delivered, refusing to take off the non-
suit. Then followed exceptions in detail, and a motion to
dissolve the injunction restraining the defendant from possession brought on another spirited war of words, and confused the case into another postponement. Finally the end
was reached; the injunction—which of necessity fell when
the plaintiff was ruled out of court—was dissolved; and
so the case goes to the Supreme Court for review. The
case was absolutely disposed of the first hour it was on
trial, and so it would have ended in any Eastern court;
but the judge was compelled to decide the same question
practically not less than four times, after as many fierce
discussions, before he could reach the logical, inevitable
results of his first ruling, which was conclusive of the
case. It must not be inferred that, because lawyers thus
conduct cases in a manner that would destroy any good
cause in an Eastern court, they are wanting in ability. As
a rule, the bar of Montana county-seats is as able as the
average of Eastern bars; but the latitude allowed in all
Western courts, and the circumscribed power of the judges,
seem to make it the duty of lawyers to fight a case in
every shape, and at every step, until fight is no longer possible. Speeches are not limited, nor are they held either

to the law or the evidence; and there is always a chance for the worst of cases by confusing a portion of the jury. If I had been judge the four days I attended court, I am sure that half the bar would have been in jail the first day, and probably the residue would have been stricken from the roll before I had got through. The business of the term could then have been finished up, with justice to all, in about three days; while, as things are, it will require a month or more of court, and half the cases will go over. A few weeks ago, when visiting different portions of the Territory, I saw a man, armed with his rifle, guarding his claims against the sheriff, who had been ordered by the court to have a survey made. In company with me was the judge from whose court the order had issued, and he seemed to regard it in any other light than that of a most flagrant contempt of the authority of the law. This was in Judge Munson's jurisdiction. They do not play such pranks on Judge Williston, who learned the duties and prerogatives of courts from his father,—one of Pennsylvania's best judges in the best days of her legal tribunals. I have found the same loose system of the administration of justice prevailing in Colorado, Utah, and Idaho.

While attending court, the crowded condition of the principal hotel in the city denied me a room to myself, and a good-hearted Professor* took me in and divided his narrow bed with me. We have both been delving in mines and studying the subjugation of the varied ores of Montana,— he from the stand-point of science, and I from the miners' well-earned practical knowledge. That we should talk was natural; for everybody talked around us. The thin board partitions which divided our little room from those adjoining might have made us master of many a forbidden

---

* Professor Eaton, of New York.

family topic; but we were both past romance,—he bald, and I well frosted,—and we plunged into science from mingled motives of politeness and interest. I could not unfold the walks and chases we had, in imagination, through formations now belonging only to the past, and after strange animals, wingless birds, and fantastic insects, whose history is written only in the mysterious depths of the earth; how we waded through the half-chilled fluidity of a million years ago, dug down into the Silurian and Devonian periods, gazed in wonder at the footprints of the Permian, and came up, through the scaleless fishes and curious mammalia of the Tertiary, to the advent of our race; how we chased the mammoth of Montana over plains now flung up into shapeless cliffs, and climbed the barren, scraggy rocks whose once green surface fed the monsters of forgotten ages; how we sailed on fathomless seas where now are blooming fields and swarming cities, and took in the sportive finny tribes where now we ascend miles above the receding ocean to look on nature's shifting panorama and bewildering transformations; how we peeped into the ceaseless but unconsuming fires, ever kissing the earth beneath us, followed the seams of precious metals they have thrown to the surface, and strained the favorite science of the day to explain the laws by which these hidden treasures are governed; how we paused to admire the few of living genera of animals which have survived through all the world's changes, make one bow of reverence to that single venerable family, and then move on to mourn the thousands that have passed away; how we blessed the flowers which beautify the earth, for numbering among their living a preponderance over their dead, and rejoiced that the birds of song have braved the ebbs and flows of the world's waters and its perpetual changes and have but few of their number as only of the past; and then, when weary of the romance of by-gone years, how we traveled on to that other great period, of which we read with tremulous voice, "when time shall be no more," and called up the dead of these mountain-slopes, ghastly statues of stone,—petrified by nature's great mineral fountains as perfectly as the sculptor's chisel could mould their forms from the seamless granite,—and gave them over to Him who alone can execute His immutable laws. To my companion it was an evening of grateful repose; to me, one of boundless interest; and thus we wandered until I gave way to the demands of weary nature, to be startled out of fitful dozes by the savage whirl of some leviathan of the deep, or the ferocious assault of some mammoth we had brought to bay. But, when awakened, the hoarse voice of the infuriated monster mellowed down into the gentle tones of my unflagging Professor. At last he sprang to the floor and seized his glass. "The moon is here: it is said that one of her craters has fallen in. Let—me—see." And with his glass carefully adjusted, bearing upon the Queen of Night, I left him for the land of dreams.

The delay of the courts consigned me to idleness, and I strolled through the city from corner to corner and crowd to crowd to hasten the sluggish hours. Passing a well-known saloon, a close-cropped head, pleasant face, and muscular frame confronted me. A hand as black as jet, from the application of chemicals, was thrown most familiarly on my shoulder, and I was thus addressed : "Colonel, I'm goin' to lam Jim Dwyer on the 25th of October,—goin' to be a gentlemanly mill,—the most respectable bruise ever we've had in the Territory; and I want you and Governor Smith to be referees or judges. What d'ye say?" From the statement made, I knew for the first time that my familiar friend was Con. Orem, a hero of the prize-ring,

who is now in training for his coming fight with Dwyer.
To the best of my knowledge, I had never met him before,
but his manner was so free and sociable that I almost
wondered whether I had not been his partner in some of
his former "mills." His countenance sparkled with genuine good-fellowship, despite his brutal profession; and, in
obedience to the customs of the country, I treated the
proposition with respect. I did not know but that Con.
had, like myself, been in some State legislature, and that
he could justly claim a mutual sympathy because of common misfortune in reputation. I informed him, therefore,
that I would consult Governor Smith, and we would
answer at an early day. "Colonel Sanders," said he,
"read the rules of the ring for me at my last fight; and if
you want to bet fifty, just go it on me," he added, with an
expressive wink meant to assure me that the wager would
be a safe one. We shook hands and parted, as I declined
his proffered treat at the bar; and, as I have not yet had
time to consult with the worthy Executive, the honor of
presiding over the fight is still to be accepted or declined.
It is most probable, however, that I will have other en-
gagements on that day.

Reading a paragraph in one of the papers to-day, recalled
to my mind very vividly a most impressive incident of the
early and dark days of the rebellion. When Baltimore
treason severed communication between the loyal North
and the national capital, and the stoutest-hearted quailed
under the impenetrable gloom that enveloped us, I was in
constant council day and night with three men in Harrisburg who were struggling in the very depths of despair to
bring a ray of hope upon the country's cause. Governor
Curtin, ever noble among the noblest in the day of trial,
and Colonel Scott, as faithful as he was boundless in resources, were two of the three upon whom devolved the

grave responsibility of acting for an imperiled nation without advices from its head. By them sat a young officer, whose fine face seemed to knit with firmer purpose as cloud piled upon cloud, and whose keen, dark eye flashed with patriotic defiance as dangers thickened around our flag. Sherman, then commanding a battery, was hurrying on from the West, and brave volunteers were swarming from every hill and valley of Pennsylvania to answer the call of their beloved Executive. I shall never forget the answer of the young officer to the question, "What shall be done?" In manner fitting the noble words he uttered, with all the ardor of a patriot, yet with the stern dignity of a true soldier, he said, "March through Baltimore. I will lead the troops through or over the ashes of Baltimore to my chief. The loyal people shall not be obstructed by treason on the highway to their beleaguered capitol." He was armed with the authority of Winfield Scott, on whose staff he was acting; and he would have marched as he proposed, had not the Annapolis route been opened and orders reached him to avoid Baltimore before he was prepared to move his forces. I saw him rise in command as the war progressed, until he wore the twin stars won in hotly-contested and skillfully-directed battles. I afterward saw him fall before the verdict of a court-martial that clouded him with dishonor and made him an alien to the nationality for which he had offered his life. I felt then that he might have erred in feeling or in judgment, but that he was faithless I could not accept, although the common peril forbade agitation for individual justice. I need hardly say I refer to the case of Fitz-John Porter. I am glad indeed to see that, in obedience to the request of many prominent men who were once his accusers, his case is likely to be submitted to another court, wherein prejudice and jealousies will not defeat a just judgment. I never met General

Porter from the beginning of the war until the day the nation was stricken in sorrow by the defeat of Rosecrans at Chickamauga. We sat together in a car when the dispatch was handed me, and, although he was then formally adjudged a stranger to his country, no one was more deeply affected by that country's disaster. In his case there should not be generosity, but there should be justice. The crimsoned surges of fraternal war have subsided. The dead cannot be restored; but if the living have been doomed to worse than death wrongfully, there can be atonement.

I see that my belligerent friend and correspondent, Mrs. Swisshelm, has succeeded in "hammering" Judge Williams into the Republican nomination for Supreme Judge, and thereby done the Republicans a kindness. She now seems to be engaged in the laudable task of "hammering" General Grant into the Republican nomination for the Presidency. Although I have been out of the current of national politics for some months, I feel warranted in saying that her pungent blows are not necessary to secure that end. He alone of our great captains, who brightened and faded in the terrible crucible of war, gave the Republic its new lease of regenerated life; and even if he erred in magnanimity when he was crowned the great victor, neither the judgment of the people nor the pen of history will so record it. No man has more resolutely and faithfully braved treason, either in the field or in the councils of the nation, than General Grant; and the time is not distant when his administration of the War Department will be accepted by all as but a new proof of his unfaltering devotion to the right. If he shall not be the next President, I think it will be because so many days have not been allotted him on earth.

I have been surprised at the earnestness with which several old friends in recent letters have inquired whether it is true, as reported, that I mean to make Montana my home. I had no such purpose when I left the "Green Spot," and have no such purpose now. Considerations not anticipated when I started for the Far West have induced me to protract my stay until next spring; and not the least of these is the decided and apparently permanent improvement in the health of those I most love. I hope in after-years, when the locomotive shall travel these mountains and the savage live only in history, to re-visit with each summer the fertile valleys and marvelous wealth of Montana; but when I seek the shelter of my own home it will be where spring and autumn wear their crowning beauties, and where old Winter is not lord of the seasons. If the same kind Providence that has thus far protected us from every danger shall so will it, the return of another spring will find me again mingling with the valued friends I left behind as I journeyed toward the setting sun.

30

LETTER XXXVII.

UNION CITY, MONTANA TERR., October 2, 1867.

How is gold produced? This question could be answered in general terms by almost any intelligent person; but there are few, without personal observation in mining-regions, who have any just conception of the intricate details necessary to the production of the precious metals. All know that millions are annually developed from the various gulches and mines in the Rocky Mountain Territories and States, and the difference between placers and quartz-mines is popularly understood; but of the skill, patience, and labor essential to produce gold, even by the simplest process, the public generally have no sort of correct appreciation.

Gulch- or placer-mining is the simplest method of taking gold from the earth. Gulches are simply the ravines into which the gold-croppings of rich leads in the mountain-cliffs are washed. Surface- or blossom-quartz is usually found on any hill in which valuable mines slumber, and the elements gradually decompose it until it separates the particles of gold from the flint or iron that holds it captive, and its specific gravity forces it not only down into the gulch, but down through the earth to the very bottom or bed-rock of the ravine. This gold, coming as it does from decomposed rock, is entirely "free gold," and has no mixture of the base metals, so that no peculiar scientific attainments are requisite to master it. Its existence in a gulch is easily ascertained by the simplest implements. A spade, pick, and pan are all that the prospector requires. His pan is made of sheet-iron, and holds about a peck. The centre of the course of the washing is found, the pan half filled with the earth, and it is washed out by dipping and whirling the pan in water until the loose earth escapes with the water, while the gold, iron, and pebbles remain. All the science necessary to save gulch-gold is the appreciation of the fact that gold is the heaviest of all substances in the earth, and will always attain the lowest point it can find. As the earth is whirled around in the water, the gold gradually settles to the bottom of the pan, and, when there is no more earth to wash out, the pebbles are picked out. A little pocket-magnet, stirred around in the pan, will take out all the iron by adhesion, and leave the pure gold or "dust." This dust varies in value according to its fineness; and its marketable price is from twelve to nineteen dollars per ounce (troy) in gold coin. The lowest standard of "dust" has some silver mixed with it; but different gulches will produce gold ranging in degrees of fineness as much as twenty per cent. Any expert dealer in gold in established mining-regions can, at a glance, usually tell the gulch from which any lot of dust has been taken. In the early settlement of all mining-countries, gold is the only legal tender in all business transactions, unless there is a special contract for currency. Every man carries a buckskin purse, and when he buys anything, from a plug of tobacco to a gold-mine, the dust is weighed out in payment at its standard value per ounce.

The various methods for separating the gold from the earth of the gulches are all exceedingly simple while the first placer-miners are working it. They usually make their own "district laws," the district embracing any particular camp or gulch. They meet in mass council, and adopt their code, their land-laws, their water-laws, and all needful regulations for their enforcement. The local or district laws have always been respected, both by Territorial and Congressional enactments,—so that no better primary title can be procured than a clear title under the district laws. When disputes arise, they try titles to claims or water either by a jury or by general meeting, as may be the adopted custom; and from the decision of the district tribunal there is no appeal. Indeed, to demur is not often even safe. The dreaded tribunal of Judge Lynch is certain to be invoked by attempted resistance to the judgment of the local court.

The claims are usually parcelled in lots of one hundred or two hundred feet in length, up and down the gulch, and embracing its entire width. The local laws are scrupulously careful to prevent monopoly of water, and it is economized, if scarce, so as to afford the greatest advantage to all. Each owner, or owners, of a claim (they generally mine and cabin in couples) erects a flume, or digs a ditch, through which to wash the dirt of his claim from each side down to the depth of the bed-rock. Their labor consists in simply digging the earth loose, and shoveling it into the ditch or flume, through which it is washed away, while a portion—usually about one-half—of the gold is saved by various contrivances. Sometimes the bottom of the flume

is made of a thick plank, into which are bored a number
of large auger-holes, just deep enough not to go through.
The "pay-dirt" is washed down over this perforated board,
and a very large proportion of the gold will lodge in the
holes. They will, of course, first fill up with sand; but
the gold will find the least depression in the surface over
which it is passing, and work down through the sand and
earth to the bottom of the holes. At the foot of the sluice
or flume a cross-piece is usually placed, about an inch thick,
to make a ripple; and sometimes cross-pieces are placed at
every ten or twenty feet, so that the earth passes over a
succession of ripples. The ripples lodge a quantity of the
earth, the gold sinks down in it to the bottom, and there
remains until there is a clean-up. Sometimes small boxes
are placed at the end of the ditch or flume, into which the
water and earth empty, and, while the earth washes out by
the continuous current, the gold lodges safely in the bottom. In some instances a quantity of quicksilver is poured
into the boxes to amalgamate the gold. The finest particle
of gold, unless covered with iron, will amalgamate with
the mercury at once, and cannot be separated from it until
the mercury is strained out through buckskin. Copper
plates, amalgamated with quicksilver, are also sometimes
used in gulch-mining, but not generally. The bottom of
the flume is covered with copper, and the copper coated
completely with quicksilver; the earth is then washed
over it, and fine particles of gold will amalgamate on the
plate. When the general clean-up is made—usually once in
one or two weeks—the various boxes, ripples, holes, etc.
for catching the gold are emptied, and "panned out," by
washing the earth and gravel away, and the pure gold will
be found in the bottom of the pan.

The gulch-miners work their claims very imperfectly.
It is deemed a safe calculation that they leave quite as

much in the earth as they extract, and more systematic men with heavy capital follow them, buy up the abandoned claims for miles together, and sometimes concentrate a whole gulch in one company. They often bring water for miles by flumes, and cut a bed-rock flume the whole length of their claims, through which they conduct a strong stream of water. Into this they throw the whole earth of the gulch, and often bring down the whole hill-sides into the flume by hydraulic power. They save the gold as the earth passes through the flume, on the same principles as their predecessors did, only with much more system and completeness. This secondary process of gulch-mining is just now in its zenith in Montana, and this year it will yield millions of gold.

But the most important and permanent mining-interest is the reduction of gold and silver quartz, and the separation of the precious metals from the rock. I have seen this process from the mines to the retort, both in Colorado and Montana; and it is a study that must interest any observer. The gold and silver mines do not differ essentially from the general laws which govern mineral and coal leads in the States, and they are worked in the same manner. When opened properly, they are clearly defined as a rule, have fixed walls with regular pitches, and can be followed by experienced men with great certainty. In most of the mines practical Cornishmen direct the development of the leads. Shafts are sunk about six feet square, usually on the leads, the sides well timbered, and when a certain depth is attained—from forty to sixty feet—a level is run both ways from the shafts, and all the ore above the level is "stoped out." Instead of working down from the top, the miners work up from the bottom. They run a "drift" from the bottom of the shaft out under the ore as far as may be expedient, make a floor of firm

timbers, so as to protect them when they make·their next
level below, and then dig or blast the ore down overhead.
They select the ore from the rock and earth as it falls
down, and wheel it out to the shaft for hoisting up, while
the refuse drops under their feet and keeps them up to
their stope all the time. When they have worked up as
far as there is ore, they go down with their shaft twenty
or forty feet more, drift out again, timber as before, and
then stope up to the floor of the first level, and so on indefinitely. The miners work day and night in "shifts,"
changing from day-to night-work every one or two weeks.
There is no day in the mines : night is perpetual. They
work by the light of sperm candles, and for a candlestick
they use a lump of soft kneaded clay, in which they imbed
the lower end of the candle, and they shift it at pleasure
by sticking the clay against a rock. Wherever it is placed
it adheres: so that handling, changing, and using this
light most advantageously involves no trouble. At first
the ore is hoisted from shafts by a common windlass; but,
as a greater depth is attained, horse-power is attached
to a "whim" for the purpose, and often steam-engines
are used. Foul air is always encountered more or less
as shafts descend. As long as the miner's candle will
burn brightly, he can feel sure that the air is pure; but
when it burns in a sickly manner or goes out, he is admonished of the danger. The engine is then employed to
force a current of fresh air through pipes to the bottom
of the shaft, and the foul air is driven out. Water is
sometimes very troublesome in shafts, and pumps have to
be worked by steam to keep it out of the way of the
miners. The better method of mining, where the mines
lie in hills, is by tunnels,—horizontal shafts run into the
ground from the hill-side until the lead is struck. The
earth is run out on a little hand-car and dumped down at

the mouth of the tunnel. When quartz is found, the miners work up from the tunnel, as they stope out a level in a shaft, and car out only the valuable ore. Water cannot impede mining by tunnel, as it drains all the water to the mouth, and air-chambers are also placed in the bottom of the tunnel, and sometimes above also, by which pure air can be preserved to a great depth. When the tunnel becomes too deep for supplying pure air from the mouth, an air-shaft is worked up perpendicularly to the surface. A constant current of air is thus secured, and the tunnel can then be driven for hundreds of feet again. The miners not only dig the ore, but they select it carefully from the granite. An experienced miner will distinguish quartz as soon as he gets his hands on it, and needs no particular examination to determine its quality. He is familiar with the peculiarities of the lead he is working, and can tell at once whether a rock is granite or first- or second-class quartz. This requires considerable practical experience. I have seen gold-quartz of every conceivable color and formation,—white crystal, cold gray, all shades of blue, yellow, and pink, and every shade of dark to jet-black. Quartz is usually very rich when gold can be detected in it with the naked eye. Miners understand what particular formations carry the gold; and they seldom err in estimating its value. In sulphurets the iron will glisten with a brilliancy that makes any inexperienced observer pronounce it gold; but the gold is infused in the iron in very fine particles, and seldom can be seen at all. Occasionally nugget-gold will be found in quartz; but it is only in rare specimens of uncommon richness that the gold appears in that way. The average cost of mining ore in Colorado I would estimate at five dollars per ton. In Montana it costs probably eight dollars per ton; but its development will be cheapened as it is systematized.

When the ore is mined, it is delivered to the mill either by wagons or railways, where it is broken about as fine as stone is usually broken on a good turnpike road. This is sometimes done by a machine, called a "cracker;" but usually by hand with the common sledge. It is then ready for crushing; and the process in most general use is the stamp-mill. Each mill has from two to six "batteries;" each battery having five stamps, which consist of heavy, round bars of iron, set perpendicularly, widening at the bottom, on which is fitted a steel shoe. Beneath the shoe is a steel die, firmly imbedded, on which the stamp drops. It is hoisted by each revolution of the machinery to a certain point, whirling partly around as it hoists; and its force consists simply in the drop of its weight upon the die. Each battery is surrounded with an iron frame or box, into which the ore is thrown and a strong stream of water pours constantly. On the outer side of the battery, the water issues through a screen or sieve, and with it is carried the fine quartz as it is pulverized, so that feeding goes on constantly to supply the place of the fine quartz as it escapes. In the battery is placed a quantity of quicksilver, with which a large proportion of the gold amalgamates as the rock is crushed, and is held there until the "clean-up." Many particles of the gold, however, escape with the fine quartz through the screen before it is brought in contact with the mercury; and, in order to catch it, the water and quartz from the latter are run over copper plates, from two to four feet wide, and ten to twenty in length, amalgamated with quicksilver. If the plate is properly coated, every particle of free gold will reach the bed of the plate in passing over it, and safely lodge in the mercury; but, if the gold is impregnated with the base metals, it will not amalgamate with the mercury. It will pass over the plates and sink in the boxes or ripples (such

as are used in gulch-mining, and before described), while
the light earth and sand will wash away. These mixtures
of gold with the base metals are called sulphurets; and
they have been worked successfully in Montana thus far by
arastras or barrels. An arastra is simply a carefully-laid
bed of stone, about eight or ten feet in diameter, encircled
with a wooden rim; an upright shaft stands in the centre,
with two arms extending out, to each of which is attached
a heavy rock with a smooth under-face. It is so attached
as to be raised a little in front, while the main weight of
the rock drags on the stone floor. Into this bed from three
to five hundred pounds or more of sulphurets are thrown,
quicksilver is added, and a stream of water is turned on to
it. A mule is hitched to the shaft on a floor above, and
he drags the headstones around over the sulphurets until
they are pulverized into almost impalpable powder; and
then they are panned out, just as prospectors pan earth in
gulches, or sluiced off over amalgamated plates. Some
stamp-mills have metal pans, in which their tailings, or
sulphurets, are worked on the principle of the arastra; and
other mills have wrought-iron barrels about three feet in
diameter, and five feet long, in which are half a dozen or
more large metal balls. The sulphurets are put in the barrels, about three hundred pounds to each, and the barrels
run about twenty revolutions per minute. The constant
shifting of the tailings and rolling of the balls rapidly reduce the base metals and separate the gold, which amalgamates with the mercury mixed with it in the barrels.
By these different processes the mills are usually run
about twenty-four hours on a charge; and then the results
are sluiced off and panned out by the ordinary panning
process. In Colorado the gold is mainly found so mixed
with the base metals as to defy reduction and amalgamation; hence the signal failure of mining-operations there

thus far ; but this season will, I believe, thoroughly master
their most refractory ores, and enable that rich Territory
to resume its former yield of millions annually. In Montana the ores have thus far been easily mastered. Another process for crushing the ores is the Chilian mill,—
consisting of heavy metal pans, five feet in diameter, in
which massive metal wheels revolve, weighing from one
to two tons each. A current of water flows constantly
into each pan, the main body of the gold is amalgamated
with the mercury in the pans, and the fine quartz issues
through screens over amalgamated plates, just as in stamp-
mills. This process of crushing is, I think, preferable to
that of the stamp-mills, and will do more work with less
power and wear and tear of machinery; but it requires
more care and skill in its use, and for that reason is not so
acceptable. There are no other processes for crushing
ores that have attained any measure of confidence; but
there are innumerable patents for separating the gold after
the ore is crushed. Silver-ores are usually roasted before
crushing; and gold-ores intermixed with silver are also
improved for reduction by roasting. Silver-ores containing forty per cent. or more of lead can be reduced readily
by smelting, as the lead serves to flux the ore; but if less
than forty per cent. of lead is found in it, it cannot be
smelted in this section so as to pay. Lead is worth from
thirty to seventy cents per pound, and salt ten dollars per
hundred pounds. The ingredients are too costly as yet
for the reduction of any other than the galena silver-
ores, excepting by the ordinary crushing and amalga-
mating process in use to produce free gold. In Colorado
some of their refractory ores are smelted, and the gold,
silver, copper, etc. all run out in bars together and then
shipped to Swansea for separation; but I do not know
the measure of success that has attended the effort. The

Consolidated Gregory Company of Colorado is working by this process, but has as yet paid no dividends.

After a run has been made in a quartz-mill (usually from one to three weeks), they clean up. The batteries or pans are run down low, and then the mercury and remaining fine quartz scooped out for the process of panning. A small pan is filled with the quartz and quicksilver out of the battery, and whirled around in the water until the sand and earth are washed out, and nothing but the mercury (holding the gold) and heavy sulphurets remain. The quicksilver is then poured out from under the particles of ore and iron, a magnet is run through it to separate the particles of pure iron, and the residue, which contains gold in iron, is pulverized in a hard mortar, and what little gold can be saved is gathered in mercury. The amalgamated plates, over which the pulverized ore has been passed, are then carefully scraped with square pieces of rubber, and the gold (mixed with mercury) is added to the mercury from the batteries. The tailings caught in the boxes and ripples are then emptied, to be worked over in an arastra or barrels. The quicksilver gathered from the plates and batteries then contains all the gold saved by the run; but the gold is in invisible particles in the mercury. The mercury is then strained out of the gold through buckskin, leaving so many ounces of "amalgam" as the clean-up. The amalgam is worth from five to seven dollars per ounce, depending upon the fine or the coarse quality of the gold —the gold that is coarsest in its particles being the most valuable, as the mercury can be better strained out of it.

The amalgam is about the consistency of thick meal mush, and nearly the same color,—the gold giving the mercury a soft, yellow color. It has yet to be retorted before it is pure gold. The amalgam is placed in a little iron box, much like a brick-mould, full of fine needle-holes. The box

is so constructed as to allow the lid to be pressed down
with clamps and screws until the amalgam is compressed
in the smallest possible space. It is then set inside of another iron box, three times its size, and a lid fitted on it
perfectly air-tight, by means of clay joints. In the top of
the larger box there is a hole, probably an inch in diameter,
to which is attached a pipe that comes down to the level
of the bottom of the box, at a distance of probably three
feet. The box is then set in a small furnace, and the end
of the pipe placed in a tub of water. A hot fire is made
around the box until it is heated to a red heat, when
the heat evaporates the quicksilver, in the inner box,
through the needle-holes into the larger box, whence it
escapes as vapor through the pipe into the water, where
it congeals, and is found in the bottom of the tub, pure
quicksilver again. This heat is continued until all the
quicksilver is evaporated from the gold and congealed
in the tub, when the box is taken out, cooled, opened,
and in the inner box will be found a little brick, probably
half the size of an ordinary building-brick, the fruits of
mining, hauling, stamping, panning, etc. twenty, forty, or,
it may be, one hundred tons of ore. The brick is assayed
to ascertain its actual value, and is then ready for coining,
or for manufacture into any of the thousands of articles for
which gold is used In this patient, laborious manner, this
country is now producing from seventy to one hundred
millions of the precious metals annually, at as little profit
just now, taken as a whole, as any other branch of industry can complain of; but ten years hence the yield should
be nearly double, without a material increase in the gross
cost of its production.

LETTER XXXVIII.

The Indian Question.—Failure of the Indian Campaign.—The
Military Expeditions fruitless.—Fearful Extent of Savagery
on the Plains.—Five Thousand Whites murdered in a Year.—
Official Libels upon the People of the West.—The Military and
Indian Agents the Great Obstacles to Peace.—No Peaceable In-
dians on the Plains.—What Professed Peaceable Indians do.—
The Butchers of Fort Phil. Kearney in Council with the Mili-
tary.—No Demand for Punishment.—The Crows and Black-
feet.—The Struggle between the Indian and the White Man.—
How Civilization is arrested by the Savage.—The Pioneers
will advance, whether protected or not.—How to avert Exter-
mination.—Abolish Agencies.—Cease treating with Indians.—
Choose Competent Military Commanders.—Select Western
Troops to fight Hostile Tribes.—Proposed Surrender of the
Bozeman Route a Crime.—Manifest Destiny.

UNION CITY, MONTANA TERR., October 21, 1867.

BETWEEN confused and conflicting telegraphic reports
from the Plains, letters from army correspondents in the
field with Terry, Augur, and Hancock, and official reports
of military commanders, commissioners, agents, and contractors, the "Tribune" confesses to a want of proper understanding of the Indian question. As it is seldom that
any two reports, letters, or official opinions agree, it is most
natural that the public should almost despair of any happy
solution of this vexed problem. I do not assume to understand it better than generals and others who are presumed
to have the very best facilities for comprehending it; but
some things are patent to all Western residents, who have

(354)

every interest in peace, and from that stand-point I shall write.

Some things relating to what is called the Indian war, the public, East and West, cannot fail to understand. It is known to all that General Sherman has had ten thousand troops on the Plains and Upper Missouri since April last; that they are costing the government probably five hundred thousand dollars a week; that no battle has been fought with the hostile tribes ; that no thoroughfare has been protected, and that, relying upon the proffered protection of the army, huudreds of emigrants and settlers have fallen victims to the scalping-knife. So much has passed into history, and must be familiar to all intelligent readers. How many lives have been thus wantonly sacrificed, the nation will never know. Most of them have fallen without survivors to tell the story of their sad fate. I notice that Governor Crawford, of Kansas, estimates the butcheries of settlers and emigrants during the past year at five thousand ; and the calculation has been received in the East with general distrust. Those who have spent any considerable time in the West have good reason to know that the number given is not too large. I do not take up a paper published between the Plains and Oregon that does not record some fiendish savagery of the Indians ; and there is hardly a cabin on the Platte or the Smoky Hill route that has not the memory of the slain interwoven with its history.

The people of the Far West have good reason to feel sorely aggrieved by the persistent and often malicious misrepresentations of their actions and purposes. They, as a rule, have to suffer exposure to the scalping-knife, and are generally rewarded for their heroism and sacrifices by studied calumny. The people of the Far West are not Indian traders, Indian speculators, or Indian thieves. They open mines and gather harvests after patient toil and incalculable privations ; and of all men they most desire peace with the savage. But they have no official relations with the government; and, when their voices are raised in obedience to the law of self-preservation, there are swarms of government officials, known as Indian agents,—but, as a class, mere Indian speculators and thieves,—who are prompt to falsify the condition and perils of the pioneers, and their influence has been fearfully potential in controlling the Indian policy of the government. They are always on the ground, always ready to propose a treaty, and have chiefs trained to play the proper part to betray the authorities into a fresh supply of arms and ammunition and thus inaugurate a series of fresh murders. They have millions at stake. They can afford to pay well—and do pay well—to subsidize government officials to let this carnival of blood go on. Every fresh outbreak is imputed to the perfidy of the whites, and the end is compensation for Indian atrocities and increased annuities for agents to steal. Turn to an official report made to the government in July or August last, in which an army-officer declared that the Indians of the Plains had been peaceable, and faithfully observed their treaties, until the Bozeman or Powder River route was opened against their protest in the summer of 1866. As that officer was on the Plains, he cannot plead ignorance in extenuation of his falsehoods. To say that he is a simpleton would be the sublimity of charity; for he must have seen the rude graves, for three hundred miles, of the victims of the Indian butchery of January, 1865. The Platte route was raided from Living Spring—fifty miles east of Denver—almost to the Missouri; and, when the savages had completed their bloody march, the garrison at Fort Sedgwick remained almost alone on the entire line, and the village of Julesburg was burned and the settlers murdered under the very guns of the fort. Hollen Godfrey ("Old Wicked") was the only ranchman who successfully defended his home. For six weeks no mails passed over the route, and all the settlers, with the exception of a very few who made miraculous escapes by flight, were killed, scalped, and terribly mutilated, and their wives and daughters reserved for a still more horrible captivity. At that time the Powder River route had not been opened or garrisoned by the government. A few emigrants had passed over it and had maintained friendly relations with the Indians. No pretense of bad faith on the part of the government or emigrants was heard of; yet the Indians, in violation of their treaties, swept the Plains, in January, 1865, from the mountains to the Little Blue, when there was not a white man between Laramie and the Gallatin. The official report made last summer, stating that the Indians were wantonly provoked to hostilities by the government taking possession of the Powder River route, was, therefore, deliberately false; for the author could not have been mistaken, and in no way can it be reconciled with integrity.

I beg to impress this important and, to Western men, self-evident truth upon your readers and the national authorities,—*that there are no friendly Indians on the Plains.* There has been no peace since the settlement of Colorado, although hostile tribes have not confederated to make war until recently. There is not a single nomadic tribe east of the mountains that is at heart friendly with the whites, —not one that does not, when opportunity is offered with apparent safety, steal, and murder if necessary, and often murder wantonly. The Utes, Crows, and some others are the implacable foes of the Sioux and Cheyennes. They have no traditions of peace between their tribes, and they hate each other with a hatred more deadly than

31*

they can cherish for the whites. The so-called peaceable tribes are, therefore, only those who are in perpetual, exterminating strife with the tribes openly at war with the government. There were no peaceable tribes in the mountains, or on the Pacific slopes, until they were taught submission by the most relentless warfare. Wassakie's little band at Fort Bridger is peaceable; but he mourns more than half his warriors slain in battle. The Bannocks and Snakes were taught peace by bloody discomfiture, leaving them only the alternative of peace or extermination. The battalions and batteries of Harney and Connor persuaded the fragments of these tribes to bow to the progress of the pale-faces. White Antelope, who was killed with most of his band at Sand Creek by Colonel Chivington, was professedly at peace with the whites. I do not believe that he meant to be at war. I cannot justify the indiscriminate massacre of his band, nor do the people of Colorado; for that massacre blasted all Colonel Chivington's political aspirations. But of the more than a dozen of credible men I have met personally, who participated in that affair, every one has assured me that they found many white female scalps in possession of the dead, and every species of plunder taken from the whites. They were, in the government sense, peaceable Indians; but among them, with the knowledge of all, were the most remorseless murderers, who were shielded by Antelope and his followers. Spotted Tail and his band are peaceable, in the popular acceptation of the term; but General Sherman must know—for General Augur is my authority for saying it—that in his band are a number who participated in the Fort Phil. Kearney massacre. No demand is made upon him for the delivery of the savages who butchered and mutilated, too horribly to mention, the captives from that ill-fated garrison. He was recently in council with General Sherman, and demanded and received powder and ball for those murderers as a preliminary to peace,—as the beginning of a treaty. Spotted Tail may appear to conclude a treaty; but where will be the Phil. Kearney savages who have just been freshly supplied with arms and ammunition by General Sherman? How many severed trunks or bleaching skeletons will be found as mute but eloquent monuments of this fatal folly? Governor Smith, of this Territory, assured me a few days ago that three of the murderers of Colonel Bozeman came in and received their annuities recently at Fort Benton, and bore their gifts straightway to the hostile camps. Two of them were sons of a chief who professes to be at peace with the whites. He does the part of diplomacy, while his sons and followers rob and butcher. A large portion of the annuities received by his tribe go to those who are on the war-path; and he shields the fraud and aids the merciless enemy. Of course General Smith and his subordinates did not know the Bozeman murderers at the time; but nearly or quite every Indian present did know them, but all shielded them from detection until they were safely in the hostile country. The Crows profess to be at peace. The Sioux are their conquerors, and they hate them. While they have no love for the whites, they will attempt to keep within the pale of peace as long as the whites are at war with their enemies. They murdered Colonel Bozeman, and hundreds of others have fallen to glut their thirst for the blood of the whites. The Blackfeet have committed numerous and most atrocious murders in Montana this season. In one instance they butchered a man on the highway to Fort Benton. They, too, are at peace; but no murderer of the whites can be brought to justice by their aid or with their approval. Of all the Indians on the plains the Sioux and Cheyennes are the no-

blest; and the only chief who possesses any of the traditionary chivalry of the red man is Red Cloud. The Sioux
and Cheyennes proclaim war : they confess that there can
be no peace between the tribes of the Plains and the pale-
faces, and they profess what they practice,—war to the
death. Red Cloud refused to join in the treaty at Laramie
in 1866. He said that the Indians must fight successfully `
or starve by submission, for the whites would soon destroy
all their game. He declared extermination to be preferable to submission; and he brandishes his blade for a
struggle in which he expects to fall, and thereby reach the
fabled hunting grounds,—the Indian's future resting-place.
He is the master-spirit, the controlling genius, of the war;
and while he lives the whites will have an open, deadly
foe.

The Indian, in his nomadic state, must henceforth be at
war with the white man; and one or the other must recede. The time was when he could be at peace, when his
hunting grounds were not encroached upon by the march
of civilization, and he met his rivals only on his borders
to traffic with them. Now the surges of progress break
upon his buffalo and deer from both the Atlantic and the
Pacific. Railroads are soon to unite the East and the West
in iron bonds. The miner and the ranchman are in almost
every valley and gulch of the mountains, laying the foundations for future empires; and the Indian must conform
to civilization, or pass away before the inexorable logic of
events. He will not civilize : must all civilization therefore be arrested in the heart of the continent? If so, the
sentimentalism of many Eastern journals, the imbecility
that has marked our recent military campaigns, and the
teachings of the swindling agents, whose richest profits
are crimsoned with the blood of the pioneers, are leading
the government wisely. If not, fresh graves will cease to

ridge the Plains, and peace will come only when such councils and counselors are discarded. The military commander who hopes to plant the hostile tribes between the mountains and the Missouri in peace knows nothing of the people, resources, or destiny of the Great West. The savage must leave it, or die. So fate has written, in characters so legible that "the wayfaring man, though a fool," should understand them, and so enduring that all the power of the government caunot efface them. Already the miner is in the Wind River, the Big Horn, the Yellowstone, and the Muscleshell ranges. The iron horse will soon be at Cheyenne, and settlements and camps will move northward. From the Upper Missouri the tide of empire is westward; and a mail-route now traverses the northern portion of Montana, with the Mississippi as its starting-point. In less than another decade, the Northern Pacific Railroad will connect St. Paul with Puget Sound, and whirl passengers from the Atlantic to the Pacific thirty hours earlier than can the Central; and the commerce of the ancient empires will pass through these mountain-valleys and gorges to our centres of trade and to Europe. The most salubrious climate of the North is on this line. The buffalo migrates northward from the Platte to the genial winters and succulent grasses of the Yellowstone. West of the Rocky range the Missoula Valley yields the finest vegetables, fruits, and field-crops. On its direct line eastward is almost a continuous succession of the most fruitful valleys, from the Missoula, by water-grade, to the Deer Lodge; thence to the Big Hole over to the range by almost imperceptible grade; then to the Jefferson, which joins the Gallatin at the head of the Missouri; thence up the Gallatin to the Yellowstone, and onward to the eastern tide of civilization from the Missouri and the Platte. Nor will the scream of the locomo-

tive be unanswered, as it annihilates time and space in its
westward flight. On the eastern slope of the mountains
his iron track will be laid, and the Montana transit will
fly along the foot-hills to the Gallatin or the Prickly Pear.
In this region are the most productive valleys, the finest
pasturage, numerous mountain-streams, rich mineral deposits, and the best timber on the eastern plains. To possess and improve these varied sources of wealth, pioneers
are streaming from the Missouri and from the mountains.
It is the progress of destiny; and no interest of the barbarian can arrest it. Our government should soon learn,
what every day has been teaching with increased emphasis
each year, that, with or without its aid, the settler will
reap golden harvests in that region, and pass over the
graves of his fallen but ever-avenged comrades, until he
adds fresh stars to the galaxy of States. He will not
found empire upon wrong. It will be the well-earned triumph over wrong, over unyielding barbarism and studied
atrocity. The Indian has become the foe of peace, the foe
of humanity, the foe of civilization. He might have abided
with and acquired all with profit, and preserved his race
indefinitely; but every effort to better his condition has
been responded to with savage treachery and with defiance of all the instincts of chivalry and mercy. His chief
ambition is not merely to murder alike innocent and guilty,
friend and foe, but he is master of the most exquisite tor-
tures to practice upon his victims. He dooms his female
captives to wrongs so cruel that language is beggared to
portray them; and his proudest trophies are the silken
tresses of the wives and daughters of the pale-faces.
With them his dusky bride is ever wooed triumphantly.
I do not delineate isolated characters among the sons
of the forest, upon whom the blissfully ignorant muse has
wasted so much sweetness. All are cruel, barbarous,

treacherous, thriftless,—at war with every principle of enlightened progress and every advance of Christian civilization.

Do not understand me as assuming that extermination is the only remedy. The government, by its persistent folly, may make that the only remedy, by making it the only safety of the settlers; but it should not be so. If Sherman commands on the Plains, calls councils to threaten the savages in words they well know to be meaningless, and closes with the distribution of powder and ball, extermination will come. The army will not accomplish it by deeds of valor, but will be the chief agency in making it imperative. If the festering sores, in the shape of Indian agents, which are polluting both the savages and every channel of power within their reach, are permitted to remain, extermination is inevitable. But if a wise, honest policy is adopted and firmly maintained, the Indian will live and the white man will have peace. To effect this, there must be radical changes.

- *First.* The whole system of Indian agencies must be swept away. With one accord they espouse the cause of the savage to plunder him. They are, as a class, pestiferous thieves and heartless falsifiers, and are justly responsible for half the graves which dot the Plains. They violate the faith of the government to increase their peculations, and encourage war to plunder both camps. They know that Indian wars, so far, have been but appalling murders on the part of the savages, resulting in increased annuities for them to steal. They are the great curse of the West, and have become a blistering stain upon our national reputation.

Second. The government should cease to propose councils or treaties with the Indians of the Plains. They are common enemies, and have forfeited all rights by their proverbial inhumanity. They believe that the government fears them, and they have no respect for treaty obligations. They meet generals, but feel not their swords. They see armies marshaled against them in grand array, but they evade them until they can be murdered in detail. They violate treaties whenever want or revenge demands it, and have thus far, in this war, been well paid for every fresh atrocity. Why, therefore, should they observe faith? Why should they respect and fear the government? For each Indian that has fallen they have scalped ten of Sherman's warriors, and a score of emigrants and settlers besides. The government can have peace only by determining on its policy and then firmly enforcing it with liberality and humanity, as becomes a great government. It must regard them as subject to its will, and not as a treaty-making power; for the Indian is a barbarian, and a stranger to the responsibilities imposed by treaties. The government must *determine*, not *propose*, the solution of this vexed question, whose history is so fearfully stained with innocent blood. The Indians should be told that they must surrender the Plains, and remove south, to a genial climate, where cattle and corn can be raised in the midst of their idleness. They should be sent where civilization will not encroach upon them, and there let them be the recipients of any measure of governmental beneficence. No councils should be held with them, except to notify them of the purpose of the government and the period allowed for their removal. Let them understand that refusal will be war, and war in their own way, until there is submission. What I mean by war in their own way is not a premium for "scalps with the ears on," but that every violation of humane warfare shall be fearfully atoned for by any of the guilty tribe that may be captured, and that Western troops shall be their foes in battle. The Indian will then obey, and will live until his natural debaucheries obliterate this blot upon mankind.

Third. Send competent military men, who have some sympathy with the struggling pioneers of civilization, to enforce the policy of the government. Send General Phil. Sheridan, General Conner, and General Harney to declare to the Indians the purposes of the government, and they will understand what it means. They will be treated humanely, and, as a rule, will go in peace. When they are fixed upon their reservations, let the Indian Bureau be transferred to the War Department, and there will be direct responsibility and justice to all.

Fourth. If any Indians refuse to leave the Plains, do not repeat the costly and bloody farce of sending regular troops to enforce obedience. After a generous policy has been proffered them, let each Western State or Territory be authorized to raise the number of troops necessary to clear the savages from its borders. The cost will not be one dollar for ten required to perform the same task with the regular army. The Indians will not wait for the advent of the mountain-troops : they will go ; for their choice will be to go or die. There will be no Sherman pow-wows ; no silly pleadings ; no idle threats ; no distribution of ammunition to conciliate them. It will be war from the start, and war in earnest,—just what the Indians cannot endure. For every act of inhumanity to a prisoner there will be terrible retribution. Less than four hundred Montana volunteers protected the whole eastern border of the settlements last summer. The Gallatin Valley is the most fruitful in Montana, and it swarms with the finest stock. It is but a few miles from the hostile country, separated by a low mountain-range, through which there are many passes ; but the settlers were safe, for no hostile Indian could enter the valley and hope to escape with his

32

life.   Nor did the duties of these volunteers end with protecting one hundred miles of exposed borders.   Fort Smith,
with its garrison of nearly two hundred men, was besieged
by the savages.   Captain De Lacy, with forty-five mountain-volunteers, marched two hundred and fifty miles through
the hostile country with a train for the relief of the fort.
The savages could not surprise him, they dared not fight
him, and they allowed him to go and return in peace.   The
Indian wants no war with the mountain-volunteers, each
of whom has some murdered comrade to avenge.

The proposed surrender of the Bozeman or Powder River
route as an Indian reservation would be a stupendous
folly : worse—it would be a crime.   Those who have advised its abandonment either want a war of extermination
or know nothing of the value of the route.   Those who say
it is not needed have studied the West to little purpose, or
belong to the white vampires of the Plains.   It is the
natural route to Montana, and the only practicable route
overland.   By it Montana is reached without crossing the
Rocky range ; by the other overland routes south the
mountains must be crossed twice.   It traverses the eastern
base of the mountains, has fine streams and pasturage, and
is the only route that has those priceless advantages.   It
will not only be the great highway between Montana and
the East, but it must soon have a profitable railroad to
connect the rich valleys and mines of this Territory with
the western centres of trade.   Its bountiful crops, precious
metals, and genial climate will soon make continuous settlements from the Gallatin until the waves of progress
from East to West join in the mountain-valleys.   No tribe
can justly claim it.   It was stolen by the Crows, and they
in turn were despoiled by the Sioux.   To whom should it
be given as a reservation ?   No tribe now in existence
could get other than the thief's title to it, or claim it on any

higher right. No savage now owns it; and it is not only absurd, it is simply impossible, to surrender it to the savage merely because he is a savage. The pioneers of the West will open this route, will keep it open, will settle on it, will work its mines and reap its harvests, whether the government abandons it or not. It is now just enough under military control to prevent settlers from protecting themselves. The mere abandonment of the forts and route by the national authorities would be of little consequence; but the effort to surrender it to the Indians by treaty and exclude the whites from it, as has been proposed, would be a foolish attempt on the part of the government to do an impossible thing. If the government can do no more for the people of Montana, let it withdraw from the contest for supremacy on the Plains, and there will be early and enduring peace; for it will be the peace of death to the savage. One or the other race must reign here; both cannot. Which it will be, requires no prophetic pen to determine. After all our weak and costly diplomacy, the inevitable end will be reached, and the nomadic tribes will fade away, either through war or through peace, and leave their hunting grounds to make golden fields for their pale-faced rivals.

LETTER XXXIX.

UNION CITY, MONTANA TERR., October 28, 1867.

You may have read the story of a second Evangeline, that went the rounds of the papers last summer, telling how a devoted German beauty came, unattended, from her far-off European home to find her devoted lover in the mountain-fastnesses of Montana. I have seen it copied into a dozen Eastern journals to show how romance pales before the stranger truths of history in the Far West. It told how the " trysting-place" of the lovers was near to " Bingen on the Rhine ;" how the ambitious Teuton gave a sad embrace and a long farewell to his affianced, as he crossed the trackless ocean and traversed the plains and bluffs of the new continent in search of the fabled wealth of the Rocky Mountains, and how he sighed for his fair

(368)

partner as the melancholy whispers of the pines tuned his heart to sadness. Three long, dismal winters whitened the valleys, silvered the mountain-peaks, and sang their hoarse melodies around the cliffs of Montana, before the faithful lovers could again clasp each other in their arms. But German love was proof against the assaults of time and the fretful anxieties of distance. Last spring the daughter of the Rhine started on her weary journey, without companionship. Patiently and hopefully she crossed the Atlantic, swept westward to the Father of Waters, thence threaded more than three thousand miles of the angry flood of the Missouri, and at last met her faithful bridegroom in Helena, where the twain were made one. The story ends in a neat little white-washed cabin, close under the grim shadows of "Old Baldy," not two miles distant, where I have visited Lewis Vogel and his happy bride in their mountain-home. He is superintendent of the Lucas Mining-Company, and is a highly-educated and accomplished gentleman.

The quiet, sober ways of Union City were sadly broken up on Friday last. It was the day of the prize-fight near Virginia, in which my particular friend Con. Orem and Jim Dwyer were the heroes of the "mill." What is here called the lingering prejudices of early education prevented me from witnessing the outpouring of the "roughs" and "sports" of Montana. I had declined the honor of calling the time and deciding the complicated questions of the ring for the combatants, and had almost forgotten all about it until Friday morning left me deserted. The mines were empty, the teams were not visible winding around the hills, and only here and there was to be seen a disconsolate son of the mountains. They had taken "French

32*

leave" as the surest way of getting off, under the leader-
ship of "Tim," the jolly Irish miner, whose face ever
flashes sunbeams of genuine Irish wit to break the monotony of mountain-life. He would miss a meal any time
to oblige a friend; but to ask "Tim" to miss a fight would
be "sorrow's crown of sorrow." The fight was to come
off at noon, and the delegation was expected to return
early in the evening. Lincoln Avenue, the Broadway of
Union City, was brilliant until late bedtime, as the
"batches" sat about their cheerful pine-fires awaiting news
from the champions of the manly art. But the long, lingering twilight at last withdrew its mellow beauties from
the track of the fugitive sun, and midnight came without
tidings from the seat of war. One of our restless Pennsylvania boys, who must either have a share of every fight
or a side bet on the result, finally got twenty-five dollars
staked on his favorite bruiser, and then turned in for a
sleepless night. On Saturday the Donkey Express, run
by the hero of the knife and cleaver, brought us our usual
supply of steaks, roasts, and pudding; and with it came the
first news of the "mill" from the still exasperated driver.
He had been to see the fight; and, with a degree of disgust that fearfully taxed his powers of malediction, he
denounced the whole affair as a stupendous "bilk,"—a
mere swindle to get winter's grub. "Fought two hours,"
said he, as he nervously licked his pencil-point to make
his pass-book entries legible, and fairly hissed his scorn,
"and nobody hurt! Con.'s eye swollen, his nose knocked
in a little, and his lip cut—that's all; and Dwyer hadn't a
bit of blood about him." He had paid five dollars to see
the affair, and he felt that he was swindled because no eyes
had been gouged out, or that nobody had been killed. With
steadily increasing indignation, he crammed his book into
his hat, and whirled his lash about his donkeys with vicious

energy, because he had been denied his expected flow of
blood at the prize-fight. After forty rounds had been fought,
the "mill" was adjourned by the sheriff of the county,
who acted as referee, until nine o'clock on Saturday morning, and "Tim" and his disciples had to see it out. They
returned sadly disjointed in spirits and by spirits, and
brought the intelligence that Con. could not come to time
in the morning, and Dwyer carried off the belt. Most of
them pronounced the whole thing a swindle; and, in order
not to be entirely disappointed, they had, under the inspi-
ration of Montana strychnine, improvised sundry "mills"
on private account. But for that, "Tim" would have returned broken-hearted. His description of the fight was
less lucid than original; but Dwyer was an old chum, and
"Tim" was proud of the victory. I think it probable
that there was some collusion between the combatants, as
the bets were much the heaviest in favor of Con., and he
was not visibly disabled the first day. The sale of tickets
of admission realized over four thousand dollars; and
probably fifty thousand dollars was staked on the fight.
"Heaven's last best gift to man" was represented in the
crowd, inside of the inclosure; and "Hit him in the eye,
Jimmy," and "Peg him on the kisser," were the words of
cheer the fair ones gave to Dwyer as he sparred with his
antagonist.

"Business is business" in Montana. They have original
ways in everything. Graves are as much an article of
merchandise as brooms, picks, and calico. I notice in one
Montana paper that "ready-made coffins and saw-bucks"
can be had at O'Neill's; and Courtwaite has "ready-made
graves" for the miners of Deer Lodge. "Wilson's Kiyuse
Cocktails" are declared "a sure thing for the blues." Stray
wives figure almost as often in the advertisements as stray
cattle; and summons in divorce are about as numerous as

the notices of hymeneal knots. The last two legislatures of the Territory devoted most of their deliberations to the passage of divorce-bills. Many of the divorced parties married again; and Congress laid its mailed hand upon the territorial statutes and swept them from existence by a single section. The result is that we have numerous wives with duplicate husbands, and husbands with duplicate wives; but such little irregularities do not ruffle society out here, where the air is so thin. "Business is business," whether in matrimony, a prize-fight, a horse-race, a vigilance-swing, or a Sunday auction.

One of the social curiosities of this region is the Chinese population. There are one hundred or more of them , in and about Virginia, and twice as many in Helena. They gather in the mining-camps and devote their energies to working abandoned claims and washing for the miners. They are all from Chinese Tartary, and are mostly peons, or practically slaves to the Chinese overseer who represents the company that sent them abroad. Each colony has an overseer or superintendent, and to him they all report their operations, and deposit with him a certain portion, or the whole, of their earnings. They are, as a rule, industrious and inoffensive. Some of them are addicted to intemperance, and all love games of chance; but, upon the whole, they are economical, and save money every week. The Chinese women in the Territory are all owned by Chinamen; and they are sold or bartered like any merchantable commodity. Some are utterly abandoned; and all are strangers to virtue. The Chinese bring with them, and sacredly maintain, all their religious superstitions. Every Chinaman and Chinawoman must be finally buried in the Celestial Empire; and it is the duty of the master of the colony to see that all have the rites of sepulture in their own flowery kingdom, without which they believe that none can be happy hereafter. The few Chinese buried here during the last summer have recently been exhumed, and are now on their way to their chosen resting-place They do not allow the dead to be entombed without a bountiful supply of the good things of life. With the body they deposit, with necessary dishes, spoons and knives and forks, pork, rice, sugar, sweetmeats, candles, money, and everything needful for a pleasant journey; and the clothing and furniture of the deceased are destroyed in a bonfire. When the body is removed from the temporary grave, slips of paper, with Chinese hieroglyphics written on them, are strewn along the way, to guide the wandering spirit to the last abode of its mortal tenement, so that no confusion may occur when mortality and immortality are to be again united. The popular prejudice against them is very strong, and they are compelled to subordinate themselves in all respects to the interests of the mining population. They are not allowed to work placer-diggings until the whites desert them; and then they must avoid all disputes with the ruling race, or they will be "cleaned out to bed-rock."

I incline just now to think better of the Mormons than I did. I have for some weeks been reading in the Eastern papers the notices of delicious strawberries, grapes, pears, and apples, until vexation made me hurriedly skip all such paragraphs. A few days ago the teamster dumped a large box into the office, marked as expressed from Salt Lake, but without anything on the outside to indicate its contents or value. I at first thought that Brother Brigham had been preserving my letters and concluded to acknowledge the favor by an infernal machine. A short council was held over the suspicious stranger; and finally one of the boys concluded to "go for it anyhow." The top came off without any explosion or sulphurous fumes, and, when

he withdrew his arm, a large cluster of elegant grapes was
suspended from his "bunch of fives." It was the first advent of a box of grapes into Union City; and, as there
were fifty pounds in the cargo, the evening was devoted to
luxury. A kind friend, with whom I had taken various
dishes of luscious strawberries when in Salt Lake last
spring, had thought of me generously as he was reveling
in the rich offerings of the Mormon vines; and he sent
the box four hundred miles by stage to mingle the luxuries
of civilization with the sterile cliffs of the Rocky range.
Although the welcome gift did not come from one of the
Mormon faith, I could not but thank Mormon industry
and thrift for the matchless fruits they now gather where
once was the Great Desert of the Plains.

Master Bruin visited us last week, but did not tarry
long. He came over the steep bluff close by, viewed the
encroachments of his enemy upon his favorite retreats, and
then trotted off in disgust. Scarcely had he appeared upon
the hill, when a rifle came from every cabin, and a dozen
well-armed men were after him. He had the advantage,
however, as he was on the summit of the cliff, while his
pursuers had to climb nearly one thousand feet; and he
was selfish enough to run away all alone, when he could
have had plenty of company and a spirited fight. But,
like General Sherman, he did not choose to have war; and
he hied to the willows of the Madison. We had visions of
bear-steaks, bear-roasts, bear baked, bear fried, bear stewed,
and bear with hominy; but his bearship had visions of
another winter snooze, and went his way. The cinnamon
and grizzly bear are numerous here, and very savage. No
single hunter is safe in encountering one, unless he can
break the fore-shoulder at the first fire, or escape up a tree.
As I have not lost any bears, I'll not hunt them. Bear-
meat, with elk, moose, deer, antelope, mountain-sheep, and

grouse, are now abundant in the city markets at reasonable prices. In a month more, game will sell cheaper than beef, as most persons soon weary of it. The Territory has this year produced enormous crops of potatoes, cabbages, turnips, and onions, and quite enough beef and flour to supply the wants of the population; and the miners will enjoy a plentiful winter.

LETTER XL.

UNION CITY, MONTANA TERR., November 9, 1867.

I HAD the pleasure recently of taking Colonel John X.
Beidler by the hand; and I need hardly say that the greet-
ing was mutually cordial. I had not seen him for twelve
years, when he was known to the people of Chambersburg
as an excellent maker of brooms, cocktails, and juleps, and
a fellow of infinite jest. He has grown stouter, but not
any taller, since he has been living in the mountains; and
he still carries the old merry twinkle of the eye that made
his face beam with good humor when he was among us in
the "Green Spot." Time has not entirely spared him, and
his still youthful face has its furrows, and his locks are
sprinkled with silver; but he is as active and jolly as ever,
and pursues the ceaseless, restless tenor of his way from
one end of the Territory to the other. A white slouch hat
with an immense brim; loose frock-coat with ponderous
pockets; pants and vest of the same cloth, loosely cut;
high-topped boots; the inevitable woolen shirt; a brace of

(376)

faithful pistols in his belt, and a huge "Arkansas tooth-pick," or bowie-knife, in a leather sheath, compose the "outfit" of this mysterious and almost ubiquitous person-age. He is always in a hurry; never stops to talk, un-less it is "business," or to pay a hasty tribute to valued friendship; and whence he comes or whither he goes but few know. He is the great detective of the mountain-regions; works up every important theft, runs down every murderer; pursues every criminal who flees to escape jus-tice; "spots" wrong-doers often before they mature their villainy, and disperses their bands; takes a turn at the Indians occasionally, usually at the cost of savage scalps; runs the militia when in the field; and can tell of every den of iniquity in the Territory, name its occupants, and sum up the record of their previous crimes. When im-portant trains are to be guarded, he is called to the task; and his presence with a picked command has always pre-vented attack. Two years ago he escorted a train with two millions of gold over the Bozeman route, and the same season he guarded a train that carried a ton of gold from Confederate Gulch to Fort Benton.

We had a long talk over old times and old friends, and then he hurried off on his favorite mission. He had spurred his "kiyuse" from Helena to Virginia—a distance of one hundred and thirty miles over the steep mountain-ranges—in fifteen hours, and was ready to go one hundred and thirty miles more in less time, if necessary. To speak of him here as Colonel Beidler, or Mr. Beidler, would make Montana people stare, and most likely provoke the inquiry, "Is he any relation of X?" When "X" is spoken of, every one at once understands who is meant. He has no other name here, unless in official documents as United States Collec-tor of the Port of Helena, Deputy United States Marshal, or colonel of the militia. When he "goes for" a desperado,

33

he generally takes him "without papers," as he terms it; and when he commands, no one has yet been reckless enough to question his authority or dispute his power. He has hung some thirty of the most lawless men the continent could produce, and has arrested hundreds, often in distant regions and without assistance, and has never been repulsed. Many have tried to "get the drop on him;" but in vain. Quick as the lightning's flash his pistol is drawn and cocked, and a movement looking to resistance is death. As an expert in the use of the pistol, he has no rival since the notorious Plummer was executed by his hands. He is evidently in love with his exciting life, and already complains that Montana is "dull" in his line. He despises petty law-breakers, and bags a murderer or a first-class wholesale thief with the satisfaction of a practiced sportsman bagging his favorite game. But he still has enough to do to satisfy any ordinary ambition; for not a week passes without his name figuring in the reports of justice. A Helena paper of a recent date has the following notices of him, from which it may be inferred how "dull" his business is:

" CAN'T TELL.—Certain facts in our possession, very suggestive of the Hangman's Tree and hemp, we are not permitted to speak of at present. We saw 'X' pull a man off his horse the other day, and—that's all!"

There was doubtless a short shrift and a hasty funeral without cards. Again:

" MORE BOGUS.—Joe Logan was arrested a week ago by 'X,' for manufacturing bogus gold dust. He was yesterday turned over to the Territorial authorities."

And again:

" ESCAPED.—A candidate for hempen honors escaped last night at twelve o'clock. 'X' is in the saddle."

" X" returned; but no one has taken the trouble to inquire as to the whereabouts of the "candidate for hempen honors." He may be living; but, if so, he is out of the jurisdiction of the unseen tribunal whose death-sentence is often carried by "X" and relentlessly executed where none but the Great Judge is witness. It is never done without trial and condemnation; but of that trial and terrible judgment the desperado seldom knows until his doom is pronounced by him who executes its mandates. The foregoing items are from a single number of the Helena Tri-Weekly "Herald;" and he appears in like manner in almost every issue when he is not absent on "business." He has acquired a clever competence, and is more universally esteemed by good citizens than any other resident of the Territory. Like nearly every one in the mountains, he talks of "going home" every spring and fall; but, like many others who settled here with the first tide, he will be more likely to land in Walrussia than in the States. I presume that he would hardly toss a copper between solitary confinement and transportation to Pennsylvania. He is still unmarried, and his home is anywhere under the shelter of the deep, blue-vaulted dome that encircles the mountains.

The Montana legislature met last week. The Senate—or Council, as it is called—consists of seven, and the House of thirteen members. This county (Madison) elected the lone-star Republican legislator chosen in the entire Territory; and he was ruled out. His majority was not disputed; but they decided that they did not need him, and vacated his place. Both branches are, therefore, unanimously Democratic, as they call it East; but the name is not in favor with most of its adherents here. They would much prefer to rally under the name "Confederate," and unfurl the flag that would truly symbolize their principles, but for the weak prejudices of their party friends in

other northern portions of the Union, where things are called
by diplomatic names. Senator Davis, of this district,—an
ex-rebel officer and a paroled prisoner of war,—was chosen
president of the first legislative tribunal of Montana by a
unanimous vote. Senator Watson, also of this district,
contested the honor of the permanent presidency of the
body; but he had been a legislator in Pennsylvania
(from Washington county), and his State had furnished
three hundred thousand loyal soldiers, and none to the
banners of crime: hence he was not eligible. One of positive rebel proclivities was demanded, and easily obtained;
and he succeeded two to one. The principal work of the
session will be to nullify the acts of Congress as far as
possible, and restore the laws recently annulled by the
national authority. The only question is, whether they
will be re-enacted by a sweeping statute of a single section, after the fashion of the Border Ruffian legislature of
Kansas, or be considered separately. They have but forty
days to perform their legislative functions, and they will
probably nullify the act of Congress in a statute of about
three lines. In the South, rebel officers of certain grades
cannot vote or hold office. In Montana they vote, and
control and fill most of the important public trusts. A
registry law, with an iron-clad oath, would be of little use,
and would simply multiply perjury. They vote in a very
free-and-easy manner in the mountains. A resident can
vote at any poll in the Territory, no matter where he may
have his home, and they do not often take the trouble to
swear voters. It is needless to say that many "vote early,
vote often, and see that their neighbors vote," besides occasionally voting for them, in Montana elections. Cavanaugh had more majority in several precincts than there
were men, women, and children within the limits of the
polls. They cheated just for the love of it; for a fair elec-

tion would have given the Democracy as much majority as they needed for every purpose. Such little irregularities as voting several times, upsetting the ballot-box in a row, and making the count suit the tastes of the controlling parties, are not considered worth complaining about. By-and-by railroads, free schools, and progressive agriculture, mining and commerce, will come along; and there are better days and better government in store for Montana.

Old Winter has established his despotic empire in our midst, and he howls his hoarse murmurs about us with pitiless disregard of the comfort of the mountaineers. We do not mind his calm frosts. The mercury may go down nearly to zero, as it has done several times recently, and no one will think the weather cold; but when the angry tempest takes up the dry snow in its winds and flings it in mad confusion hither and thither, we are glad to surrender the contest. While the brief summers are most delightful, usually clear, calm, and balmy as Eastern spring, winter crowns his grim visage with almost perpetual scowls and storm, and the snows are but feathers on his breath. The valleys below us are still bare, though bleached to repulsive barrenness, but up in the mountains all is robed in white; and until another long winter drags its weary months along, we will have but the green tops of the straggling pines to break the painful monotony of the frosty mountain-crown. But here, as elsewhere, nature is beneficent in her laws. The latitude demands nearly half the year for winter. The earth, parched by dewless and rainless summers, refuses to rear the forest to soften the gleam of the winter's sun; and the Storm-King generously clouds his rays and protects the residents of the mountain-gorges. If the winters were calm and clear as the summers, few eyes would survive the blinding glare of the sun upon the unbroken coat of snow. It is wisely ordered, therefore,

33*

that the clouds and storm shall rule through winter's
reign; and, when exceptional clear days fling their brilliant beams over the whitened, glassy earth, green or
smoked spectacles are necessary to those exposed to the
sun, if the eyes would be protected from serious injury.
Many Indians suffer from impaired sight, and some from
total blindness, by exposure in mild winters. In the valleys the snow disappears almost as rapidly as it falls,
excepting in unusually severe cold spells; but in the
mountains, where Indians winter for game, they have perpetual snow from early fall until late spring.

Another peculiarity of the winters in the Rocky Mountains is the insensibility of residents to cold. The air is
so dry and pure that the cold is not felt as it is in the
East. When the thermometer is down to zero, it is not
considered unpleasant for out-door work unless there is a
violent storm; and men wear fewer clothes, and suffer less,
than do the people of Pennsylvania in ordinary winters.
Overcoats are seldom worn, save by travelers. The chief
care that persons exposed to the cold must exercise, is to
guard against freezing their feet, limbs, hands, and ears
without any knowledge of it until they get to the fire; and
it is not uncommon for persons to freeze to death without
any appreciation of their danger. Any one about to start
on a journey in very cold weather should ascertain the
range of the thermometer, and calculate, before he starts,
how long he can safely expose himself; for he cannot trust
to his suffering to admonish him when to cease the struggle with cold. Many Eastern troops have been frozen
without any sense of danger; and even experienced residents have suffered a like fate. The dry frost sends the
chilled blood gradually and without pain to the heart, the
circulation narrows imperceptibly, and, with no admonition
to the traveler used to the damp, stinging winters of the

East, and without serious discomfort, the life-fountain is congealed in the icy embrace of death. Rheumatism is unknown in this climate,—excepting among miners who work in wet placer-diggings in winter ; and even among them it is very rare. I have not seen a single resident of Montana who was suffering from a cold,—the complaint so common, and so fatal, in the East. Not a case of consumption has been contracted in the Territory. Persons suffering from it in the incipient stages have invariably been cured ; and those who had reached the secondary stage have been apparently hastened to the grave. The infirm of Montana are those who came here the victims of fatal disease, or who are suffering from some of the many accidents incident to new mining-countries. There are asthmatic patients here who would be glad to "go home," but dare not. After breathing the pure, invigorating air of the mountains, they would return only to die Mountain-fevers occasionally result from exposure; and they are the most obstinate cases Far-Western physicians have to treat. They are now seldom fatal ; but, even after the tedious course of the fever is run, patients rally more slowly than fever-subjects in the States. I doubt whether any other portion of the world can excel Montana in healthful climate ; and the time is not far distant when it will be one of the great resorts of the continent.

LETTER XLI.

VIRGINIA CITY, MONTANA TERR., November 20, 1867.

AFTER six weeks' sojourn in the mountains, I have
made a hasty visit to the capital, to see the legislature,
the courts, and the fashions, and chat with my new Western friends on the corners.   The weather is beautiful,
the sun uncomfortably warm, after it dissipates the morning chill, and we seek the shady sides as we cluster on
and whittle off store-boxes and discuss current events.
My particular friend Con. Orem is out again, with one of
his optics still a little the worse for his "mill" with
Dwyer; but he has given me the most positive assurance
that he will whip Dwyer the next time.   His failure in
the ring has broken his prestige and naturally diminished
the trade at his bar.   He has therefore hauled off for repairs, and rented his saloon for the House of Representatives.   The favorite sons of Montana, to the number of

(384)

thirteen, gather in there at ten every morning, to give
laws to the forty thousand people of the Territory. A
cheap double ingrain carpet is spread over half the room
where the members sit, and one of Con.'s private poker
rooms has been metamorphosed into a platform for the
Speaker of the House. A rudely-carved and daubed
eagle, with wide-spread pinions, is suspended back of the
Speaker's chair; and, in order that irreverent strangers
may know the solemn presence they attain when they
jostle in by mistake to imbibe one of Con.'s "smashes,"
the eagle supports a painted placard declaring the sacred
purpose to which the room has been dedicated. The
Council, corresponding with our Senate in Pennsylvania,
sits a few doors from the House, in the loft of a store. It
consists of seven members, of whom four constitute a
quorum. Like the House, but a portion of the room is
covered with cheap carpet; and the members sit around
the stove, smoking, whittling, and cracking jokes, while
the ordinary routine of legislative business is going on. I
noticed but one man in either branch who had left a State
reputation behind him when he came to Montana. I refer
to Hon. Semple Orr, of Missouri, who was once an unsuccessful candidate for Governor in that State. Taken
as a body, the legislature falls below mediocrity, although
every county in the Territory has first-class men who
would serve the forty days if called upon. Here, as elsewhere, however, politics is a trade, and is not cultivated
for the lesser honors by the best men.

I am glad to say that Virginia City is materially improving in morals. Last Sunday I did not see a single
street-auction, and not more than half as many stores were
open as I noticed the first Sunday I spent here in June
last. Bishop Tuttle, of the Episcopal Church, has performed a vast work in his mountain-diocese. He came

here about midsummer, and has traversed the Territories
of Montana, Idaho, and Utah, visiting all the important
camps and settlements, and waging a most vigorous offensive warfare against the rule of the prince of darkness.
He is able, eloquent, sociable, practical, and untiring, and
rears an altar to the living God wherever he finds mortals
to gather around it.   He is equally at home in the chapel
and in the cabin of the lowly; is never unmindful of his
great calling, and exhorts to righteousness wherever he
goes.   I judge that he would preach at a prize-fight if he
could get a start between the rounds, and dismiss the
"mill" summarily with a prayer; and so highly is he
respected, as a sincere and consistent Christian, that he is
beloved by the most abandoned.   Instead of turning the
restless tide of men to be found here away from him by the
denunciations of the law, he preaches the atonement, visits
the sick, mingles his prayers with the appeals of the sor-
rowing, and tries to get a Bible into the hands of every wan-
derer, and a primer into those of every child.   Here, where
skill is as essential to a successful ministry as are piety
and brains, he seems to be matchless in his work.   A good
politician was spoiled when he entered the pulpit; but, as
good politicians are comparatively plenty, while efficient
ministers are scarce, I am glad that it has fallen to his lot
to teach holier things.   He has an able ally in the Methodists,—the pioneers of Protestantism in new countries;
but he wisely aims to educate the rising generation of the
mountains, while the Methodists teach only in their Sab-
bath-schools as yet.   It is a remarkable fact that the
Catholics have been the first to occupy the whole Far-
Western region.   They have not only churches in almost
every camp, but their teachers come with their missionaries, and they are educating fully one-half the children of
the Territories who are educated at all.   More than a

century ago they extended their missions from Mexico up
through what is now Utah, New Mexico, Arizona, and
California; and, once established, they rarely abandon a
field. The Methodists come after them, and hurl their
thunders against the Pope; but, while they proselyte a
few, the priests are gradually, but surely, leading the
minds of the young to their peculiar faith, and they
reap rich harvests for their labors. Bishop Tuttle is
founding schools wherever practicable, and has already
established a number where the Catholics have hitherto had no competitors. If he will spend five years
in the mountains, he will be the great benefactor of this
people, and must have many stars for his crown. The
only violent innovation upon the sanctity of the Sabbath
that occurred here last Sunday was a negro prize-fight
that came off behind the hill close to the city. A funeral
had gathered the idlers around the Catholic church; but,
while the services were in progress, a whisper of the fight
passed around, and when the priest was through, half his
audience was missing. It did not break up the funeral,
sadly as it thinned the ranks of the procession; but it did
break up the fight. The sheriff noticed the movement,
and followed, and his unexpected presence dispersed the
unlawful assembly, most unexpectedly to himself. The
principals and bottle-holders did not wait to see whether
the sheriff came as a spectator or as an officer of the law,
and the bruise was called a draw as the colored gentry
gave leg-bail. As funerals and prize-fights are about
equally rare in this section, they had nearly an even
chance for the crowd on the score of novelty; but the fight
drew rather the best. The bishop will have things mended
in a moral way by another year, and Sunday in Virginia
City will be as quiet and orderly as in Chambersburg.

The most important criminal trial that has ever occurred

in Montana closed here on Saturday evening; and I witnessed the last day of it. The ablest lawyers were engaged,—Colonels Sanders and Wolfork for the defense, and
Colonel May, with District Attorney Shober, for the prosecution. Professor Hodge, of New York, was tried for the
murder of Mr. Moore; and the high personal and scientific
standing of the accused attracted public interest to the case.
I might say that he was acquitted of course, as no capital
conviction has yet occurred in the Territory, although there
have been some fifty trials for homicide; but the defense
had a good cause, and he was acquitted justly. The four
speeches of the attorneys occupied ten hours,—two and a
half hours each; and, as no good lawyer could talk that long
on a case with less than a dozen important witnesses, they
naturally made half their speeches on the case and the
other half on each other. It seems that they had to talk
their time out, or expose themselves to the imputation of
inability to do justice to their cause; and before the long
argument was closed, some bad blood and more bad
whisky got into it. Derringers and revolvers were therefore in demand before the mellow mountain-twilight had
disappeared. An entertainment given impromptu to Professor Hodge, at the hotel where I was staying, severed
the incensed combatants, and we all made merry over
the congratulations and repeatedly proposed health of the
rescued professor. The wine not only effervesced in the
bottles, but it seemed to effervesce in the secondary stage
as well; and we had toasts and eloquence and drinks until
the drinks and eloquence began to multiply themselves
by compound rules, and anywhere outside of the mountains I would have called the party hilarious. Finally the
bottles became awkward; they would tumble over, no one
knew why, and as often attempt to stand on the top as on
the bottom; the wine was wayward as untamed lightning

and would run almost everywhere but in the glasses; the glasses would not hold still for the bottles, and seemed to break now and then most unaccountably; the waiters would mistake the smoker's nose for his cigar or pipe, and add a fresh blossom to it,—until finally confusion brought on a general engagement, when "Nick Berry," the deputy sheriff, whose glass-ware had committed more than its share of blunders, declared the entertainment closed in consequence of the immediate approach of Sunday. I have yet to hear of the first man who got away with his own hat; and the inference is irresistible that the hats were on a spree while the social party was in progress. The next day, being Sunday, the belligerent attorneys had leisure, and some time in the course of the morning they each re-collected that there were mortal injuries to be atoned for, and three braces of pistols, well loaded and capped, swung in as many coat-tails. Industriously did the embryo combatants search for each other; but they always happened to roam on different streets, and the sun went down on their unappeased wrath. Judge Williston and I walked the streets for several hours, expecting to come across a first-class funeral. He had new clothes on, and he considered it most fortunate that he could be on hand in faultless black. As a sort of honorary member of the bar, I had thought out the points of a speech to be delivered to the mourning brethren of the profession in case of a fatal en-counter; and the judge was just in trim to preside with the dignity demanded by the solemnity of the occasion. But the next morning the war was over; two of the bel-ligerents had, in their haste for an "eye-opener," taken a "smile" together before their slumbering pugnacity was aroused, and Peace spread her silvered wings over the bar and the bars of the capital.

The weather has been remarkably fine in the mountains

this fall. With the exception of several snow-storms, we have had more genial days than I have ever known in Pennsylvania. During this month the thermometer, marked at noon and at six, morning and evening, has averaged a fraction over forty-seven degrees; and up in Union City, seven thousand five hundred feet above the sea, the days have been the most pleasant I have ever enjoyed in any climate. It was so in the fall of 1863, and the succeeding winter was very mild, with brief exceptional cold spells; but the last two winters were long and severe. The Indians and old mountaineers all predict that the coming winter will be unusually moderate; and I hope that they may not prove false prophets. The people, however, calculate on long winters, and prepare for them. There are more social amusements in this city than in any town treble its size in the States. The Governor and his lady give a public reception every week in the largest room that can be found, and several hundred attend regularly. A formal bow to the Governor and his wife, and a shake of their hands, end all ceremony, and thenceforth the attendants promenade, waltz, polka, or join cotillons, to elegant music, at pleasure. When I left, at midnight, there seemed to be no abatement in the dance. I could not join, as, while little was done for the cultivation of my head when young, the heels were totally neglected; and I was entertained by the perspiring dancers as they would drop out to gather breath. They have other social assemblies which meet weekly and vary the entertainment between lectures and dancing. I believe that all meetings in this region, excepting at church and funerals, end in a dance, no matter how they begin. The people of the mountains enjoy life, and never discount trouble. When it comes, they meet it manfully, and with the first ray of sunshine they leave their sorrows behind them, and move on to gather the flowers from the sunny sides of the rugged journey.

LETTER XLII.

The Heroes of Civilization in Montana.—Colonel Wilbur F. Sanders, the Volunteer Advocate of the People.—His Defense of
Order and Signal Triumph over Crime.—The Trial and Execution of George Ives.—His Position at the Bar.—Leading the
Forlorn Hope of Republicanism.—Colonel George L. Shoup,
the Hero of Sand Creek.—His History of that Battle.—His Integrity, Courage, and Benevolence.—Colonel Neil Howie.—His
Capture of "Dutch John."—He commands the Montana Militia.—His Defense of the Gallatin Border.—Restrained from
Offensive Movements.—The Tides of Fickle Fortune in the
Mountains.—The Discoverer of the Comstock Mine.

VIRGINIA CITY, MONTANA TERR., November 25, 1867.

WHILE every new country has its heroes whose names
are justly inscribed on the scroll of fame, it is not uncommon
for the deeds of some of the most useful and heroic to be
unknown beyond the limited circles in which they move.
Colonel Beidler figures in every Montana newspaper, because he is ever crossing the path of noted criminals, and
the records of crime necessarily perpetuate and widen his
fame. While others who stood by his side in the darkest
days of trial, and performed acts of noblest heroism, have
withdrawn to the quiet channels of business, he has continued on the war-path against desperadoes, and stands
without a rival as the terrible messenger of justice. Of him
I have written before and with more minuteness, because
of the interest his personal acquaintance in Franklin
county attaches to his history; and I now turn to pay a

(391)

hasty tribute to several others who justly rank among the heroic of the mountain-regions.

Colonel Wilbur F. Sanders was one of the first permanent settlers of Montana. He had previously served with marked gallantry in the Union army, until broken health compelled him to abandon a calling that enlisted his whole heart and was an inviting theatre for his manly courage. When Governor Edgerton, his uncle, was appointed Governor of the Territory, Colonel Sanders came with him, in search of health, adventure, and fortune. He had already attained a high position at the Ohio bar, for one of his years ; and on his arrival he devoted himself to the practice of his profession. He was here before the courts were organized, and took a prominent part in introducing forms of law, and in winning for them that respect so often denied in new countries, but so essential to the order and safety of society. When he came, Plummer was in the zenith of his power, and the whole energy of the law was paralyzed by desperate and corrupt officers charged with its execution. Crime was supreme and defiant. Murders were committed in open day, without fear of retribution, and robberies were almost of hourly occurrence. A reign of terror spread its dark pall over the camps and settlements of Montana, and none dared to demand the punishment of the criminals who publicly gloried in their evil deeds. In the fall of 1863 the forbearance of the better class of citizens was exhausted, and the resistance to crime took form in the organization of a vigilance committee. The desperadoes were confederated by oaths and signs ; they knew their men, and could command them at any point in the shortest possible period ready for action. But the very perils which beset the effort to redeem Montana from the thraldom of crime made strong men stronger, and, with the highest resolve to do and dare for the right, George Ives, one of the desperado leaders, was arrested and arraigned before a court of the people. Several thousand spectators were present, all armed; but how many of them were ready to obey the secret signal of Plummer's band and murder the chief actors, no one friendly to order could judge. With their lives in their hands they erected the new altar of justice, selected a jury of twenty-four true men to pass upon the guilt of the prisoner, and called for a prosecutor. It was the most perilous of all the positions in the court, and men naturally hesitated. A young advocate, tall and slender in stature, but with intelligence and determination written in every feature of his face, came forward, and, in the name of the people, charged that George Ives was a murderer and unfit to live. His bearing told, more eloquently than could language, that either himself or the criminal must die; and his clear voice rang out over the plain as he pleaded the cause of order with a fervor and ability that thrilled the audience, and paralyzed the majority who had come determined to save their companion by fresh murder if necessary. The jury rendered their verdict, declaring the prisoner guilty. It was confidently expected by his friends that the most the court would dare to do would be to pronounce the sentence of banishment; but they little knew the earnestness of the citizens. While the desperadoes were clamoring for the submission of the sentence to the audience, the tall, gaunt form of the young prosecutor appeared on a wagon, and, with his eyes flashing his invincible will, he moved that "George Ives be *forthwith* hung by the neck until he is dead!" Before the well-organized friends of the accused recovered from this bold and unexpected movement, the motion was carried; and not until the sudden clicks of the guns of the guard were heard simultaneously with the order to "fall back from the pris-

oner," did they appreciate that their comrade was doomed
to die. With matchless skill the advocate for the people
had carried his case to judgment, and the murderers were
appalled as in less than an hour they saw Ives drop in the
death-noose. The people, clad in the strong armor of justice, had triumphed in the very presence of the heroes of
crime; and the execution of the stern judgment fore-
shadowed the fate of all the robber's band. Before another autumn chilled the mountain-breezes, not one of
them was among the living. The young advocate who
thus braved defiant crime in the very citadel of its power,
and hurled back the fearful tide of disorder, was Colonel
Sanders; and he is to-day beloved by every good citizen,
and hated by every wrong-doer, for his sublime heroism
in behalf of the right. He is still at the bar, and tries one
side of every important case in his district. The traces of
his early efforts against the lawless are still visible in his
peerless invective when it is warranted at the bar; but he
is known to be brave to a fault, and as generous and noble
as he is brave, and pretenders do not seek notoriety by
testing the qualities of his manhood. He is still in the
prime of life, and, but for his fidelity to peace and order,
and his earnest devotion to his country's cause, he would
have been in Congress from the organization of the Territory, and continued to represent Montana until he voluntarily surrendered the trust. He has twice led the forlorn
hope of the Republicans,—first in 1864, and again in 1867;
and, in the face of predominant treason, he has been boldly
faithful to freedom and to all the logical results of treason's
bloody failure. With abiding faith in the ultimate triumph
of correct principles, he will battle on until churches and
schools and railroads come to his aid and give victory to
a better civilization. When that triumph shall have been
won, he will be the crowning victor, and wear its richest
laurels.

Colonel George L. Shoup, the hero of Sand Creek, Colorado, is now a citizen of Montana. You might meet him every day for a year and not know where he has been, what he has done, and what his purposes are, unless closely questioned. He is tall, well formed, has a countenance that denotes unmistakably the integrity of all his actions, and his soft blue eyes and pleasant, unaffected manners stamp him as anything but a man of cruel instincts. He has spent many years in the mountains, has amassed an ample fortune, and mingles with his business many generous deeds of which the world knows not. On but one subject can he be aroused out of the even tenor of his way. When you speak of "friendly Indians" in his presence, his eyes kindle and his reserve is broken. It is the key that unlocks the only passion that is stronger than himself. He has spent the most of his days in the Indian country, and has never harmed them save in self-defense. The degraded fragmentary bands which wander about Salmon River, where he does business, never appeal to his generosity in vain; but he well knows that they will steal and murder when they think they can do so with safety. He has been among all the tribes, and has but one story for the race,—that they will murder wantonly when they can hope to escape detection. He credits them with no friendship for the whites beyond what is dictated by fear. He was in Colorado when the horrible butcheries of 1863 aroused the settlers to the deepest hostility, and he raised a regiment to serve in the Indian war. At the battle of Sand Creek, known East as the Chivington massacre, he was in immediate command, and directed the movements of the troops in the engagement. It would have been well for the government, and for the people of the Far West, had his judgment been accepted and his actions approved; but dishonest Indians, and still worse

Indian agents, urged that the Sand Creek Indians were not hostile, and Congress paid them for their loss of stolen property, and atoned for their loss of warriors by generous annuities. Colonel Shoup has informed me—and his veracity has never been impeached where he is known—that among the killed was one leader of an Indian band that had robbed a train but a short time before; that he recovered horses and mules belonging to different trains previously captured by Indians; that three scalps from white women, not yet dry, were seen and examined by himself and others, and that a vast amount of other plunder, taken from trains and families, was found in their camp. The battle, he admits, was a butchery, and because it could be nothing less. By the side of the warriors the squaws and children, old enough to fight, fought with the desperation of fiends; and the battle could not cease until the Indians were killed, because they would not surrender. Children were killed because they were within the Indian rifle-pits, and could not wholly escape. In government circles he would be called a murderer, and an instigator of war with the Indians; but where he is known his valor, integrity, and humanity are regarded as the conspicuous traits of his character. He is not a contractor nor a politician, and he could buy anything in the Montana market to-day twenty per cent. lower than could the general government, because his credit is better and his faith unbroken. When Montana shall have passed through the hard ordeal that must form a part of the history of all new Territories, her peaceful and prosperous advancement will be greatly indebted to the unpretending but efficient efforts of Colonel Shoup.

Colonel Neil Howie, United States Marshal of the Territory, is another of those who have marked the history of Montana with creditable fame. He was a resident here in the dark days when the desperate struggle between order and chaos came; and in the midst of the conflict, when every active friend of society was pointed out for sacrifice, he performed the most conspicuous act of individual heroism that is recorded in the many noble acts of noble men in the mountains. "Dutch John," one of the most merciless outlaws, who had committed a number of atrocious murders, was met on the highway by Colonel Howie and his train. In vain did the colonel appeal to his men to aid him in arresting the desperado; and finally, when he saw that assistance could not be had, he resolved to arrest him single-handed or die in the attempt. He followed the criminal, and, when seen, his errand could not be misunderstood. When the rifle of the murderer was about to be leveled, quick as the lightning's flash Howie's trusty pistol was drawn, and any effort at resistance would have been instant death. He had "the drop," and there could then be no contest. He captured the villain, and brought him to the gallows. He is of medium size, much the build of Colonel Beidler, but a little taller, and is quite muscular. He has the inevitable blue eyes which seem to prevail among the heroes of the West, and as genial and amiable a face as could be found in a thousand. During the last summer he commanded the Montana volunteers; and his name was a host in protecting the exposed valleys. General Sherman might have been at Bozeman City with five thousand troops, and the people of the Gallatin could not have escaped the scalping-knife of the savage; but Colonel Howie, with less than four hundred men, protected one hundred miles of exposed frontier but a little distance from the hostile tribes. The Indians knew that he was on the defensive, and would so remain unless they inaugurated war against the settlers. They knew also that, if provoked to move against them, he would give them war in their own way,—just such war as the Indian will never invite; and there was peace here while the hostile bands traveled one thousand miles to assail regular troops. A scoutiug-party was sent out by Colonel Howie to ascertain the movements of the Indians. The party was assailed by a large band, and two killed and three wounded. Colonel Howie, with thirty men from his command, rescued the wounded and recovered the dead in the face of three hundred savages. The next day a reinforcement of a hundred men joined him; but he dared not advance, for Terry had forbidden it, lest he should bring on an Indian war; and he returned to his camp fretting like a caged eagle over the imbecility of great commanders. He is now back from the field, as the Indians, under the policy of buying peace with money, ammunition, arms, etc., will keep quiet during the winter, when they could be fought successfully; and next spring he will doubtless return to the border to protect the settlers, while the regular army will waste millions, protract the war, and sacrifice fresh thousands of emigrants and residents to military stupidity and Indian savagery. He is now quietly performing his duties as United States Marshal, with Colonel Beidler as his assistant, and is honored by all classes for his high social qualities and true heroism.

The history of many men in the mining-regions would make romance pale before the truthful portrayal of personal adventure and the variable tides of fortune. The name of Comstock is known in every business-circle on the continent. The celebrated Comstock mine in Nevada, now operated by companies whose stocks command from thirty to forty millions on the market, was discovered by an old prospector of that name, who sold his interest for less than three thousand dollars, part of which was paid in trade. When in Deer Lodge, last August, I found him gaining a precarious subsistence by working in the gulches of that county. The tide in his affairs was not "taken at the flood;" and he is in poverty while millions have been made by others as the fruits of his labors. "Every one has his chance some time," is a saying of the miners; and it is in the main true. I have scarcely found a miner, among the hundreds I have seen, who did not at one time or another have fortune within his reach. Many have acquired a competence, and wasted it as rapidly as it was gathered; and nearly all have had opportunities which, if properly used, would have given success. But, with all the fortunes they have acquired, and all they have had within their grasp, there are very few indeed who could leave the mines better off than they came. They linger from spring to fall, and from fall to spring, always hoping to gather wealth and return to old friends; but disappointments follow in continued succession, or dissipation defies the best resolves, and they remain, and will remain, until, after "life's fitful fever," they will sleep in the unmarked tombs of the mountains.

LETTER XLIII.

The Pacific Railroads.—The Central Route.—Its Impassable Snows.—The Great Achievement of a Pacific Railroad.—The Northern Pacific Railroad Line.—The Growth of the Northwestern Territories.—A Continuous Line of Civilization from the Atlantic to Puget Sound.—Advantage of Distance in the Northern Route.— The Western Terminus nearer the Asiatic Commercial Ports than San Francisco.—It crosses the Great Rivers of the West.—Advantage in its Construction. —Climate on the Northern Route.—Lower Altitude.—Succession of Hot Springs.—The Incalculable Development it will inspire.— Changes in the Present Centres of Trade.—The Commerce of the World will pay Tribute to the Northern Railroad.

UNION CITY, MONTANA TERR., December 2, 1867.

THE nation has wisely given its credit to make the great Central Pacific Railroad line an established fact. Already the iron horse climbs the Sierra Nevadas from the golden slopes of California, and traverses the Eastern Plains from the Missouri to the base of the mountains at Cheyenne. The year 1870 will unite the Union and the Central iron bonds across the continent in the valley of Utah, and the tourist may then worship one Sabbath in Boston and the next in San Francisco. In the mean time the line from St. Louis is moving westward by the Smoky Hill to Denver, and thence it will turn south, through New Mexico and Arizona, to the Gulf of Mexico, or northwest, along the eastern foot-hills, through the fertile valleys of the Bozeman route, to the Northern line on the Yellowstone or Gallatin.

(400)

While the construction of the Central line was the first necessity of the nation, the rapid march of progress to the north has left it as but the secondary highway from the Atlantic to the Pacific. Its distance is some five hundred miles more ; its grades heavier ; its highest altitude nearly three thousand feet greater ; its snows deeper ; its winters much more severe ; and from the eastern base of the Rocky range to the western base of the Sierra Nevada—a distance of probably twelve hundred miles—the valley of the Utah alone is productive of freights, while for not less than four months of the year five hundred miles of the road will be often impassable. I crossed the summit of the Rocky range at Bridger's Pass in a terrible snow-storm on the 6th of June, and on the 9th passed over five feet of snow on the Wasatch range. But I hope that our proverbial energy and perseverance will at least measurably overcome these adverse elements. Whether it shall be done or not, this great highway was an imperative necessity, and Congress, and those who have prosecuted the enterprise with such wonderful celerity, deserve the gratitude of the nation. It will make new fields to blossom where now are waste and desolation, bring fresh thousands of pioneers in the valleys and mountains along its line, and develop new sources of industry and new mines of wealth, until the bleak cliffs and the "American Desert" unite in swelling the triumphant progress of the New World. So much has been well done. The credit of the government, so liberally given when the undertaking was a doubtful one, has not drained the Treasury of any of its sadly-needed revenues, and the time is past when national responsibility need be apprehended. The railroad will be more than able to maintain its own credit and care for its liabilities, both government and corporate ; and the nation is greatly enriched, without the danger of loss.

35

But, since the construction of the Central line has been determined upon, the march of civilization has not been sluggish in the North. Montana has opened with her thirty or forty thousand population, and has contributed one hundred million dollars of gold to the wealth of the world. Idaho has nearly an equal population, and is pouring out her millions annually of the precious metals. West of the mountains, Oregon and Washington have far advanced in agriculture, in addition to their mineral wealth. Hundreds of miles to the north is our newly-acquired Russian America, with its mines, lumber, furs, and fish; while between lie the British Possessions, bidding us to prepare for protection to our extended borders. Nor has the march of progress been wholly to the Far Northwest. From the centre of Montana, and from the Missouri and the Platte, the tide of civilization has been coursing onward, until the pioneers are scattered through the hills and valleys from the Gallatin to the mouth of the Yellowstone, and from the Upper Missouri to the Eastern plains. When the Central route is blockaded by snows, the sturdy ranchmen of Montana are herding their flocks in the mild climate of the Gallatin and far down the Yellowstone, and will bring them back in the spring for the butcher's block. There is now an almost continuous line of people and commerce from the Atlantic to Puget Sound; and, but for the scalping-knife of the savage, towns would be reared as by magic, and the bleached plains of to-day would wave with golden harvests in another year.

The construction of the Northern Pacific Railroad will enable New York to reach the Pacific in less than three thousand miles, while to San Francisco the distance is nearly three thousand five hundred. From an apparently reliable work before me (Hall's "Guide to the Great West"), the exact difference in favor of the Northern route over the Central is five hundred and forty-two miles from Boston, five hundred and twenty-five from New York, four hundred and eighty-five from Cincinnati, three hundred and sixty-four from St. Louis, five hundred and forty-two from Chicago; and from every port east of New Orleans the difference is from one hundred and twenty to over five hundred miles in favor of this line. This great disparity in the distances of the two routes must, in itself, tell decidedly in their relative success when both are completed; and it should now be conclusive of the immediate construction of the Northern Pacific Road, if all other advantages were only equal. But in every other essential respect the Northern route has substantial advantages over the Central. The New York, Philadelphia, and Boston merchants will not only reach the Pacific five hundred miles quicker than by the Central, but when at Puget Sound they are several hundred miles nearer the centres of trade in Australia, China, and Japan; and the English merchant will reach the trade of China, across our continent, in nearly half the time he now reaches it by Suez. In 1860 the value of English exports to China was nearly thirty million dollars, and the imports from Shanghai—the nearest important port in China from Puget Sound—to England were over thirty million pounds of tea and twenty thousand bales of silk, and twenty million pounds of tea and two thousand bales of silk to the United States. Puget Sound has spacious harbors as secure as any on either coast, and is surrounded with fine timber and immense beds of excellent coal, from which California draws her main supply. A prosperous and progressing agriculture is back of it in Oregon, Washington, and Montana; and the finest water-powers give promise of extensive manufacturing in the future.

But the shorter line between the Atlantic and the Pacific, and from thence to China and Japan, is not the only mate-

rial advantage in favor of the Northern route. It crosses
the great rivers, the great "natural highways" of trade,
and the cost and time necessary to its construction are
thereby sensibly diminished. The Central line had to be
built from but two points,—the Missouri and the Sacra-
mento. No intermediate point could be supplied with
iron, timber, machinery, provisions, etc.; and the two parties must patiently plod on until they meet. There are no
rivers by which material can be transported to any part of
the route, and every pound of iron for the middle portion
of the road has to cross the Rocky range from the Missouri, or plow the ocean to San Francisco, thence to cross
the Sierra Nevada. On the Northern route, parties can
work east and west from the Missouri, others can work
east and west from the Yellowstone, and others can work
east and west from the Columbia, and all can be supplied
with iron, locomotives, provisions, and all necessary material at comparatively low-cost. There are but few sections
on the route that will not supply an abundance of good
timber. The great mountains can be crossed at a much
lower altitude and with better grade than on the Central;
and the cost of grading the entire road will not much ex-
ceed two-thirds the cost of grading the other. I would regard it as a safe estimate that the cost of the road per mile
will be fully twenty per cent. less than that of the Central.

One of the essential advantages of the Northern route
is its climate. The Big-Hole Pass, regarded as the greatest obstacle in winter, is now traveled by teams all seasons
of the year; and the testimony of old residents, who have
traversed the mountains for a quarter of a century, is that
the snow is not a serious impediment on the proposed line.
Captain Mullan, who opened the wagon-road to the Pacific,
and wintered in the mountains, says, in his official report,
that " the snow will offer no great obstacle to travel with

horses or locomotives from the Missouri to the Columbia."
On the continuous line of valleys from the Yellowstone to
Missoula—nearly one-third the distance of the entire line,
and in the heart of the mountains—stock is grazed every
winter without hay or feed. The buffalo migrates north
to the sweeter grasses and more salubrious climate of the
Yellowstone, and Missoula raises the earliest and finest
vegetables of any of the mountain-valleys, and is now growing fruit under the very frowns of the Bitter Root and
Rocky ranges. The base of the mountains on this line
has the same mean temperature as is found on the Missouri,
seven degrees farther south. Hot springs abound on almost
all the waters in this region. The Madison has a school
of boiling geysers for its source. They fling their columns
up from thirty to eighty feet in the air, and soften the atmosphere for miles around and for an incredible distance
along its course. The Yellowstone has many such springs,
of varied temperatures, emptying into its waters. I have
found these hot springs in every valley; and their effect
upon the climate is wonderful. Captain Mullan, speaking
of them, says, " On either side, north and south, are
walls of cold air, and which are so clearly perceptible that
you always detect the river when you are on its shores."
A writer in the " Atlantic Monthly" describes these currents as " a river of hot wind, which is not only one of the
most remarkable features of the climatology of the continent, but which is destined to have a great bearing upon
the civilization of this portion of the continent. They
sweep through the passes with the precision and regularity
of the Gulf Stream of the Atlantic." Thus, while the passes
in the British Possessions, where these currents are not
known, are closed by snow in winter, the passes on the
line of the Northern route seldom present over two feet of
snow to contend with.

35*

There is another consideration that should determine the action of the government in favor of the construction of this road. It is the incalculable development of material and permanent wealth it must effect. I have traversed the chief valleys of Montana, from the eastern extremity of the Gallatin to the western extremity of the Deer Lodge, and saw them when their rich harvest was ready for the reaper. I have tasted the luscious fruits of Missoula, still farther west, and heard the reports of those who have explored the Yellowstone in all seasons of the year. The fruitfulness of these valleys, with the rudest cultivation, would be accepted by most Eastern readers as a romance, if truthfully portrayed. The country from St. Paul to the Missouri, on a western line, is well known; and from the Missouri to the Yellowstone, on the same line, there are few obstacles to a railroad; while valuable farming-lands and timber are found most of the way. From the point where the Yellowstone is reached, it would seem that Nature had marked out this great highway to the Pacific. Before the fertile plains and rich mines of Montana were known, it was supposed that the railroad must run north of the Missouri to Fort Benton; but no such route can be contemplated now. The Yellowstone Valley, the richest and most genial of any east of Missoula, can be followed to the Gallatin divide, which can be crossed at such a grade as is not now considered excessive. Then the route runs down through the fruitful farms of the Gallatin Valley to the head of the Missouri, when it crosses to the Jefferson Valley and ascends through prosperous settlements to its head, where lines of agricultural communities spread out on the Stinking Water and Beaverhead. Thence it ascends the Big Hole Valley, following the water-grade of the river, until the summit of the Rocky range is attained almost imperceptibly, with pioneers already near neighbors on both sides.

From the summit the magnificent Deer Lodge Valley opens, and descends by easy, regular grade for one hundred miles, with large herds and fine farms dotting it from one end to the other. I do not pretend to sufficient knowledge of the country to indicate the line west of Deer Lodge Valley; but it must cross the luxuriant Missoula Valley, and thence mainly follow the waters to the Western Sea. Competent men differ as to the route; but all agree that it need not be circuitous or difficult. Thus for hundreds of miles, in the very heart of the Rocky Mountains, the Northern Pacific Railroad will pass through the most productive valleys of the continent, and rear State after State, with swarming populations and boundless wealth, to give prosperity and power to the Union. Unlike the sterile, repulsive mountains on the Central route, the valleys of Montana will send to the markets of the East and West the rich offerings of their fields and mines; and one of our chief sources of productive greatness will be here, where but a few years ago the savage ruled the Northern wilderness and plains.

This great improvement will revolutionize the present centres of trade in the mountain-regions; and the future metropolis of Montana commerce is now marked by but a few widely-scattered cabins. Helena, the present chief mart of business, will be isolated and left to depend upon its local interests. Virginia City will also be off the great highway, and localized in its traffic even more than now. Fort Benton will recede to a mere frontier military-post, and a few straggling steamers will land there to supply the soldiers and the settlers on the river. The centre of trade will gravitate to the Gallatin Valley, and it will be the depot for the North, whence light boats will transport from the railroad to the falls above Benton. Goods can be shipped up the Missouri and Yellowstone to the railroad, without encountering the perils of the Upper Missouri, and the head of navigation will be practically where the railroad crosses the Yellowstone. No commerce will pass above the mouth of the Yellowstone, excepting what the posts and few pioneers on the river may demand; and the Upper Missouri will be left to its alternating angry surges and low waters for ages to come. From the Yellowstone steamers will ascend the Big Horn to supply the future settlements of Big Horn and Wind River Valleys, where the most fertile lands and valuable mineral deposits are found; and they in turn will pour out their streams of wealth to the railroad. The now immense lumber-trade of the Mississippi, which has all the region west of its waters and east of the mountains to supply, will be narrowed down to its own natural boundaries; while the Missouri and the railroad will bear the fine timber of Eastern Montana to cheapen improvement in Nebraska and Western Iowa. Mining-camps, now called cities, will fade from the maps as progress reverses primitive settlements into permanent channels, and the future capital of the future Golden State will overlook the union of the waters of the mountain-valleys, as they mingle in soft murmurs in the sinuous course of the Missouri.

If 1870 shall see the locomotive sweep from Omaha to San Francisco, 1871 should hear its shrill song reverberate over the plains and through the mountains from St. Paul to Puget Sound; and while the Central will be hastening its share of travel and freight across the New World, the growing tide of trade will sweep through these rich valleys until every nation shall pay tribute to the Northern Pacific Railroad. It will bring not only the matchless wealth of the new Northwest, but the commerce of the ancient empires will pass us as it seeks the Eastern cities and Europe toward the rising instead of the setting sun; and the crowning pride of the Republic will be this great artery of national and commercial life.

LETTER XLIV.

VIRGINIA CITY, MONTANA TERR., December 6, 1867.

I HAVE had a truce of a week with the mountains and
mines, and devoted it to the sights, the fashions, the
amusements and social enjoyments of the capital. The
theatre, under the direction of the jolly Langrishe, has
been running clever audiences. Ingomar has illustrated
to the accomplished circles of Virginia the ways and tastes
of the barbarian. Claude Melnotte has confirmed the old
adage that the course of true love does not always run
smooth. Pretty much everybody goes to the theatre; and
the "Pony," just opposite, clears the cobwebs out of the
throats of the people between the acts. Pleasure and business are happily mingled in Western life. When the cur-
tain falls the glasses rise, and are emptied between social
greetings and commercial contracts. At the "Pony" may
be seen the dignitaries of the Territory and city, the mem-

bers of the bar, the men of business, and around them the inevitable and ubiquitous "bummers," all smiling together, and discussing Montana liquors, Indians, politics, and the last murder or prize-fight. The legislature is also running, and is one of the standard amusements of the city. They pass bills as they like, when they like, and construe the Constitution and the organic acts to suit every exigency as it arises. They have decided claims to originality, alike in their orthography and in the construction of sections. Most of their laws have to be reworded before they can be intelligently construed ; and then it is not always a possible task. After three sessions had been held in the Territory, a commission was appointed to examine the statutes they had enacted, correct their spelling, and ascertain to what extent they were unintelligible or in conflict with the organic act or with each other. The commission waded through the duty assigned them, with very unsatisfactory results ; and one of the board finally cut the Gordian knot by persuading Congress to annul the laws. The present legislature has, therefore, turned a new leaf, and must go over all the old ground, as the people of the Territory—or rather the controlling portion of them—demand that the legislature shall now annul the act of Congress by re-enacting the annulled laws. As Congress pays them their salaries, they are bothered how to do it and appear not to do it; and this nice distinction taxes the genius of the legislature overmuch. The result is that their forty days are nearly out, and they have done little or nothing. An extraordinary session is now inevitable, and the city will have the legislative Solons in their midst for another forty days. In order to facilitate legislation, a Third House has been organized, embracing most of the leading men residing here. It meets in the Representative Hall, and is presided over by a member of the regular House. Judge

Williston, Major Bruce, and myself were put in general nomination for the office of page, and, after an animated contest, Major Bruce was chosen. As he is editor of the Democratic organ here, the House was doubtless unwilling to incur his displeasure, and Williston and I think that the issue was controlled rather by the major's position than by the merits of the several aspirants. Senator Orr, who missed the Governorship of Missouri because "the other fellow" got the most votes, is acting as Executive of the auxiliary government; and he delivered an elaborate message, after which he served in the capacity of a legislator. I noticed particularly his statistics on the subject of education, gathered from the report of the Superintendent of Instruction, who signed his mark to the document. He reports the number of children, of all colors, admitted to the schools at thirty-seven and a half; and he gives the number preparing to graduate for the gallows, the penitentiary, and the legislature as exactly the same number to the fraction. The notices of bills, resolutions considered, and reports from committees were decidedly entertaining; and wit and jest, often more pungent than chaste, had the largest license, and took the utmost liberty with names and reputations. Then we have the courts, another unfailing source of amusement, where legal gladiators play fastastic tricks before the shade of Blackstone. At the last row among the members of the bar, the judge took a hand so far as to fine one of the belligerents ten dollars, and followed it up by fining a remiss juror fifteen dollars. One of the tip-staves will probably come in next for a fine of twenty-five dollars: so that the thing is getting gradually under way.

The jurors complained this week that they could not get suitable sticks to whittle; and the deputy sheriff now passes a soft pine board along the jury as soon as they are sworn, and each one splits off a piece corresponding with his appetite in that line.

We have also the levees or receptions every week by the Governor and other officials. They are popularly known as "levels," or "deceptions," and since they have been so denominated they draw well. Last night Secretary Tufts gave his "level;" and, as he is a bachelor, the question of selecting a fair partner to accompany him in state became a very serious one. In order to avoid invidious distinctions, he drew lots, and won the Governor's wife, who promptly accepted and graced the occasion with her presence and smiles. I borrowed a "boiled shirt," after much tribulation on account of my "heft," and plunged in with a Byron collar and polished boots,—and also the other necessary apparel. Over two hundred people were in attendance, nearly one-half of them ladies, and they tripped the light fantastic toe until the "wee sma' hours" admonished them that it was time to disperse.

Nor does our list of amusements end with dances in honor of our officials. The "hurdy-gurdy" still has its place in the capital, and on the most public corner of the city. It has lost much of its old-time spirit, and will soon be only of the past. I visited one for the first time, recently. Four girls, about fifty men, an Irish fiddler, a bar-keeper, and a bar, constituted the outfit. The gents were charged fifty cents each for a dance with the fair damsels, and after the dance they were required to pay a like sum at the bar for drinks for themselves and partners. I noticed that the girls were as prompt at the bar as they were on the floor. Money is scarce among the miners, and it was at times difficult for the "last best gift" to get the set made up. They would pass through the crowd exhausting their powers of persuasion to get the sterner sex to participate. One—not fair, but fat and forty—insisted that I should join in the festivities of the occasion; but I modestly declined, saying that I never danced, to which

she replied, with the bewitching air of the sex, "D——n
it, don't tell me *you* don't dance; I've *saw* you dance forty
times." There I was, with a borrowed white shirt on,
and liable to be taken for anybody but myself; so I did not
deny the soft impeachment, lest I should fail to persuade
my tender accuser of my proper identity, but declined all
controversy on the subject. She then squared herself in
the middle of the room, and extended a general invitation,
saying, "I'd like to see the color of the fellow's hair who'll
dance with me." A long, lank miner, with unkempt beard,
sporting a cigar at an angle of forty-five degrees toward
his nose, accepted the challenge, and the dance went on as
I went out.

A few years ago, when Alder Gulch was yielding
thousands of dollars daily from the placer-mines, the
hurdy-gurdy was the great institution of the mining-
camps. Virginia then had half a dozen regular houses of
the kind open nightly; and, as men were more numerous
here then than now, and women not so plenty, a dollar in
dust was freely paid for the pleasure of a dance with anything that could lay just claims to female apparel. Nor
did the abandoned only attend them. It was not uncommon for virtuous women, whose husbands had not been
fortunate in the mines, to go occasionally to provide themselves with the necessaries of life; and, rough as the
mining-population was at that day, they always treated
with proper respect such frequenters of the hurdy-gurdy,
and made it a point to contribute liberally to their wants.
At that time a dance in a hurdy-gurdy was good for a "clean
up" in the morning of from fifty to one hundred dollars in
gold-dust, by panning out the sweepings from the floor.
Dust was the only circulating medium; and, as the party
would get hilarious over the dance and beer, the gold-dust
would be scattered rather promiscuously in making pay-

ments.   Gambling, prostitution, dancing, and drinking
were sometimes combined in one establishment ; and, when
it is considered that the miners had then no other places of
resort for amusement, it is not surprising that few of them
saved any of their earnings.   But the days of the hurdy-
gurdy are gone, and gone forever, in this region.   Only here
and there sickly, spiritless caricatures of it remain ; and they
will soon fade away before the progress of civilization.

The people of the West learn from the Eastern papers
that the Indian war is over,—that it has been happily concluded by treaties made by General Sherman.   Strange
indeed is it that intelligent people in the States believe
such silly statements, and approve of the fatal folly of the
commanders, in the face of the fact that the same farce
has been repeated every year since the whites have peopled
the Plains.   Every year we have had a war, and every
year a treaty.   Several effectual treaties have been made
in the last ten years, but the government makes no more
of the kind.   General Conner forged one out by his artillery at Bear River, and made the Bannocks peaceable, because the few who survived were too feeble to fight.   General Harney did the same thing at Elk Horn ; and Colonel
Chivington repeated it, only a little more so, at Sand
Creek.   No Indians who have had war from earnest and
competent commanders have been willing to renew hostilities ; but all the hostile tribes know that the present commanders take much more care of the savages than they do
of the whites, and they rob and murder without fear of
consequences.   All they desire is that regular troops occupy the West, and war is the most profitable enterprise
they can embark in.

During the last three years we have had war, on a large
or small scale, every summer, and regularly paid the Indians in the fall for their atrocities.   The government paid

over two millions for the Colorado war, and then paid the
Indians half a million or so for their losses,—thus carrying on the war on both sides. In 1865 the savages raided
the Platte from Denver almost to the Missouri, and, in the
spring of 1866, General Sherman passed by the charred
walls of the murdered settlers' cabins, and their rude
graves, and reported that the Indians were not hostile, and
had not been so, excepting when provoked to it by the
whites. He declared that there were no tribes at war;
and he proceeded to make a treaty giving the Indians arms
and ammunition, with which they immediately went to
war again. Next they butchered his Phil. Kearney garrison, and have murdered hundreds of settlers and emigrants
last summer, often in sight of his troops, and stolen or destroyed millions of property; but he still insists that there
is no war, and has just closed the campaign by another
treaty, and given them clothing, provisions, arms, ammunition, etc. to keep them during the winter and start them on
the war-path again in the spring. He was cheated in his
first effort at diplomacy with the savages, and has persisted
in his error, even when every day brought its mangled
dead to teach him his fatal mistake. When he was treating
with the chiefs of the Sioux at Laramie, a band of their warriors attempted to raid the Gallatin Valley, but were repulsed by Colonel Howie's volunteers; and the Indians
had no other motive in making a treaty than to have clothing, provisions, arms, and ammunition for the winter and
to start them in the spring. They prefer war in the summer, when they can swarm over the plains and through
the mountains to gratify their taste for plunder and vengeance. They do not fear any number of regular troops,
for they can easily evade them when they wish to do so,
and they are always ready to cut off small bodies in detail.
Besides, every war they make in the summer results in

ample supplies in the fall, when they retire from their profitable campaigns to winter in comfortable indolence. In the
winter they cannot wage war. Their ponies are poor and
have no feed, and they cannot depend upon supplying themselves on the march. Any vigorous, competent commander
would hunt them in their villages now, and conquer them;
but Sherman forbids it. They are therefore ready to make
a sham peace every fall, as they have done for years; and
the wrong has just been repeated, as if the government
had no other duties in the West. The Indians are all hostile when they dare be so. They would be more than
untutored mortals if they were otherwise. They see the
pale-faces covering the plains and valleys, dispersing their
game, and they foresee the destiny that awaits them,—the
choice between civilization or death. They are all bar-
barians in instinct and taste. They will not work, and they
love to rob, torture, and kill. They have no appreciation
of faith, and make treaties just as they spy an enemy's
camp. They are debauched, degraded, and merciless, and
they regard civilization as their deadly foe. He who treats
with them, therefore, after a summer of hostilities, is either
a fool or a knave; and he who knows and defends them is
worse than both. Ten thousand troops have been west of
the Missouri the last season. What has been done? The
Indians took special care to murder and plunder in the very
presence of the troops. What retribution has been visited
upon them? what lines have been protected? what lives
preserved? Millions of money have been expended: what
account can be rendered for it? These are bitter words,—
more painful to me than they can be to any others; but
they are the words of truth and soberness. I entreat the
government to recall the troops from the West. With one
voice the suffering people of the plains and mountains desire it. They have submitted to military authority, and

sought to make it effective; but they have advised and appealed in vain. Let the millions wasted last season be saved, hereafter, by the withdrawal of the regular troops, and let competent and honest officers be sent to organize mountain-troops when hostilities are commenced again. Colorado will gladly protect Colorado, with one man for every ten Sherman has there; Montana will protect Montana in like manner; and there will be no war, if the Indians must brave the pioneers. There will be peace; for then there must be peace or death. Soon railroads will traverse the now crimsoned plains, and settlers and miners will force out the slumbering wealth hitherto sacrificed to savagery, and safety and prosperity will bless the noble people of the Great West.*

---

* General Sheridan has made some equally effective treaties recently, by decisive battles, and there is now some prospect of peace for the West.

36*

Holiday in the Rocky Mountains.—A Genial Christmas-Day.—
Sumptuous Dinners and a Jolly Dance.—The Ball.—New-Year's
Day.—A Field-Day of Frolic.—The First Call.—The Egg-nog
analyzed.—Hospitality of the Capital.—The Babies.—A Prize-
Fight in the House of Representatives.—"Teddy" and "Chick"
have a "Mill."—Con. Orem seconds Teddy, and wins, after a
Protracted Contest.—A Row in the Ring.—"Teddy" the Hero
of the Theatre and the "Pony."—The Evening Supper.—The
Professor's Speech.

VIRGINIA CITY, MONTANA TERR., January 4, 1868.

HOLIDAYS in the Rocky Mountains are the most festive
of all our festive occasions. Dull care is thrown far in the
background, and business is subordinated to social and
general enjoyment. Christmas was one of the balmiest
days I ever witnessed in any climate. I sat most of the
day in an office with the windows and doors open; and
fire would have been uncomfortable. The air was as soft
as Eastern spring, and the sun shone out upon the hills and
cliffs with such warmth as to start their winter crowns of
snow in murmuring streamlets down their rugged sides.
The city was gay throughout. The mines had poured
forth their sturdy men to have a holiday frolic, and "The
Pony" (the chief saloon) had crowded tables from early
morn until the "wee sma' hours" told that another Christmas had departed. The street-auctions were unusually
lively; the stores were swarming with customers of all

(418)

classes, from the unshorn and unshaven mountaineer to the fashionable belle; the "sports" had their lively games, and billiards attracted nearly all the dignitaries of state to try their skill. Sumptuous dinners were spread in various uninviting-looking shanties, and fair hands and fascinating faces inside made guests forget the rude architecture that encircled them. In the evening mine host, Chapin, of the Planters', gave a ball, and one hundred jolly people responded. Tickets were twenty dollars each; but the supply was unequal to the demand. A second floor over one of the large store-rooms was fitted up most tastefully for the occasion. Evergreens and flowers were festooned around the walls, and the Stars and Stripes hung in graceful folds over the orchestra. For the first time in the Far West I found nearly as many ladies as gentlemen at the ball; but they varied rather more in their ages than is usual in Eastern gatherings of the kind. Young misses of ten and twelve years not unfrequently aided to fill up the dance, and, as a rule, did their part very well; while my partner in the only active participation I had in the ball (the promenade to supper) was a grandmother who owned to nearly sixty winters. She was, like all Western ladies, fond of social parties, and looked with just pride upon her children and grandchildren as they "tripped the light fantastic toe" to the best of music. Supper came with midnight; and it would have done credit to any Eastern town of thrice our population. Oyster soup opened the course, —the oysters having been shipped three thousand miles. Elegant salads, delicious jellies, game of all kinds, candies manufactured here into temples and monuments, almost every variety of fruits, and sparkling wines, combined to tempt the appetite; and a jollier party I never saw sit down to a repast. While there was a freedom from the severe

exactions of social rules in the East, there was the most
scrupulous care on the part of all to restrain social freedom
within the bounds of propriety. After an hour at the
table, the middle-aged portion of the party returned to the
ball-room, while the old folks and little ones retired to
their homes. Altogether, it was one of the most agreeable
gatherings I have ever witnessed; and it was enjoyed by
most of the company as only Western people can enjoy
social parties. With all the freedom of Western life, I
have never seen a man intoxicated at a ball or other social
meeting; and the sincere cordiality evinced by the ladies
to each other would be an improvement on the more cultivated customs of the East.

Between Christmas and New-Year the city was unusually lively. The streets were gay with beauty and fashion,
and in the evening merry music and the dance were always
to be found under some of the many hospitable roofs of the
town. Colonel Beidler was here, having a good time
visiting old friends; and Colonel Howie was also among
the guests, enjoying the festivities of the capital. We spent
many pleasant hours, during leisure afternoons, hearing
Colonels Sanders, Beidler, Howie, Hall, and others fight
over again the desperate battles they had had to give order
and safety the victory over organized crime.

Finally New-Year's morning dawned upon the little
mountain-capital ; and it was by general consent laid out
for a field-day of frolic. A party, embracing the heads of
Church and State,—Bishop, Executive, Chief Justice,
Secretary, Marshal, Professor, and some others of us who
classed as high-privates,—started out to inaugurate New-
Year calls. We naturally enough first paid our respects
to the family of one of the distinguished officials, and found
that our call was not unexpected. A huge bowl of foam-

ing egg-nog was set out on the centre-table; and we were made welcome, and accepted accordingly. We spent half an hour or so with the fair hostess, when the professor decided, from the confusion of tongues, that an analysis of the beverage was a necessity; and, after a careful and scientific investigation, he reported that the egg-nog consisted of three gallons of whisky, one egg, and a little cream. I can vouch for the bishop retiring in as good order as he came; but of the others, including the writer, it is not necessary to speak. There was some inexplicable confusion in fitting our hats as we started; but it may be explained by the very thin air of the mountains flying to our heads. We did not get over half the city until the walking became very hard for our party, owing to the condition of the streets, and other causes; and it was found impossible to conclude the calls on foot. A few inches of snow had fallen the day before, and Colonel Beidler, always ready for an emergency, called out a four-horse team and sled, in which we completed the New-Year calls. It was not so difficult to get from house to house, but it was very tedious and tiresome getting in and out of the sleigh so often,—so much so, indeed, that several of the party turned up missing on final roll-call. We had many a song and many a speech, and the jingling of glasses told of the gushing hospitality that welcomed the party at every house. The chief justice gave a story and a song, and was gravely lectured because there was no baby in the house. Neither host, nor hostess, nor distinguished guest, received the lavish compliments of the season that were given to the future statesmen and mothers of the mountains now boasting of swaddling clothes. One not yet a week old received the homage of the distinguished party, as the nurse guarded the cradle with mingled devotion and pride. Several were christened in the round,—not by the bishop in an official way, but in most instances with Biblical names.

At last the team was brought up before the hall used by the House of Representatives. Colonel Beidler was sitting with the driver, and, with a merry twinkle of the eye, he said, "Fun ahead, boys: let's have a hand at it;" and he called our attention to a rude placard on the door, stating that a sparring-match would come off at about that time. "All hands come in," said the colonel; and he looked especially for the bishop. "Just a little fun in the manly art," he added; but the bishop pleaded an engagement, and, with a kind farewell and a pleasant bow, he left us. The legislature had adjourned, and the hall of the House had been converted into a regular ring: the floor was covered with several inches of sawdust, a circle of rude board seats had been thrown around the ring, and what I supposed to be a sparring-match was to be exhibited at the moderate price of one dollar a head. "It's to be a square fight, and there will be fun," said Beidler; but still I did not comprehend the entertainment to which we were invited. After the Orem and Dwyer fight, the legislature had passed a law forbidding public exhibitions of the manly art, unless the contestants wore gloves,—intending, of course, that the heavily-padded boxing-gloves should be used. Upon entering the hall, there was every indication of serious business on hand. A ring, some fifteen feet in diameter, was formed, and in it were four men. In one corner was Con. Orem, stripped to his under-shirt, with an assortment of bottles, sponges, etc.; and by his side was sitting a little, smooth-faced fellow, wrapped in a blanket, looking like anything else than a hero of the prize-ring. He answered to the euphonious title of "Teddy," although English-born, and weighed one hundred and twenty-four

pounds. In the opposite corner was a sluggish-looking
Hibernian, probably ten pounds heavier than "Teddy,"
but evidently lacking the action of his opponent. With
him was also his second. He was placarded as "The
Michigan Chick;" and they had met to have a square set-
to, according to the rules of the ring, for one hundred dollars a side. Both had thin, close-fitting buckskin gloves
on; and they were to fight in that way, to bring themselves
within the letter of the law. Packed in the hall were over
one hundred of the "roughs" of the mines; and I confess
that I did not feel comfortable as I surveyed the desperate
countenances and the glistening revolvers with which I
was surrounded. Regarding discretion as the better part
of valor, I suggested to Colonel Beidler that we had better
retire; but he would not entertain the proposition at all.
"Stay close by me, and there's no danger," was his reply.
I had seen almost every phase of mountain-life but a fight;
and I concluded that I would see it out and take the
chances of getting away alive. My old friend Con. Orem,
who was to fight "Teddy," gave me a comfortable seat
close by his corner, and reminded me that I was about to
witness a most artistic exhibition of the manly art. "Is
it to be a serious fight?" I asked. "You *bet!*" was Con.'s
significant reply. A distinguished military gentleman was
chosen umpire, and in a few minutes he called "time."
Instantly "Teddy" and "Chick" flung off their blankets
and stood up in fighting-trim,—naked to the waist, and
clad only in woolen drawers and light shoes. "Teddy"
stripped as delicately as a woman. His skin was soft and
fair, and his waist was exceedingly slender; but he had a
full chest, and when he threw out his arms on guard he
displayed a degree of muscle that indicated no easy victory for his opponent. "Chick" was leaner, but had su-

perfluous flesh, and was evidently quite young, as was manifest when he put himself in position for action. He betrayed evident timidity, and was heavy in his movements; but he seemed to have the physical power to crush his foe with one stroke, if he could only get it fairly home upon him. They advanced to the centre when time was called, and shook hands with a grim smile that was mutual, and the fight commenced. Both fought shy for a considerable time, and "Teddy" soon gave evidence of superior tact and training generally. "If he only has the endurance to protract the fight, he will lam the 'Chick' certain, you bet," said Orem, while he was bathing his principal after the first harmless round. And he was right. Fifty rounds were fought, and fully an hour had been employed in mauling each other's mugs, when both showed evident symptoms of grief, and would have been glad to call it a draw; but considerable money was staked, and their reputation as professional pugilists was involved, and they had to go through until one or the other was vanquished. Soon after, the "Chick" got in a fearful blow on "Teddy," and, as he reeled to his corner, the crowd evidently believed the fight to be ended. The odds had been bet on "Teddy," and a rush was made into the ring to break up the fight in a general row, so that the bets might be "declared off;" and instantly fifty pistols clicked and were drawn, most of which seemed to be pointed directly at me. I could not get out, and could not dodge: so I had to nerve myself to face the consequences. Colonel Beidler at once sprang into the ring, drew his revolvers, and declared that he would kill the first man who attempted to interfere with the fight. All well understood that when Beidler's pistol was drawn it meant business; and the ring was almost instantly cleared, leaving him standing alone in the centre. "Boys," said he, "this must be a fair fight. Go on with the show!" and time was promptly called again. It was perhaps fortunate for "Teddy" that the interruption occurred; for it gave him considerable time to recover from the serious blow he had received, and he came up to the scratch smiling again, but fought thereafter with the greatest care, striking out only when he considered the blow certain to tell. I noticed that he struck the "Chick" seventeen times on the right eye in seven rounds, and closed it,—when he commenced pounding the left optic. "Chick" generally closed because of his superior strength, and took "Teddy" in chancery frequently, but often with more cost to his own ribs than to "Teddy's" mug. Finally, after a fight of one hour and forty-two minutes, embracing sixty-seven rounds, "Teddy" got in a terrible blow over "Chick's" heart, and sent him spinning to his corner like a top. The sponge was at once thrown up, and "Teddy" was victor. I went to "Chick's" corner, and found him in a most distressed condition. His face was battered almost into a jelly, one eye was entirely closed, and the other nearly shut. The gloves had prevented the skin from being cut, and he was forced to seek relief at once by the free use of the lance to get the blood from his face. His nostrils were closed with clotted blood, and his mouth was full of dark, thick blood. "I am too young," he said. "I should have known better. But I will whip him yet," was his remark, as he was led away by his friends. The crowd at once dispersed peaceably, and that night "Teddy" was the lion of the theatre, and participated in numerous drinks in honor of himself, at the "Pony," between acts.

An elegant reunion supper at the "Planters'" was the next entertainment; and both wit and wine sparkled freely while we partook of the grateful mountain-repast. His

37

Excellency, Governor Green Clay Smith, presided, and
each in turn spoke as his humor prompted him. No ex-
cuses were accepted, and each had to take his part in the
oratory of the evening. The Professor's speech was rather
of the pantomimic order; but, as all knew what he meant
to say, he was appreciated and generously applauded.
Several brilliant open-door parties closed the festivities of
New-Year's Day, and none could complain that there had
not been a general recognition of the Christmas holidays
in the mountains.

LETTER XLVI.

BEAR RIVER, UTAH TERR., January 10, 1868.

HOMEWARD-BOUND at last! The evening of the 5th I spent with old mountain-friends, around the hospitable board of Colonel Sanders; and the hours hurried by with unwelcome speed, as we discussed the past and the future of the brave mountain-people. I saved an hour for a quiet chat with Captain Mills, at his plain but ever-inviting table of exchanges; and politics and mines were forgotten as we wandered back to the familiar scenes and friends of Pennsylvania. He is doing a great work in the struggle of Western civilization, and his genius sparkles in the columns of the "Post" with a brilliancy that would do credit to journalism in any section of the country. Midnight stole upon us unconsciously, and, with mutual good wishes for long life and happiness, I hurried off to rest a few hours before starting on a winter stage-ride of one thousand miles over the Rocky Mountains. At four in the morning I was called; and, after a hasty break-

(427)

fast, the tedious work of preparing for a struggle with the terrible storm-king of the mountains was to be done. The bright weather of Christmas had departed, and one of the "cold snaps" was upon us. The mercury was down to twenty-six degrees below zero in Virginia City; and we accepted it as an admonition that the Rocky range would welcome us with old Winter's severest frost. Besides, the mountain-roads might become impassable, and the possibility of detention in snow-drifts, with the temperature from twenty to forty degrees below zero, made passengers thoughtful to protect themselves as completely as possible. With double woolen underclothing, a heavy winter suit, a blanket overcoat, a pair of heavy California blankets fully half an inch thick and large enough to envelop the whole body, an immense buffalo robe, double woolen socks, buckskin moccasins, and buffalo boots, all carefully wrapped in gunny-sack, for the feet, I felt that the worst of winter storms might be defied. The ears, face, and hands were well protected by furs; and, when nine of us were crowded into a mountain-coach, we decided that Winter must play some most fantastic tricks to conquer us.

Just as the first dim rays of the god of day were gilding the hoary mountain-tops, the driver took his seat, cracked his whip, and we whirled out of Virginia to climb the innumerable cliffs and ranges which stood between us and home. A light coat of snow covered the valleys, and the frost-bound roads answered in sharp, screeching song as the coach-wheels crushed the ice beneath us. Down through Nevada and Junction Cities we hurried along, until the open valley of the Stinking Water enabled us to turn south toward the frowning battlements of mountains which lay across our path. The sun had reached nearly midway on his westward course; but his rays were too feeble to moderate the keen, sullen chill that enveloped us. There was not a cloud in the sky, but the atmosphere was thick with frost, and throughout the day the sun was unfelt. The horses were whitened with the frozen perspiration, and their nostrils were covered with ice, their warm breath congealing before it escaped. The mustaches and whiskers of the driver and passengers were all frozen into uniform whiteness. But we had started out to face Winter in his angriest mood, and were fully prepared for it. One hapless miner who joined us at Helena Junction, and who was but poorly clad for such a journey, was crowded in the middle, where our large blankets and robes could envelop him in their ample folds. A jollier party I never traveled with; and, as it had been made up to be congenial, we resolved that, let the storm rage as it might, we would have a good time as long as possible, and never borrow trouble. The amiable Professor flanked me on the left, to equalize my size by his want of excessive avoirdupois, and his quiet jokes, along with the rollicking Irish lad of Western telegraphs and song, were like the mellow, still wine after the sparkling champagne. A little of the best brandy the mountains could furnish was snugly stowed away in almost every overcoat; and, as we captured the station-fires while the horses were exchanged, bottles of bitters were passed around, and generally accepted in moderation.

About one o'clock we landed at the first "home-station," at Beaver-Head Rock, and an old-fashioned Eastern open fire greeted us and made us forgetful of the frost, while the landlady prepared us an excellent dinner. During the afternoon we crossed a portion of the Beaver-Head Valley, and found herds of fine cattle grazing, apparently indifferent to the severe snap of winter that was upon them. The whole day's journey presented nothing of special interest that the

37*

letters have not already described, and night brought us to the celebrated Rattlesnake Cliffs, on the Beaver-Head River, where we were to rest until morning. The night was perfectly clear, and the thick frosted atmosphere of the valleys had been dissipated as we reached the foot-hills of the Rocky range. Although the mercury stood at thirty degrees below zero, I took a stroll, in the matchless starlight of the mountains, to look at the towering walls of seamless granite which almost hung over the little cabin in which we were quartered. The Beaver-Head ran too fresh and rapid for the ice to conquer it, and it dashed by in murmuring melody to chill in the embrace of Winter in the valley below. In every direction nothing was visible but the rude cliffs and frost-bound waste of the mountain-spurs; and the stillness was inexpressibly painful,—not even a withered leaf to answer the soft stir of the mountain-breeze; my own footsteps seemed to break harshly upon the melancholy solitude that reigned around me. Away to the northwest the silver brightness of a snow-capped peak told that the moon was climbing the eastern slopes to fling a halo of mellowest beauty over the domes of peerless white, and, as she progressed in her steady course, to scatter alternate lights and shadows over the confused ranges and winding ravines of the Rocky Mountains.

A good supper and a comfortable fire made us all cheerful, and the king of song made the little station-house melodious and hastened the flight of the long winter evening. By ten o'clock we were all comfortably in our rude but welcome bed, consisting of robes and blankets spread on the floor as close to the stove as we could venture to sleep with safety. Before daylight we were called to prepare for breakfast, and, after doing ample justice to the morning meal and rehabilitating ourselves in our ponderous suits, we started to climb the Rocky range. Our

progress was not rapid, as the hard hills and the snow compelled us to make haste slowly. There was too much snow
in many places for the coach, and not enough in other
places for runners. We had, therefore, to climb the range
patiently. The road wound round the hills in the most
tortuous manner, and on either side of us the rocky cliffs
towered thousands of feet above us. At noon we reached
Old Barrack Junction, and found a single-roomed cabin,
doing duty alternately as a carpenter-shop, kitchen, dining-
room, and bed-chamber. A tolerable dinner was prepared,
and enjoyed by the company; but the badly-frozen hands
of the driver who should have taken us on, was not a
pleasant reminder of the cold snaps of the mountains.
His fingers were swollen to thrice their natural propor-
tions, and, just before we started, he was coolly debating
with the landlord whether the fingers must be amputated.
Our locomotion was sensibly improved at that point, by
our getting a sleigh in exchange for the unwieldy coach;
but we had to increase our care to guard against freezing
our faces, ears, and hands, as we were entirely exposed
to the keen, stinging winds of the mountain-summit.
We drew our robes over our heads, leaving but a little
opening through which to see out; and, with that precaution, and carefully avoiding to face the wind, we got along
with comparative comfort and entire safety. The drivers
seemed to be indifferent to the fearful cold to which they
were exposed; but they were well protected. They wear a
full suit of buckskin underclothing over a like suit of
woolen. It preserves the heat of the body, and is the
best protection against the searching winds which play
with pitiless fury on the mountains. They can readily
protect the face and ears by furs, and the feet by socks,
moccasins, buffalo-boots, and gunny-sacks; but their hands
are greatly exposed, as they cannot encumber their fingers

with clumsy gloves. They always hold and manage all the lines with one hand, and must have the free use of their fingers. They wear silk gloves next the skin, and unlined buckskin over them, which constitute the best pro. tection they can provide; but it is often inadequate. In four days' drive I did not find a single home-station where there was not some driver or stable-man who had been more or less frozen during the last week. One man, who had to follow some straying horses, had both his feet so badly frozen that he hardly hoped to save them from amputation.

The afternoon drive was on the summit of the Rocky range, and our road was over a succession of abrupt cliffs and deep snow-drifts. The snow is as dry as sand, and does not beat down like snow in the East. It is so light that the least breeze drifts it, and it sweeps along in low clouds and drops into every ravine or depression it crosses. The road is marked by long willow branches, stuck in the snow where drifts occur; and both horses and driver understand that the beaten track must be closely kept. Daily travel packs it like stiff sand, and the road can be traveled safely; but if horses or sleigh get off the track they plunge into the unresisting snow, and it is often difficult to extricate them. Twice we had to unhitch the whole team, to get the horses out of the loose snow into the beaten road again. At times we went dashing over snow-drifts as high as the telegraph-poles, and the trained horses seemed to be intent only on guarding against missing the track. If one of them finds a foot sinking, he will jerk it up suddenly and shy off toward his mate, and generally save himself. So rapidly and continuously does the snow drift, that the road becomes trackless in a few minutes after a team has passed, and, but for the willows to mark the way, travel would be impossible. Only well-trained horses can be driven at all over the drifted portions of the mountains. Evening brought us to the most forlorn station on the whole mountain-route; and, as if to teach the sublimest contradiction, it is called "Pleasant Valley." I found it better kept, however, than in June last, and, but for the cloudless but howling storm that raged about it, I might have thought kindly of it. It is on the top of the Rocky range, in what is known as Pleasant Valley Pass; and near it the headwaters of the Snake and Missouri Rivers divide. The station is a rude little cabin, in a deep ravine, between two steep cliffs, and the snow was banked up in little mountains around it. Here we reached the lowest temperature I have ever experienced. From nine P.M. until after daylight, it was forty degrees below zero, as indicated by spirit thermometers; and I need not say that we cultivated the fire with tireless devotion. An excellent supper was served, and several of us made the acquaintance of the obliging landlady while we visited the kitchen to bathe our feet in fresh water to fortify them against the ordeal of the next day's drive. She was once in comfortable circumstances in Alexandria, Virginia; but rebellion took husband, home, and all she owned and loved. With some friends she made her way to the mountains, to begin life anew, and she is now earning one hundred and twenty-five dollars per month keeping the station. Although a stranger to labor until war left her bereft of property and blighted in her affections, she resolved to be dependent only upon herself; and she now welcomes the traveler with cheerful smiles to her humble but hospitable home.

After supper we brought the trained lightning into requisition, through the kindness of the operator, and chatted with friends in Virginia, Helena, Salt Lake, etc., and found how the weather-king was likely to receive us on our next day's journey. From all the same answer came,

—" The coldest night of the season." The Professor dis-
coursed upon the philosophy of maintaining animal
warmth under difficulties, and every precaution was carefully studied and prepared for.   A song closed the evening
festivities, and, throwing off all care until the morrow, we
disposed ourselves around the stove for a comfortable
sleep.   We had breakfast at four, and all took an extra
cup of strong, hot coffee to enable us to brave the piercing
frost without.   At five we started in an open sleigh on
our journey.   Not a face was visible in the crowd.   The
driver had a fur mask over his face, and the passengers
looked like so many blocks covered with robes.   We crowded
down in the bottom of the sleigh, and took the robes of the
middle men to cover the heads of the entire party.   Thus
fortified, winter's fiercest blasts swept over us harmlessly,
and we soon began to flatter ourselves that we could be
indifferent to the temperature of the mountains.   But, just
as day was breaking in the east, the sleigh got off the
beaten road, and we were tumbled pell-mell into snow up
to our waists.   Some went down head-foremost, and but
for their robes would scarcely have left their boots above
the snow.   I was thrown from the further side, and was
almost entirely buried before I realized that anything had
happened.   Fortunately, the dry snow shakes off like dust;
and we soon had the sleigh righted up and ourselves re-
packed in the bottom of it.   But it was a terrible ordeal ;
for our hands were almost frozen, even in our fur gloves,
before we got restored to our places.   Three upsets before
ten o'clock relieved the monotony of this memorable morning ride, and we all suffered intensely by the few minutes'
exposure to the wind and snow necessitated by our unwilling somersaults.   We did not even venture out to warm ourselves at the stations while the horses were changed, and
the driver took the wise precaution to avoid fire during the

whole fifty miles of his drive. The experienced and prudent mountaineer always avoids whisky and fire until his day's exposure is ended. Noon brought us out into Snake River Valley, and we had a tolerable dinner at "Hole in the Sand" station. We had got down from the summit, and the temperature had moderated some fifteen degrees,—making the weather what we regarded as decidedly pleasant. We took the coach again at this station, and found no difficulty in keeping comfortable in the close apartment, packed in as we were with blankets and robes. We could again venture to look out without getting our noses frostbitten ; and, as our faces no longer needed to be covered, conversation and cheerfulness again took possession of our little circle. Evening brought us to Eagle Rock Lodge, already described in these letters ; and we had a fine supper, a pleasant evening, and a comfortable sleep. In the morning we continued our way through Snake River Valley to Ross's Fork, near old Fort Hall, where we had a good dinner. Fresh pork, venison, potatoes, and cabbage, with delicious bread and coffee, tempted us to eat the worth of the one dollar and fifty cents demanded, and we pushed on through Pont Neuf Cañon, Robbers' Roost, and other inviting localities, memorable for mountain robberies and murders, until we landed in Marsh Valley, at " Ruddy's," about eleven o'clock. Late as it was, we had a bountiful warm supper, after which we went to bed in our robes, and rose at two in the morning for breakfast, in order to make the long drive to this place in good time. The roads were bad, and we had to move slowly. The weather had continued to moderate ; and when we reached the Josephite Mormon (anti-polygamy) settlement at Malade, for dinner, we could air ourselves on the streets without blankets. We spent an hour with the Hickory Mormons, and then pushed off for Bear River. The mosquitoes which swarmed about

us in June had succumbed to winter, and we found a large
two-story hotel at the place, instead of the little bank cabin
that welcomed us to myriads of gnats and other winged
blood-letters on our outward journey. We were joined
here by the passengers from Idaho, and fresh acquaintances added to the zest of an evening chat. One by one
they have dropped off from song and story to bed, until I
remain alone; and, with this hasty sketch of our five days'
journey over the Rocky range, I resign myself, with my
companions, to rest.

LETTER XLVII.

An Early Start from Bear River.—The Great Salt Lake.—Character of its Tributaries and its Waters.—Dinner at Ogden.—Arrival at Salt Lake City.—The Townsend House.—The Landlord and his Three Wives.—Kindness and Hospitality of the Mormons.—Mormon Drinking-Houses, Billiard-Rooms, and Currency.—The Law against Polygamy practically a Dead Letter.—Solution of the Vexed Problem.

SALT LAKE CITY, UTAH TERR., January 12, 1868.

WE had pleasant beds and a good night's sleep at the new Bear River Hotel, and a tempting breakfast before daylight. It is a long drive from there to this city; and, with just snow enough to make staging rough and hard, and not enough to run the coach on sleds, we had a heavy day's drive to reach here on schedule time,—six in the evening. Before it was light enough to recognize each other in the coach, we were snugly crowded in, and started at a gay gallop to ascend the very abrupt hill which forms the southern bank of the river. Once on its summit, we had an open and almost level valley ahead of us, and we swept along at the rate of eight miles an hour, regardless of the icy roughness of the road. Soon we were again in view of the Great Salt Lake, with its broad unruffled surface, and without a particle of ice on its waters. It is changeless in all seasons. Its banks never overflow, no matter how rapidly its mountain-tributaries rise; nor does its volume of water diminish in the severest drought.

38   (437)

Whither its vast but unknown outlet courses in its hidden path to the sea, no one pretends to know; but that it must have a large subterranean passage to the Pacific is not a matter of doubt.   Four large rivers empty into it,— the Bear, the Weber, the Ogden, and the Jordan, their combined waters being greater than the waters of the Susquehanna at Harrisburg; and, although all are the freshest of streams, the water of the lake is the most briny known in any large body in the world.   Three gallons of water will evaporate into one gallon of pure salt.   Of course no toilers of the sea inhabit it.   Cattle cross some of its arms to reach the nutritious pastures on the lake-islands, where fresh water also abounds, and boats bear ambitious tourists from island to island to inspect the wonders of this singular inland sea; but no commerce floats upon it.   It extends nearly eighty miles north and south, and about thirty miles east and west, with occasional flat meadows and towering mountains scattered through it.   Now that it will soon be accessible in a few days from the Eastern cities, and scientific men can make a pleasant summer tour to this beautiful valley, before many years elapse the invisible currents of this large body of water will be positively traced, and the point of outlet ascertained.

We arrived at Ogden City for dinner, and enjoyed the hospitality of one of Bishop West's eight wives.   The weather was still cold,—the thermometer ranging below zero; but we were all well protected, had level roads, and had rather an agreeable journey through the Mormon settlements to the chief city of the Saints.   We arrived here last evening punctually on time, and took quarters at the Townsend House. It is owned and kept by Bishop Townsend, and is all that the traveler could wish for as a place of entertainment.   The rooms are large, well ventilated, and cleverly furnished, and the table is bountifully and creditably supplied. The bishop is the lord and master of three wives, and is an enthusiastic disciple of the polygamic faith. His first wife is not visible to the guests of the house; and how much the advent of the plural sisters has to do with her retirement, I can only guess. The second wife is the landlady,—a clever, agreeable Danish woman, and evidently a thorough housekeeper. She was one of the very few Mormon wives I found ready to chat with visitors; but the one unpleasant domestic subject was never introduced. The third wife is a young madam still in her teens, and monopolizes the tender attentions of her lord. She lives in a separate establishment; and the playing of the piano by the second wife all last night in the parlor immediately under my chamber was explained by the clerk as the result of the absence of the bishop, who was enjoying the latest-found charms of his increased household.

I had studied the Mormons socially when here in June last; and in these letters will be found the convictions then accepted. They have not been in any degree changed. Notwithstanding the freedom with which I discussed the objectionable features of Mormon life, I have been welcomed again with unaffected kindness and hospitality; and the same dignitaries of the Church have renewed the old discussion with me in the most friendly way. I spent last evening seeing the evening retreats of the Saints. Two drinking-saloons are allowed in this city of twenty thousand people, and they pay a license to the city of three hundred dollars per month. One of the saloons has a billiard-room attached; and, in addition to the license for selling liquors, a special license of $33.33⅓ a month is paid to the city on each of the nine tables. Here the Gentiles and strangers gather in, and it is a reunion every evening for some old friends who have long been parted in their mountain-adventures. Here and there through the crowd could be seen a Jack-Mormon (the term applied to adhering Saints who care more for Mormon trade than Mormon religion); but I did not see a single prominent Mormon during the two hours I spent there. Brigham Young recognizes the necessity for drinking-houses and billiards; but he well understands that responsibility for abuse in the sale of liquor can be counted on only by limiting the houses to the smallest possible number. To do this, he makes the license thirty-six hundred dollars per annum; and but two houses can afford to pay it. He thus gets the maximum of revenue from the minimum of sources. Another large source of revenue is in Mormon currency. Notwithstanding the acts of Congress taxing all but national currency practically out of existence, the corporation of Salt Lake City (or, in fact, Brigham Young) has a considerable volume of currency out, that closely resembles our greenbacks. It passes in all branches of trade as acceptably as regular national bank-paper, and I presume must, in some way, escape national taxation.

I have so fully discussed the social features of polygamy heretofore that I will not again refer to them; but the solution of this vexed problem has caused me much reflection since my visit here last summer. We have passed laws prohibiting polygamy, pronouncing it a crime, and defining its punishment; but the laws have been as dead letters on our national statute-books, with not even the pretense of respecting them by this peculiar people. Indeed, in all my conversations with the leading Mormons, they declare with one accord that the laws against polygamy cannot and shall not be enforced. It is vain for a faithful Governor to appeal to the legislature; for it is entirely Mormon. It is idle for law-abiding judges to charge Mormon grand juries that they are criminals, and ask them to find true bills against themselves; and, even if a conviction could be attained, sentence could not be enforced. Until I mingled with the Mormon people and ascertained their infatuated devotion to their Church, I felt that our government was remiss in not enforcing the laws against polygamy at any cost; but since I have been here I have been staggered at the contemplation of the probable results of such a policy. The leaders are shrewd, cunning men, and do not mean to surrender their power over a deluded people. As a class, they would, I have no doubt, surrender their cities and fields to devastation, and start for new homes in some inaccessible wilderness, rather than submit to force. Of the one hundred thousand population of Utah, ninety-two thousand are Mormons; and of that number nine-tenths have implicit faith in the Mormon religion. It is a faith, too, that reason cannot unsettle; and persecution, or what they would regard as persecution, would but intensify it. They have well considered the subject; and it is their high resolve that they may be driven from their favorite valley and their property sacrificed, but that they will not submit to any encroachment upon what they claim to be their right to worship according to the dictates of their consciences.

But for the fact that the surges of Christian progress are already breaking against this hitherto impregnable rock of blasphemy and fanaticism, I should hesitate to offer any solution of the vexed question. But the Pacific Railroad will cross this country in less than two years more, and each day is now practically shortening the distance and lessening the dangers of a tour across the continent. When the people of the East get to understand that here are opportunities for industry and enterprise such as the old settlements cannot present, and when five days' travel will land emigrants in Utah, I look for a heavy influx of settlers who will antagonize the Mormon faith; aud the discovery of rich mines in the surrounding mountains will precipitate a population before which the Mormons cannot stand. Whether vice or virtue come to mingle with this people, the antagonism is the same. Virtue will reform, vice will attack, and both will gradually but surely dethrone polygamy.

The time is not yet for effective legislation on the subject; but it cannot be far distant. When the railroad is completed, and the tide of fresh population sets in for Utah, then Congress may render essential aid in wiping out this fearful blot upon our fame. No half-way measures will be availing when the effort is to be made. Laws must not only be enacted, but they must be enforced. It cannot be done in a day, and perhaps not in a year; but it can be done. There must be fifty thousand anti-Mormon people in Utah before laws against polygamy can be effective. There must be social, political, and business power to aid the law in asserting and maintaining its majesty. Then, if defiance continues, as hitherto and now, Congress can lay a heavy hand upon the polygamists and attain substantial results thereby. If all else fails, the denial of the right to vote, to hold office, to acquire title under the pre-emption and homestead laws, and to sit as jurors, may become a necessity, and accomplish what milder measures have failed to secure. There will be a desperate struggle for polygamy; but I am hopeful that the rapid infusion of a new element into Mormon society will gradually prepare them for the change, and submission will ultimately follow. The time has come when this problem must be solved. It is now about to be brought face to face with civilization; and our laws should conform to the new order of things and aid enlightened progress in this reform. In no other way can it be effected, unless by a prodigious war and pursuing the criminals with flame and sword; and that cannot be sanctioned. To be successful, the remedy must be a peaceful one; and I shall anxiously await the day when the westward march of liberal Christianity, going hand in hand with law, shall remove this stain from our national escutcheon.

LETTER XLVIII.

CHEYENNE, DAKOTA TERR., January 18, 1868.

ON the morning of the 12th we bade a second farewell to the City of the Saints, and started for a winter journey of over five hundred miles across the Rocky Mountains again. The journey from Montana to the East by Utah involves crossing the Rocky Mountains twice from base to base; and the tourist starting from Deer Lodge, Montana, for the East must cross the Rocky range three times. The mountains bend far to the west as they cross the northern part of the United States, leaving Virginia City, Helena, and most of the settled portion of Montana east of the Rocky range, although far west of the eastern side of the mountains at Denver. The Rocky range divides Montana, leaving Deer Lodge and Missoula counties west of it. Starting at Virginia City, therefore, we are on the eastern side of the Rocky range, and get on

(444)

the western side as we journey south into Idaho and Utah. At Salt Lake City we must cross the mountains again to get to this point. Thus in a journey of three thousand miles by stage through the mountains I have crossed them six times from base to base, and at four different passes,— viz.: Bridger, Pleasant Valley, Big Hole, and Mullen's. Bridger and Pleasant Valley Passes were crossed twice each in the journey.

Although I had crossed the mountains from here to Salt Lake in June last, I found but little sign of summer; and, upon the whole, the winter trip was decidedly the most pleasant. The most pitiless snow-storm I was ever exposed to was on the summit of the range on the 7th of June; and the ravages of the Indians all around us did not add to the comfort of the journey. But the winter trip was comparatively pleasant. We all looked for cold weather and but moderate accommodations; and we did not realize more than we expected in the disagreeable line. Indeed, in some respects it was a very pleasant part of the mountain-journey. We had a jolly company, were not uncomfortably crowded, and the line and stations were in comparatively good condition. We had no vexatious delays, only two or three innocent upsets, and the "home-stations" generally welcomed us to acceptable meals.

Instead of crossing the Wasatch range by Parley Cañon, as we did when going west, we were taken through Weber Cañon, where the Weber River has cut its way through the towering mountain that impeded its outlet to the Utah basin. The fall of the river is very rapid in most places. The bed of the stream is narrow, and the water foams and dashes along, often undermining huge rocks and hurling them down with the irresistible tide. We dined on tolerable fare at the mouth of the cañon, and started in a comfortable sleigh to follow the sinuosities of our narrow road along the river-bank. At times perpendicular walls of rock, nearly a thousand feet high, were on one side of us, and the boisterous river close by us on the other side; and in several instances the frowning rocks reached out over us,—the water having washed away a portion of the foundation where the narrow stage-road is now located. In some twenty miles nothing is presented to the traveler but the bleakest of mountain-cliffs, abrupt ravines, and the ceaseless roaring of the angry waters of the Weber as they dash onward to the plain.

It was after dark when we arrived at Weber, fifty miles from Salt Lake, and the most eastern settlement of the Mormons. We had an hour to enjoy a good supper and a bright open fire, when we started for a night-drive through the celebrated Echo Cañon, already described in these letters. We all got comfortably wrapped up in our blankets and robes for sleep. Conversation had entirely died out, and all were enjoying or coaxing slumber. Suddenly we all landed, in most ungraceful attitudes, in a snow-bank on the hill-side, and passengers, robes, blankets, trunks, bottles, etc. were mixed up in the greatest confusion. The sleigh had upset when making a rapid turn in the road, and we were pitched more than a rod before we fell. Fortunately, no serious damage was sustained by any one, and we gathered ourselves and our baggage up as best we could, shook the dry snow off, and nestled down again for rest. Before midnight a heavy snow-storm set in, and the road soon became invisible to the driver. He stopped several times to reconnoitre; and I could hear his expressions, rather more emphatic than elegant, evidently indicating that he had lost his way. After wandering around for two hours, he finally reached the next station, and there we met the western-bound coach laid up for the

night,—the driver having also lost his way, and decided
to wait for daylight. There was no comfortable room for
the passengers, and, after lounging about for an hour or
more, our party insisted upon going on; and the driver at
last consented to do so.

Before daylight we reached the summit just west of
Bear River, and there we suddenly emerged from the
snow-storm into bright starlight, with a cloudless sky
above us, while the storm-king was hurling the tempest on
every side of us below. We stopped the sleigh, and all
got out to enjoy the scene above the clouds, and called
upon Professor Eaton for an explanatory speech. He responded in his happiest style, and a miniature town-meet-
ing was thus improvised on the mountain-top to hear and
applaud the theory of storms and clouds.

Just as the first appearance of day was visible in the
east, we landed at Bear River, and remained for breakfast. After a good warming and a clever meal, we
started again, to climb the Quaking Asp Divide, the
highest range of the Rocky Mountains crossed by the
stage-route between this place and Salt Lake. The
morning was intensely cold, and the fine, dry snow
was flying in clouds, which blinded the driver and passengers. Where the snow-drifts were deep, in the numerous ravines or depressions, the road was marked by
willow sprigs, and the horses kept the beaten track. Little
driving was required, and the long slope of changeless
white, without even a bush to break the monotony of the
view, seemed almost endless, as we slowly climbed it.
What appeared to be but a steep incline of a few miles
proved to be a weary journey of ten miles, and we most
gladly welcomed the sight of the rude station that stood
out on the hill-side to brave the merciless storms which
play almost perpetually around it. The warm stove was

a welcome acquaintance, and we clustered around it to thaw ourselves out.

After crossing the Quaking Asp Divide, we had a delightful drive over Bridger Plain, and the middle of the afternoon brought us to the little mountain-city known as Fort Bridger. My old friend, Judge Carter, was absent; but a fine station-house, with several apartments, and all with cheerful fires sparkling on the hearth, made us most comfortable, and furnished an excellent dinner.

At this place we came under the whip of the celebrated Hank Conner,—the gayest, the jolliest, the most reckless, and yet one of the most expert drivers on the entire route. Hank is a splendid specimen of Western manhood. Tall, well proportioned, active as a cat, his face beaming with intelligence and humor, he is a perfect monarch when he is seated on the box, with his hat perched saucily on the side of his head, his lines perfectly in hand, and his long lash tapered with the keen, silken cracker. While he chatted with us before the fire, he was busy finishing a new whip, and, from the sly expression of his face rather than from anything he said, it was manifest that he meant to give us a ride to be remembered. He had given me notice, when I went west, that he hoped to have a chance to give me a display of his skill; and now the opportunity had come. Jolly John Creighton was one of the party; and Hank had an old score to settle with him also. It was evident that a merry ride was before us, and we resolved to take things as they came, and to die rather than "squeal,"—to use a Westernism.

About four o'clock we started for a sixty-mile drive to Green River. The road, for thirty miles, was over a level plain. The sleighing was elegant, and we traveled along at the rate of twelve miles an hour. Soon after dark we got into a succession of bluffs; but still we went along

pleasantly, until we came to the last station west of Green
River. So far, Hank had been jolly and talkative, but he
had not been able to "sweat" us, as he had threatened.
We began to hope that we would escape; but at the last
station a confusion of bluffs were dimly visible in the moonlight, and I feared that Hank's time had come. I walked
carelessly around the team as the men were hitching up,
and professed to amuse myself petting the sociable stable-
dog; but I was carefully surveying the restive bronchos
(wild horses) led out for Hank's last drive.

"Lively team, Hank," I remarked, with well-affected
indifference.

"They're lightning," was Hank's laconic but expressive
answer.

"How is the road to the river?" I ventured to ask, next.

"It's hell," was his significant response.

Creighton and I held a hasty council of war, and decided
that one of us should take the front and the other the rear
seat in the sleigh on opposite sides, so that we could lean
out and probably save an upset. The six bronchos pranced
around until Hank took his seat, when, with the yell, "Git!"
his long lash swung out over the team, and the crack of his
silk resounded through the mountain-cliffs. The horses
sprang off and dashed down the steep hill with frightful
speed. The off-wheeler soon became dissatisfied with the
race, and commenced violent kicking, to which Hank responded by the free use of the whip; but the broncho
kicked away until he had about dissolved himself of harness, when Hank pulled up the team, and, with a growling
curse at the vicious horse, he got out to hitch him up again.
It required two of the passengers to hold the team while
the obstreperous wheeler was being reharnessed; but soon
the job was completed, and Hank whirled and cracked his
whip more viciously than ever. A long, rough hill was

before us, with snow-drifts and sharp curves around the cliffs; but through and around all he dashed as if some mountain-fiend was chasing him. Several times he well-nigh had the sleigh over, but Creighton and I would swing out and save it when just on the balance. Before we reached the foot of the hill, the lead-pole attaching the front horses to the team broke loose; but Hank did not stop for such trifles. Away he dashed with part of the team detached from the other horses and held only by the lines, his whip cracking and flashing over the frightened bronchos, and now and then, as bare spots of road were reached, a streak of fire streamed behind us for rods, as if some demon of the wilderness was on our track. Not a word was spoken by the passengers: all were fixed in the determination that Hank might break a few necks or limbs, but that none should recognize anything unusual in his fancy midnight drive. At the foot of the hill he pulled up again, getting the horses in a bunch, and attempted to re-hitch the leaders. It required all the passengers to hold the team while Hank was reuniting them, and, that done, he cracked his whip again and started off with increased desperation. A single expostulation would doubtless have satisfied him and given us peace. We all wanted the mad drive to end, and I think that each hoped that one of the others would speak; but no one proved equal to the surren-der of his pride to his fears. There was, therefore, nothing left but to meet it as bravely as possible; and we made the twelve-mile drive over the worst of mountain-road without an intimation from one of the passengers that anything was wrong.

At last the foaming and steaming horses galloped up before the station at Green River, and the silence on the subject of the drive was unbroken until we sat down to our one o'clock supper. Hank could keep silent no longer. We had beaten him at his own game; and he was deeply mortified. Finally he said, "Colonel, I was a little *slower* on my last heat than usual. Hope you were not impatient at the delay." "Certainly not," I answered. "Considering the bad roads and the lateness of the hour, you did reasonably well." Not even a smile accompanied the remarks on either side; and soon after we all bade Hank good-by with a hearty shake of the hand.

I have so fully described the Bitter Creek region and Bridger Pass in letters last spring, that I will not refer to them again. No incidents worthy of note occurred on the route, until at Sulphur Spring we were joined by a lady with a rollicking baby. She certainly could not complain of our want of gallantry. We first offered the whole sleigh to the baby, and as much of it as the mother wanted for herself. Two passengers were detailed to take special care of the young mountaineer; and they were relieved from station to station. Never were mother and child made more welcome, and the best of our blankets and robes encircled them. Who they were, or to whom they belonged, we never inquired. They were as an oasis in the desert; and we left them at Dale City, with an individual blessing from each of us.

Last night we emerged from the mountains; and I felt some reluctance at the idea of giving up the old stage-coach. It had been my friend for many months, and my companion through all my long mountain-travels. I had learned to love it, to sleep comfortably in it, and to enjoy the hospitality it secured me. But the land of civilization had again been reached, as I fully realized when near the city. I heard again the almost-forgotten scream of the locomotive-whistle. For eight months I had not heard it; and when I had left the iron horse on my westward journey it had but reached the Platte, three hundred miles farther toward the rising sun. At three this morning we whirled into Cheyenne; and I woke up to see a city of five thousand people. On the 9th of June last, when I was at Virginia Dale, some thirty miles west of this place, the Indians had attacked the engineer corps about where Cheyenne stands. There was then not a habitation visible on this inhospitable plain. Now the locomotive sings his rude song daily, and five thousand of the fastest people of the continent dwell here for the time being. They have no law but the law of the people, and a lifeless body suspended to a post this morning occasioned no comment, unless among strangers. The law of self-preservation is the supreme law, and there is a short shrift for the freebooter.

To-morrow I start for home. It is now but a journey of three and a half days from the Rocky Mountains to Harrisburg. I have had eight months of the most delightful adventure in the mountains; and my three thousand miles of journey through them will ever be among the most grateful recollections of my life.

APPENDIX.

THE OVERLAND STAGE LINE.

Letter No. 18, commencing on page 275, is given as originally published in the New York "Tribune," without omissions or modification.

Wells, Fargo & Co. complained that it did their company great injustice, and formally notified the publishers of the "Tribune" that, unless my alleged misstatements were corrected, an action for libel would follow. No retraction or apology was given for the publication, and no libel suit followed. I met one of the officers of the company after my return, and the whole subject was fully and frankly discussed. The facts, as I gave them from personal observation, he did not question; but he made some explanations which I deem it due to the company now to give with the letter. He informed me that the government had never paid for any horses taken by the Indians. On that point I was doubtless mistaken. He claimed, however, that, under their contract, Congress was bound to pay for all stock they have lost or may lose because of inadequate protection to the route. He fully disabused my mind respecting the alleged neglect of the company to provide for their stock. They came into possession of the line late in the fall of 1866,—too late to procure ample supplies of feed; and the loss of their stock on the Plains compelled them to use every horse they could get, and they very naturally used the least valuable in the mountain-region, where the stock was most exposed, and where proper care could not be taken of them. I am convinced that I did the company injustice in assuming that the capture of their crippled and worthless stock was deliberately planned. While I cannot hold the company as excusable, I am glad to relieve them from the

(453)

grave imputation of inviting Indian raids by intentionally exposing their worn-down horses. I believed then, as did their own agents, and business-men generally on the line, that they were clearing from $500,000 to $1,000,000 annually, and felt that they could afford to make much better provision for their stock and greatly enhance the safety and comfort of passengers. The fact that the shares of the company have fallen sixty per cent. since the spring of 1867, and that (as I have been assured by an officer of the company) the line was run at a heavy loss in 1867–8, relieves them from the charge of illiberality. The obnoxious law, prohibiting the transmission of books, papers, and pamphlets by mail, has been repealed since my letter was written, and that serious ground of complaint is removed. Desiring to be just, I have thought it best to give the letter just as it was written, together with this note of explanation. When I returned over the same route in the winter of 1868, I found the whole line well stocked and abundantly supplied.

THE INDIAN QUESTION.

The letter No. 38, commencing on page 354, was written after the most careful reflection upon the subject, and also after opportunity had been afforded for very thorough observation of the actual condition of both settlers and the nomadic tribes in the Far West. As will be seen by reference to the first letters written west of the Missouri, I shared the humanitarian views of most Eastern people in looking to the solution of the Indian problem ; and it was with great reluctance that I accepted the convictions of the Western people as just. In this I was not singular. But few who have acquired personal knowledge of the actual condition of the two races on the plains and in the mountain-valleys have been able to maintain their opinions formed in the East. At the time these letters were written, the military were nearly as much at war with the settlers as were the Indians. Since then our commanders have attained a better understanding of the two races; and the result is the prospect of permanent peace.

In General Sherman's official report, made November 1, 1868, he recites some of the revolting atrocities of the savages, and adds, "I recite these facts with some precision, because they are proved beyond dispute; and, up to the very moment of their departure from Pawnee Fork, *no Indian alleges any but the kindest treatment on the part of the agents of the general government, of our soldiers, or of the frontier people,* with one exception, Agent Leavenworth."

Speaking of the regular army, he says, "The soldiers, *not only from a natural aversion to an Indian war,* which is all work and no glory, but under positive orders from me, had borne with all manner of insult and provocation, in hopes that very soon the measures of the Peace Commission would culminate in the withdrawal of these savages from the neighborhood of our posts, roads, and settlements, and thereby end all farther trouble."

Again he says, "I am fully aware that many of our good people, far removed from contact with these Indians, and dwelling with a painful interest on past events, such as are described to have occurred in Minnesota in 1863 and at the Chivington massacre in 1864, believe that the whites are always in the wrong, and that the Indians have been forced to resort to war in self-defense, by actual want or by reason of our selfishness. *I am more than convinced that such is not the case in the present instance;* and I hope I have made it plain."

The Indian war of 1868–9 is but a continuation of the war of 1865–8, and its prosecution, in studied savagery, has never been abated since the terrible sweep of the Indians from the mountains down the Platte Valley nearly to the Missouri, in the winter of 1865. Had General Sherman's report of 1868 been made three years ago, and the campaigns of 1866–7 been conducted as Sheridan has conducted his campaign just closed, many thousands of frontier lives and millions of property would have been saved. It was true then, as General Sherman acknowledges now in his report, that "*it is idle for us longer to attempt to occupy the Plains in common with these Indians. . . .* Therefore a joint occupation of that district of country by these two classes of people (settlers and savages), with such opposing interests, *is a simple impossibility, and the Indians must yield;*" and there would have been peace long since, had not soldiers with "a natural aversion to an Indian war" been in the field, and a systematic effort been made to do what is now a confessed impossibility—make the industrious pioneer and the indolent, thieving, and treacherous savage live in peace together. General Sherman now solves the problem as I begged him to solve it in 1867; and Sheridan's recent victories would have been pronounced repetitions of Sand Creek, had not the government slowly and reluctautly learned that Sand Creek, Elk Horn, and Bear River (where decisive battles were fought by Chivington, Harney, and Conner) are the only monuments of peace known in the history of the settlement of the mountain Territories. I have referred to General Sherman's report to show that in the treatment of the Indian question in these letters I have been fully sustained by the civil and military authorities, and that my statements, which were deemed harsh at the time by many Eastern readers, were fully warranted, and have been fully vindicated.

THE END.